JUDGE
ME NOT

By

RJ Layer

Bella
BOOKS

2014

Copyright © 2014 by RJ Layer

Bella Books, Inc.
P.O. Box 10543
Tallahassee, FL 32302

First Bella Books Edition 2014

Editor: Medora MacDougall
Cover Designer: Judith Fellows

ISBN: 978-1-59493-376-9

PUBLISHER'S NOTE

Other Bella Books by RJ Layer

The Real Story

Dedication

For Lori—forever and always—enough.

About the Author

Born and raised in the "Heart" of the Midwest, RJ still resides there with her partner of twenty-five years, their feathered chatterbox and two furry feline rescues. She loves to work at writing a lesbian story that will capture the heart of the romantic. In addition to traveling to new places, RJ can be found relaxing in the rolling hills on the water. Their hideaway is the perfect place for dreaming up engaging characters and moving stories. She also loves taking photos and enjoys reading every free minute she can find.

Acknowledgment

I want to again thank Karin Kallmaker and Linda Hill for making possible the opportunity to share my passion for writing. Bella's dedication to bring lesbian literature to readers is coveted, and I count myself fortunate to be part of the Bella family. Patricia Fuller said, "Writing without revising is the literary equivalent of waltzing out of the house in your underwear." And for that I give a million thank-yous to editor extraordinaire, Medora MacDougall, for helping me cover my exposed parts. Your expertise, motivation and gentle guidance inspire me to improve my craft with every word.

A heartfelt thank you to my family for a lifetime of love. Thanks to the ultimate lesbian resource connection, the "Women Outback," Alex, Mayra, Dori, Jennifer, Jules and Just Kim. Peeps rock!

And, Lori—my one—my all—my new wife.

CHAPTER ONE

Jeremy stood in the doorway, impatiently awaiting instruction while Lane listened to some nitwit contractor blather on about delays in having Judge Morrison, an acquaintance of her father's, rescind a financial judgment imposed on him. This was the fourth time in as many hours she had summoned him to her office.

She cupped her hand over the mouthpiece. "Call my father and the restaurant and push dinner back an hour." She tapped a perfectly manicured nail on the stack of papers in front of her. "I have to rule on this tomorrow morning." She slowly rolled her eyes to the desk clock. "If I can get this insolent jackass off the phone, and please, Jeremy, no more calls."

He started to leave, but stopped. "Don't forget your date for drinks."

She moved her hand back to cover the phone. "I guess you're going to have to push that back too. Or—cancel?"

His head shook adamantly. "Oh, don't you dare. If you don't make this date, I quit." He cocked his hip, dropping a hand on it.

She closed her eyes and expelled a long breath. "Fine, change it." She waved her hand dismissively.

District Court Judge Elane Stanford, or Lane as most knew her, was one of a handful of judges in the city on the fast track for greater attainments. Actually, she'd been fast tracking for as long as she could remember.

Jeremy returned. "Everything's been rescheduled for this evening. I'm out of here." A curt nod was the only thank-you he received. "Please don't forget your date later." She raised her eyes from her papers to glare at him. "If you don't get laid soon and release some of that…" he waved his hand dramatically, "I *will* cease to work for you." She scowled at his retreating form.

When she heard the outer office door close, she squirmed in her chair. "Great," she muttered. She hadn't seen anyone in weeks, maybe a month. She couldn't even recall the last one. She went back to the papers. After several more minutes, unable to concentrate, she got up and went to the closet adjacent to her private bathroom. She poured vodka into a short glass, added two olives and leaned against the mini-bar. Arms crossed over her chest, she held the glass poised to drink.

When she made herself do so, she recognized the building tension Jeremy had pointed out. Staying busy with work and other activities had kept her focused and usually kept her from thinking about it. She sipped her drink. Jeremy's reminder had now put it front and center in her mind—or someplace a bit lower in her anatomy. She took another drink, but it couldn't tamp down her building need. "Shit!" Returning the glass to the bar, she closed the door. There would be no concentrating on the damned brief now, she reasoned as she returned everything to the file and slipped it into her briefcase. She'd have to make it late night reading after, hopefully, someone released her pressure valve.

The maître d' spotted Lane the moment she entered the Eclipse restaurant on the tenth floor of the KEM building and took her directly to the best table in the house, the one with the magnificent view of the Ohio River as it meandered along downtown Columbia's waterfront. With great effort, her father stood as she approached, as did the man seated with him. Once the same height as Lane, her father now appeared shorter and frail for his relatively young age of sixty-six. Side by side in their dark power suits, they looked formidable. Weston resembled a pasty old Republican in Lane's eyes, while her darker coloring, hair and eyes came from her mother's Mediterranean roots.

She kissed his cheek and murmured, "Hi, Daddy," making certain no one else heard the endearment.

He would never allow such things. After all, he was Weston Stanford III. He had a reputation to maintain as a former State of Ohio Supreme Court Justice. Health issues had forced him from the position he'd devoted his life to achieving. But he had Lane. She would follow in his footsteps. He was going to make sure of that. And if his influence held, he'd see her bring even more glory to the Stanford name—and help their state, which to his chagrin had helped put the first African American in the White House, return to a bright red hue.

He took her hands in his. "You look well." His tone was gruff—he was a man of few words. He always told Lane as a child, "Say what you mean. Don't pad your speech with a lot of words because you think it will make you sound intelligent. People respect directness. Say only what you expect or intend." Growing up, she had never had reason to question his intelligence, expectations, intentions or power. She wanted to follow in his footsteps in every respect, including the lofty goal of becoming one of the youngest women to sit on a State Supreme Court. And beyond that…well, the sky was the limit.

He released her hands and waved a shaking, wrinkled one to the man beside him. "This is Thomas Beckman. His company is City Development." Lane offered him a firm handshake. "My daughter, Judge Lane Stanford."

The dinner was pleasant enough. They talked mostly about the business of developing areas that had fallen victim to a faltering economy, with Beckman explaining how profitable it could be to build in these areas if one could persuade city officials and committees to get banks and financial institutions to let the run-down real estate go for peanuts. They danced around the subject of politics very briefly. Lane knew the purpose of this introduction was for her to meet another powerful businessman in the city and a potential backer for her political aspirations.

After dinner Lane stood, offering another firm handshake.

Thomas Beckman said, "I'm sure our paths will cross again. It was very nice to meet you."

Lane nodded, following her father's simple advice. "And you."

* * *

Randall was waiting across the street when she emerged at nine. "Where to, ma'am?"

"Home," she sighed. "I'm calling it a night."

"Very well, ma'am."

Randall had been driving her for nearly six months. She debated trying to break him of the "ma'am" habit, but decided it was an improbability. He was about her father's age and undoubtedly raised to be respectful. As long as he continued to be discreet, something paramount in her drivers, she'd live with his habit.

A moment later her phone rang. She answered tersely. "I'm on my way now."

"I have a life too, you know? You should be here already," Jeremy huffed.

"I'm only fifteen minutes away. Keep your pants on."

"Being late does not make a good first impression."

Sometimes you are such a drama queen. "Please pass an apology along to my guest. You can leave. It's not as though there's china or crystal to steal. I think I'm capable of making a simple introduction and lasting first impression."

She rode the elevator up to the eighth-floor penthouse, quickly changing into a casual pair of slacks and blouse. She removed her hair clip, shaking her head to let her hair fall loosely to her shoulders, and took the back stairs to the fifth floor, entering through the rear door. Her "date" was comfortably seated on the couch. Lane paused to take in the red hair and milky white skin—and the breasts nearly spilling over the top of her tight dress. She took another moment to mentally undress the woman before stepping into the room.

"I'm sorry you had to wait. I had this other thing." She hooked her thumb over her shoulder. From behind the bar she gave the woman her most engaging smile. "Can I freshen up your drink?"

She raised her champagne flute. "I'm fine, thank you."

Indeed you are, Lane thought, pouring her own drink. "I hope Jeremy took care of you before he left."

The woman offered a dazzling smile. "He did. He's such a charming young man."

"That he is." *But only with other people.* Settling on the couch, Lane extended her hand. "Hi, I'm Renee."

The redhead slipped her delicate hand into Lane's. "Caroline. Jeremy told me you were very attractive and I would enjoy meeting you." She had a sexy smile. "So far, I'd say he's right..."

"I'm flattered you think so. And you are..." Lane lightly rubbed her thumb over the back of Caroline's hand, "quite a beauty."

Blushing slightly, Caroline took a quick sip of champagne. When Lane sat back, Caroline too eased back into the cushions. "I'd like you

Jeremy would have already shown up, told Henry, the doorman, that he was expecting a date, ridden the elevator up, exited via the rear stairs to the parking garage and left undetected, leading the doorman to assume Jeremy was in the apartment.

Lane's heartbeat sped up and a tingle caressed her skin when she opened the door. Caroline's eyes traveled down her body and a slow smile spread over her face, registering her approval of Lane's outfit, a black silk vest and matching slacks. Simple but elegant, it was designed to get out of quickly. Lane gave an approving nod in turn, taking in Caroline's revealing emerald-green blouse and a tight, oh so short, black leather skirt that showed more thigh than it hid. Three-inch heels gave an illusion of never-ending legs.

Lane took her hand gently, drawing her inside. "I'm going to have difficulty concentrating on food with a distraction like you."

Caroline slipped a finger in the top of Lane's vest to stroke between her breasts. "I could say the same."

Lane wanted to back Caroline against the door and take her right there. She preferred to show women class and civility, however, before she shook them to their core. She led her to the bar. "What can I get you? There's champagne, several different wines and any kind of liquor you can imagine."

Caroline slipped onto the barstool, giving Lane a glimpse of even more leg before she tugged her skirt down. Lane forced herself around the bar to put a barrier between them. Caroline leaned an elbow on the bar, settled her chin into her palm and gazed lustfully at her.

"What are you having?"

Lane looked at her empty glass. "I'm having vodka neat with a couple of olives."

Caroline tapped a glossy red nail on the bar as she considered. "Vodka's fine—if you can leave out the olives and splash it with something tasty."

Lane added a bit of cranberry juice to two fingers of her favorite Czar's Gold Russian vodka and handed the cocktail to Caroline, fighting the desire that the word "tasty," falling from Caroline's perfectly painted lips, had amped up in her.

"Thanks." Caroline tipped her glass toward Lane. "It smells heavenly in here. You cook?"

"No, but I have a palate for good food and know the finest places in the city to find it." She picked up her fresh drink. "Speaking of food, shall we?" She waved in the direction of the formally set dining table.

During dinner, she kept the conversation on Caroline, her job and generally safe topics like music and movies. When she went to the kitchen to start coffee to go with a decadent dessert, Caroline slipped in with her and rubbed against Lane's backside.

Her voice was sultry as she whispered, "I can think of at least one thing I'd rather have for dessert that's calorie free." She raked her nails down Lane's spine.

Lane turned slowly, watching with narrowed eyes as Caroline drew long thin fingers up her thigh toward her throbbing center. "If you make me come, I'll fuck you until you beg me to stop."

Caroline took Lane's hand and pulled her to the kitchen door. "Take me to your bed."

In the bedroom, Lane removed Caroline's blouse and skirt, leaving her covered only by the tiniest bit of lace, and laid her back on the bed. She slowly unbuttoned her vest, her body flushing with arousal as her eyes roamed over Caroline's voluptuous form. When Caroline licked her luscious lips, Lane knew she couldn't wait any longer. Quickly shedding her slacks, she stretched out beside her and hungrily found her lips.

"You're incredibly beautiful." She met Caroline's eyes briefly before moving her lips to her ear and whispering, "I want to taste every inch of you."

Caroline hooked her leg over Lane's, pulling Lane on top of her. Desire burned brightly in her eyes. "Talk is cheap, darling."

Lane skillfully stroked and kissed her way down Caroline's soft, pale skin, expertly wrenching cries of ecstasy from her. When Lane slithered back up her body, Caroline stroked her to a quick and furious orgasm. Lane dropped over onto her back, panting for breath. This was the way she wanted it. Hard, fast, with her in control. The way she needed it—without complications.

Caroline cooed, "Was that good for you?"

"Mmm…" Lane murmured. "I want to fuck now." She climbed off the bed. "Don't move. I'll be right back."

In response, Caroline drew her fingers seductively up the inside of her thigh.

Lane disappeared down the hall into the bathroom, returning a few minutes later clad in her robe. Lying beside Caroline, she parted the robe slightly. "Can you handle this?"

Caroline eyed the phallus harnessed between Lane's thighs with a pleased smile. She parted her legs, pulling Lane between them.

Lane could barely contain herself as she entered Caroline and began matching the rhythm of her hips.

Caroline gasped. "Oh yes, Renee…" She dug her nails into Lane's backside. "That's it." She panted. "Oh, God, yes…"

When Caroline came again, Lane gently collapsed on top of her. "You okay?"

Caroline's breath was ragged. "Better…than okay."

"Do you want me out of you?"

Caroline shook her head "no" and held Lane tight against her. "You're not quitting, are you?"

Lane smiled seductively. "Honey, I'm only getting started."

An hour later, after Lane smothered Caroline's scream with her mouth, Caroline rolled on her side breathing hard. Propping her head in her hand she stroked Lane's breasts, arousing her nipples.

"You're an incredible lover, darling. Much as I hate to leave your bed, however, I do have to go. I'm meeting my parents for breakfast in the morning, and I need my rest after all this." Lane gazed at her voluptuous breasts and creamy skin as she began a search for her clothes. Once dressed, she perched on the edge of the bed. "I hate leaving you here looking so tempting…" She moved her hand slowly under the harness to cup Lane's heat, a smile teasing her lips. "…and so wet." She paused. "Will I see you again?"

Lane briefly pressed Caroline's hand against her crotch, removed it and placed it to her lips giving it a lingering kiss. "You can bank on it."

Caroline smiled at her play on words, leaning over to place a light kiss on her lips. "You've got my number."

Lane woke hours later when she turned over and the harness pinched her tender flesh. She removed it and, padding to the bar naked, poured herself a drink before moving the dishes from their dinner into the kitchen. She was exhausted. The redhead had far more stamina than Lane had expected. There was no way she was going to dress in order to make the climb up three flights. She wondered briefly if that meant she was getting too old for her lifestyle. She polished off her drink, set the glass on the nightstand and slipped between the sheets. As one hand caressed a breast and the other moved slowly down her body, she knew the answer was, absolutely, "no."

* * *

She called Caroline the following day when she thought the redhead would be brunching with her parents, taking care as always to dial *67 first to keep her name and number from appearing if she had Caller ID. She didn't want to speak to her, only to leave a message. As her voice mail greeting played through, the sultry voice in the recording took her back to last night. At the tone, Lane spoke low and throaty. "Caroline, it's Renee. I hope you found last night as thoroughly enjoyable as I did. I'd like to have another date...I think we kind of clicked, and I'd like to explore things further if you're up for it. I'll call some evening next week. Enjoy your day."

Her day, unfortunately, was going to be filled with reviewing briefs—and not the fun, skimpy, lacy kind. Her life was about her goals and ambition. There was only a very small amount of room in it for women. Definitely not enough for anything resembling a monogamous relationship, which involved emotions and other baggage she wasn't interested in carrying. She didn't do loving-kindness. During his first year in her employ, in fact, mincing no words, Jeremy had stated flatly that she had ice water running in her veins, a judgment he'd rendered on the heels of a case she prosecuted in which she interrogated a female witness relentlessly, bringing her to tears with every question asked.

It was all about control in the bedroom too. She didn't want a lover for life. She wanted a woman to dominate, someone who craved sex with her with such intensity that she held all the power. The easier they were to control, the longer she tended to keep them around, but even those didn't last that long. Ironically, she couldn't quite foster respect for a woman who couldn't or wouldn't take charge at least once in a while. So eventually they all got cast aside. Caroline was likely to suffer the same fate, but in the meantime, she was in for the ride of her life.

CHAPTER TWO

When Lane called Caroline Wednesday evening, she was caught off guard by how her voice reignited her desire. "I'd like to make a date with you for the weekend, but I'm not sure I can wait that long to see you."

"You don't say," came Caroline's blasé response.

Blasé was good, an indication she wouldn't likely become clingy. "Yes..." Lane cleared her throat, "you are such a beautifully sexy woman. The thought of you naked in my bed makes me...well, I'm sure you know how it makes me."

"Hmm...and what does the thought of me naked in *my* bed do?"

Lane smiled. "Makes me thirsty for a taste of you."

"Maybe you should consider driving over here to quench that thirst."

Cat and mouse—Lane loved games. She was incredibly competitive, however, always playing to win. "Perhaps I will. What's your address?"

The suburbs, Lane thought when she heard the address. Of course. How quaint was it that the pretty little banker lived in the 'burbs. Her neighbors probably thought of her as every guy's dream wife. If they only knew.

"And Renee...?" Caroline's voice startled her from her thoughts.

"Hmm."

"I'll have the door unlocked, because I *will* be naked in my bed."

The anticipation started a hum low in Lane's body as she stood. "See you soon."

She shed her suit and tucked a long-sleeved dark gray Henley into tight blue jeans. Putting her hair in a ponytail, she pulled it through the cut out in the back of her navy blue Columbia State ball cap. All in all, with her five-foot-ten frame, she looked fairly butch. It would be an effective enough disguise, she decided, surveying herself in the mirror. She hoped Caroline wouldn't be put off by it, but she needed to reduce the chance that some nosy neighbor might recognize her. Grabbing her keys, she headed down to the garage where she hopped in the Mazda MX-5 Miata roadster she rarely had the opportunity to drive. She recalled with a smile how upset her father had been when she bought it last year, citing how inappropriate it would be for a judge to be seen in a sports car. Against his best advice, she'd fallen in love with the Stormy Blue Mica color and made the purchase.

After driving past the house once she turned around and parked a few doors down across the street. The only visible light glowed softly from what she presumed was Caroline's bedroom window so she wiggled down into the soft leather seat to watch and wait. She surveyed the neighborhood, scrutinizing houses one by one before directing her gaze back to Caroline's. Nearly twenty-five minutes later, she saw what she'd been waiting for. The light came up in the front room and she could see Caroline's silhouette through the sheer curtains. She was pacing.

Lane hurried to the door, rapping lightly before letting herself in. "I'm sorry I took so…"

Her words trickled off when Caroline turned to face her. She hoped her mouth hadn't dropped open. Caroline wore a short, royal blue robe. Her hair hung around her shoulders, almost touching the top of her breasts. Lane's fingers twitched involuntarily. Caroline crossed one arm under her breasts, nearly pushing them from the loosely tied satin, and raised the small glass in her other hand.

"I was having a little drink. Would you like something?"

Lane swallowed, licking her lips. "Sure, whatever you're having is fine." She knew as she said it that all she really wanted to taste was Caroline.

"It's sherry."

Lane nodded. Caroline motioned her to the sofa, where Lane shrugged out of her jacket, sinking into the soft cushions. While pouring

the drink from the other side of a counter that divided the living room from the kitchen, Caroline commented, "You look different tonight. Sort of...boyish. But cute. Did you have a ball game?"

"Is it a problem?" Caroline shook her head but continued to gaze intently at her.

Made nervous by Caroline's questioning, cat-like eyes, Lane rose and crossed the room to get a closer look at a collage of photos hanging on the wall. Caroline wasn't in any of them, she noticed. She felt the heat between them as the redhead stepped near, pushing the drink glass into her hand before lightly tapping hers to Lane's.

"Cheers."

Lane took the tiniest sip of the warm liquor. "You're a photographer?"

"I like to take pictures, but I'm no photographer." Caroline set her drink and Lane's on the entry table. "Listen, Renee, I like small talk as much as the next girl, but we both know you came here for one reason."

She turned Lane toward her, planting luscious lips on hers and pressing her breasts firmly into Lane's chest. When Lane pulled Caroline's hips against her, she quickly ended the arousing kiss.

She hooked a finger in the unbuttoned top of Lane's shirt. "I'm sure you know what I want." She gave a tug. "Come on."

Lane followed like an obedient puppy down the hall to the dimly lit bedroom. She pulled her cap off as Caroline tugged the shirt over her head. Lane began her apology again. "I'm sorry I was so long getting here..."

Caroline hushed her with a finger to her lips. "It doesn't matter now, does it? You're here and I want..." Her hands moved lightly over Lane's breasts, grazing her nipples, prompting their immediate response. "I *need*," she said, reaching for the button on Lane's jeans. "I need you to fuck me. Now."

Lane stopped Caroline's hand as it caught hold of her zipper. "All in good time, my beauty." With her hands on Caroline's hips she walked her backward to the bed. "I have needs too." Lane steered her down on the bed, sliding the robe from her shoulders. "I'm dying to taste you." Lane's lips began their journey below Caroline's ear, traveling down the long soft column of her neck until they reached the valley between her breasts. Caroline emitted several tiny moans.

Lane worked her into a frenzy, taking her close to climax and backing off until Caroline finally gasped, "Oh please, Renee," firmly pushing Lane's head to her throbbing center. A moment later, Lane

had her bucking so wildly she had to hold tightly around Caroline's thighs to keep from being thrown off the bed.

"Oh God," Caroline rasped. "How do you do that?"

Lane nipped at her thighs. "It's not hard." She stroked her tongue once more over Caroline's swollen clit before moving up her body. "You taste amazing." She settled her lips over a rock-hard nipple, sucking lightly.

Caroline moaned, "Yes," reaching for the hand that continued to stroke her wetness. "And now I need you to fuck me like I know you can."

Lane entered her and proceeded to give her what she was begging for. Rocking against Caroline's thigh she got herself off, hard, moments before Caroline screamed again. She rested her head on Caroline's chest, magnifying the thundering of her heartbeat.

Between gasps, Caroline said, "I want...you now."

Lane licked and sucked the soft flesh of Caroline's breast. "Not necessary."

Caroline slid her fingers lazily through Lane's hair. "I want to make you come."

Lane lifted her head, meeting hazy green eyes. With a smile, she said, "You already have."

Caroline tugged her up until they were face to face. "I want to watch you come."

Lane brushed a kiss across her cheek. "I'm not sure it's possible."

Caroline maneuvered the zipper down on her jeans, moving her hand under Lane's underwear and into her slippery arousal. Lane flinched at the first touch against her hard pulsing flesh.

Caroline whispered, "Where's your friend?"

"Home. I wasn't sure how welcome it would be tonight."

Caroline wrapped a leg around Lane, pulling her close as her hand continued to stroke. "For future reference, you may bring any friends you'd like to share with me anytime." She smiled seductively at Lane.

"I'll keep that in mind." Lane pushed up, pulling away from Caroline's hand. "Now, though, I have to get going." When Caroline reached for her again, Lane rolled quickly out of reach. "I have work I need to finish tonight and a busy day tomorrow."

Caroline rolled onto her side, watching as Lane slowly rezipped her pants and searched the floor for her shirt. "You have a magnificent body, but I bet you hear that all the time."

Lane shook her head. She stroked her fingers over Caroline's hip and down her thigh as she sat on the edge of the bed. "And you…you have an insanely beautiful body."

"So…will I still see you this weekend?"

Lane tried to recall her schedule. She knew there was something early Saturday evening, a dinner or fund-raiser she was expected to attend. "I have a busy one, but I'll be sure to save some time for you." When she stood, Caroline caught her hand. "It might have to be late Saturday evening. I can't squeeze in dinner, but maybe dessert."

"I love dessert."

* * *

Lane called Caroline Friday evening. "I have a dinner commitment I can't get out of tomorrow, but I want to get together afterward, if you'd like."

"All right. Did you want to meet somewhere?"

"How about if I come by your place?"

"Perfect. Then I won't have to figure out what to wear. What time can I expect you?"

"Between eight thirty and nine. Or is that too late?" Lane asked.

Caroline laughed. "It's Saturday night, darling. It's never too late."

"I'll see you tomorrow."

"Yes, goodnight, Renee." Her breathy words sent a shiver up Lane's spine and a rush of blood between her thighs.

"Goodnight, Caroline."

* * *

Halfway through dinner Lane stifled a yawn. Her table was full of old, hard of hearing "blowhards." She smiled politely and nodded at the appropriate times, but her mind was elsewhere. She swirled a spoon in her coffee, conceding that she'd have to get used to these affairs. They were routine in public life. If she wanted to sit on the highest court in the state, she needed to rub elbows regularly with the important figures in the city. She declined the sinful dessert being offered in lieu of the more sinful one scheduled for later. She just wanted to get the hell out of there.

As she inched her way toward the back of the room, a hand caught her arm. *Damn*, she thought. *So close.* She eyed the door.

"Judge Stanford, so good to see you this evening," Bruce Spencer said.

Lane forced a smile. "Bruce," she nodded, "good to see you again too." Having seen him earlier during dinner, she wasn't surprised to find him lurking in the shadows, but she had hoped to avoid him.

He gently took her elbow. "I was hoping we could talk," he said, steering her toward the door. "Somewhere private," he said quietly.

She decided to get it over with. "Of course. I was leaving. You can walk me out."

He pulled her to one side in the lobby, pinning her in with his towering hulk. She listened intently. She had heard from others that he demanded attention and respect, and although it probably was merely talk, she didn't want to test the rumors that he could make people…disappear. When he was this close, in her space, it was all too easy to believe the talk could be true.

Fifteen minutes later, with an anxiety she'd only experienced around her father, she interrupted him. "Bruce, I'm sorry, but I really must be running. I'm late for an appointment." She held her breath, quickly adding, "Can I get you to call me Monday morning when we can discuss this with all the attention it warrants?"

After cocking his head, he returned her smile. "Of course, of course." He took a step back, waving his hand toward the entrance. "I forget how busy you public servants are." He opened and held the outer door for her. "I'll call you Monday." As she handed her ticket to the valet, he said, "And Judge…?" She glanced back at him nervously. "Enjoy your weekend."

"Thank you, Bruce. Enjoy yours too." She took a deep breath. Another questionable favor to be done for yet another one of her father's good ol' boys. She sighed.

Racing her car down the street, she dug her cell phone out of the console to call Caroline and apologize for being late. "Damn!" The battery was dead again. She needed to remember to have Jeremy get her a new one. This one didn't seem to last more than an hour or two. She rummaged in the console and glove box for her charger. She cursed again, recalling it was stashed in her briefcase.

She whipped her car into Caroline's driveway, grabbing the bag off the passenger seat and hoping she'd be forgiven for her tardiness. The house was dark except for a very faint light coming from the hallway. She knocked before trying the doorknob. It was locked. She waited a moment. She waited another before checking her watch in the glow from the streetlight. It was almost a quarter of ten. "Shit,"

she mumbled, wondering if Caroline had given up and gone out. She knocked again and waited. It served her right if she had. You couldn't keep a beautiful woman like Caroline waiting around on a Saturday night.

As she turned to step off the porch, a porchlight glared to life behind her. In its harsh light Lane saw Caroline standing inside the door blowing on the nails of her left hand. She looked irrefutably displeased. Lane knew she'd have to call upon every skill she'd honed as a litigator to get out of this. She didn't smile, although the magnificent sight in front of her made her want to. Caroline looked tantalizing in a black lace and satin teddy that revealed more than a hint of cleavage.

Stepping through the door, she said, "God, Caroline, I am so sorry I'm late." She held out a bottle of expensive champagne and hoped the tone she used to seek her father's forgiveness would serve her here as well. Caroline stood rigidly, eying her defiantly. "I'm having the shittiest evening, and my phone died so I couldn't even call to let you know I was running late."

"I don't appreciate being kept waiting," Caroline said coolly. "I gave up on you fifteen minutes ago and decided to do my nails." She continued to eye Lane critically. "Just what every girl wants to do on a Saturday night." She reached her right hand toward Lane. "As you can see, I'm only halfway done, so I guess you'll have to wait now."

Lane took Caroline's long, elegant and—oh, yes—talented fingers in her hand. "I could do that for you." Caroline arched a brow. "I'm not too bad with nail polish." Lane pulled her to the counter between the kitchen and living room. "Please, sit." Lane raised the bag in her hand. "Allow me to pamper you." She moved into the kitchen. "Where are your glasses?"

She popped the cork on the champagne, filled two glasses and clinked hers to Caroline's. "To beautiful women—who should never be kept waiting." When the sexy redhead gave her a slow smile, Lane knew she'd charmed her pants off. Well, not pants, because she wasn't wearing any, but she hoped before long that she'd be ripping the lacy little teddy off. "Where's the polish so I can finish your nails?" Lane lightly stroked her finger over Caroline's delicate hand.

"The bedroom." Her lips curled slightly. "You know where that is."

When Lane returned down the hallway, Caroline had hungry eyes fixed on her. She brushed her hand lightly over the sleek black linen of Lane's pantsuit. "I have to say I do prefer this look, so powerful and commanding, over the tomboy outfit of the other night."

After her nails had dried and she finished her glass of champagne, Caroline touched her fingertip to Lane's hand, which was wrapped around a champagne flute. "You know, Renee, I bet you could think of a few other ways to apologize for making me wait."

"I can think of more than a few." Taking Caroline's hand, Lane drew her off her stool and led her to her bed, her arousal growing with every step.

Around one o'clock, after Lane had pulled several orgasms from Caroline and she started to drift off, Lane began dressing.

"You know you don't have to leave. You can stay the night."

Lane never spent the night with a woman. She hadn't awakened in a woman's arms in the morning since her first and only relationship back in college. She wasn't going to change those habits now. When she sat on the edge of the bed, Caroline rolled against her thigh.

"Tell me I won't have to wait until next weekend to see you again." She rubbed her hand up Lane's thigh, dangerously close to her crotch.

Lane pushed back errant locks of hair hiding Caroline's face. "I'm not sure what my schedule is for the week yet."

Caroline softly traced the line between Lane's thigh and hip. "Call me after you get to work Monday and let's see if I can talk you into a dinner some evening this week."

Clearly, Caroline was hooked. It gave her a heady feeling, potent and powerful. Lane leaned down. "Maybe you can." Their lips touched briefly. Lane stood before Caroline could entice her back into bed. "I'll call," she said before disappearing through the door.

CHAPTER THREE

After going over her schedule for the week with Jeremy on Monday and alerting him to the expected call from Bruce Spencer, Lane decided Tuesday evening was her best chance to hook up again with Caroline. She was scheduled to have dinner with a group of gals at six, acquaintances she'd accumulated over the years through various social affairs. She'd have to settle for only having drinks with them—she hated that, though she hardly thought she'd be missed. She called Caroline in late afternoon, leaving a message that she would call that evening.

When Caroline answered the phone Monday evening, she was gasping for breath.

"I've called at an inopportune time."

Caroline took several deep breaths. "I was on the treadmill. Believe me, I welcome the interruption."

Lane imagined her in tight spandex. "Well, it seems tomorrow evening is the only one I have any time before the weekend."

"How about coming over here and dining with me?"

"I have to meet with some people at six, but I can probably be there by seven or so."

"Seven it is then. Bring your appetite. I intend to stuff you before I work you out." Judging by her tone, Caroline seemed pleased.

"I'll do that. I'll see you tomorrow night."

* * *

The next day Lane had Randall take her home to pick up her own car before she went to meet the gals at The Inn. One of their regular haunts, the restaurant had a great wine list, a Mediterranean menu that was as eclectic as Roscoe, its owner, and a dark, but classy, warm and cozy atmosphere that made it perfect for a business meeting or informal gathering of friends.

Lane embraced Carlina, the first to arrive and, frankly, her favorite. Lane had been smitten with "Car" when they'd met at some fundraising event or another. She was a stockbroker and model-perfect with long dark hair, brown eyes, flawless skin and a tall, shapely figure. Lane would have been willing that night to give up all her career plans to go home with her and become her sex slave, but had backed off when she noticed the hunky fellow whose arm she was hanging on.

"Where are the others? I'm usually the last to arrive."

Lane tipped her head. "They're right behind you, Car. I'm surprised you didn't run into them at the hostess stand." They stood, exchanging hugs.

Emily was a pediatrician. Lane had also met her at a charity event, something for one of the local hospitals. For some reason they clicked. Emily was short, only five-three, but she had a wholesome attractiveness and a round face accentuated by bright blue eyes and blonde hair.

The last of the group was Tara. Tara was blonde too, but tall. At a glance she was sweet and kindly, but she had a reputation for chewing up IRS representatives. A tax attorney, she and Lane had met in a courtroom over a case during the first critical year that Lane had been on the bench and had hit it off instantly.

Tara, Emily and Car were the closest thing Lane had to friends. Which is to say, that while they got together regularly and shared a lot about their lives with one another, none of the others knew much about her. At least not the things that could cost a person her profession or worse.

They were ordering their drinks when first Lane, then Carlina noticed the table full of men nearby who were giving their waitress a hard time.

"Look at those Neanderthals over there groping that poor thing," Carlina said, breaking into their conversation. "I'd bet my Beemer every one of them is married too."

Lane's anger rose with each second that passed. The pretty blonde was doing her best to avoid the men's hands while doing her job, but it was a losing proposition.

When their waiter arrived a moment later with their drinks, Lane asked, "Is Roscoe here this evening?"

Carefully placing the drinks in front of each woman, he replied, "I believe he is."

Lane glared at the customer with his arm around the young woman's waist, holding her in place. "Would you ask him if he has a minute to speak with me?"

The waiter became noticeably nervous. "Uh…sure, Ms. Stanford. Is there some way I can be of assistance?" The voices of the men at the nearby table grew louder.

"No, please simply tell him I'd like a moment of his time."

The waiter scurried off and in a few minutes Roscoe, the rotund owner, came trundling over to their table.

"Lane," he nodded. "Ladies. I do hope there is no problem with your service this evening?"

Lane pushed up from her chair, towering over him in her heels. She placed a hand on his shoulder. "Our service is impeccable, as always, Roscoe." She leaned in close to speak quietly. "But that table full of jerks over there"—she inclined her head in the direction of the drunken, laughing hyenas—"is getting far better service than they deserve." Roscoe glanced toward the noise and back to Lane. "Do you suppose you could arrange for the young lady to serve our table instead and maybe give them the oldest male waiter working this evening?"

He looked quickly again at the table of men. "Of course, of course. Thank you for bringing this to my attention."

"Always glad to help."

She watched as he waddled over to the wait station, speaking first to the young woman and next to a fortyish-looking fellow. When the blonde looked toward their table, Lane simply smiled, but when the waitress returned the smile, her heart literally skipped a beat. It raced inexplicably as she made her way to their table.

"Good evening, ladies, my name is Ali. Can I get anyone another drink?"

Lane raised her glass, offering the beautiful, blue-eyed waitress an appreciative gaze. "Czar's Gold vodka straight up with two olives, Ali, and thank you," she ordered, even though she hadn't intended to have another drink.

When no one else requested another, the waitress asked, "Have you ladies decided what you want to order or do you need a few more minutes?"

Carlina spoke up, flashing the blonde an engaging smile. "I think we would like a little more time."

Lane couldn't help but watch as Ali walked away. She was short, no more than five and a half feet, if that, but she moved with grace and… confidence. She seemed on some level wiser than her young age would indicate. Her uniform of white shirt, black pants and shoes wasn't particularly flattering, but neither did it hide a figure that appeared to be very shapely.

After a minute she told the girls, "Well, ladies, I'm sorry to say that I won't be joining you for dinner. I have another engagement I simply can't miss." She checked her watch. "Actually, I should be leaving in five minutes." She watched intently as the blonde started their way, carrying her fresh drink. "On the upside, that means you'll have a lot of time to talk about yours truly this evening."

"Thank you," she said as the waitress set the drink down. She looked up at her…and froze. Her eyes were amazing, so deep a blue that Lane felt herself falling into them. And they sparkled like the tiny sapphire posts that adorned her ears.

Eventually, out of nowhere, she heard Tara calling her name. "Lane…hello." Lane glanced around dazedly, ascertaining that the waitress was gone, and averted her eyes. "Are you okay?" Tara asked.

"Of course I'm fine," Lane responded automatically. She quickly took a swallow from her water glass, trying to douse the warmth that had unexpectedly erupted inside her.

Tara said, "I was saying, we would never talk about you behind your back, we'd do it to your face. Right, girls?" They all laughed.

"So who's the hunk you're standing us up for?" Emily asked.

Lane shook her head. "Sorry, ladies. I'm not at liberty to divulge that information."

"She's afraid one of us will steal him," Carlina said, and she sipped her drink.

"You girls wouldn't have to steal…" Lane winked. "I'd share."

They all laughed again. They had a long-standing joke about sharing men, since they had all bragged on occasion about their conquests, which inevitably led to someone drooling with interest.

The waitress reappeared. "Are you ready to order?" After looks around the table they all agreed. She started with Lane. "What can I get you?"

"Regrettably, I won't be staying for dinner," Lane said, handing her menu to her.

Ali took the menu. "I'm sorry."

"Not half as sorry as I am," Lane mumbled.

"Excuse me?"

Lane attempted to shake the nonsense from her head. "Nothing. I was thinking aloud."

Ali moved around the table, coming last to Carlina. "What can I get you?"

Carlina exhaled a sigh. "I can't decide. Is there something you'd recommend?" She batted long lashes, smiling. Lane got the distinct impression Carlina was flirting with the young woman, and for reasons she couldn't begin to understand, that bothered her.

The waitress leaned over Carlina's shoulder, touching a finger to her menu. "The salmon is one of the most popular dishes."

Carlina continued to look up at her, completely ignoring the menu. "And what is your personal favorite?" She arched a perfect brow.

She *was* flirting. Lane discovered that she was jealous—and not because the waitress had attracted Carlina's attention, but because Carlina was attracting hers. Lane tried to dismiss the possibility that she might be smitten with the young woman. Lane Stanford didn't do "smitten."

In any case, the waitress seemed thrown by Carlina's attentions. She was noticeably nervous when she quietly said, "I shouldn't say, but I really like the shrimp dish."

Carlina's gaze burned into Ali's blue eyes. "Is there anything else you like?"

Tara and Emily, deep in a discussion of their own, were oblivious to the exchange between Carlina and the waitress, which had Lane squirming in her seat, disquieted by the emotions running through her.

When the young woman left with their orders, Lane turned to Carlina. "If I didn't know better, Car, I'd swear you were flirting with her." She assumed a matter-of-fact expression that she hoped made her remarks appear to be a passing observation.

Carlina sipped her drink, eying Lane over the rim of the glass. Putting it down, she leaned toward Lane. "What's wrong with a little flirting?"

"Nothing, I suppose," Lane said with some asperity. "Isn't that what we were trying to protect her from, though, when we had her switched to this table?"

Carlina responded to the rebuke with a rueful smile. "Good point, Your Honor. Thanks for the rap on the knuckles. I'll mend my ways. Promise."

Lane took another peek at her watch and mentally cursed. Damn. It was a quarter of seven. If she left that very minute, she might only be a few minutes late, but...she didn't want to leave until she had another chance to speak to the waitress.

By the time Ali ventured back to their table, it was nearing seven. Lane stood quickly. "Well, ladies, it's been a pleasure as always. Enjoy your dinner. I'll see you again in a month or so."

Ali smiled. "Please come again when you can enjoy dinner with us."

Lane pressed more than enough money to cover her bill and a generous tip into her hand. "Thank you, I will." She had to force herself to leave.

* * *

Stepping outside of the restaurant, she pulled out her cell phone and cursed once more. It was dead—again. She rushed back inside. "Is there a phone I could use? My cell is dead." She waved the useless device in her hand. "And I have an urgent call I need to make."

The hostess smiled warmly. "Of course, Ms. Stanford." She led Lane to a small, cramped office. Handing her the receiver from the desk phone, she said, "You have to dial nine first to call out. Take your time."

After she'd closed the door, Lane realized Caroline's number was in her phone. Her very dead phone. "Damn it to hell!" she exclaimed as she slammed down the receiver and raced from the office. "Thanks," she called to the hostess as she breezed past her. She managed to make the twenty-five-minute drive to Caroline's in under twenty minutes, but it didn't matter, she was nearly half an hour late, and after Saturday night's debacle, she was certain Caroline would be furious.

She knocked lightly and tried the knob. When it turned, she pushed inside, but before she could utter a word, she was preempted by the sound of glass shattering a few feet from where she stood. She froze, fixing her gaze on the redhead staring her down with anger burning in her eyes. She slowly raised her hands. "Caroline, I'm so sorry." She took a step into the living room. "I tried to call, but my cell was dead again, and I couldn't use the landline because your number…"

Caroline cocked her arm and hurled another glass in Lane's direction, screaming as it shattered, "You are so damned inconsiderate. I've never met a man that has anything on you!"

Lane took another tentative step. "But Caroline…"

Caroline yelled, "Don't 'but' me. You think all I have to do is stand around waiting for you to grace me with your presence?"

When she raised yet another glass, Lane yelled, "Caroline, please stop breaking your glassware."

She loudly slammed it on the counter. "I had a nice dinner prepared for us. You were supposed to be here half an hour ago. If you had called, I could have saved it, but that would require a certain amount of consideration, something you've shown damn little of."

Lane was finding it harder and harder to breathe. This woman, who she had thought was so fun and free-spirited, was becoming stifling. Lane would be ridding herself of her posthaste. First, though, she had to get her settled down, make sure the break, when it came, would be a clean one.

She lowered her eyes. "I'm really very sorry, Caroline." She tried to sound as contrite as she could. "Can I make it up to you by taking you to dinner somewhere?"

Caroline stepped from behind the counter wearing only heels below the lacy apron covering her blouse and what appeared to be a thong. "Do I look like I'm dressed to go out?"

"No…no, you don't," Lane said, swallowing hard. "You look ready to be devoured." She touched her hand to her stomach. "And I'm starving."

"You think you can waltz in here and have your way with me after I ruined dinner waiting on you?"

She approached Caroline cautiously, running a fingertip up her smooth thigh to a bare hip. In a sultry tone, she said, "What I wouldn't give to feast on you." She leaned in and nipped at Caroline's neck, making her gasp. "Come on…let me make you forget all about dinner," she murmured, her breath hot against Caroline's skin.

Caroline grabbed Lane's hand and forced it to the warm, wet spot between her legs. "Just fuck me, Renee. Now, dammit. Before I change my mind."

Lane did as instructed, taking her right there between the kitchen and living room. When she finished, Caroline lay breathless on the counter amidst the dishes she'd not yet broken. In the bedroom later, Lane wrenched several more orgasms from her.

When Caroline asked when she'd see her again, Lane answered evasively. As she kissed the enticing redhead goodbye, she knew this would be their last time together. She paused in the doorway for a last look before slipping out into the night. She'd miss the sex with Caroline, but as hot as it was, it wasn't worth the burden and demands. This evening had certainly shown her that.

CHAPTER FOUR

The following morning Lane summoned Jeremy the minute he arrived. "Close the door," she commanded. She stopped him shy of taking a seat. "This will only take a second." He looked at her with apprehension. Her eyes remained fixed on the papers in front of her. "I need you to clean out the apartment."

Jeremy's jaw dropped. "But…I…I thought…"

She raised her hand. "It doesn't work. Would you please see to it that it's handled? Thank you."

Jeremy shook his head. "Okay." He hesitated briefly. "Anything else?"

She glanced up, feeling her jaw tighten. "No." The metamorphosis had occurred. She was back to her unemotional, icy persona. He left without another word.

When she breezed out of her office heading to court, he called out, "The apartment has been cleaned. And I have to say that woman's language could put yours to shame."

She didn't bother with a response.

* * *

Lane was poring over the mountain of work on her desk when her phone rang about six thirty. Jeremy's cell number showed on the screen. She wondered if she'd forgotten an appointment.

She answered, "Jeremy…"

"You've got to get over to the apartment now. She's gone ballistic and won't leave until she talks to you in person."

"What are you talking about, Jeremy? And speak up, I can barely hear you."

"Caroline is here, at the apartment. Henry called me two minutes after I walked in my place and said there was a 'raving redhead' in the lobby who wouldn't leave until she spoke to Renee in person. He assumed I had been careless enough to let two of my women find out about each other. I rushed over and brought her upstairs so she wouldn't attract more attention than she already has. God, I'm sure he thinks I'm the biggest cad in town."

Lane began stuffing papers in her briefcase. "I've got to call the car service to cancel my car. I'll grab a cab."

"I'll call the car service. Just please get here before she tears me to pieces."

"Fine, fine," she said as she locked the door behind her. "I'll be there as soon as I can."

* * *

The minute the door lock clicked and Lane rushed in, Jeremy set his glass down on the coffee table and exited.

She dropped her briefcase in a chair on her way to the bar. "Would you like something to drink?"

"Hell no!" Caroline yelled, coming to the counter. "What I want is an explanation for why you had your sidekick dump me."

Lane poured herself some vodka and took a slow, steady sip, before asking, "Would you like to break some of my expensive glassware?"

"Do you want to answer my fucking question?"

Lane took another sip and leaned over the bar toward Caroline. "You're smart and beautiful, and I can personally attest to how magnificent you are in bed…"

"But?"

Lane shrugged. "I…I'm not thinking it's right for me." She prayed she'd read Caroline correctly. "I want more. I think I'm ready to settle down. You know, adopt a few kids and start a family. I wasn't feeling"—she waved a hand between them—"that we were headed that direction." She took another sip of her drink. "Did I read things wrong? Is that a possibility?" Lane worked to fill her expression with pure sincerity.

Caroline shook her head. "No, you didn't read it wrong. I'm young. I have a lot of oats left to sow. And I'm not sure I ever want to do that family thing with children."

Lane concealed her pleasure. There was a reason she was successful in her career. She was a masterful manipulator. Calling up the heartache of her mother's passing, she turned eyes glistening with tears to meet Caroline's. She touched Caroline's hand. "I really am sorry it didn't work out." Caroline met Lane's eyes with a sympathetic gaze. "And I'm sorry I didn't have the courage to break it off myself."

Caroline placed her other hand atop Lane's and squeezed. "It's okay, darling." She stroked her fingers over Lane's cheek. "I do hope you find your happily ever after."

Lane caught Caroline's hand as she drew it away, pressing the palm to her lips. She asked meekly, "Are you sure we can't have more than a physical relationship?" Lane could tell by the pull of Caroline's hand that she was ready to bolt.

"I'm sorry, Renee, but no." She smiled. "You only show this tough exterior, but you're a real softie at heart. It's very endearing." She tilted her head. "Unfortunately, I don't think I'm meant for endearing." She gathered up her purse, hanging it on her shoulder. "Perhaps we'll run into each other out and about sometime."

Lane nodded as Caroline left, closing the door with a click. Smiling, Lane raised her glass in salute to her skills.

* * *

No sooner had she entered the penthouse from the back stairs when she heard a knock at the front door. She froze. *No, she couldn't possibly know where I live.* She moved soundlessly to the peephole, holding her breath until she spied Jeremy in the hallway.

"What?" She jerked open the door, turning her back on him as she headed to the kitchen.

He stomped along behind her. "I have a life, you know, and I don't appreciate being dragged into the middle of all the drama you create in yours."

She stopped him in the doorway with a glare and pulled the vodka bottle from the cupboard. "Did you come up here to submit your resignation?"

"Well, no..." he sputtered. "I don't know how you do it. Don't you ever want to find one person to settle down with?"

She leaned against the kitchen counter. "Why do I need the complication of a relationship? I get what I need without the commitments and demands."

He sighed. "Don't you want someone to hold every night, to wake up with and share your life with?"

"Not really." She shrugged, sipping the drink she had poured for herself. "I've spent enough time in courtrooms to know that relationships are nothing more than big complications. I prefer to keep things simple, as they are."

"This one certainly wasn't simple."

She drained the glass. "A rarity. They usually walk away without looking back."

He shook his head. "I guess it's true what they say about redheads being hotheaded. I've got to go. I'm supposed to meet some people"— he checked his watch—"ten minutes ago."

* * *

She was back from court by three the next day, which gave her time to sift through at least part of the mounting pile on her desk. She'd been working on it for little more than an hour when Jeremy knocked and poked his head in.

"I know you said no interruptions, and I'm sorry, but your father called and said you're to meet him for dinner tonight." Lane closed her eyes, exhaling slowly. "He said for you to pick the place. I'm to call him back with the arrangements, but he said, and I quote"—Jeremy mimicked his deep gruff voice—"'it's vital to her future.'" He tapped his pen on the notepad. "Where shall I make your reservation?"

Lane found the habit annoying as hell. "See if you can get us a table at The Inn."

"Oh, I'm sure Roscoe will find you a spot." He spun dramatically and left.

Damn, Lane thought. She'd hoped to start catching up on everything that accumulated in the last few days.

He came back ten minutes later. "Your reservation is for six thirty and he'll meet you there."

"Can you call the car service? They had me down for seven. If they can't cover with my regular driver, cancel, and I'll get a cab."

"Already done, Randall will be here at six. I'm out of here in ten unless you need something else." Shaking her head, she offered a "thanks."

She wondered during the ride to the restaurant what had possessed her father to demand a meeting on such short notice. She was surprised to see him seated alone when the hostess led her to the table.

She put a hand on his shoulder before he could get up, leaning over and placing a kiss on his cheek. "Hi, Daddy. To what do I owe this unexpected surprise?" She sat across the small table.

"Tom Beckman called me to say you haven't been in touch."

She fiddled with the silverware. No one but her father made her nervous. Mustering a modicum of confidence, she said, "I've been incredibly swamped the last few weeks." She heard the trepidation in her voice, but she doubted that he did. His hearing wasn't nearly as sharp as it had been when he was on the bench.

He cleared his throat. "Be that as it may, you need to get acquainted with Thomas, and the sooner the better for you in the long run."

Lane caught the waiter's attention and noticed the waitress from Tuesday evening, who was waiting a table across the restaurant. While her eyes traveled over the young woman's firm backside, her mind roamed to other places.

"If you don't get serious about things, you'll never get further than you are."

Lane refocused her eyes on the dark ones staring at her from across the table. "I know." She nodded, reassuringly. "I've had a couple of cases lately that have monopolized my time, but I have him at the top of my list."

He sipped his drink. "Very well. I'll let him know he can expect to hear from you within a week."

Terrific, she thought. *Now I have the added pressure of another demand on my time.* She set aside her irritation long enough to enjoy dinner with him, talking about business and politics—and stealing as many glances as she dared at the attractive blonde. When they were finished and their bill was settled, her father insisted Lane walk him out. Holding onto his arm, she chanced another look at the waitress and was, to her surprise, rewarded with a smile in return. Lane's heart skipped a few beats as she stepped into the night with her father.

* * *

Lane never fantasized about women, but as far behind and as busy as she was with work and other commitments, all weekend she kept conjuring up images of the waitress. She couldn't stop thinking about her, and she didn't even know if she was gay.

By the following Tuesday, she'd become so distracted thinking about the woman, she decided to go see her. While waiting for her car to arrive, she phoned and asked the hostess if she could get a small table by seven thirty. She assured her they'd find one.

Once she was at the restaurant, she sat at the bar and ordered a drink. She didn't make a habit of doing that. It wouldn't do to be thought of as a judge with a drinking problem. Not that her drinking *was* a problem.

Finally the blonde stepped up to the wait station beside the seat Lane occupied.

"Ali, right?"

She answered Lane cautiously. "That's right."

Lane couldn't take her eyes off the blue ones looking back at her. "You served my friends and me last week."

Ali looked her over closely and then smiled. Lane thought she would melt off the barstool. "Oh yeah. You're the ones that got me moved from that table of Neanderthals, so thanks. You ladies were definitely more pleasant to serve." She took the drinks offered by the bartender. "Have a good evening."

Lane couldn't keep from watching her in the mirror behind the bar as she walked away, and for a moment at least she didn't care if anyone noticed. The nearness of the beautiful blue-eyed blonde had caused a pulsing between her thighs and an elevated pounding in her chest, leaving her feeling slightly dizzy. The sensation in her lower body was all too familiar, but the other—that was something totally foreign.

Someone was watching her, Ali thought. Learning to sense that had saved her from many a danger in the past and wasn't something she'd soon forget. It had to be the gorgeous dark-haired woman who'd spoken to her when she picked up that last drink order. Attention that ardent from a total stranger made her feel uneasy, even though, when she finally did catch the woman's intense gaze, she simply smiled at her. When her break came, she made her way across the restaurant to the table she was dining at.

"Well, hello again."

Ali scanned the handsome face, its eyes even darker than the perfect dark hair that framed it. "Do I know you from somewhere? Or should I ask if you know me from somewhere?"

"No." The woman shook her head slowly. "I'm certain if I had met you before last week, I wouldn't have forgotten." She set her elbow on the table and rested her chin in her hand.

"It's just a little…" Ali didn't want to offend a regular customer, but she couldn't shake off the nervousness her scrutiny had produced.

"I'm sorry if my staring has made you uncomfortable." Lane hesitated. "You're so beautiful…I couldn't help myself."

Ali's cheeks warmed, and she looked immediately at her feet. "I, uh…" Slowly she raised her eyes. "I don't exactly know what to say to that."

The woman slipped a card from her purse and offered it to her. "Say you'll have dinner with me."

Ali's hand trembled slightly as she took the card, which contained only, "Elane R. Stanford, Esquire" and a phone number, along with a logo she recognized as the scales of justice.

"My friends call me Lane. I hope you will too."

Slowly returning her gaze to the lawyer, she said, "There's, uh… someone."

"I'm only asking you for dinner." Lane leaned back confidently. "You might enjoy it."

Ali glanced again at the card. "I don't think so, but thank you for the invitation." She slid the card into her back pocket. To her relief the woman didn't seem to be bothered by the rejection.

"Think about it, there's no pressure. You have my number. Call if you change your mind." She smiled warmly, which made her eyes twinkle in the dim light.

The expression reflected something more than the lawyer said, something vaguely familiar to Ali. It seemed, as impossible as it was to imagine, like sincerity. There had been few people in her past who ever seemed sincere. A lawyer was the last person she expected it from.

Ali swallowed a knot of fear. "Well, anyway, enjoy your evening."

She hid in the corner of the kitchen for several minutes, staring at the card the woman had given her. She couldn't help being suspicious of a lawyer offering to take her to dinner. "Come on," she murmured under her breath. *I wasn't born yesterday.*

The woman had definitely pinged her gaydar. But she knew better than to think someone so attractive would ask her on a date. People like her were here to serve people like…she glanced at the card again…like Elane R. Stanford, Esquire. People like Ms. Stanford didn't date waitresses. They dated women like the brunette she was with last week. Oh, she thought, that table of women must have been lesbian couples. Two blondes and two dark-haired women and maybe not in that combination, but all obviously successful, powerful women and all clearly out of her league.

Tucking the card into her back pocket, she peeked through the kitchen doors to see if the lady lawyer was still at her table. Whew. She was gone. She returned to work, still uneasy about the feelings the woman had stirred in her.

CHAPTER FIVE

Thomas Beckman and Lane were scheduled for a dinner meeting the following Thursday. Discretion was key when it came to the company she kept publicly so the reservation was at a small, dark restaurant across the river. It would pass Beckman's scrutiny, but most importantly, she'd never seen anyone there that she recognized or anyone who seemed to recognize her. Jeremy arranged everything. She needed only to show up.

She wanted to drink until she was drunk as he talked. It was the same stuff she'd heard from every other "important contact" her father insisted she align with to gain political footholds for her future. Her father was determined to see his daughter seated in a higher-ranking position and the sooner the better. She was ready, he said. She had his powerful, commanding ambition, not the romantic, daydreaming passion of her mother.

What her father thought about her not yet having married at the age of thirty-six or even been engaged, she couldn't guess. She was reasonably sure he didn't have a clue about her sexuality, though she wondered if that was a conscious choice on his part or naïvete. He probably assumed she was putting her career and success above all. He'd managed the last twenty-eight years without a woman taking care of him. Why would she need a man to take care of her?

All that was fine with her, frankly. When events required them, she could arrange to be accompanied by a smart, handsome male escort. But marriage, well, that wasn't in the plan. Not hers anyway.

She was never happier to have anything end than the dinner with Thomas Beckman, self-made businessman and self-centered creep. His parting handshake and slimy smile had made Lane want to wash not only her hands but her brain. Instead, she went home, put her feet up and had a drink. It wasn't difficult to erase Beckman from her memory as it turned out. Five minutes after she kicked off her shoes and savored a long, sip of her favorite vodka, her mind was filled with thoughts of Ali, the lovely blonde waitress.

She smiled. She was a beauty. And likely hiding a hell of a body under that uniform. Young, though. In her mid-twenties, probably? She hadn't been with anyone that age since her college days. She couldn't figure out why she found her so appealing. It felt like more than sexual attraction. But what that might be eluded her. The more she thought about Ali, though, the more she felt—something.

* * *

She tried keeping the young woman off her mind by staying busy, but when the long days ended and she was tired and alone, she couldn't banish the thoughts of her. She saw herself holding Ali—intimately—and that aroused so much more than her libido. When two weeks passed without a word, she had Jeremy make a reservation for her at Roscoe's on Thursday evening. If she couldn't get Ali to have dinner with her, she could at least find out why. Maybe then she could rid herself of this fixation.

Lane kept an eye on the blonde beauty as she worked her section of the restaurant, a grouping of half a dozen tables. When Ali finally looked her way, Lane nodded, eliciting from Ali a slight tip of her head and smile in return. *Hmm*, Lane thought. *Maybe I should simply show up here several times a week for dinner and stare at her until she accepts my invitation.*

After taking as much time as she dared with her meal, Lane stood to leave. When she was a few steps short of the hostess stand, a voice so soft Lane wasn't sure she'd heard it said, "Excuse me." She ignored it, continuing over the restaurant's polished black pebble tile floors through a stone arch toward the door until she heard it again, accompanied by the lightest touch to her elbow.

Lane's heart leapt to her throat as she slowly turned to meet the amazing blue eyes looking up into hers. "Yes?"

"I'm curious. Why would you want to have dinner with a lowly waitress?"

Lane fell back on well-honed courtroom skills. "Your job is your contribution to a working society. We all have one. All equally important." She lifted a brow. "I'm intrigued. I'd like to know more about you."

"I'd like to know more about you." As the lawyer said this, she leaned in so close to her that Ali could smell her expensive perfume and get a peek at the flawless skin where the top of Lane's blouse formed a V, revealing subtle cleavage. In a hushed tone, she added, "And I think you're the most beautiful woman I've ever seen." She leaned back. Her smile was completely disarming. "If you're not inclined or have other persuasions, I will certainly understand."

Ali found herself mesmerized by the dark, mysterious eyes looking into hers. There was something hidden in their depths, but she couldn't begin to guess what it might be. This woman was sophisticated and charming beyond belief. Ali had never had anyone remotely like her give her the time of day.

"I have to be running." Lane drew a noticeably deep breath. "You have my number if you decide you want to have dinner sometime." Lane tipped her head. "Call me."

Ali smiled. "I just might."

Lane stepped from the restaurant, gasping for a gulp of the fresh night air. She couldn't recall a time she'd become breathless from simply talking with a woman. "God, she's beautiful," she whispered under her breath.

"Ma'am?" Randall asked as he opened and held the car door for her.

"Nothing, Randall…" Her stomach fluttered as she slid into the car. "Nothing," she murmured.

After slipping behind the wheel, he met her eyes in the rearview mirror. "Where to now, ma'am?"

"Across the river to Sixteenth and Concord. And I'll need you to drop my things with my doorman. I'll catch a cab home."

He started the engine. "Yes, ma'am."

She removed the sunglasses from the breast pocket of her suit jacket and pulled all the cash she had out of her wallet, shoving it into her pants pockets. If Jeremy found out what she was about to do he'd have a stroke. He was fast tracking to be her campaign manager when the time came for her to make another run. Something like this would send him over the edge.

"Don't get out," she ordered Randall when he stopped the car. "Your discretion is appreciated." She saw the affirmative nod of his head as she climbed out into the night.

Sliding the sunglasses in place, she pressed some bills into the sweaty palm waiting inside the door. Taking her time, she made her way through the overcrowded and dank little hole-in-the-wall to the only spot open along the bar. The rock music roared as she leaned over to yell her drink order to the bartender. A twenty-something blonde, Lane guessed, with hair spiked so short you could see her scalp and a cute, round face sullied by a piercing in her brow and another that split the middle of her bottom lip. Lane knew full well what purpose a lip or tongue piercing served. She, however, would continue to rely on her God-given talents. After all, she'd never had any complaints.

Lane slid the money across the bar to the punked-out woman and sipped the vodka. She raised the glass in salute, and the bartender smiled and wiggled the brow with the earring before moving down the bar. Lane rested her back on the bar, surveying the sea of bodies as if she were looking over land for purchase. She watched the torsos gyrating on the dance floor intently but didn't find a single woman who attracted the slightest bit of interest. Thirty minutes later, as she finished her second drink and was about to ask the bartender to call her a cab, taking her usual precautions about where she summoned cabs to, a raven-haired woman in three-inch spike heels pressed ever so slightly against her.

"Excuse me." Lane turned to find eyes as dark as a moonless night gazing at her. "Are you waiting for someone?"

Lane turned back to the bar. "Only you, darling." The bartender reappeared, and Lane indicated her empty glass and the woman's beside it.

The woman stretched up to get closer. "Let's go where we can talk." She leaned back.

"Lead the way."

Making their way through the throngs of women, Lane brushed breasts—and more than a few derrières—as the woman led her toward a long hallway past the end of the bar. To the left was a double doorway into a room filled with women crowded around pool tables. On the right were restrooms and, further down, before the hall ended at a steel exit door, doors marked STORAGE and OFFICE.

They stopped in the empty hall beyond the restrooms. Leaning a shoulder against the wall, the stranger sipped her drink, and said to Lane, "Now we can talk without screaming."

Talk was the last thing Lane wanted to do. She leaned close, extending her long, strong fingers. "Hi, I'm Renee. You're incredibly beautiful, and I'd actually enjoy making you scream." The thought of having those glistening red lips pressed to her neck while her probing fingers wandered elsewhere made Lane ache.

The woman took Lane's offered hand, holding it gently. "I'm Sophie. You sure don't mess around."

Lane kept the hand in hers, stroking her thumb over its soft flesh. Smiling seductively, she said, "Life's too short not to stop and smell the roses." She leaned closer, placing her lips a breath away from Sophie's ear. "Or stroke their velvet petals." She heard the sharp intake of air the same moment Sophie's hand squeezed hers. Lane took a step back and watched as the dark eyes grew wanton. "Do you have a car?"

Slowly moving her head side to side, Sophie drew Lane further down the hall into a deeper shadow. She placed their drink glasses on the floor, encircling Lane's waist with her hands and insinuating her leg between Lane's thighs. "We don't need a car." She slid one hand from around Lane's waist to her crotch.

Lane flinched at the touch before catching Sophie's wrist and pulling her hand away. She cupped Sophie's full breasts, roughly rubbing her thumbs over the nipples, turning them to hard pebbles. Sophie groaned and rocked hard against Lane's muscled thigh. Lane lowered her mouth to Sophie's ear again to murmur, "I'll fuck you right here if that's what you want."

Sophie responded by pulling Lane's hand from her breast and pushing it toward her waistband. Lane found her center hot and incredibly wet. She dropped her head against Lane's shoulder, holding tightly to her hips to steady herself. Lane whispered, "Don't worry, I've got you." When she spread her legs further, Lane's strong fingers glided easily into her.

Sophie threw her head back, panting, "Oh, yes…yes…yes…" She came in a shudder, burying her face against Lane's neck to muffle her loud moans. Her body shook one final time as Lane withdrew from her. When her breathing slowed enough to speak, she muttered, "My God, that was…"

When Sophie reached for the button of Lane's pants she quickly stopped her. In a low tone, she purred, "I'm good, darling. I came watching you."

* * *

Her shift finally over, Ali again pulled the lawyer's card from her pocket. It was beginning to show wear from being slipped in and out and being fingered as she had considered the possible motivations for the dinner invitation. She'd hoped the lawyer's response to the question she'd asked earlier would give her an idea if she were out to make trouble for her. But she'd only sensed attraction. Her hands grew sweaty as she remembered how the woman said she was beautiful. No one had ever said those words to her like that. So...sincerely. She'd been told she was pretty and she believed that, but "beautiful," the way the woman said it and looked at her with those dark bedroom eyes— that had been more like a soft caress.

If they passed on the street, Ali would be more likely to pick Lane out as a model than as a lesbian. She certainly was as beautiful as ones she'd seen in magazines. She didn't look at all like the lesbians she knew, not in her expensively tailored pantsuit and shoulder-length hair. *Imposing.* Ali decided that word was the best way to describe her. Powerful-looking, but no, not necessarily gay. One of those bi-curious women maybe.

In any case, it didn't much matter, because like she told the lawyer, there was already someone else. She slipped into the manager's office and dialed the number. It rang and rang for several minutes but was never answered. She didn't expect it would be. She'd sneak in before her shift tomorrow and try again.

CHAPTER SIX

"Wow," Jeremy said, taking a seat opposite Lane the following morning. "Sleepless night?" He indicated his eyes with two fingers.

She pulled a compact mirror from her lap drawer. "What on earth are you talking about?" Her eyes were clear as glass.

Leaning forward and moving his index finger in a half circle, he said, "The dark circles. Late meeting?"

She looked closer, seeing the faint shadows under her eyes now that he mentioned them. She thought she'd covered them, but in the harsh light of the office they were quite noticeable. Expressionless, she looked back at him. "Price of business." A warm sensation surged through her at the thought of what she'd actually done the previous night and early morning with the insatiable Sophie.

Following sex in the bar's hallway, they'd finished their drinks and crowded onto the dance floor where Sophie grinded on Lane's thigh until she was sure she could feel Sophie's wetness soaking through her slacks. Lane suggested they go to Sophie's place and while Sophie was telling her friends she was leaving, Lane had the bartender call a cab.

Lane had wanted to take her in the back of the cab. Wanted to free her full breasts from their constraints and get her off again. She knew people behaved that way. She'd been witness to those kinds of confessions in court. Instead she'd simply stroked Sophie's thigh, in long, slow movements, keeping the fire burning. When they reached her tiny apartment in a run-down neighborhood, Lane pinned her to the doorframe.

"Tell me what you want and I'll give it to you," Lane recognized the deep and throaty sound in her voice. She was aroused.

"Anything?" Sophie asked between gasps as Lane bit the tender flesh of her neck.

Lane pulled her hard onto her thigh. "If I can, yes."

Sophie slipped from the press of Lane's body and dragged her down a short hallway to a bedroom. Beneath the dim light on the bedside table she pulled open a drawer. When she turned to Lane, a sizeable strap-on dangled from her hand. The atmosphere became electric as Lane eyed the soft rubber in a leather harness. "Will you fuck me with this?"

Lane stepped closer. "Anyway you want me to, darling."

Their tryst lasted for hours, encompassed multiple orgasms and ended with Sophie bent over the dresser, too spent to stand on her own. Lane had had to brace herself on the dresser, for that matter, feeling her legs quivering beneath her. Half holding Sophie up, Lane guided her toward the bed.

"I want to touch you...I want...to get you off," Sophie said breathlessly.

Lane gave her a half smile. "I got off." She unbuckled the harness, dropping the apparatus next to Sophie on the bed. "I think another orgasm might kill me, but if you want to continue..."

When Sophie shook her head "no," Lane pulled on her underwear, pants, buttoned her blouse and stepped across the hall to the bathroom. As she washed her hands, she surveyed herself in the dull mirror and prayed she didn't smell too obviously of sex since she was going to have to stop and collect her things from her doorman. She stepped inside the bedroom door and swept her hand through her hair. "It's been amazing. Maybe I'll see you again sometime."

Sophie nodded. "It would be nice, but I know what this was. It's okay."

She didn't know, of course. They never understood that Lane wasn't pleasuring them out of some insatiable sexual desire. It was the conquest...that was what drove her.

Sophie padded naked to where Lane stood. Standing on her tiptoes, she moved to kiss her, but Lane turned her head so Sophie's lips landed on her firm jaw.

She dialed the cab company with Sophie's phone, stepped into the dark, dingy hallway and descended the stairs. Standing in the filthy lobby, she watched for the cab through the smudged glass of the door. She prayed it would arrive quickly. Jeremy would die if he knew what she'd done. But it would be far worse if she was mugged, beaten or something more heinous where she was and the news got out who she was.

"Lane..." His voice pierced through the fog of last night's memories. "Hello..."

She felt a light flush in her cheeks and hoped he didn't notice. "Let's get this done. I've got work."

He opened the appointment book in his lap. "Don't forget you have the fund-raiser Sunday evening for the hospital pediatric wing. Emily called to confirm and said"—he gestured with his fingers—"'you tell her I expect to see her there because I don't have a date.'"

"Fine. Please make sure all my dry cleaning has been dropped by my place."

He stood. "Sure thing, boss. Anything else?"

"Yes," she glared, "don't call me boss."

"Yes, Your Honor."

* * *

Ali snuck into the manager's office again before she started her shift the following day right before eleven. Dialing the number once more, she crossed her fingers. Busy! She hung up and watched the clock on the desk. After a minute she dialed again with the same result.

After the fourth attempt it rang, but only once before an angry female voice said, "Hello?"

Ali spoke quickly, "I need to speak to Z. It's really important."

After a hesitation the voice said, "She ain't around and you're burnin' my time."

Ali pleaded. "Can you please give her a message? I have to get a message to her."

Gruffly the woman asked, "What?"

"Can you please tell her to call Al at four, two..."

"Whoa there, Miss Thing." She cut Ali off. The woman spoke away from the mouthpiece. "Anyone got a real good memory?" After a moment, the voice said, "Go ahead, sweet thing." As Ali recited the number and gave her name as Al in the phone, the woman repeated it loudly and added, "That's for Z. Must be her other babe." She gave a loud, coarse laugh.

"Thank you," Ali said meekly, returning the phone to its base. She slipped unnoticed from the office and began helping with the lunch setup.

About four forty the tables were only sparsely filled when the manager appeared at her side. "There appears to be a rather urgent call for you."

Ali feigned utter surprise. "For me?"

He shrugged. "They asked for a blonde named 'Al.' Take it in the office and don't be long. You have customers."

She quickly placed her order in the kitchen and hurried to the office. "Hello," she answered timidly.

"Hey, doll. Somethin' urgent?" The voice, though rough, contained a hint of genuine concern.

Ali's voice trembled. "God, Z, I miss you so much."

Z chuckled. "No sense in wastin' your time doing that. It's not like we're ever going to be together again." The words stung.

"I know. It's just…" Ali sighed heavily. "I can't help it."

Z's voice softened. "Look…we talked this to death before you left. You got to move on, make a way for yourself. You know, carve out a new place for yourself in the world. I can't be around to take care of you anymore. You gotta start doing it for yourself."

The words weren't new. Ali repeated them to herself every day. She knew what she needed to do, but saying it didn't necessarily make it happen. And hearing Z's voice now, after all these months, made her long for the security of her arms and the comfort of her sure touch.

"Hey, doll, you listenin' to me?"

"Yes." Ali answered without conviction.

"Sounds like a pretty fancy place you're workin' at there."

"Yeah, imagine me in a fancy place."

Z chuckled again. "I can. You're the prettiest girl ever gave me the time of day. I can picture you somewhere fancy, dressed all nice. I bet you're real good at what you do."

Ali smiled. Z always knew how to make her feel better about herself. Tentatively she said, "There's a woman that—"

Z cut her off. "I knew you'd get hooked up with some hot chick."

"No, no," Ali said quickly. "I'm not with her. She just asked me out."

"Uh-huh." Z snickered.

"God, Z, she asked me out for dinner, but I don't know what to do. I mean, I think she only wants to have dinner, I don't even know if she's one of us, but I—"

"Listen, a woman wants to take you out to dinner, then go out for dinner. She's not a dog or a whore is she?"

Ali almost laughed. "Not hardly. She might be someone important. She looks like someone important and that's why I don't get it. She told me I was…" She hesitated, too embarrassed to repeat the words.

"Told you what?"

"She said she thought I was beautiful. So I thought maybe she's, you know, like us, I guess."

"Al, Al, you're still so naïve. A woman don't have to be a dyke to appreciate the good looks of another woman and want to hop in the sack with her. There's all kind of straight women out there lookin' for some action on both sides of the fence. She nice lookin'?"

Ali closed her eyes. "Very."

"Hell, doll, that's a no-brainer. Go out to dinner. Dinner's innocent. See what her story is. If she's interested in jumping your bones, she'll make it plain. And whether she is or ain't into women, it's still a free dinner for you. How many of them have you had since I saw you?"

"None."

"Okay, so it's all settled. I gotta get off here, someone else needs to use the phone. Maybe I'll talk to you again sometime."

Ali felt sadness settling over her. Hearing the voice that had filled her days and warmed her nights for so many years had temporarily lifted her spirits. "I'll come for a visit as soon as I save enough gas money and can afford to take a day off." It would be a five-and-a-half hour drive.

Z's voice was stone cold. "Don't." She paused. "I told you when you left we shouldn't ever see each other again. Besides…there's already someone else."

Ali's vision blurred with tears.

To add insult to injury, Z said, "You didn't think I was going to sit around here and pine away for you, did you?"

Ali sniffled. "No," she barely muttered.

"I told you, you got a chance to start all over. Go out there and get it right this time." In a harsher tone, she added, "And don't be callin' me for permission or advice for nothin' else. I got better things to do with my life than to make up your mind for you. Go out and get you some. It'll make you feel better. It always does me. Have a good life, Al."

Before Ali could utter a simple goodbye, the dial tone pierced her ear. She stood several long moments. The woman she'd devoted years to honoring, respecting and loving had just set her adrift. Z had been her rock, her protector and lover when she'd been so lost she wasn't sure she'd ever find her way. And now she felt like one of the books Z read again and again, until she knew it word for word, cover to back, and would simply return to the library for a different one. She dropped the phone on the base, patted her eyes with her sleeves, swallowed the piece of her heart that had risen to her throat and returned to work.

When her break came she went out back to the partially enclosed patio area where the smokers were forced to go to enjoy their banished habit. Fingering the worn business card again only produced fresh tears. The woman she had grown to trust and love had all but abandoned her. Maybe Z was right. Maybe she should try to start anew. There certainly wasn't anything to stop her from trying now.

* * *

Randall held the door as Lane stepped out into the comfortably warm evening air. He asked, "Ma'am?"

"Pick me up in two hours." He nodded. She mumbled as she climbed the steps of the convention hall, "I'm sure I'll be ready to leave long before then."

She was beat, having spent hours earlier at her father's, talking strategy with him and several businessmen, or "industry leaders," as they liked to think of themselves. She'd only wanted to return home and spend the evening relaxing. Instead she'd dressed up for yet another public showing. She was beginning to feel like one of the those specialty breed dogs whose owners dragged them from show to show, prancing them about in a ring to be inspected and rated. She knew it was all part of the preparation for bigger things in her future. It was too much at times. And sometimes she wanted to quit. But she couldn't. Every time she contemplated it, she could hear her father's voice belittling her for wanting to be ordinary.

Emily sidled up to her as she entered, taking her arm. "God, I'm glad you're here. I was beginning to feel like one of those tropical fish on display in a giant aquarium."

Lane patted her hand. "Good to see you, Emily. How is the business of doctoring children?"

Emily tugged her in the direction of the bar. "If tonight's turnout is any indication, I'd say it's about to become better than ever."

When they had their drinks, Emily led her over to a group and introduced her to the hospital board members. Lane checked her watch frequently throughout the evening, waiting for that magic moment when she could excuse herself to meet the waiting car. As she descended the steps, Randall promptly got out, holding the door.

"Thank you," she offered a tired smile. "Take me home, please."

Stepping out of her shoes the moment she closed the door, she made her way to the kitchen. The cell phone sitting in its charger on the counter briefly caught her eye, but didn't deter her from her intended mission. Once she'd made her drink, she unplugged it and retired to the living room couch. "Ah." Settling into the soft cushions, she brought up the screen and saw a missed call from an unknown caller and a voice mail. She deleted the call message and sipped the vodka, allowing the liquor to warm her inside as she called up her voice mail.

The unfamiliar number was announced and the message started.

"Hi…" There was a long pause, then, "Uh, this is Ali from The Inn restaurant…You asked me to dinner sometime and, well…I figured it's dinner, right, so…why not have some interesting conversation with a very attractive woman."

A smile claimed Lane's mouth.

"Anyway, you're obviously busy right now, and unfortunately there's not a number you can call me back at, so I'll try and call you again." The message ended.

Lane's heart raced. No phone number? She couldn't call her back. Or could she? She pulled up the call log on her phone and punched the redial button.

After several rings, the phone was answered. "The Inn, this is Suzanne. How may I help you?"

Damn, Lane thought. "I'm sorry, I've misdialed." She ended the call and tossed the phone on the coffee table.

* * *

Ali didn't call back on Monday. Lane would have known because she had her phone on vibrate in her pocket while in court.

When she didn't call again on Tuesday, Lane made a decision as she climbed in the car to go home. "I need to go by The Inn, long enough to run in. I won't be but a few minutes."

"Yes, ma'am."

Waiting anxiously for the hostess at the stand, she finally asked, "Is Ali working this evening?"

Suzanne hesitated before answering. "Yes, I'm sure she is. Is there something I can help you with, Ms. Stanford?"

"No. I'd like to speak with her for a moment if you'd locate her for me."

Suzanne straightened a stack of menus. "Of course, I'll be right back."

Lane was surprised at the flutter in her stomach when she saw Ali rounding the corner. She'd had plenty of physical responses to beautiful women before, but nothing like this one.

Ali smiled. "Hey."

Lane felt her lips curve involuntarily in response. "Hi." She motioned to a spot a few feet from the hostess stand. "Do you have a minute?"

Ali nodded. "I was going to call you again. I just don't have my own phone yet and I work a lot of hours…" Lane interrupted.

"I was close and thought I'd try to catch you here since you didn't have a number for me to call you back at…" A sudden, uneasy silence descended on them. Lane had never been at a loss for words. But the deep blue eyes looking up at her at that moment seemed to have short-circuited her brain. She blinked several times, attempting to reboot it.

"So…about dinner?" Ali's smile made the blood flowing through Lane's veins feel like liquid fire.

"I have no doubt your schedule is as busy as mine." Lane wanted in no way to belittle her waitress job. "Why don't you give me an idea when you're free and I'll see about working my schedule around it."

"I have Friday off this week." Ali blew out a long breath. "The first one I've had off in a month, but if Friday's not good, we can try another time."

Lane racked her brain, unable to remember what the rest of her week was like. "It's not out of the question, but I really need to consult my assistant to be certain."

"Oh, sure." Ali waved a hand. "I understand."

Lane smiled. "I will, and I'll…"

Ali had turned away, saying, "I have to get back to work. Let me know." She smiled over her shoulder at Lane.

Lane nodded a "yes." Back in the car she fumbled her phone from the briefcase and speed-dialed Jeremy.

"What did I forget now?" he answered, irritated.

Lane ignored his tone. "Do you know what my schedule is this Friday evening?"

He laughed. "You're joking, right?" He answered himself. "Of course you're not joking. What do you think I am, your walking Day Planner?" Lane heard a male voice in the background and Jeremy's became muffled.

She apologized. "I'm sorry I interrupted. I thought perhaps you might remember."

Jeremy's voice softened. "I want to say you have something at five or six, but I'm not sure."

Lane hated that her life had become so hectic she could no longer keep track of it. She hung up in frustration and pressed the button to lower the privacy window.

"Ma'am," Randall responded.

Lane leaned forward. "I need to go back by my office for something before I go home, please."

"Yes, ma'am." The window slowly rose as she sat back, anxious to know what was in store for Friday night.

She quickly flipped the planner on Jeremy's desk open to Friday's date. "Damn," she muttered, seeing a notation there for drinks at six o'clock with some corporate guy in town for a convention. With such appointments, drinks were typically followed by dinner. *Well, not* this *Friday.* No, her dinner Friday would be with a perky blonde who had eyes big and blue enough to swim in.

She rummaged through Jeremy's desk drawers until she came up with a blank envelope. Tearing a sheet of paper from his steno pad, she wrote, "Ali, I can be available for dinner Friday evening between seven fifteen and seven thirty if that's not too late for you. If that doesn't work, let me know and we'll try another time—Lane." Stuffing the note in the envelope, she wrote Ali's name on it in her elegant script. When the car pulled in front of her building, she handed Randall the envelope, along with a fifty-dollar tip.

"I need you to drop this at The Inn for me, please." He took the envelope. "Thank you, Randall, and please use this to take your lovely wife out to dinner."

He tipped his head. "Have a good evening, ma'am."

CHAPTER SEVEN

Ali called the following day as Lane returned to her office.

"Hi! It's Ali."

"Hello." Lane smiled at the cheery voice. "Your timing is impeccable." She closed the door and leaned against it. She felt that little flutter in her stomach again.

"Friday night is good, if you still want to have dinner."

Lane inhaled a calming breath. She hoped her voice sounded calmer than she felt. "Of course I do. Why would I change…?" She stopped. "Never mind. Where shall I pick you up?" Ali gave the address. "Actually, my car will pick you up at seven fifteen, after which you'll pick me up at seven thirty. Unfortunately I have a meeting I'm not able to cancel."

"No problem," Ali replied. "You have a car, and what, someone else drives it?"

"Yes and no." Lane chuckled. "I do have a car, but I use a car service if I might be drinking. I do try to be a law-abiding citizen."

"Me too."

"That's another thing we have in common then."

"Uh…what's the first?"

Lane pushed off the door. "We both work hard for a living." She plopped down in her chair. For the first time all day she felt relaxed.

"Oh, yeah." An uncomfortable long pause followed Ali's reply. "Uh, so...I guess I'll see you Friday evening at seven thirty and someone else at seven fifteen. Um, I don't have anything very fancy to wear, so..." Ali sounded nervous now.

"Whatever you have will be fine." Lane confirmed the address again. "My regular driver is Randall. He'll be driving us Friday evening."

"Good to know. So I'll see you Friday," Ali repeated.

"Yes." Lane caught herself doodling on the folder lying in front of her. "And Ali..."

"Yes?"

Her voice was low. "I'm really looking forward to dinner."

"Yeah, me too."

* * *

Anxious barely described how Lane was feeling Friday evening, sitting at the bar area of the mega-hotel. She tried to listen to the man and his associates, but in the last ten minutes she was sure she'd checked her watch a half dozen times. She had advised them when she arrived that she had another engagement at seven thirty.

Finally an agonizing hour and a half later, she was able to leave. She spied Randall across the street as she exited, standing at the ready by the car's back door. He tipped his head in greeting.

The first thing Lane's gaze settled on in the car's interior light was the sparkling blue eyes looking back at her and next the perfect soft lips that formed an infectious smile.

They parted slowly as Ali said, "Hi."

"Hello." Lane allowed her eyes to travel to the turquoise blouse that stretched across Ali's breasts, disappearing into the waistband of a black skirt that barely covered her smooth, shapely thighs. Lane swallowed the desire that rose inside. She wanted to pull Ali into her arms. Kiss her perfect lips and caress her smooth skin.

"I do hope you're hungry. I didn't get lunch today and I wouldn't want you to confuse me with a hungry bear at our *first* dinner." At Ali's questioning look, she added, "I can't imagine I won't want to have dinner with you again. And again."

While they rode through the evening traffic, they exchanged nervous conversation about the weather and a few current pop musicians. Lane thought the last time she'd felt so jittery had been in high school. Ah yes, the first time she kissed a girl. The wonder and sensation of it far surpassed the terror she experienced leading up to it. It was more than she could ever have imagined.

At the restaurant, Randall barely had the door open when Lane hopped out, eager to have an excuse to stare into Ali's mesmerizing eyes. She extended her hand to Ali as she got out, the brief, innocent touch sending a shiver through her that rocked her insides.

"Ma'am?" Randall asked.

"Uh…" Lane stuttered uncharacteristically before glancing at her watch. It was nearly eight. "We should be ready by nine thirty." He nodded. "Thank you, Randall."

She held open the door to the dimly lit restaurant, taking the opportunity to once more appreciate the view of Ali from behind. When Ali confessed to being a lightweight drinker, Lane ordered them each a glass of wine, promising not to get her drunk.

Clinking her glass with Ali's, she said, "To meeting new and interesting people."

"Here's to…" Ali said, taking a sip. "Mmm." Her tongue slid along her upper lip. "That's pretty good." Lane couldn't help but wonder how sweet the wine on those lips might taste if she had the opportunity to kiss them.

After they ordered, Ali rested her arms on the table, wrapping her delicate fingers around the stem of the wineglass. The candlelight danced in her eyes as she confessed, "I feel kind of underdressed for this place."

Lane's eyes never left Ali's. "You look amazing, for here or anywhere." She grasped the lapel of her jacket. She was wearing a gray pinstriped pantsuit with a burgundy silk blouse, picked to remind the men she'd met with earlier of her position and power. "I went straight to my meeting from work, so I didn't get a chance to change. I actually feel overdressed."

"You could take off the jacket," Ali offered. "And unbutton another button or two on your blouse…to get more comfortable, I mean." Ali quickly raised the glass to her mouth as her cheeks colored with a blush.

Ali's probably unintentionally suggestive tone had made Lane's entire body flush. She followed her sartorial suggestions, turning up the cuffs on her blouse as well, and leaned her arms on the table. Normally at this point on a first date, she'd be trying to impress the woman with her authority and influence. She had no desire to do that with Ali. More than anything else, she wanted her to be completely at ease.

Lane Stanford was clearly out of Ali's league, but she wanted to see where the woman expected this date to go. As Z said, it could mean a fresh start as well as a free meal. Lane's intent gaze fell frequently on her as the evening progressed, but it didn't make Ali feel uneasy the way she'd thought it might in anticipation of their dinner. The unpleasant experiences she'd had in her young life had sharpened her senses about people. It didn't feel like Lane was any kind of threat. To the contrary, Ali felt unusually comfortable being with her. She hoped Lane's motivation for asking her out really was because she was attracted to her. It was certainly the reason Ali had accepted.

They talked easily over dinner and while sharing a decadent dessert, Ali couldn't take her eyes off her. Lane was eloquent in her movements, and her dark eyes were filled with captivating mystery. Ali had an overwhelming yearning to touch her, caress her skin and taste her lips. A desire long denied had been rekindled.

Lane tipped her head. "What?"

Ali blinked. "I'm sorry?"

"No need to be. You looked rather intent on something."

Ali took a quick sip of water, trying to calm the jitters spreading through her. She leaned over the table, speaking quietly. "I'm surprised, I guess."

"By?" Lane asked.

Ali took her time, not wanting to sound mistrustful. "You're a lawyer, and by all appearances a powerful one." She tilted her head. "But you seem so laid-back and down to earth. I guess I thought lawyers were all really intense."

"You've met a lot of lawyers in your young life?"

Ali shook her head, frowning. "Only a couple in person. I've watched a lot on TV, though."

Lane's mouth curved into a tiny smile. "Lawyers are like actors in the courtroom. We have to perform for a judge, often a jury, and sometimes our own clients. It's like most jobs. We all have to put on certain façades at work sometimes." She emptied her wineglass and dabbed at her mouth with her napkin.

"Right, looks can be deceiving."

Lane nodded. "Exactly." Putting her napkin down, she glanced at her watch. "Are you ready?" It was almost nine thirty. "Randall is probably waiting on us."

Ali smiled one of those brilliant smiles Lane had been enjoying all evening. "Sure."

Lane again took the opportunity to walk behind her on their way out, trying to sort out her thoughts. Ali aroused far more than sexual desire in her. She didn't just want to fuck her until she begged Lane to stop. She wanted...more. The feeling, completely foreign, was a little unsettling.

"Where to, ma'am?" Randall asked as Ali climbed into the car.

"To Ms. Castle's, where you picked her up," Lane answered, joining her date in the car. All too soon, they stopped not far from Roscoe's restaurant on a street that housed old industrial buildings. Lane knew some had been developed into low-end loft spaces.

Opening her own door, Lane told Randall, "We're fine, thanks." He returned to his seat. Standing outside the car in the dim streetlight, Lane said, "I'll walk you in."

"No," Ali said quickly. She touched Lane's arm lightly. "I mean, that's okay. I'd rather you not see my place." She shrugged. "It's not the greatest."

Lane watched her curiously. "All right then, I'll say goodnight here."

Ali had thought after the flirting and the intense looks she'd been giving her that Lane Stanford would want something. She knew she certainly did. Repeatedly throughout dinner as she had looked into the dark, mysterious eyes across the table from her, she had felt a familiar twinge between her thighs. It was as if the smoldering eyes were caressing her skin. She ached to be touched by Lane's long, elegant fingers.

Lane's voice startled her from her reverie. "I'd like to see you again."

"Okay. Uh, let me know." Ali tipped her head. "I had a really nice time. Thank you for dinner." She bit into her bottom lip.

"My schedule is somewhat flexible. Since I can't call you, how about you let me know when you're available and we'll see what we can work out." Ali nodded. "Are you sure you don't want me to walk you up to your door?" Lane glanced around them.

"No, not necessary, but thanks."

"Well, goodnight, Ali. I had a wonderful time and I look forward to our next meeting."

Lane put herself in the car before she could think twice about abandoning such a beautiful woman at the curb.

Randall lowered the partition when he heard the car door close. "Where to, ma'am?"

She blew out a breath. "Take me home."

"Yes, ma'am." He raised the partition again, leaving her to her thoughts.

* * *

Lane failed miserably at not thinking about Ali Castle and waiting for her to call. She couldn't recall a time she wanted to be with a woman as much as she wanted to be with her. She certainly couldn't understand why she felt she'd be satisfied simply being around her. She wasn't consumed with the desire to rip her clothes off. No, what Lane was feeling toward the blonde beauty was something completely unfamiliar.

She was listening to a defense attorney declare his client's innocence when her phone vibrated under her robe. As inconspicuously as she could, she maneuvered the phone out for a glimpse. The screen registered an unknown caller. She smiled ever so slightly as she returned it to her pocket, waiting for the voice mail alert. When it followed a moment later, she checked the time. It was nearing ten. The second the attorney quit talking, she called for a short recess.

Retreating to the tiny private office behind her courtroom, she called up her voice mail. The recorded voice was perky. "Lane, hi, it's Ali. I'm scheduled off next Tuesday, the whole day. I'm sure you're pretty busy as a lawyer and all, but if you want to go out for dinner again or something I'd be up for that. Let me know. Uh, you can call the restaurant to get hold of me if you want." There was a pause and for a second Lane thought that was it. Then Ali's voice purred, "I really had a great time Friday night, you know, just talking and dinner. So, uh, well, I hope we get to do it again."

When the bailiff knocked, Lane felt more relaxed than she had since Friday. As she left the court building at a quarter of five, rushing across town to meet her father for dinner, she called her office.

"Judge Lane Stanford's office. How may I help you?"

Hearing her powerful title never ceased to thrill her. "Jeremy, I need you to clear as much of my schedule as possible next Tuesday."

"Okaaaay…" He drew the word out, making clear his avid interest. "What are we going to schedule in place of what you want to cancel?"

"You're not going to have to schedule anything. I need to take some personal time. I absolutely need you to free up my afternoon and evening if there's anything. I don't care what it is, get me the time."

"Well, there's nothing I can do about the afternoon because you have the Mercer trial starting on Monday. So the day is going to be up to you. As far as the evening, you have a dinner meeting scheduled with Tom Beckman from City Development."

"Shit," Lane muttered into the phone.

"You have some time Friday evening. You want me to try and reschedule Beckman for then?"

Lane thought only a moment. "Sure," she answered. "Friday's fine."

"I'll see what I can do. I assume if Friday's out, I should schedule him for your next available evening?"

"Yes, and please let me know as soon as possible. If he demands this meeting, I might have to work something else out."

"Sure thing, boss."

She cringed. She hated when he called her that, but he knew that.

* * *

Jeremy sat across the desk from her on Wednesday morning. "So what did you manage with Beckman?"

He flipped open his notepad. "Friday's no good. He said to call the middle of next week to see what you two could coordinate."

"Thank you, and make absolutely sure to keep next Tuesday evening free."

He made a note. "Anything you need me to set up for you for Tuesday evening?" He appeared indifferent as he asked.

"No." Her response didn't leave room for question.

Jeremy persisted. "Perhaps I can help you arrange your last-minute plans."

She glared at him. "I told you on the phone last night that I wanted to take some personal time." She added in a coarser tone, "I don't need your help with that."

Many might have flinched at the bite of her words, but he'd obviously become calloused. "Court's at ten this morning." He left without so much as a glance back.

Lane made two decisions. First was that when the trial started on Monday she'd notify the attorneys that they would be adjourning Tuesday at lunchtime. The other decision she acted on at five minutes after seven when she instructed Randall to deliver her to The Inn for a quick drink before her late dinner engagement with members of the city's planning commission.

She sat at the bar where she'd have the best view of the wait staff as they came from the dining room for drinks, hoping to catch Ali's eye without drawing too much attention to herself. Ten minutes later Ali came in with a drink order.

As Ali put her order in, she sensed someone's eyes on her. When she caught sight of Lane at the far end of the bar looking back at her, she couldn't help but smile. She watched as a smile spread slowly across Lane's face in response. Ali was suddenly warm and tingly. Anchored in the moment she was sharing with the mysterious, attractive lawyer, she stood unmoving. When the bartender interrupted with her drink order, she raised her index finger. Lane nodded.

When she returned, she saw Lane checking her watch, her drink all but gone. She approached without Lane's notice, lightly touching her hand to Lane's back as she stepped in close beside her.

"Hi!" she said, feeling bubbly and giving Lane another smile.

"Hello." Lane's voice was pitched smooth and low. It made Ali want to slide her hand under the designer jacket Lane was wearing and caress the silk of the blouse where it touched her skin.

"I'm sorry you have to come by here to get hold of me. I'm saving to buy me a phone. Anyway, I was only going to wait 'til the weekend and I was going to try calling you again."

Lane's lips curved pleasingly. "That's quite all right. I love this place, and it was on the way to my appointment."

Ali envied the person who got to spend the evening with Lane.

Lane tapped a long perfect nail on her watch. "I do have to be running, but I hoped to make some plans for Tuesday."

"Great!"

"I'll be free around lunchtime. So how about if I pick you up and we plan to make a day of it?"

"I'm in. Where and what time?"

"Let's say twelve thirty. And I'll pick you up at your place."

Ali pursed her lips. "You know, I'll probably use the morning to run errands, so you can just pick me up here. Out front, I mean."

"Are you sure? I'm pretty sure I can find your place again."

"No, out front is fine." She motioned toward the door.

Lane drained her glass, turning slightly. "All right I'll see you out front Tuesday at twelve thirty."

"How should I dress?"

Lane pursed her lips. "Casual and comfortable."

Ali gave a nod. When Lane stood, there was little space between them. They were standing so close she could have easily placed her hands on Lane's waist and pulled their bodies together, but she clenched her hands. She was on the clock. Smiling at Lane, she stepped backward, giving her room to leave. "See you Tuesday."

Lane tipped her head before disappearing into the dinner crowd gathered at the front of the restaurant.

CHAPTER EIGHT

Lane informed the attorneys in the Mercer trial Monday about the early recess the following day. Tuesday's noon break couldn't come soon enough. She disappeared into her private office behind the courtroom and changed clothes, attempting to move inconspicuously from the courtroom to her car, which was parked in the adjoining garage.

Ali was waiting on the sidewalk in front of The Inn when Lane turned the corner. She was wearing shorts that hit midthigh and a sleeveless, stretch V-neck top that left little question she was all woman. With her hair pulled back and wearing a pair of low-heeled sandals, she looked like some high school sweetheart waiting on her date. The thought made her conscious of their apparent age difference. She'd never experienced an infatuation with someone as young as Ali appeared. When Lane pulled to the curb, Ali turned smiling, bright eyes on her. She reached across the seat, opening the passenger door.

"Good afternoon." She hoped her anxiousness wasn't apparent.

"Hi!" Ali replied in her ever-cheery tone, settling into the soft leather and reaching for the seat belt. "Nice car."

"Thanks. My father hates it. It's my adult rebellion."

Ali turned sideways in the seat. "Mine's a '98 Escort, a real beater," she said, running her hand along the edge of the seat.

"But it serves its purpose?" Lane glanced at her and back to the road.

"Yeah, it gets me where I need to go." Ali hooked her fingers inside the hem of her shorts, catching the edge of the fabric in her nails. "So…can I ask where we're going?"

"It depends."

Lane's response made Ali suddenly feel ill at ease, her stomach full of butterflies. She wondered if her original assumption about the lawyer's motives had been right after all. Was Lane about to take her somewhere she didn't want to go?

"Have you had lunch yet? I know you said you were running errands this morning." Lane's voice was light, unthreatening.

"Uh, no. I kind of ran out of time," Ali responded, still uneasy.

"Perfect, I know a wonderful place we can lunch." She checked the dash clock. "If you don't mind a late lunch, that is."

Ali shrugged. "Fine by me." Her uneasiness melted away, replaced by a feeling of being pampered. It was a feeling that was foreign to her, but one she decided she liked—a lot.

For the next hour and ten minutes their conversation centered on benign topics, interspersed with moments of silence where the only sound was the purr of the car's engine and the road passing under its wheels.

When Lane finally pulled off the highway into the parking lot of a nondescript roadside diner, she said, "I hope you're not a health food nut." Ali shook her head. "Good, because they have the best food here and not a bit of it's good for you." She opened and held the passenger door. "And they have the most amazing desserts."

"Do you have any time constraints today?" Lane asked after paying their check.

"Nope, I only have to be back to work tomorrow by ten thirty." Ali felt like adding, "I'm all yours till then."

They drove another forty-five minutes before Lane left the highway for a rural route. Ten minutes later, out of the dense woods on the narrow road emerged a palatial-looking mansion. Ali thought it resembled a picture she'd seen of the Kennedys' Massachusetts estate. It was bigger than huge and, well, awesome looking. She noticed immediately that there were more than a dozen cars in a parking lot off to one side and thought there must be a lot of people working inside to keep the place up.

"I hope you don't mind my bringing you here. It's so wonderfully relaxing." Lane slipped her keys in a pocket. "I don't get enough opportunities to do that, and…" She met Ali's eyes. "It's so beautiful." She gazed around a few seconds before returning her eyes to Ali's. "Like you."

Ali smiled shyly. This was so new for her, getting this kind of attention from someone that she hardly knew. She followed automatically as Lane led the way around the side of the mansion on a cobblestone path. It wound through lush foliage, eventually ending at a massive courtyard ablaze with late summer flowers of every color and strategically placed bushes. It was picture-perfect, Ali thought, a flawless blend of color, a landscape she'd love to capture on canvas someday. The beauty and serenity of the place were almost tangible.

"Wow, this place is great."

Lane stopped in the middle of the courtyard, making a complete turn, trying to see it through Ali's eyes. "I have a far better appreciation for this place now than I did when I was young." She inhaled a deep breath of the fragrant air. "I know why Mother used to love it so much." She continued across the courtyard to yet another stone path and into more lush foliage, which gave way to a scattering of trees and peeks of blue water beyond a sandy beach. The stone path became a boardwalk that veered right and eventually turned toward the water.

The memories flooded back in a torrent. Lane hadn't been here since she was starting high school. The memory of her mother had still been far too painful for her to appreciate what it was her mother had enjoyed so much about the place. Now, as an adult living a fast-paced, demanding life, she could better understand the desire to spend time in a place that was so peaceful, so calming, and allowed a person to look within herself.

Her last visit had been terribly conflicting for her in other ways too. It was the summer she finally admitted to herself that she didn't want to be like the rest of the girls. She didn't want to pine away for some boy who thought girls should bow at his feet. Nor was she interested in smart and considerate boys. In fact, she didn't want a boy at all. She wanted a girl. She had met one that summer too, near the end of her three-week stay with her aunt, uncle and two cousins. The flash of memory was so vivid she could still see her face. Jenny...her name was Jenny, and she had been Lane's first.

The warm fingers on Lane's arm made her jump. "Are you okay?"

Lane touched her hand to Ali's, holding lightly onto her forearm as she mentally shook the memory away. "Yes...I'm sorry. I got lost in the past for a moment." She continued down the boardwalk and out onto a finger of the empty docks. She motioned to a bench attached securely to the one that faced the water. "Would you mind if we sat for a few minutes?"

"Okay." Ali watched Lane stare out over the water. "This is your tour." The sun was warm and the water sparkled as it rippled under a light breeze. When the silence stretched too long, Ali asked, "You said your mother *used* to love this place. Does that mean she doesn't come here any more?"

"No." Lane's head shook slowly before she turned to face Ali. "She passed away when I was young."

Ali gasped. "Oh, God, I'm sorry."

Lane's eyes softened. "It's okay. It was so many years ago. I was just eight."

Ali's gaze on her was kind and caring, and for a brief moment Lane felt that little ache in her heart that she had experienced so often after her mother had passed. The ache that brought the tears she had to learn to hide from her father.

He'd been comforting at first, had given her what he thought to be a reasonable time to get used to the fact she'd lost her mother. When she cried, he'd tell her, "There, there now, it's going to be okay," and wrap her in his arms and hold her until she stopped. After six months, though, he became impatient with her and would say, "Lane, your mother is gone. I miss her too, but we've got to pull ourselves up by our bootstraps and go on. She wouldn't want you sitting around, crying all the time."

Lane learned to hide her tears, even from the nanny, because she reported everything to her father. Over time, she'd become almost completely self-reliant and had distanced herself from anything that resembled feelings. The few she'd managed to hang on to were tucked safely away. Until today.

As she sat here now, with Ali's tender blue eyes gazing deep into her soul, Lane felt a tiny, familiar, but long ago forgotten emotion. Although she felt very vulnerable with Ali, she also sensed it was safe to expose to her a part of her no one had seen since her mother. She realized in that moment that she could care about Ali in a way that she hadn't cared about anyone in twenty-eight years.

Ali's face was filled with concern. Lane touched her thigh. "Really, it's okay. You didn't say anything wrong."

Ali wanted to believe her, but she'd always felt like she was jinxed with saying, and particularly doing, the wrong thing at the wrong time. Timidly, she said, "It must have been special to share this place with your mom. So…was this like your family vacation place or something? You know, Mom, Dad and the kids?"

Lane laughed. "Oh, no. My father never had the time to get away with us, and I'm an only child, so it was only us girls." Ali saw Lane's expression brighten if only briefly. "No, the judge has never even seen this place."

Ali's eyes went wide in surprise. "Your dad's…"—she barely squeaked out the words—"he's a judge?"

Lane regarded Ali. "He's retired now, but yes, he was a judge for as long as I can remember."

Ali hoped that she'd hid her surprise and dismay. She took a shallow breath, holding it as Lane's face took on a look of intensity.

"Ali, I'm a judge too. I hope that's not a problem for you. Like yours, it's my job. Someone has to sit on the bench to ensure the laws are enforced and justice is served. My father saw to it that that someone was me. I get to make the tough decisions. Lucky me." She chuckled. "I sincerely hope this won't prevent us from continuing to see each other."

Ali searched the dark eyes searching hers. She considered her instincts about people to be pretty dead-on now, and she wasn't getting any kind of bad vibe from Lane. Surely if this woman had some other agenda, she wouldn't be feeling like she wanted to kiss her. On the other hand, lawyers and judges sometimes took the easy way out. They weren't all the perfect pursuers of justice they showed on TV.

With only mild apprehension, she said, "Like you said, it's a job." She shrugged. "I don't see why it should matter." At the same time, she reminded herself that she would be foolish if she didn't keep her guard up.

Revealing the truth about her work before things went any further gave Lane an odd sense of comfort. Another unfamiliar feeling, but one she liked.

"That's terrific, because I really like you, Ali, and I'd definitely like to keep seeing you." Ali's eyes sparkled in the sunlight. "You feel like walking around some?"

"Sure."

Lane veered left on the boardwalk and continued on past the sandy beach area where the woods began again, Ali following close behind. At the tree line the wooden walkway ended and a narrow dirt path began.

"There are paths everywhere around the lake," Lane said over her shoulder. "I think I can still remember my way around. I hope so anyway." She ducked a low hanging limb. "Well, I've shared one of my big secrets. Why don't you tell me something juicy about yourself."

"Well…" Ali worried at her lower lip, obviously giving the question a lot of thought. So much thought, in fact, that she ended up stumbling on an exposed root. She caught herself at the last moment, but her face was tight and red with embarrassment—and something else?—when she looked up at Lane. Lane paused when the path widened so Ali could walk beside her again.

"I have this crazy dream of someday being an artist," she said finally.

Lane turned to her. "Having dreams is what inspires us to achieve greater things. What's so crazy about yours?"

"I don't know." Ali shrugged. "Maybe the fact that I'm twenty-six and I'm working as a waitress. I can't afford a phone, let alone go to school and take any classes." She shook her head, frowning. "I don't have a great feeling about it. Think I might have to find a new dream."

Lane stepped within inches of Ali and grasped her hand. "You should never abandon your dreams."

Ali's hand trembled slightly in Lane's. "I…uh," Ali tried her voice again. "Okay. I guess you're right."

Looking down at the hand she held, Lane lightly rubbed her thumb over its soft skin. "You know this is the first place that I ever kissed a girl."

Ali's eyes went wide. "No kidding?"

Lane's eyes met hers. "No kidding."

Joking and clearly nervous, Ali asked, "What's the chances?"

Lane's lips twitched. "That I would come here again with a beautiful woman like you?" She lowered her head slightly. "Or that I would want like hell to kiss you?"

Ali's only response was to push up on her toes to meet Lane's inviting lips. After a long moment, gasping, she pulled back. They gazed, wordlessly, at each other.

Lane's body flushed with a desire she had never experienced from simply kissing a woman. This wasn't the hammering hunger she usually felt. It was something more, something much deeper…something intimate. Yes. That's what it was—intimate. Lane didn't want to merely have sex with Ali. She wanted to touch every part of her, *feel* every part of her, inside and out. And the scariest part was that she wanted Ali to feel the same way about her. It was beyond terrifying to admit that she wanted to feel loved. The way her mother had always made her feel. Because feeling that kind of connection would inevitably lead to pain, the way her mother's sudden passing had.

She took a shaky breath before sliding her arm around Ali's waist and pulling their bodies together. She searched her blue eyes briefly for regret and claimed her lips again. When Lane's tongue delved into the warmth of her mouth and Ali moaned, Lane felt a pressure, first in her chest, like someone had hold of her heart and was squeezing it gently. As it spread lower, she moved her foot between Ali's and Ali pressed firmly against her thigh. She stopped questioning then and simply allowed herself to feel. The kiss became urgent, leaving both women gasping for breath. Lane finally pulled back, fighting a force that seemed stronger than she knew herself to be. She released Ali, taking a step back.

"I'm sorry. That was rather presumptuous of me."

Ali leaned toward Lane, hooking her finger inside the front of Lane's shirt, preventing her from moving farther away. "Don't be. I'm an adult. I could have stopped you." She hesitated. "I didn't want to."

"Yes, well, in any case I don't think this is a place we should be caught making out like a couple of teenagers."

"Okay." Ali gave her a sultry smile. "Where then?"

As much as Lane wanted to pin Ali to the tree behind her and kiss her senseless, she knew she couldn't behave as she had that summer so many years ago. Even this far from the city, knowing that no one here knew who she was, Lane couldn't ignore her better judgment.

She tipped her head. "Why don't we continue our walk for now?"

"Sure."

They walked on, stopping at one point at the southern end of the lake when Ali said, "You know, I swear I keep hearing things hitting the ground."

Lane looked up before scouring the ground around them. After a moment she stepped a dozen or so feet off the path and retrieved something from the ground. Returning to the path she slipped one hand in her pocket and extended the other to Ali. She took the smooth round, brown object from Lane's hand and turned it over repeatedly.

"They say a buckeye is good luck."

"Oh, um yeah." Ali rolled it around in her palm before closing her fingers over it. "Well, I sure can use all the luck I can get."

Lane fingered the one she had slipped into her own pocket. She wasn't a believer in luck. She'd been taught good fortune came with dedication to hard work. But, she thought as she rubbed the smooth nut between her fingers, maybe, just maybe, meeting Ali was lucky.

They arrived back at the sandy beach from the other direction. A number of times during the nearly two-mile walk Ali brushed against Lane where the path narrowed, sending shivers racing through her.

"Why don't we stop in the restaurant here for a drink of something cold before we head out?" Lane suggested.

While they sat in the shade on the outside patio sipping iced tea, Lane got Ali talking about her dream of becoming an artist. She didn't recall ever hearing anyone talk with so much passion about something.

She also couldn't remember ever feeling so relaxed while enjoying the company of anyone. It was a challenge not to sit and stare at her like a lovesick puppy. For the first time in a long, long time, she stopped caring about the fact that she wasn't controlling things and allowed herself to simply go with the flow.

* * *

As evening approached, Lane drove to the college town of Oakland, where she had spent time when she was younger. It wasn't where she had attended school, but a place she'd frequented after college. Around seven they stopped at a small, nondescript café/restaurant for dinner. The place was quiet and, despite the small-town atmosphere, no one seemed to pay any attention to two women staring lustfully across the table at each other or the occasional mostly innocent touching of their hands.

As they left the restaurant, Lane asked, "Are you in a rush to get home or would you like to have a drink before we make the drive?"

"Whatever you want to do is fine. I'm all yours until ten thirty tomorrow."

"Good." Lane grinned. She felt like a twenty-something-year-old again. "Let's walk. It's only a couple of blocks."

At first glance, "The Wet Spot" appeared to be a regular corner bar, complete with darkened street-front windows filled with neon beer signs. The fact that all the customers turned out to be women suggested otherwise. Ali noticed as Lane cupped her elbow to steer her toward the opposite end of the bar, they were gay women.

Her heart leapt with excitement. She'd never been in a gay bar. While her one and only previous sexual relationship had been with a woman, it had been private, covert. There were no public displays, and the intimate moments occurred only late at night when they were shrouded by darkness. She'd sometimes wondered during those years if she was even a lesbian or if the relationship was simply one of convenience. That question, though, had been answered the minute she laid eyes on Lane and they spoke for the first time. And when they had kissed earlier in the woods—that kiss had melted every part of her.

She was having a hard time believing it, but she thought there'd been something there for Lane too. When those dark, mysterious eyes looked at her, they told Ali that Lane wanted her. The way men wanted women. Seeing that filled her with a ravenous hunger. She wanted Lane to steer the direction of this, though, whatever it was. She was beginning to trust her, wanted to believe her intentions were honest.

Lane motioned Ali to an empty stool. Standing very near, she said over the jukebox noise, "I hope you don't mind this place." Ali shook her head. "It's a favorite haunt from years ago." Lane leaned her elbow on the bar.

"You make it sound like you've been around forever."

Lane laughed lightly. "I can assure you I've got more years on you than I want to admit." Lane waved over the Goth-looking bartender and ordered a glass of wine for Ali and a club soda. "Don't want to drink and drive." She cocked her head. "Have to uphold the law and all that."

* * *

They talked, about everything and nothing, nothing important anyway or serious. After a while, Lane noticed a drop-dead gorgeous butch eyeing them from the other end of the bar. As she discreetly observed her, it became clear she was interested in Ali. A wave of protectiveness took over and when a slow ballad began to blare from the jukebox and several women moved lazily onto the tiny dance floor across the room, Lane lightly touched her hand to Ali's back.

"Would you like to dance?"

"I would."

Lane slipped her arm possessively around Ali as they moved to the floor.

There Ali turned, reached her arms around Lane's neck and tipped her head back. "I hope you're leading."

Lane merely smiled, placing her hands at Ali's waist, beginning a slow movement. Ali shivered in response, and Lane slid her hands to the small of her back. Ali tightened her arms around Lane's neck, pressing along the length of her body, and placed her cheek against Lane's chest. The move set Lane on fire. God, the thought of touching her, skin to skin, made Lane ache like she never had before.

Neither of them spoke as the song played on. The connection and movement of their bodies against one another and together was all the communication they needed. And it was telling Lane that Ali wanted her as much as she wanted Ali. When the song ended and was replaced by something fast and raucous, Lane groaned inwardly. The only thing she wanted to do at that moment was lie naked with Ali and please her in every way imaginable. Ali was different from every other woman she'd slept with, though, and that difference made Lane want to go slow. "We probably should get out of here."

She had never before considered the possibility of having one person in her life forever. The women she'd met, slept with, had brief affairs with had only wanted one thing from her, sex. That and whatever luxuries Lane bestowed on them. Ali, though… She seemed content simply to be in Lane's company.

As for how being with Ali made her feel…being around her made her feel caring and cared for in a special way. The way she had when she was a young girl. Before her father had turned her into the stonehearted adult she'd become.

Lane was in control of her raging libido again by the time they reached the car. It didn't last long.

"You know, I wanted to kiss you so bad in there when we were dancing." Ali raked her index finger up and down Lane's forearm, raising goose flesh on her skin as it passed.

Lane met Ali's intent gaze and leaned toward her in the car's darkened interior. She quickly closed the distance, capturing Lane's mouth in a hungry kiss. Passion enveloped Lane like flame consuming dry kindling, and she allowed her hand to massage the length of Ali's thigh before traveling up and cupping one of her full breasts. Her heart thundered in her chest and every part of her became liquid fire, burning a path to her center.

When Ali pushed Lane's hand toward her parted thighs, though, Lane abruptly pulled away, ending the kiss. She looked into Ali's eyes, which were clouded, she saw, with the same desire that was consuming her. God, Lane realized, she wanted her more than she'd ever wanted a woman in her life. But not like this—not like she would with any other woman. She didn't want their first time to be simply about sex. She wanted more. She wasn't exactly sure what that "more" was, but it clearly wasn't something that happened in a parked car.

In a hoarse whisper she said, "We can't do this now…not here."

Ali bit her lip, slowly nodding her head.

Their eyes stayed locked together for another long moment, the message telepathing between them evident. This was going to happen. It was only a matter of when and where. Lane imagined something romantic, like a scene from a well-scripted movie. She forced herself to start the car. As they drove slowly through town, Ali reached across and rested her hand on Lane's thigh. Lane glanced at it briefly before placing her own on top, curling her fingers under to hold it firmly.

Yes, this was going to happen, and when it did it would be more special than anything Lane had ever known.

* * *

As the car slowed on the highway off-ramp, Lane turned toward Ali's side of town. Lane felt confident she had made her intentions known, and she hoped Ali wasn't opposed to taking things slow, even after two dates. Lesbians had a habit of jumping into things, relationships, living spaces or lives, too quickly. That was the stereotype, at least, and she couldn't exactly refute it. After all, when had she ever *not* immediately hopped into bed with someone she was attracted to? But this—this could be serious, special, and Lane wanted to take her time. At the same time and for the same reason, being someone who was prudent about protecting her name and reputation, she decided she needed to know more about the beautiful blonde before things went much further.

"I hope you don't mind if we end our evening. I have an early court time tomorrow and some preparing to do yet tonight."

Ali squeezed Lane's thigh where her hand still rested. "Not at all. I can't imagine how busy the life of a judge is."

Lane glanced at her silhouette in the dark. "Well, hopefully I do enough good to make up for all the time and sacrifice." She pulled the car up to the now-familiar building but didn't turn the engine off. "I'm not going to offer to walk you up tonight because if I do, I'm afraid I won't be able to leave." She took Ali's hand, lifting it to her lips. *God, this is killing me.* Ali's skin was velvety soft and her scent as fresh as the garden they'd walked through earlier.

Ali shivered at the touch of Lane's lips on her skin. She squirmed. "I know." She could barely speak. "And I wouldn't let you."

Lane held onto her hand, her eyes still locked on Ali's. "If...there was any question, I do want to see you again."

Ali nodded. "I can call you when I know my next day off."

Lane smiled as she reached over and popped open the glove box. She held out the phone. "And I'll be able to call you back."

"I can't take that."

"Please, it's an inexpensive pre-paid one. Even if we only have one more date it's not a big deal. But," she tipped her head, "I don't think that's going to be the case. Please take it. I want to be able call and talk to you."

Ali took it reluctantly. "Okay. I promise not to use it except to call you."

"Call whomever you wish. I like knowing that I can call you." Lane relaxed. The prospect of dating Ali seemed more real now that there was this thread connecting them. "My cell number is already programmed in for you."

"Okay." Ali slipped the phone into her back pocket. "Thanks." Before reaching for the door handle, she leaned over and kissed Lane. The kiss should have been brief, but when it lingered, Lane again showed some restraint and pulled away. "I'll call as soon as I see the new work schedule."

"I'll be waiting."

CHAPTER NINE

Lane was beginning to think Ali wouldn't call. She didn't want to believe Ali was going to skip out on her. She wanted to give her the benefit of the doubt. She was finishing dinner with a local entrepreneur and his partner on Friday evening when the phone vibrated in her pocket. She took a discreet peek at the screen, her heart racing when she saw the caller ID of *1*.

Phone in hand, she pushed back from the table. "Excuse me, gentlemen, but I need to take this call." She quickly hit the answer button as she stepped away. "Hello."

"Hi!" Ali's voice bubbled. "It's me."

As Lane passed the kitchen on her way toward the restrooms, a door burst open. Loud shouts and the clanging of pans made it impossible to hear. Stepping partway down the narrow hallway, she asked, "I'm sorry, you were saying?" Two boisterous men exited the men's room a few feet away, nearly running into her.

There was a hesitation. "Oh, I'm sorry. You're out...I don't know why...silly me to think you'd be sitting home on a Friday night."

Lane had to put her finger in her ear to hear as several raucous young females squeezed past her. "It's business," she said, "and it should be concluded shortly since my car will be here at nine. I can call you back when I get out of here if that's not too late?"

Ali chuckled. "No, nine isn't past my bedtime."

"I thought maybe since you have to work tomorrow…you do have to work tomorrow…oh, never mind me. I'll call you back when I'm finished here." Lane was nervous. Nervous! She didn't do nervous… especially with women.

"That's fine, I'm not going anywhere. Call when you have a few minutes. I'll be waiting."

"I'll talk to you soon."

The men wanted her to stay for drinks, but Lane explained she had another commitment and her car was likely waiting. She didn't want to spend another minute with them. She wanted to talk to Ali.

Randall held her door. "Where to, ma'am?"

She was scrolling for Ali's number as she slid in. "Nowhere yet, Randall." He climbed into the driver's seat and waited.

Ali answered before the second ring finished. "Hi!"

The sound of her voice made Lane's pulse quicken. "Hello." There was a long pause. "I assume you were calling to let me know when your next day off is."

"Uh, yeah," Ali hesitated, "and it's not until Thursday."

"Oh," was all Lane could manage.

"Yeah, my schedule kind of sucks most of the time. I'm pretty much on the bottom of the ladder here, but it's a good paying job."

Lane respected that she was making her own way. "What are you doing now?"

"Talking to you."

Lane chuckled. "No, I mean if I were to say…come by and pick you up, would you have a drink with me?"

"Sure," Ali said eagerly.

"We'll be there in about twenty minutes. Okay?"

"Great." Ali's voice was light, melodious. "Pick me up at the corner by the restaurant. I feel like a little fresh air."

"See you soon." Lane lowered the partition as she tucked the phone away.

"Ma'am?"

"Please take me to The Inn. We're picking up my friend, Ms. Castle."

"Certainly, ma'am."

Ali was waiting when the familiar car pulled to the curb. She immediately opened the door, calling across the roof to Randall, "I got it," before hopping in beside Lane. She wanted to jump in her lap, kiss her ardently, but she didn't want to mess things up. As hard as it was to resist the dark-haired, dark-eyed woman in the power suit, she vowed to hold to her original plan of letting Lane set the pace.

Lane leaned over, kissing her lightly, a simple brush of soft lips before once again lowering the partition. "We're going to my building." She handed her key card to him and powered the privacy window back up so quickly that they caught only the "yes" of Randall's response.

"You have your own building?" Ali asked, eyes wide.

"Not mine, no. I merely live in it."

Randall pulled the car to the elevator in the garage and held the door. Upon exiting and before he could ask, Lane said, "Please return here at eleven to pick up Ms. Castle and drive her home."

He slipped her key card into his pocket and nodded. "Yes, ma'am."

Lane fumbled through her bag for her keys while they waited for the elevator. She steered Ali in ahead of her, pressed the button, and the doors swept closed behind them. On the fifth floor she unlocked the rear door to the apartment, waving Ali inside.

"Wow, nice place."

Lane tossed her keys and jacket on the entry table, dropped her bag beside it and led Ali down the hall. "Make yourself comfortable," she said, kicking off her heels as she made her way around the bar.

Ali stepped toward the couch, taking in the fashionably decorated room before moving to the bar. "Okay if I sit here?" She ran her hand over the leather seatback of the barstool.

"Sure." Lane surveyed the contents of the bar. "I can offer you anything but beer." Tilting her head, she narrowed her eyes. "But you don't strike me as a beer drinker."

"No." Ali shook her head. "I can have whatever you're having. You don't need to fuss."

Lane placed the liquor bottle on the bar. "I'm drinking vodka straight up with a couple of olives. Are you sure about that?" Ali wrinkled her nose and Lane laughed lightly. "I have a number of different wines, or I could blend you a daiquiri or margarita if you'd like."

"Don't go to a lot of trouble. Some wine's fine as long as it isn't real dry."

Lane looked at the glass-fronted mini-fridge before opening the door. "I've got the perfect one." She poured a glass, sliding it across to Ali. "This is supposed to be a little sweet." She winked. "Like you."

Ali took a sip, running her tongue over her upper lip after she swallowed. "Umm, you're right about the sweetness."

"Do you mind if I taste?"

Ali pushed the glass toward her, but Lane leaned over the bar, lightly running her tongue over Ali's lips before kissing her briefly. Her heart pumped double time as she leaned back slightly. "I agree, 'umm' would be the correct description. That's tasty." She gave Ali a subtle smile.

Ali quickly hooked her hand around Lane's neck and pulled her back in for a fevered kiss.

Lane braced her hands on the bar, allowing Ali to take control. The kiss felt like it lasted a lifetime, but in fact took only a minute. They parted, both breathing heavily. The look in Ali's eyes said, "Take me."

"Maybe we should move into the living room where we can be more comfortable," Lane suggested.

She poured herself a drink and moved to the couch. Ali stepped out of her sandals before sitting close to her with her feet tucked under her jean-clad legs. Holding the crystal wineglass in one hand, she placed the other on Lane's thigh, brushing lightly over the expensive fabric of her slacks.

Ali's light touch quickened Lane's pulse. This never happened. She never felt this out of control with a woman. She was never this aroused until she was literally "fucking" a woman. Yet another first since meeting the beautiful Ali Castle.

"Your suit is beautiful." Ali lightly ran her fingers up the silken sleeve of Lane's blouse. "Is this what you wear under your black robe?"

"As opposed to what?"

Ali smiled enticingly. "Oh, I've heard some judges wear little...or nothing." She fingered the collar of the blouse and allowed her hand to brush over Lane's breast as she pulled it away to raise the wineglass to her lips with both hands. She watched Lane over the rim of the glass as she sipped.

Lane sensed her control slipping further under Ali's seductive gaze. Ali's eyes had turned a deep shade of violet, and it was as if the energy around them shifted. "Is everything okay?"

Ali placed the glass on the coffee table and turned back to meet Lane's eyes. "You give off this dark, mysterious vibe, and I've gotta say

I'm a little intimidated." Her shoulder lifted slightly. "I'm sure you have hordes of women trying to get a date with you."

Lane took a long drink, allowing the warm burn to spread slowly and soften the edges before she responded. "I admit I've been with a few women. My track record certainly isn't anything to be proud of."

Oh, God. Who is this person using me as a mouthpiece? I'm trying to come off as someone with a heart and soul when all I've ever been was a woman about the conquest. And the tougher to conquer the more rewarding the success. How many have there actually been? Far too many to count.

This business of caring about someone and the accompanying emotions were keeping her off balance and leaving her feeling at a serious disadvantage. She decided to speak from her heart, something else that was completely unfamiliar.

"I can honestly say that I've never met a woman who has captivated me as you have." She set her glass on the table and turned to face Ali. "The truth is I'm a little nervous with you too." Lane struggled to talk past the knot in her throat. "I'm afraid I'm going to mess this up."

Ali touched her fingers lightly to Lane's jaw. "I don't think you can." She slipped her hand around her neck and pulled Lane in, kissing her with an intensity that sent fire all the way to her toes.

Lane's hand slid up to cup her breast, holding the weight in her palm. When Ali moaned in her mouth, Lane's fingers caught the already hard peak through thin fabric. Ali pushed into her hand. Lane slipped the thin straps holding the top off her shoulders, along with her bra straps, moving her hand inside to cup the warm flesh.

Ali pulled her lips away, leaning her forehead against Lane's. "Oh God, that feels so good." Lane tweaked her hardened nipple. "Ah... and I've been imagining what your hands would feel like." Her lips found Lane's again.

Ali slipped her hand between Lane's thighs, brushing her fingers over her crotch. Lane abruptly ended the kiss and caught Ali's wandering hand gently, raising it to her lips.

"I'm sorry, I didn't mean—"Ali said, confused.

Lane quickly cupped her chin, running her thumb over soft lips. "You didn't." Her gaze held Ali's. "I don't want to rush this...it should be special." She glanced at her watch. "Besides, Randall will be back for you soon." She stroked her fingers down the column of Ali's neck, briefly pausing where her pulse beat rapidly. Lane's fingers hovered above the valley between her breasts. "As I said, I don't want to rush this. I want to take an entire night, or day, to make love to you." Lane cocked her head.

What could Ali say to that? She was nuts for Lane. She'd never felt the kind of desire she made her feel. Her previous lover had definitely made her lust for sex and the physical gratification it unleashed, but this was something entirely different. Lane had called it "lovemaking." Ali could only imagine what something more intense and deeply satisfying than what she'd shared with Z could be. She could wait.

She slowly nodded a "yes." She took Lane's hand. "I may not be sophisticated, but I'm not a nymphomaniac either."

"I wasn't implying you were."

"Can we...?" She shrugged. "I don't know...make out some more before I have to go? I really like kissing you." She felt her cheeks warm. "It makes my head feel all fuzzy and my insides shake."

That's two of us. Lane leaned in, capturing Ali's mouth again. The feel of Ali's tongue, searching, imploring, overwhelmed her—consumed her.

She repositioned Ali's straps before escorting her to the garage at a few minutes shy of eleven. Randall was already parked close by, leaning next to the rear passenger door. He returned Lane's card to her when they walked over.

"Thank you, Randall. Goodnight."

"Ma'am, I'll see you tomorrow evening at six."

"Yes." Lane held the door open as Ali got situated and Randall returned to his seat. Lane leaned in, giving Ali a quick peck on the lips. "I'll talk to you soon."

Ali nodded. "You're not going out with another woman tomorrow night are you?"

Lane laughed lightly. "No, you're the only woman I want."

Ali touched Lane's hand as she moved away. "Call me?"

"You can count on it."

* * *

Lane returned home from the fund-raiser the following night around ten thirty. Knowing the restaurant wouldn't be closed and Ali was likely still on the clock, she made a drink and called to leave a message. She settled into her king-sized bed with her drink and a file containing a petition for the trial that would begin following the

Mercer trial. The ringing phone woke her. She snatched it up, trying to sound alert.

"Hi!" Ali's voice came softly to Lane.

"Good evening." Lane glanced at the bedside clock to confirm it was in fact still night.

"Sorry to call so late."

"That's quite all right."

"I thought I should try and catch you tomorrow." Ali hesitated. "I didn't want to wait that long to talk to you…I couldn't quit thinking about you all day today."

Lane's heart rate quickened. "I can honestly say that you've been on my mind today as well."

Lane heard Ali's quiet sigh. "I'm glad you called tonight."

"So how was your day?"

"Long, grueling, like most. Thank God it's over. And how was your thing, whatever it was?"

Lane laughed. "It was a fund-raiser and, like your workday, long and grueling. I'd have rather spent the evening at Roscoe's, keeping my eye on you."

"So why did you go?"

Lane wondered how to answer. She decided that honestly was the only way, if she intended to have any kind of relationship with Ali. "In my position there are certain things that are expected, certain appearances people expect you to make. Do you understand what that means?"

Ali laughed. "Yeah, I bet it means you're in the closet, for one thing. Which means I won't have to go to any of those high society parties with you if we keep seeing each other."

"That's a harsh way to view it, but unfortunately true. I'm sorry. I do have certain appearances to keep up if I expect to move ahead in my career. I hope it doesn't present a problem."

Ali paused only a second. "Nah, I'm not big on flaunting my sexuality, and besides, I don't really have any friends to blab to about it anyway. Your secret is safe with me."

Lane was not in the habit of trusting women. To the women she dated, she was just Renee. But Ali was different, had been from the first time they'd met. She could be trusted. Lane felt it to her core. It was the reason she'd been more honest with Ali than she'd ever been with any other women, the reason that she'd told Ali her real name.

Which could be dangerous. They'd done little more than kiss, though, so she didn't think she'd created any kind of PR nightmare.

Still… She made a mental note to call her old friend, John Woods, a retired cop. You couldn't be too safe, no matter how honest and seemingly innocent a person appeared. Wasn't she an excellent example of that, an expert at hiding truths and agendas?

"So, Thursday is your next day off. I'm pretty sure I won't be able to play hooky again, but I'd like to have dinner. Would you consider dinner again?"

"Hmm…that depends."

"On?"

"On whether dinner might include a decadent dessert."

Lane could hear the smile in Ali's voice. Seductive innuendo, that was something she was familiar with. "I can arrange for any dessert that might please your palate. Whatever you're in the mood for."

"I'm thinking something darkly rich, warm and mouth-watering."

"I…" Desire rose quickly, nearly consuming Lane. "Perhaps we can discuss that during dinner. Will that work?"

"Absolutely. When and where?"

"I'll call in the next few days, once I know how long my Thursday's going to be. A late dinner won't be a problem?"

"Nope, you pick, time and place." The timbre of Ali's voice dropped. "I'll go willingly, I promise."

Lane's body flushed. Perhaps she could make this a night they'd both remember for a long time to come. Aching to touch Ali, Lane kept her voice even and calm. "I like willing. I can probably let you know by Tuesday."

"Can't wait, Lane," Ali cooed. "Talk to you later."

"Goodnight, Ali."

CHAPTER TEN

Lane contacted John Woods Monday morning. Even as she passed along the small amount of information she had on Ms. Ali Castle, she felt confident John would come up with little or nothing that was alarming. Without waiting to hear back from him, she called Ali Wednesday evening and left a message to please call about their dinner date. She was lying in bed looking over some work when the phone rang a little after eleven thirty.

"Good evening," she answered, keeping her voice low and deep.

"Hi! So, dinner tomorrow..." Ali sounded tired. "When and where?"

Lane was hesitant. She was worried that Ali might find a quiet dinner at the apartment too...simple. "I thought we could have dinner at my apartment."

"Sounds good. So you cook too?"

Lane chuckled. "No, but I know nearly all the best chefs in the city, so I can promise you won't be disappointed with dinner."

"I have no doubt about that. And, uh, we will be discussing dessert during or after dinner?"

"Yes, we will *discuss* it."

"What time do you want me there?"

"Let's say seven. All right?"

"Sounds good."

"Seven it is. I have to ask you a favor, and I need to share a confidence."

"Uh…sure. Like I said, I can keep your secret."

Lane proceeded tentatively. "The doormen for our building think my assistant, Jeremy, lives in this apartment. That's a story for another time. In any case, in order to keep my private life very private I would ask you to tell the doorman you're here to see Jeremy. He will, of course, give you a smug smile and check you out. I apologize it has to be so secretive, but it really is imperative for maintaining my privacy. I hope you can understand that."

"Sure, no problem. I just tell the door guy I'm there to see Jeremy in apartment…I forget the number."

"Five-oh-four. Jeremy will notify the doorman to expect you."

"Okay. Anything I should bring?"

"Only your beautiful self."

"Hum…I guess I'm going to have to search my wardrobe for something special so you won't be disappointed."

"I don't think you could disappoint me, Ali Castle. I'll send Randall to pick you up around six thirty at your place."

"No, uh, could you have him pick me up at the corner by the restaurant where he did the last time?"

"Sure." Lane scribbled a note to call the car service herself, speak with Jeremy and arrange delivery of their dinner. "I will see you tomorrow evening at seven."

"I can't wait. I've been missing you a lot since last Friday."

"I've missed you as well. I'm looking forward to seeing you again tomorrow. Goodnight, Ali."

"Night."

* * *

Following a light rap on the door, Jeremy popped into her office Thursday morning. Lane launched into her list for him. "First of all, I need you to stop by my building and let the doorman on duty know you're expecting a guest at seven this evening." When he opened his mouth, she held up a hand. "Save your questions. I need you to call Donnatelli's and order a dinner for two to be delivered by six or six thirty. Make it the spinach and cheese-stuffed shells with all the extras. And I need you to pick up a prepaid credit card for one hundred dollars for me—no, make that one-fifty—and I need that before the end of the day. Now, what do you need to know?"

His mouth hanging open, he huffed a sigh. "Well, who is she?"

"For the time being, no one you need to know."

He narrowed his eyes. "You better not tell me you picked up a woman while out cruising a bar."

"I wouldn't, I didn't, she's not a barfly."

He frowned, creasing his otherwise smooth forehead. "And yet you're not going to tell me a single thing."

Lane hesitated. "She's a beautiful blonde, smart and intriguing. That's all you need to know."

Jeremy smiled. "You like her."

Lane tried to appear unaffected by his comment.

He repeated, "You really like this woman, don't you?"

She frowned. "You know exactly what I like, Jeremy." She waved him off. "Take care of those things and quit trying to analyze me."

He smirked.

Lane left shortly after five, giving Randall his instructions as he drove. She'd have plenty of time to shower and dress before the dinner arrived. She was surprised to meet Jeremy at the front doors.

"Mission accomplished," he whispered as he passed her and was gone.

Lane dug in her closet until she found what she was after—a well-worn pair of blue jeans that she was confident would still fit her slim figure. She wanted this evening to be casual. She wanted Ali to feel relaxed and comfortable.

Randall arrived promptly to pick Ali up at six thirty. When he stopped shortly afterward, parking in front of an upscale fashion boutique, she assumed they were picking Lane up. When he got out and opened her door, she looked at him in confusion.

Randall held out a plastic card. "Ms. Stanford wishes for you to shop for something you'd like to wear to dinner."

Ali stammered as she climbed out, "But I'm supposed to be there at seven."

Randall nodded with his usual impassive expression. "Ms. Stanford says that you should take all the time you want shopping. I'll wait right here and she will gladly hold dinner until you arrive."

As Ali strolled into the store, which was of a caliber she had never shopped in, she wondered if she should be insulted by Lane's gesture. She decided finally that if Lane didn't mind contributing to her own downfall, she wasn't going to mind either. Because if Lane didn't make a move tonight, she was going to seduce her. She didn't want to wait any longer. The way Lane looked at her, the way she sounded when she spoke in that rich, low voice made Ali's insides tremble. It aroused her more than she'd ever imagined possible.

She fingered the sleeve of a blouse that felt silky as strands of her hair. She needed to pick something that looked sophisticated, but sexy in an understated way. She settled on a tight little black dress with spaghetti straps that stopped inches above her knees. She hoped Lane would be pleased. Pleased enough to want her out of the little black number before the night was over.

Having money to spare on the credit card, Ali asked Randall if they could stop at a flower shop on the way to Lane's.

"Yes, ma'am. I know just the place."

Feeling like someone's very special someone for the first time in her life, Ali exited the car in front of Lane's building, grasping the wrapped bundle of fresh-cut flowers. Their fragrance filled her senses as she stepped into the posh lobby.

The gray-haired man in a jacket and tie behind the desk looked her up and down before asking, "Can I help you, miss?"

Ali smiled. "I'm here to see Jeremy, apartment five-oh-four."

He looked at a notebook on the desk. "Yes, Mr. Jeremy said to expect you." He jumped from behind the desk and rushed to the elevator to punch the button. As the doors swooshed open, he said, "And may I say, you look quite lovely this evening."

She smiled again, stepping inside, feeling his eyes still on her. It'd been a while, but she recognized that kind of leer. She took calming breaths as the elevator rose, suddenly feeling more nervous than she had on her first date with Lane. Would the flowers seem silly or a bit overboard? Why she was so worried? The attraction between them was undeniable. Lane's restraint couldn't hide the desire bubbling below the surface. Ali wanted to break through that, shatter it. She stood in front of the door for several moments, calming her nerves, before pressing the buzzer.

The door opened and there was Lane, looking more tantalizing than any meal Ali could imagine. She was wearing a navy cashmere sweater, sleeves pushed up her forearms, blues jeans, of all things, and comfortable-looking leather loafers. Her dark hair was down and brushing the top of her broad shoulders. She wore the barest amount of makeup. The look was casual and yet still elegant, sophisticated. If she couldn't have this woman tonight, if she couldn't seduce her into submission, Ali thought with a grin, she should take a vow of celibacy.

Ali's smile snapped Lane out of a trancelike stare. "I'm sorry, please come in." She shook her head, trying to clear it. Ali was the most beautiful woman Lane had ever seen.

"I don't know if you like flowers…" Ali extended the bouquet to Lane as she entered.

She took them, lightly touching Ali's fingers. "They're beautiful." She leaned down, brushing her lips over Ali's. "But not nearly as beautiful as you."

"Thank you." Ali smoothed a hand over the silky fabric covering her hip. "You approve?"

Lane's lips twitched. "Very much so." What she'd done—buying a date a dress—was pretty presumptuous, she realized now. She'd never done anything like it before, in fact. But wow! She took Ali's hand. "Come on, let's have a sip of something before we eat."

Lane didn't care for mixed drinks. In fact, she preferred her liquor very straight. But she had prepared margaritas, wanting to have something Ali might like. She had also set dinner up for them at the counter between the kitchen and dining area. No formalities for this evening.

She was right. The narrow counter made the dinner more intimate. So intimate, in fact, that it was hard to focus on eating. Finally Ali laid down her fork and pushed aside her plate. "We were supposed to discuss dessert during dinner."

Lane met her eyes. "That we were." She dabbed her napkin over her lips. "I have a number of things for you to choose from."

Ali reached across the space between them, her fingers slipping between Lane's fingers. "There's only one thing I'm interested in."

She watched Ali's fingers caress her own. "And what would that be?"

"I want to taste your lips"—Ali touched her tongue to her own upper lip—"and I want to feel those lips on my skin…anywhere you want to put them."

Wordlessly, Lane came around the counter and turned Ali to face her, moving her thigh between Ali's knees and cupping her face. "I want to devour every inch of you." She touched her lips briefly to the corner of Ali's mouth, murmuring, "Very…very slowly." She kissed the other side. "I want to please you every possible way."

Ali's knees tightened against Lane's thigh. "Please touch me," she whispered.

Lane leaned back, gazing a second into the luminescent blue of Ali's eyes before kissing a spot below her ear and slowly working her lips down the side of her neck. Ali tossed her head back with a gasp, and Lane slipped the thin dress straps off her shoulders. She kissed one shoulder, then the other, and brought her hands up to cup Ali's breasts in the slinky black material.

Ali slid her arms around Lane's neck, pulling her into a fiery kiss. When it ended, she dropped her forehead against Lane's chest. "I want you so bad I don't think I can wait." She reached for the top of Lane's jeans, rasping, "I have to touch you." When Lane caught her hand, Ali pleaded, "Please, let me touch you."

Without a thought, Lane relented, something else she'd never done before. Ali released the button, unzipping the jeans while Lane braced her hands on the counter. She groaned as Ali's hand passed beneath her silky underwear and found her wetness. "Oh, God, Lane, you feel so good."

Lane's legs stiffened as an unstoppable wave of pleasure weakened every part of her. She didn't fight the loss of control. She couldn't. Powerful, take-charge, in-control Judge Lane Stanford was presently someone else—somewhere else. In a few short weeks, Ali had managed to crack the shell inside which Lane had protected herself for all these years. And it didn't matter.

Ali stroked her as Lane's hips rocked. She leaned close, her hot breath touching Lane's ear. "You're close, aren't you? I can feel it."

Lane gasped, "Yes."

Ali murmured, "Come for me, baby."

"Yes," Lane barely managed, shuddering against Ali's hand.

"That feels amazing."

Lane steadied herself on shaky legs, trying to catch her breath. She drew her fingers along Ali's jaw, down her neck, stopping only when she touched the top of her breasts. "You..."—she drew her fingers lightly across the top of one breast—"are amazing." She inhaled deeply. Cupping Ali's breast, she grazed her thumb over its already erect nipple. Leaning close, she said softly, "And now I want to touch you." She slipped a hand under the hem of the dress. "And taste you." Her tongue danced down the side of Ali's neck. Ali pulled Lane's hips between her legs. Lane drew back enough to look in her eyes, which were burning like blue flames. "I want to do this right." She took Ali's hand, guiding her off the stool toward the short hallway.

Lane turned on a low-level bedside light and returned to Ali. "You are so incredibly beautiful." She cupped her face, kissing her lips tenderly. "I want to touch every exquisite inch of you." Lane kicked off her shoes before laying Ali gently back onto the bed.

Ali captured Lane's mouth in a searing kiss, while Lane's hand traveled slowly up the inside of her thigh until her fingers grazed a damp triangle of fabric. She leaned back slightly, watching the desire that burned in Ali's eyes. "God, I've wanted to touch you like this since the first time I saw you." She deftly worked her hand inside the skimpy panties, eliciting a barely audible whimper when her fingers brushed over her clit. Lane lowered her head to place feather-light kisses on Ali's cheek and chin. "You feel so good." She kissed along her jaw. "I think I could come again from simply touching you."

Ali threaded her fingers in Lane's hair, guiding her lips to her breasts. "That feels so good," she managed hoarsely. "I'm so close." Ali rode Lane's fingers as she pleaded, "Yes, oh, please, don't stop."

Lane thought her heart might explode as she held Ali so close to ecstasy. She wanted to melt into Ali so she could feel her orgasm inside herself. She'd never felt so intimately connected with a woman in her life. And that's what this was…intimacy. Not sex for a physical release, but something much deeper, something…something emotional. Lane stilled her hand, gazing at Ali's face.

Ali immediately reached for Lane's motionless hand. "Oh, God, what's wrong?" she gasped.

"I want…" Lane kissed between Ali's breasts. "I don't want to rush this. I want to savor you."

Ali attempted a smile. "Oh, baby." She clenched her thighs and pushed against Lane's hand. "Can you do that later? I need to come so badly I can barely breathe."

Lane felt so vulnerable, so not in control. "Promise?" Her voice sounded so unlike her…timid.

Ali's expression grew tender as she stroked Lane's hair. "I promise, baby, I promise." She pushed again against Lane's hand. "Please…"

Lane stroked and kissed, easily bringing Ali to orgasm. She cried out, collapsing back onto the bed and moving her fingers again into Lane's hair. "God, that felt so good," she panted. "I've been dying for you to do that."

Lane tugged up the dress hem, encouraging Ali to lift her hips and quickly relieved her of it. She kissed Ali's stomach before sliding off the bed and shedding her own clothes. "I've only started," she said, returning to lie beside her, kissing her stomach again, making the muscles there twitch. "And I want so much more of you."

Ali's eyes, filled with craving, looked back at her and through labored breath, she said, "I don't think I can come again, but I don't mind trying."

Lane smiled, moved up the bed, molding her body tightly to Ali's side. Draping her arm across Ali's waist, she held her close, marveling again at the connection she felt with her. And fighting the fear that caused.

Ali was different, special. Lane was beginning to care very deeply for her. But her brain was firing little warnings. A serious relationship with a woman would be dangerous, even disastrous, for her career and future, she knew that. With Ali, though, she wasn't feeling any of the self-preservation instincts she'd had in the past.

Maybe, Lane reasoned, it was Ali's innocence and vulnerability. Could she be a lover for the long haul? Like—a partner? God, Lane realized. This was the first time in her life she'd ever considered making a life with someone. Was that even possible?

Ali groaned in response to Lane's light strokes up and down her side and pulled Lane's mouth to hers for a brief kiss. "I want to make you come again."

Lane rolled over to partially cover her, slipping her thigh between Ali's. Her clit went rigid at the feel of Ali's hot slickness on her own thigh. She thrust against Ali. "I don't think that's going to be a problem." Ali brought Lane's mouth to hers again, kissing her feverishly as she worked her hand between them. Lane groaned, "Ah, Jesus," rocking with each movement of Ali's fingers, the pulse throbbing intensely between her legs. When Ali plunged her tongue into Lane's mouth, it carried her over like a wave crashing onto the beach. She growled Ali's name before dropping her head against her neck.

"You are," Lane murmured breathlessly, "so incredibly amazing."

Ali turned her head, lightly kissing Lane's forehead. *Wow,* she thought, *I brought Z to orgasm before and never received more than a grunted "thanks."* She'd never had anyone make her feel special, like she was worth something, the way Lane did. She was barely aware of Lane's lips moving down her body to the top of her thigh. Lane's cheek brushing across her damp curls. Lane turned her head, whispering, "So beautiful," before lowering her mouth to her.

Ali cried out, "Oh, yes..." Her voice faltered as Lane's fingers slowly entered her and the orgasm swept her over the edge.

Lane again moved to Ali's side, wrapping a protective arm around her waist and burying her face against her neck. She kissed Ali's damp skin lightly.

Ali moaned as she clenched her thighs against an aftershock spurred by the thought of Lane's mouth on her heated skin. She'd never had an orgasm like this before either, so intensely…intimate. And now, Lane had her wrapped in her arms. No one had ever had sex with her and held her after. It was terrifying, but somehow at the same time comforting. They lay in the embrace while their breathing slowly returned to normal.

"I probably should get going," Ali said, breaking the hypnotic silence. "I'm sure you have to be up early for work."

Lane leaned back. "I do." She tightened her arm around Ali's waist. "But you don't have to leave," she said, placing a tender kiss on Ali's shoulder. "Unless you need to. Or want to."

Ali turned toward her. Lane's eyes were black as the night outside. She couldn't read anything in their dark depths. "If you want me to stay, I'd like to," she said with some trepidation, stroking her fingers along Lane's strong jawline.

"I like you, Ali Castle, and I'd like you to stay the night with me." Lane took Ali's hand and placed a kiss in her palm. "I'd like that a lot." She ignored the alarms blaring in her head as she pulled a corner of the comforter over them, wrapping them like a cocoon. The rational side of Lane's brain warned her that her behavior was dangerous, careless. Getting too involved with a woman, especially one who knew her real name, was equivalent to playing with fire. It could burn her house down, scorching her too, if she weren't careful. Her emotions were in control of her body at the moment, however. She couldn't deny the pull of this woman. She didn't want to. After thirty-six years, she wanted more than a one-night stand or a week-long affair. A lot more, she decided. In fact, she wanted it all. Wrapped in Ali's warm embrace, she drifted off.

CHAPTER ELEVEN

Lane startled from sleep when Ali stirred and murmured softly. The momentary confusion she felt as to why she was waking with a woman in her arms evaporated as she breathed in Ali's scent and memories of last night's pleasures came flooding back. Ali had touched something deep inside her, something she wanted never to give up.

She did, however, have to get up, she realized—the clock on the nightstand read five minutes past six—or she'd be late for work. Without disturbing Ali, she slipped from the bed, gathered up her clothes and quietly left the room. After dressing hurriedly in the bathroom, she ran up to the penthouse. She grabbed some bills off the dresser and a notepad and pen before stopping in the kitchen to put on some coffee. Ten minutes later, back down in the apartment, she tiptoed into the bedroom, placing the note and the cash on the nightstand. She stood at the side of the bed several minutes before quietly removing herself from the room. She wanted to kiss Ali, but she didn't want to wake her. She looked like an angel, lying in sleep, her blonde locks framing her adorable face. *An angel from heaven*, Lane thought. For a fleeting moment she had the surreal thought that her mother had sent Ali to her. She shook her head, laughing to herself as she rushed back upstairs to get ready for work.

* * *

Ali woke in an empty bed at around eight thirty. She experienced a moment of panic, but then the sleep cleared from her head and she recognized where she was. She'd slept so soundly she hadn't heard Lane leave. As she dropped her legs over the edge of the mattress, she spotted the note on the nightstand.

"Ali," she read, "last night was too incredible for words. You are an amazing and beautiful woman. It took every ounce of self-control not to wake you with my lips caressing your delicate skin."

Ali's thighs clenched at the memory of Lane's mouth on her.

"I realize we both have very busy and hectic schedules, but I do want to see you again. Soon. Let me know when you're free and I will move heaven and earth to accommodate your schedule. I hope to see you soon—Lane."

Under the first note, there was another one folded around some bills. "Cab fare. Tell the doorman that Jeremy said he would call you a cab." She smiled. Lane Stanford was nothing like the only other judge she'd met. She was kind, considerate, tender—and a selfless and passionate lover.

She padded naked to the living room to retrieve the phone from her purse. In the bathroom she found a robe hanging on a hook. She caught a whiff of Lane's scent as she pulled it on. "Oh, God," she muttered. "You make me want you so bad." She wandered to the kitchen next, where she found another brief note. "Coffee's ready to brew." She hit the button and dialed Lane's number.

The vibrating in her pocket startled Lane. Ali's ID appeared on the screen. "Good morning, beautiful."

"Good morning."

Lane pushed back from her desk, leaning back in her chair. "I trust you slept well." She heard Ali's sigh.

"I slept like a baby. Your bed is like sleeping on a cloud."

Lane felt the stirrings of desire again. "In that case, I'm hoping you'll want to do it again." She paused. "Soon."

"There's a very good chance you'll get exactly what you're hoping for." Ali's voice purred through the phone. Lane had to fan her warming face with a folder. "I could get used to this. You better be careful, you'll spoil me."

She heard the coffeemaker gurgle and the last place Lane wanted to be was in her office. She wanted to be home having breakfast with Ali and perhaps Ali for breakfast.

"The work schedule should be posted today for the next week. I can call you later and let you know what I'm working." Lane didn't respond. "Lane?"

"Hum…" Lane replied distractedly.

"I'm sorry, if I'm interrupting some important business, you should have said so."

Lane mentally shook herself from her daydream. "No, I'm sorry. I allowed my mind to wander for a moment. You were saying?"

"That I will know my schedule later today and I can let you know if you want to make some plans to do something."

Lane realized her hand was unconsciously moving dangerously close to the heat radiating between her legs. *A little self-control*, she admonished. "Yes, by all means let me know, and we'll plan another date."

"You can't imagine how much I'd like that." Ali's voice purred.

Lane clenched her thighs. "Actually, I can." *For once in my lonely life.* "I'll think of somewhere special we can go."

"Or," Ali interrupted, "we can stay in and order out." Ali slid her hand inside the robe and cupped her own breast. "I really like having you all to myself." She liked being with Lane alone in the apartment. She'd never been with a woman before, not "that way," in a place she felt safe and comfortable. Ali knew she could get used to the feeling.

"I think we need to end this conversation before I develop some sudden illness and have to come home."

"If you do, I promise I'll be waiting to take care of you."

Lane groaned. "Oh, God, Ali, you are far too tempting for my own good."

"I'm sorry."

"Ali, don't ever say you're sorry." Lane practically whispered. "It's… you're so…" She didn't finish. "Let me know your schedule once you have it and we'll plan something."

"Okay, I'll talk to you later."

"Bye, Ali." And with that Lane was gone.

* * *

It was well into the afternoon before she could concentrate long enough to get any work done. Thoughts of Ali were ever present in her mind, causing her pulse to jump without warning or triggering that funny flutter in her stomach. She was telling herself—again—to buckle down when Jeremy interrupted.

"There's a John Woods here. He doesn't have an appointment, but he said you would want to see him."

She'd completely forgotten about the assignment she'd given John. She couldn't believe he'd dig up anything scandalous, but…better safe than sorry. "Send him in."

She motioned John to a chair. "I didn't think I'd hear back from you."

He dropped his six-foot-two, broad-shouldered linebacker frame into one of the chairs across the desk. He ran a hand across his buzzed off sandy hair before saying, "There's not much to report. That's kind of the problem."

Lane, suddenly anxious, watched as he fished a piece of paper from the inside pocket of his jacket. Unfolding it, he slid it across the desk.

"I came up with very little from the name and address you provided. In fact, doing the basic searches I couldn't find anything going back more than about six months. That was when she purchased the '98 Ford Escort listed there. She had a couple of jobs working at fast-food places before she started working at that restaurant a few months after the car purchase."

Lane emitted a heavy sigh as she read the next piece of information.

He continued, "And yes, that address you gave me is a vacant building. No living spaces, not a single tenant in the whole place. It seemed off to me that someone would try to pass that off as their address." He shifted nervously. "Which is why, even though you didn't ask me to, I followed her."

Lane laid down his report, her eyes intent on his, waiting for the other shoe to drop.

He hesitated…too long. "From what I can tell it appears she's living out of her car parked in the alley behind the restaurant where she works. There's a rolled up sleeping bag behind the driver's seat and the floor in front and behind the passenger's seat looks like a hotel laundry cart."

Shocked didn't begin to describe how Lane felt at hearing John's news. Ali Castle was homeless? It was the last thing she had expected.

She finally nodded. "All right. Thanks, John." She reached into her case for her wallet and handed him several hundred dollars in cash. "Please keep looking. I can't imagine she simply materialized six months ago. Everybody has a background, some kind of history. Keep me posted."

He slipped the cash in his pocket. "Sure thing, Lane." He made his way to the door. "I'll be in touch."

She'd been distracted before thinking about Ali, but now, well, she was completely unnerved.

Homeless. How could Ali possibly be homeless and I didn't pick up on it? She didn't look like the homeless people she'd ever seen. Homeless meant living on the streets, wearing dirty clothes and not bathing. Not possible, she thought, remembering vividly the taste of Ali's soft skin last night. No, she definitely bathes.

She pulled out her cell to call Ali, knowing full well she'd be working. The message she left was brief. "Ali, hi, it's Lane. I know you're busy working so maybe you can call me back when you get a break." She hoped her voice didn't hint at the anguish she felt roiling in the pit of her stomach.

She watched the clock for thirty minutes before standing and pacing the area behind her desk. Each time she passed and glanced at the piece of paper lying in the middle of her desk all she could envision in her mind was the word "homeless." There had to be a plausible explanation...had to be. Her instincts were better than that. Weren't they? John had to be wrong. She might not live at the address she'd delivered her to, but she couldn't be living in a damn car. And then, like a slap in the face, it hit her. She's living with someone, living somewhere else. "Ah, Christ!" She recalled the first time she invited Ali for dinner and Ali had said there was "someone."

Her mind was a million miles away when Jeremy knocked and poked his head in. "I'm out of here." She looked at him blankly. "Don't forget you have that dinner meeting at six." She nodded. "Okay, your car will be here in forty minutes and I'll see you Monday." When she only nodded again, he stepped inside and closed the door. "Lane..."

"Hmm..."

"You okay? Because you look...I don't know...I've never seen you look like this before."

She placed her hand to her neck, barely nodding her head. "Yes," she said, noticing that her voice was hoarse. "I think I might be coming down with something. I'll be fine."

He placed his hand on the doorknob. "Well, take yourself straight home after your dinner and go right to bed. I seem to recall you have some charity event tomorrow evening too."

She regained a momentary thread of control. "I'll be sure to do that, Mr. Mom," she said, offering him a wry smile.

"Anyway, have a good weekend." With that, he left her to her worry.

* * *

Lane was beyond distracted as the car moved through the evening traffic, unsure if it was luck or not when her cell phone rang as they approached the restaurant.

"Hello," she said, hoping her voice didn't betray her mood.

"Hi, it's me." Ali's voice bubbled as usual.

She called to Randall through the open privacy window. "I have a call I have to take before I go in if you want to pull into the lot." Without waiting for his reply, she raised the window and returned to Ali's call.

"Sounds like you're still working. Do you want me to call later?"

"No," Lane said, more abruptly than she intended. "I'm sorry. I have a million things on my mind at the moment."

Ali's voice was carefree. "It's okay. I imagine you've got lots going all the time."

"Yes, well, in any case, I was calling to see if I could swing by your place and pick you up after work and grab a drink somewhere."

"Sure, but you can just pick me up here. My car's actually been acting funny, so one of the busboys and his friend are going to look at it for me."

"How were you going to get home?"

"Um, well, I figured I'd walk. It's really not that far."

"I realize you're young and probably fearless compared to me, but I'm a little uncomfortable with the thought of you walking in that neighborhood at night. I can't imagine it's safe. So promise me, if you have an issue with your car, you'll let me know. I can ensure you get to and from where you need to safely."

"Gee, Lane—"

"No," Lane cut her off. "Please, Ali, if we're going to date I don't want to worry about your safety if I can help."

"Okay, but they're supposed to have it fixed for me early tomorrow."

"What time should I pick you up?"

"I should be done by about eleven thirty."

"All right. I'll see you at the restaurant."

"Okay. And Lane…"

"Yes?"

"I'm glad you called. I've been thinking about you all day."

Lane said only, "I'll see you later," before ending the call. She wanted to tell Ali she'd been thinking of her as well, but given the news she'd received from John earlier, she wasn't sure her tone would convey enthusiasm instead of anxiety.

Concentration was difficult during her dinner meeting with the city's two largest developers. She feigned attention as they spouted grandiose plans for developing some of the rundown areas of the city, but the truth was she couldn't have cared less. For the first time since she'd been elected to the bench, she was having trouble looking ahead. This situation she'd allowed herself to fall into felt a lot like quicksand, with the potential to suck her under and swamp anything resembling a future for her.

By eight thirty when she could endure no more, she made her excuses and left. Randall was parked in the lot next to the building, and she actually managed to sneak up on him, although that wasn't her intention. When he heard her try the door handle, he immediately jumped out.

"I'm very sorry, ma'am." He held the door for her. "You should have called so I could pick you up out front."

"It's fine, Randall," she said distractedly as she slid into the seat. "Take me home, please."

"Yes, ma'am." He gently closed the door.

* * *

Up in her penthouse she made a drink, changed into comfortable clothes and settled on the sofa in her living room, which had been decked out by one of the trendiest interior decorators in the city. It was too lavish for her tastes, but her father had insisted. It was grating on her more than usual tonight, as she contemplated Ali's living conditions. She managed to stay put nearly ten minutes before getting antsy and going to her home office. After more than a half hour of trying to concentrate on one thing without success, she headed to the kitchen to put on some coffee.

She felt as though an alien had taken possession of her. She couldn't recall ever being so out of it, in fact, since her mother had passed away. No, Weston Stanford III's lessons and lectures were deeply embedded in her core. She had never before allowed anything, especially a woman, to divert her focus from her work and where that laser-beamed focus would take her. And yet somehow, in a matter of a few weeks, Ali had managed to undermine all that.

At ten forty-five she tore out of the garage in the Miata, needing the fresh air that swirled around her as she entered the expressway to open the car up for a few miles and kill some time. She pulled to the curb across from the restaurant early, parked and watched the entrance compulsively. Finally, at eleven thirty-five the front door pushed open and Ali exited. Lane's heart leapt at the sight of her.

"Hi!" Ali gave a wave as she crossed the street and opened the passenger side door. Her eyes sparkled in the car's interior light before it faded. She leaned across the console and touched her lips to Lane's. The kiss, as quick as it was, raised goose flesh on Lane's skin. She sat back. "Sorry. I smell like fish. Normally I'd shower before meeting anyone."

As she turned the ignition key, Lane wondered exactly where it was that Ali might have showered. "I thought we'd have a drink at my place if that's all right with you."

Ali slipped her hand onto Lane's thigh. "Okay by me." She hefted the oversize bag she'd dropped on the car's floor. "I do at least have a change of clothes so I don't have to smell like Roscoe's red snapper special."

She carried a bag of spare clothes around with her. *How convenient*, Lane thought. The ride back to the apartment was peppered with long silences with Ali initiating most of the conversation that did take place.

After a quiet ride up in the elevator from the garage, Lane said, "You can shower before you change if you'd like. There are towels in the bathroom linen closet. Help yourself."

Ali caught Lane's hand before she stepped toward the bar. "Are you okay, Lane? 'Cause you don't seem like yourself tonight."

Lane didn't allow her gaze to waver from the deep blue of Ali's eyes. Squeezing her hand reassuringly, she said, "I'm fine. It's been a very long week for me and it's not over yet."

The corners of Ali's mouth curved up. "Well, maybe I can help relieve some of the stress weighing on you." She stepped away, slowly pulling her hand from Lane's. "After I freshen up."

Lane was seated on the couch when Ali returned, wearing a simple white V-neck T-shirt and black skintight jogging pants and combing her fingers through her damp hair. She looked adorable, Lane thought. Very innocent.

"Sorry for the clothes," she said, pulling at the hem of the T-shirt, "I wasn't planning on seeing you when I threw these in my bag this morning."

Lane's inquisitiveness overrode her intention to be diplomatic. "What was it that you were planning for that outfit?"

Ali glanced briefly at her well-worn clothes, wondering at the edge in Lane's voice and met her eyes again. She saw something dark in their depths, and it wasn't desire.

Lane was turned off by her thrift store clothing, she decided. They hardly compared to a judge's wardrobe. Still...

"I hadn't really planned anything. I knew I had to walk home tonight, so I figured I might as well be comfortable."

Lane nodded. "I hope you feel better having gotten the restaurant grime washed away."

Ali rested her hand on Lane's thigh. "I do. Thank you for letting me shower." When Lane only nodded again, Ali got the sense once more that something was off. They sat in silence until she couldn't stand it any longer. She turned to face Lane. "I feel like there's something wrong." She motioned between them. "Have I done something? Are you mad at me for something?"

Lane asked, "Are you living with someone?"

Ali shook her head, confused by the question. "No."

"It seems like you go out of your way to keep me away from your place." She shrugged. "Like maybe you're hiding something or someone there."

Ali lowered her head. "I don't really live there. I'm sorry I let you think that."

Lane hadn't been prepared for Ali's honesty. She stared at her in silence.

In a near whisper, Ali finally said, "There's nobody else, not anymore. And I don't have a place, no place except my car." She looked up at Lane, all the brightness gone from her eyes.

Lane's heart nearly broke. She had to clear her throat to speak. "Why didn't you tell me?"

Ali's eyes became liquid with tears, and her voice quivered when she responded. "Because..." She paused, trying to regain her composure as a tear slipped down her cheek. "Why would someone like you even look twice at a homeless person? Or go on a date with them? Invite them into your home?"

Lane's insides twisted. She felt no alarm, didn't feel threatened. She had only a powerful yearning to hold Ali in her arms. Here was a woman who had been surviving the best she could given her circumstances and who had asked Lane for absolutely nothing. There were plenty out there in similar situations who would take advantage of others without a second thought. But not Ali, no. And Lane was not about to shame her by asking questions and making Ali tell her everything.

Reassured now that her instincts from their first meeting had been spot on, Lane gently wiped the wet streak from her cheek.

"From the very first moment I saw you, I saw more than an incredibly beautiful woman." Lane briefly raised Ali's hand to her lips. "I saw a woman with direction and determination. The way those businessmen were acting with you disgusted me, but you handled them with a professionalism that blew me away. I detest asses like those guys."

"It's part of the job," Ali said meekly.

"I know, but it made me sick to sit there and watch them treat you that way."

"And so you had Roscoe change my tables."

"It was purely selfish on my part. I wanted to see what kind of woman could take the crap those guys were dishing out without seeming at all fazed." Lane squeezed her hand. "And…I wanted a better look." Lane leaned a little closer, stroking her thumb over Ali's hand. "I haven't regretted for a second pursuing you. Please know that you can tell me anything. You don't have to hide anything. I like you for the person you are, not whether you live somewhere nice. Understood?"

Ali nodded slowly. Lane kissed her and leaned back, stroking her fingers through Ali's still damp hair. "You'll stay here again tonight. And I'm going to work it out so you don't have to worry about where you'll be sleeping in future."

"But…"

Lane gently touched her fingers to Ali's lips. "No buts, please. I don't want to think about you sleeping in your car, God knows where. I'd never sleep another wink myself worrying about you." Ali started to protest again, but Lane stopped her. "There's no discussion. I'm pulling rank." Lane winked, finally pulling a smile from her.

"Are you going to sentence me to the bedroom for the rest of the night?" Ali's finger began drawing little circles on Lane's thigh.

"If that's what you want."

"That's what I want," Ali said, moving to straddle Lane's thighs. "That," she ground herself into Lane's crotch, "and this," she kissed Lane ravenously, rocking against her.

When Ali opened her jeans and slipped her hand inside, Lane groaned into her mouth. Ali tipped her forehead to Lane's. "God, I think I could come simply by touching you."

Lane pushed against Ali's hand. She was so close. "That's it…" she moaned. "Don't stop."

"No, baby, I won't."

Lane came hard, gasping for breath as her head dropped back against the couch. Ali continued administering gentle strokes. "I love to watch you…so intense." She rocked against her own hand. "You should feel what you've done to me."

Lane gave a lazy smile. "Believe me, I intend to." After a few more calming breaths, she removed Ali's hand, then rocked forward, cupped her hands under Ali's behind and pushed up from the couch. Ali wrapped her legs around Lane's waist, holding on while Lane carried her down the hallway. Lane kissed the hollow at the base of Ali's neck. "I'm imposing sentence now. Prepare to be punished." Lane patted her backside. When Ali dipped her head to capture her mouth, Lane's legs became unexpectedly rubbery. She wondered if she'd make it to the bed.

Punishment. The word echoed in Ali's mind even as she desperately tried pushing it away. Hadn't she been punished enough? First by a father who wouldn't let her be a regular kid. And a mother who had mirrored his hellfire and brimstone attitudes, whether out of fear of him or because she too believed all that religious garbage. Which meant she had gone off to college naive—and ended up stumbling into more trouble than she knew could exist in the world. Trying to start over, surviving in a strange place, having to live in her car, for God's sake—that had been a kind of punishment too.

Now, though, she had Lane. Lane made her feel as though life really could be the sunshine and rainbows she had dreamed of as an innocent little girl.

Lane dropped them on the bed with an "oomph." She stopped thinking and abandoned herself to sensation.

CHAPTER TWELVE

Lane went through much the same motions Saturday morning as she had the previous day—but it all felt different. Very different. She was invigorated as she climbed the stairs to the penthouse, thinking about how sound and restful her sleep had been with Ali wrapped securely in her arms. She'd never given a thought before as to whether she did—or didn't—make the women she dated feel safe. Frankly, she hadn't cared, because they served a very basic purpose for her—sex. There wasn't any doubt now, though, that Ali wasn't one of those women. She was someone Lane genuinely cared for. Lane had realized the moment Ali confessed to her homelessness that she wanted to protect her, wanted to take care of her, needed to make her feel safe in a way she herself hadn't felt in many years. That was reflected in the note she'd left Ali this morning:

Ali, I never imagined how wonderful it could feel to wake with a woman in my arms after a night of shared pleasures. Again, you don't have to worry about where you'll be sleeping from now on. Please call me later and let me know when you'll be done working tonight so I can meet you at the restaurant. I'll get things arranged. I'll be thinking of you—Lane.

Lane felt a sense of fulfillment she couldn't remember feeling since passing the bar. After that day, she knew nothing could stop her in her quest for a future filled with great accomplishment. And now…she had a feeling it could all mean so much more than she'd ever imagined.

She stepped into her private bathroom, barely recognizing the image she saw reflected there. She saw someone looking back at her who cared about someone other than herself. It was going to take some getting used to to adjust to this feeling of…she struggled to identify what she was feeling. Was this what people called happiness? She drew in and exhaled a deep breath. Would it last? she wondered. And if it did, would she ever get used to this new Lane?

While she felt like a changed woman, a part of her still wanted to proceed with caution. There were already things in the closets and drawers to give the appearance that she lived in the apartment—in the event someone she entertained decided to snoop—but before she went to pick up Ali Lane decided to move a few more clothes and personal items down from the penthouse. She allowed herself only enough time to get to the restaurant. Saturday night was probably the busiest night of the week, and she didn't want to be seen loitering in her car out on the street. She was rewarded with a huge smile when Ali came out. She strode confidently across the street as Lane lowered her window.

"Hey, baby," she said, stepping to the open window.

Lane had used the endearment herself with women, but she'd never before been anyone's "baby." She liked the feeling it gave her.

"Hi!" she replied. "You look tired."

"It's been an exhausting day. I'd rather have Saturdays off."

"Maybe I can speak to Roscoe…"

Ali crossed her arms under her breasts. "Oh, no. I don't want you using your influence to get me any special treatment. That's not why—"

"I'm sorry. Please know I would never do anything you didn't want me to."

"So…what's the plan?"

Lane handed a plastic card to her through the car window. "Get your car and let's go home."

A few blocks from the building Lane phoned her.

"Miss me that much you couldn't wait a few more minutes to talk to me?" Ali asked in a giddy tone.

Lane chuckled. "No…I mean, yes…and no." She was flustered. "After I swipe my card and enter the garage, you'll need to let the gate close before you swipe yours. I'll show you your parking spot."

"Sure thing, Lane. You're the boss," Ali said teasingly.

"I'm no one's boss," Lane said rather harshly.

"I'm sorry, Lane, I didn't mean anything by it."

Lane mumbled, "You're being ridiculous."

"What?"

"Sorry. I was talking to myself. I don't much care for that title. It's what Jeremy calls me when he's in a snippy mood." She turned at the garage entrance. "I'll see you inside." She activated the gate, waited inside until Ali had entered and pointed out the two parking spaces assigned for Apartment 504. She parked in her personal spot close to the elevator.

When she got out, Ali was already walking toward her. "Nice parking spot, but there were two together over there." She hooked her thumb in the direction she parked.

Lane steered her toward the elevator. "I pay a lot of money to have that space." And that was the truth. She instinctively started to push the number "eight" button but managed to hit the "five" before Ali noticed. Damn. This was going to be hard. This was the most involved deception she'd ever attempted and she would have to be vigilant to keep up the charade. They entered the apartment through the back door.

"I have to ask that you always enter and leave through the back door and only use the garage elevator. I need to keep my private life very private." She reached for Ali's hand. "In a perfect world, I'd parade you around on my arm, proud to have everyone know that you're with me." She placed her lips lightly on the back of Ali's hand. "But this is not a perfect world, and I have to do my best to conform to the expectations everyone has for me."

"So you have to act straight?"

"In a nutshell, yes."

"Okay," Ali agreed easily. "I can be discreet or invisible or whatever you need me to be. But before anything, I'd like to wash off the work smell. You mind if I shower real quick?"

Lane gave her hand a light tug. "I've got a better idea. Come on." She led her to the bathroom, opening the linen closet door and pulling out a bottle. "How about a nice hot soak with bubbles?" She wiggled her brows mischievously. "I can wash your back for you." Lane handed her the robe from the back of the door. "Undress. I'll start the water."

Ali made sure her fingers brushed Lane's as she took the offering. "Be right back."

When Ali returned, the bubbles were nearing the top of the tub, the water still running. Lane stood and dried her hands. "I guessed at the temperature."

Ali stepped beside the tub, slowly sliding the robe from her shoulders. When the silk pooled around her feet, Lane felt her blood pound between her legs. Ali settled into the fragrant water. "It's perfect." She slid her hands up and down her arms, drawing the bubbles over herself. She placed the bath sponge in Lane's hand. "I seem to remember an offer to wash my back."

Lane looked on in stunned silence, slowly nodding her head. Ali looked angelic, if it were possible for a living, breathing human to do so. And the passion in her eyes made Lane want to drag her from the water and take her right there on the floor. Reining in her desire, she dipped the sponge in the bathwater and slid it up Ali's back.

Ali moaned and Lane throbbed so hard between her legs it hurt. "I need you to touch me." Ali pulled Lane's hand to her breasts, her eyes glassy like she was high on something. "I'm so close."

The way I am from simply touching you, Lane thought. She slipped off the edge of the tub to her knees. Ali hooked her hand around her neck. "Need you now, Lane. Can't wait."

Lane pulled Ali to her, probing the warm confines of her mouth with her tongue. She leaned back a moment later, and Ali reached for the buttons on her shirt. Lane's eyes never left hers as she unbuttoned it, slid the fabric off her shoulders and released the front clasp of Lane's bra, exposing her breasts completely. When she cupped both in her warm, wet hands, Lane moaned audibly and her eyes fluttered closed for a moment. Lane jerked when Ali gently squeezed her oversensitized nipples.

Ali whispered, "God, I want to make you come right now." She lowered her hand to the top of Lane's slacks and looked up, seeking permission.

"Yes," Lane panted. "God, yes." Ali hurriedly unbuttoned and unzipped them. She stood on shaky legs, shedding the blouse and bra hanging on her arms, kicking her shoes aside to step out of her pants and underwear and slipping into the tub.

Ali straddled Lane's thighs, facing her. Lane slipped inside her, watching with rapture as, after a few quick strokes, she came. "Beautiful," Lane whispered. "So very, very beautiful." She smoothed her hands over her sleek backside. "And exhausted," she added, noticing that Ali was drifting off.

"Ali, sweetheart, we need to get out before we fall asleep and drown." Ali lifted her head from Lane's shoulder, her eyelids heavy. Lane gave a tiny smile. "I can see the headline now: 'Judge Found Drowned in Bathtub with Lesbian Lover.' Who knew?" She patted Ali's rump. "I have to remain in my closet, at least for now. Let me put you to bed."

Ali rose slowly from the tub, got out and toweled herself off. "I need a few minutes before I'm ready to crawl into bed."

Lane stood at the door, towel wrapped at her waist, her nipples tightening as she gazed at Ali's gloriously naked body. She didn't think she'd ever tire of seeing it. Inhaling deeply, she pulled open the door. "Take all the time you need. I'll meet you in there." She inclined her head toward the bedroom. She thought about detouring to the bar, but decided she wouldn't need a drink to fall asleep tonight. She was reclining on the pillows with the sheet pulled only to her waist when Ali came in.

"I'm not sure I can sleep with your naked body tempting me all night." Ali dropped the robe over the end of the bed and slid between the crisp, cool sheets next to Lane's warmth. "You feel so good." She wrapped an arm around Lane's waist, settling against her shoulder.

Lane stroked her fingers lightly up and down Ali's back. "I bet if you close your eyes, I can put you to sleep."

She kissed the top of her head while continuing the feather-light touch along her spine. Ali murmured again as she slipped her leg between Lane's, settling more firmly against her. Less than five minutes later Lane could tell by the steady, warm breath across her chest that she was indeed asleep. She snuggled down into the pillows herself and wrapped Ali tightly in her arm.

"You sleep, sweetheart. I'm going to take care of you," she whispered. Suddenly and completely she was overwhelmed by a torrent of emotions. The only thing she had to compare them to were the loss and loneliness she'd felt when her mother had died. But these... especially this overpowering pull to take care of someone else...they were unlike any she'd ever known. Ali Castle had gotten inside her, somewhere no other woman had before, and she didn't want Ali to leave that place anytime in the foreseeable future.

Ali stirred, moaned softly and turned over, pressing her back into Lane's side. When Lane turned on her side as well and slipped her arm around Ali's waist, she took Lane's hand and pulled it between her breasts. *God, this must be what nirvana feels like.* The bedside clock glowed one seventeen as she closed her eyes, joining Ali in a deep sleep.

* * *

Ali's voice startled Lane from her sound sleep. "Oh crap!" She opened an eye to watch as Ali scurried from the bed and started looking around desperately. "Shit!"

Lane stretched. "What's wrong?" The clock read nine forty.

Ali grabbed at the robe lying on the bed. "I'm going to be late." She stepped toward the door. "I'm on at ten thirty. Roscoe is trying out a Sunday brunch today."

Lane crawled out of bed and caught Ali at the door. "Relax, sweetheart, we'll get you there on time."

"Oh, God…" Ali exhaled, her shoulders slumping.

"What?"

Ali placed her hand against Lane's chest. "I'm late, you're standing right here…naked…and I just want to touch you."

"I'm flattered that the sight of me does this to you"—Lane stroked her fingers through Ali's disheveled hair—"but we need to get you to work so you don't get fired." When Ali sighed and reached for her anyway, Lane grabbed her hand and kissed it. "I actually have some things scheduled for today too. We'll have plenty of time later to hop back in the sack. Now, go get dressed and whatever else you need to do." She made a shooing motion. "I'll call a cab for you. They'll get you there in time."

She kissed Ali at the back door with a sense of loss. She wanted her at home, not running off to work. She wondered if she'd always feel this way. "Remember to come in through the garage when you get home."

"Sure, baby."

"I'll see you later." Lane gave her another quick peck before opening the door and sending her off.

* * *

Ali arrived home around eight. She had the cabbie drop her in front of the building next door so she could slip in through the garage and ride the elevator up without stopping at the first-floor lobby. She dropped her purse inside the spare room, used the bathroom and ventured to the kitchen, where a soft light glowed under a cabinet onto the counter. There she found a note.

"Ali, I had a dinner meeting that I would have canceled if I could have so I could be here when you arrived home." *Home*, Ali thought. She hadn't known anything resembling the comfort of a home since graduating from high school. She wondered if she would ever feel like this place was her home. She read the rest. "Dinner is at seven so I should be home about nine. Make yourself comfortable. See you soon, Lane."

Ali returned the note to the counter and pulled open the fridge. She found lots of bottled water there and little else. She moved over to the cabinets. They contained enough dishes to service any household, but no food other than a few boxes of crackers. She plucked one out, got a bottle of water from the fridge and wandered back down the hall. The only television was in the spare room, so she plopped down on the small sofa there and clicked on the remote. She flipped through the channels until a naked butt caught her eye. She watched several minutes while a voluptuous brunette with breasts larger than any Ali could imagine gave pleasure to a handsome blonde who looked like a bodybuilder. The combination wasn't particularly arousing, but the sight of the woman's tight backside and swinging breasts was. She reached for her own growing wetness, then realized where she was. How would it look for Lane to come home to find her masturbating? She ran the channels up several more before turning the TV off.

* * *

Lane got home a few minutes after nine. She smiled as she entered to find Ali propped on a barstool in a bathrobe. "Hi."

Lane dropped her purse and keys on the entry table. "What a welcome sight." Ali's arms snaked around Lane's neck, pulling her in. The kiss that followed was dizzying. She steadied herself on the bar as Ali deepened it. She couldn't recall sharing a kiss so filled with passion with anyone before Ali. She had also never met a woman that she was as willing to submit to as she did to her.

"Baby?" Ali's voice whispered soft against her lips.

"Mmm…"

"You look so hot I want to tear your clothes off, but I know you have to get up early for work."

Lane had been called a lot of things by women, "a knockout" or "attractive" usually, and more unpleasant things of late, but she'd never before been called "hot."

"It's barely past nine." She ran her fingers through Ali's silky locks. "We have time for whatever you have in mind." She kissed her briefly. "I would however ask you to refrain from the 'tearing' part with regard to my clothes."

Ali slipped her arms around Lane's waist and smiled seductively. "I'll try."

They moved to the bedroom, where Ali slowly undressed her, pushed her down on the bed and lowered herself over her body. Before Ali could move lower than Lane's breasts, however, Lane rolled her over, settling between Ali's legs.

Ali pouted. "That's really not fair. You're bigger than I am."

"And don't forget, I outrank you too." She winked. This was so much more than sex. It was slow, gentle and passionate. And it was foreign, like a different language. *This is what they call lovemaking*, she thought. The thought unsettled her. She had all kinds of new feelings for Ali, but she didn't think it could be love. Whatever it was, she decided, it was wonderful. For the third consecutive night Lane fell asleep comforted by Ali's still, sleeping body in her arms.

CHAPTER THIRTEEN

Lane sat on the edge of the bed Monday morning, gently stroking the hair from Ali's face. When she stirred, Lane placed a soft kiss at the corner of her mouth. "Good morning, beautiful," she whispered. Ali moaned. "I've got to go. I left money in the kitchen. I know there's nothing here to eat, so pick up anything you want."

"You don't have to do that," Ali said, her voice hoarse with sleep.

Lane rubbed a hand across her sheet-covered hip. "My car's waiting, I've got to run. What time are you off tonight?" Ali frowned. "Leave me a note or call." She stole another brief kiss. "I'll see you later." Ali caught Lane's hand as she stood, holding her at the bedside. When their gazes met, an ache started deep in Lane's chest. Lane gently tugged her hand away. "Sweetheart, I've got to go now."

"Thank you." She looked more innocent than a child.

Lane left quickly, the temptation to crawl back into bed almost too powerful to resist. As wonderful as it would feel to wrap Ali in an embrace, the rational portion of her brain was reminding her how little she really knew about her. She rushed out the front door, down the hall to the stairwell and up the three flights to the penthouse. She entered the penthouse from the back and exited through the front door to ride the elevator down. By the time she stepped into the building lobby, her racing heart had returned to a near normal rhythm.

Seated at her desk an hour before Jeremy would arrive, she called John Woods. "John, it's Lane. Sorry to call so early. Have you found out anything more I should know about?"

He cleared his throat. "No, Lane. I'm sorry, I haven't. It's strange… she seems to have only appeared six months ago, and that's not possible. I have a lead I'm trying to run down, though."

"All right, John. Thanks."

Before he hung up, he added, "I've never run into anything like this before. There's almost always something out there on a perp, especially in this day and age. I'll keep digging."

He thinks it's a routine investigative request and so far he hasn't tracked her back to me. Lane heaved a sigh of relief.

The rest of her day, like any other, was long and hectic. At least now she had something to look forward to at the end of it. She worked at her office until eight and picked up takeout from one of her favorite places on the ride home. Tonight was the only night until Sunday that she didn't have something scheduled. She envied Ali's life. She had little to worry about except getting to work on time. She reconsidered—well, aside from the distress involved with living in one's car. By the time Randall dropped her at the door her thoughts had moved on to the busy day ahead tomorrow.

"Evening, Ms. Stanford," Henry greeted her.

"Good evening, Henry." When the elevator arrived, she got in and punched the button for the fifth floor without even thinking. "Damn," she muttered, quickly hitting the number eight. With luck Henry wouldn't have noticed. As the doors opened and closed on five and continued up three floors, she reflected how quickly the fifth floor apartment had come to mean "home" with Ali there.

She changed quickly, grabbed a few more things from her office and made her way down the back stairs. Ali had left her a note.

Lane, I only bought a few groceries. I'll get more tomorrow if you let me know what you want. I have to close again tonight. I should be back around eleven thirty. I'll miss you today–Ali.

She sipped a drink at the bar as she worked up a shopping list. She dropped it on the kitchen counter before heading down the hall to the bedroom. She should have spent more time waiting upstairs. She was bored out of her mind. She'd remember the next time. Stripping off her clothes, she slid under the covers, her drink on the nightstand and case folders in her lap. She opened the first one, but Ali's scent on the pillows beside her proved too distracting. Concentration was impossible. Before long the pulse between her legs was providing even more distraction. She slid her hand down her body, stopping only when her fingers reached her wetness.

"Jesus," she muttered. "A little patience. You don't need to do that anymore." She tossed the first folder aside and opened the next one, hoping it would be more engrossing. That effort proved futile as well. She was unlikely, she decided, to have any luck trying to work in the bed she was sharing with Ali. She'd have to start working in the spare room across the hall.

She awoke to a sensation so pleasant she might have thought she was dreaming. The warm, naked body pressing into hers, however, was definitely not some fantasy.

"Hi, baby," came Ali's breathless whisper before she kissed Lane. "I'm sorry I woke you. I couldn't help myself." She traced her fingers lightly over Lane's already taut nipple, lowering her mouth to capture it.

Lane jerked at the tug from Ali's lips. "What time is it?"

"Almost midnight."

Lane shifted and looked in Ali's eyes. "Why so late getting home?"

"I wasn't." Ali looked confused. "I got here about eleven thirty, took a nice long shower and got ready for bed." She tilted her head. "I'm surprised you didn't hear me fumbling with my door key."

Lane tried to play off the accusatory nature of the question. "I didn't realize I could sleep so soundly." She ran a hand up and down Ali's arm. "I guess I'd better keep the doors securely locked so no one sneaks in while I'm sawing logs and makes off with you." She outlined Ali's cheek with her fingertips.

"You don't snore, and besides, my mom always used to say no one would keep me more than two minutes."

Ah ha, a kernel of information. So she didn't drop out of the sky six months ago. "Any other words of wisdom your mother imparted that you'd like to share?"

Ali gazed off distantly. "Um…'the Lord giveth and the Lord taketh away.' I think that's how it goes. And a bunch of Bible verses I'd rather not remember. So…" She looked at Lane's lips. "I guess you have to be up at the crack of dawn tomorrow like every other day."

Nodding, Lane moved her hand down across Ali's hip. "Did you have something in mind?"

As visible as a candle's flickering flame, desire burned in Ali's eyes. "I should let you go back to sleep then."

Lane's hand moved between Ali's thighs and ever so lightly brushed her wetness. An "Oh" escaped Ali's parted lips. "Or not." She threw her leg over Lane's hip, giving her the access she sought. "Oh, God," she gasped. "I can't resist you."

"Why would you want to?" Lane dipped her head, catching Ali's nipple gently between her teeth before pushing her onto her back.

"Oh…" Ali muttered again. Lane nibbled at the tender skin of her neck, stroking Ali until her body melted under her.

Afterward, Ali bit her bottom lip and gazed up at Lane. "Please, baby. I want to go down on you." She slowly withdrew Lane's fingers from her and tried to roll her over, but Lane stopped her.

"Touch me while you kiss me, sweetheart. That's more than enough."

* * *

They fell into as much of a routine as their ever-changing schedules allowed as the week progressed. By the time Saturday rolled around, however, and Ali headed off to work lunch at the restaurant, Lane was exhausted. She'd thought the physical exercise she was getting—taking the stairs several times a day and the nightly workouts with Ali between the sheets—would get her in great shape. It seemed to be having the opposite effect. She didn't know how much longer she could keep up the pace. She decided she'd better try to get some rest this afternoon, because Ali had Sunday off. They wouldn't have the whole day together since Lane was scheduled to have a lunch meeting at her father's. Ali had taken the news well, though she'd teased Lane about it.

"A 'lunch meeting'?" she said. "That kinda sounds like he's your boss or something."

Lane had chuckled. "He thinks he is, but no. He's more like a career advisor." She had explained as much as she thought wise. "As a retired State Supreme Court Justice he wants—no, let me rephrase that—he insists I follow in his footsteps."

"Wow! That's a pretty important job, isn't it?"

"It is," Lane had answered, adding that she hadn't decided definitely that was the direction she wanted her career to go. She wasn't going to tell her father that tomorrow, however. Not if she wanted to be able to spend the better part of the day with Ali after she got home. And she did. John Woods had called Friday to report that his lead had gone nowhere, but he had another to pursue out of state and would be in touch soon. Though there was nothing new on that front, she hoped that maybe—just maybe—if she and Ali could spend some of their time together talking, she might get some clues about her life prior to six months ago.

* * *

Lane arrived at her father's promptly at one o'clock, frowning as she noticed the Cadillac Escalade parked off to the side of the circular drive.

"Ms. Stanford," Jerald greeted her, pulling open the heavy door as she climbed the steps.

"Lord, Jerald, you've known me since I learned to speak. Can't you call me Lane?" His mouth drew into a tight line. She shook her head. "You could whisper it. I promise not to tell." She crossed a finger over her heart.

He cleared his throat. "Your father is waiting in the den."

Lane patted his shoulder as she passed. "Good to see you." When she entered the room her father and two other men were admiring his accolades, which were displayed prominently on the wall behind the desk. The click of the door closing behind her brought their attention around to her.

"Father." She crossed the room with a powerful and confident stride and placed a kiss on his cheek.

He responded by taking her hand. "Gentlemen, I would like to introduce you to my daughter, Judge Elane Stanford. Lane, this is Gregory Nelson of Nelson Excavating and Vinnie Conti with Marino Construction." As Lane extended her hand to each, nodding her greeting, Weston said in a gruff voice, "Let's have a drink. Talk about the state of affairs."

Lane rolled her eyes behind their backs as they moved to the bar, knowing full well the only affairs they'd be discussing would be ones that involved a lot of back scratching. But she put up with all of it, including lunchtime conversation filled with flirtations and innuendos from Vinnie whatever his name was. She wondered if he thought he might be about to get a judge in both his pocket and his bedroom. The thought of the latter disgusted her.

She excused herself at two thirty, stopping in the bathroom on her way out to wash off the sweat of Vinnie's handshake. He'd held onto her hand far too long, suggesting they have dinner some evening. She'd blown him off with a promise to check her calendar. The thought of spending an evening alone with him repulsed her.

"Miss Lane," a voice called from behind her. "You stop right there."

"Miss Clara," Lane said, turning and reaching for the old woman's hands.

Clara pulled her into a bear hug. "Where you sneaking off to without coming to say hello?"

"I have a lot on my mind."

"Tsk, tsk." She shook her head. "Miss Judge Lane, you forgettin' that I wiped your behind, scrubbed behind your ears and tended to your scrapes and scratches when you were a young 'n?"

"I'm really sorry, Miss Clara." She glanced at the enormous grandfather clock across from where she stood. "I have enough time for a cup of tea."

Clara smiled warmly as she took her hand and led her to the kitchen. She put the teakettle on and placed cups on the table. "You still take yours straight?" When Lane nodded, Clara produced a bottle of bourbon from the pantry. She poured a generous amount in both cups before returning the bottle to its secret place. When the kettle whistled, Clara placed a tea bag in her cup and topped it off with boiling water.

Once she was seated on the other side of the small butcher block table, Lane said, "Still hitting the sauce I see."

Clara winked. "Only on the most special of occasions." She raised her cup. "And you visiting is definitely one of them."

Lane touched her cup to Clara's. "I've been called any number of things, Miss Clara. I can assure you 'special' is not one of them." She chuckled.

Clara tsk'd again. "Well, you're special to me, child, always will be...So what kind of prospects you got on the marriage and family front?"

Lane phrased her statement carefully. "No real marriage material in the offing, Miss Clara, I'm sorry to report."

Clara placed a gentle hand on hers. "You know, you spent more years than I want to think about trying to fib to me. You never did get away with it now, did you?" Lane tried desperately not to let her guilt show. "Well, you're not getting any better at it. There's someone special, I can tell."

Lane shrugged, trying to formulate an answer that would be truthful without giving much away. "Honestly, Miss Clara, it's too early to say." She quickly raised the cup to her lips and took a sip.

"Okay." Clara's eyes never left Lane's. "So, tell me about her."

Lane swallowed in surprise, choked and began to cough violently. Clara came around the table and began smoothing her hand over her back.

"There, there, child. Take a deep breath." She rubbed a moment longer before going to the sink for a glass of water.

When Lane finally cleared her throat, she asked, "Why on earth would you ask me such a question?" Her voice was hoarse and raspy.

Clara leaned back, crossing her powerful arms under her large breasts, and fixed Lane with one of the "don't try me" looks that Lane remembered so well from childhood. She also recalled how wonderful it had felt when Clara had wrapped those arms around her and held her after her mother was gone.

When Clara didn't respond, Lane asked meekly, "How could you possibly know something like that about someone?"

Clara's expression softened. "Honey." She captured Lane's hand again. "Sometimes, people just feel things. I'm sure there's things you've been feeling since at least your teenage years, even if you never wanted to admit it to yourself."

Lane was flabbergasted to think Clara had always known what she thought was a deep, dark secret. Finding some courage, she decided to confide in her de facto mother. "Okay, but I wasn't lying. It really is too soon to know if it will turn into anything."

"Tell you what, honey. You bring her by sometime when your father's not around and let me have a look. I'll tell you if you should invest your dowry in her." Her smile was tender.

"I might do that," Lane said, remembering that Clara always seemed to know if the boys she occasionally brought around were suitable. She wondered now if Clara had always known she'd never find happiness with a man. She pushed her unfinished drink aside. "Now, though, I have to be running along."

Clara hooked her arm through Lane's as they strolled down the long hall, waving Jerald off as they passed the study. "I'll see her out." They stopped at the front door.

"I meant it about you bringing your friend around." Lane nodded. "I don't care nothing about what your father or anybody else wants, honey. I only want for you to be happy."

Lane quickly stanched the tears that Clara's loving words threatened to start. Tears had always elicited long lectures from her father, something she'd chosen to avoid, as she'd chosen to avoid her own personal wants.

"Thank you, Miss Clara." She kissed her forehead. "I'll be around to see you again soon."

"See to it you do. Don't make me come looking for you." She gave Lane a devil of a grin and a wink.

As she and Ali shared a quiet evening later, Lane decided not to ruin it by probing for details of her past. She couldn't remember another time in her life when she was this happy to simply share space with someone. Well, that wasn't entirely true. The times she and her mother had spent at the "castle," as Lane had named it, up at the lake—they had felt a lot like this. Yes, she recalled now, this was exactly how she'd felt then—contented.

CHAPTER FOURTEEN

"Shit!" Lane's voice echoed in the cavernous stairwell after she stumbled going upstairs to the penthouse Monday morning. When she rubbed her painful shin, her fingers came away with traces of blood. "Damn it," she mumbled, unlocking the rear door of the penthouse. "This is why I should always wear slacks."

She had a closet full of clothes in the apartment. That wasn't the reason she was running up to the penthouse each morning. She was doing that to make sure the doorman or some other busybody didn't catch her leaving from the apartment. Quickly peeling off her ruined hose and cleaning up the abrasion, she pulled on fresh stockings, traded the skirt suit for a pantsuit and rushed down to her waiting car.

"Good morning, ma'am," Randall said, greeting her with his usual early morning exuberance.

Despite the mishap on the stairs, which normally might have soured her mood for the whole day, Lane was feeling a bit exuberant too...What was that word she'd settled upon last night? Contented. That was it. No, it was more than that. She was happy. Actually *happy*. All thanks to the gorgeous woman she'd left in her bed.

"Good morning, Randall."

Happy or not, she reminded herself again that Ali was a virtual stranger and she needed to proceed cautiously. She hadn't wanted to press things yesterday, but she needed to know more about Ali's past. She'd been known as an expert interrogator in the courtroom before her election to the bench. She needed to put those interrogating skills to work again.

As she crossed her legs, the pain in her shin reminded her that Ali was not the only one hiding things. Despite the unaccustomed happiness that being with the woman brought her, she was still living half-truths with Ali.

Her Monday went south when she returned from court in the afternoon.

Jeremy trailed her into the office. "Your father has phoned twice."

She spun abruptly on her heels. "What does he want now?"

"He wants you to meet him for dinner and drinks."

Lane opened her mouth, but he rushed on. "I told him you already had a dinner commitment this evening. He said, and I quote, 'You're her damned secretary. You schedule her time. Find some for me and call me back.' And he hung up on me."

Lane blew out a breath and dropped heavily into her chair. "What do I have this evening?"

"You're supposed to meet your friends for your usual dinner thing"—his hand flitted about—"at Tango's at six thirty."

Her nails drummed on the desktop. Hadn't she just spent hours with her father yesterday?

"Do I have anything else this afternoon?" He shook his head. "Okay, call him and tell him I can meet him at five thirty in the bar at the club for a drink only and please be sure to stress the singular. Try to help him understand how busy my schedule is. And call the car service to pick me up at five." He turned to leave. "And Jeremy," he turned back, "I apologize for the way my father spoke to you." Jeremy's mouth fell open. "I'll speak to him about it this evening."

"Uh—thanks."

Ten minutes later he knocked and poked his head in. "All set. The car will be here at five and your father will be anxiously waiting for you at the club."

"How did he seem?"

Jeremy tilted his head. "You know…he was your father." He slipped out the door.

She slumped back in her chair, spinning around to look out the window. What Jeremy was implying was that Weston Stanford III was demanding, controlling and unyielding. *And he's doing his best to make you exactly like him.* Being demanding, she knew, was necessary to get a response. Being controlling was a way to keep a handle on things. But being unyielding, that required being selfish, self-centered, uncaring.

All those things described her father and—as much as she hated to admit—described her too. Her mind drifted back over the past few years. Yes, that was her. If it didn't affect her, her life or the direction of her future, she took what she wanted, when she wanted, without consideration of the impact on others. She used people as her father used her to accomplish what he couldn't for himself.

How different would her life be, she wondered, if her mother were still alive?

Her mother was a warm and caring soul. At least that's how Lane remembered her. But she also had an independent streak. She vaguely recalled an argument between her parents before that last summer trip to their special place on the lake. Weston had demanded they not go because of something important he wanted her mother to be present for. Her mother had responded without a hint of anger, but with fierce resolve, telling him to go alone or skip it altogether. She said that she gave and gave, of herself and her time, for his aspirations, but it was time for her to give her daughter the time and attention she deserved. He told her she had the rest of her life to go running off to that unheard of place in the woods. He needed her at home. She stated calmly her plans would not be changing and left the house to stroll around her lavish gardens out in the back.

Lane remembered watching him watch her mother from the windows on the staircase landing. She couldn't ever remember feeling more proud of her mother. "I wanted to be like you." She turned back to her desk. "And I'm so much like him." That truth sat heavy in her chest.

* * *

Weston was seated with a partially empty glass when she arrived. The second the waitress had left with her drink order, he said gruffly, "Thomas Beckman informed me this morning you've not met with him." He sat forward, eyes intent on her. "You can't do that to this man, Lane. He wields power that can launch political careers. Do you understand how important that is to your future?"

She felt like a child again, and she resented it. She wanted to be her mother. She wanted to say exactly what she was feeling. But she didn't. She sat silent for a long minute.

"We've had some difficulty with our schedules. You should know I have a very busy"—she made air quotes—"social calendar. And," she paused for a beat, "I'm trying to squeeze in a small amount of time to have a personal life." There. She had at least made that tiny admission. The color in his neck rose to his cheeks, causing regret to settle like lead in her stomach.

"Don't be so damned selfish, Lane. Make your calendar more accessible." It wasn't a request. "And as far as a personal life, you've got the rest of your life. Right now you need to concentrate on your political aspirations."

Right, she thought, *like Mother had the rest of her life.* But she again held her tongue. She sat mostly silent until her drink was gone while he continued to flaunt his age and wisdom over her. A quick glance at her watch told her it was time to go or be late meeting the girls. She found herself actually looking forward to their probing and prying. It would be a welcome change from his pontificating.

"I have to go." She stood. "I have another engagement." Displeasure flickered unmistakably in his dark eyes. "I will get together with Mr. Beckman as soon as our schedules allow." Her fingers lightly brushed his shoulder as she passed. "Have a good evening" was all she said. She all but threw herself into the backseat of the Town Car, wishing it had a stocked bar. Anything to douse the emotional fire raging inside her.

She waved off the hostess when she got to the restaurant, quickly making her way to the table with her friends. Each offered a friendly hug, something Lane had never welcomed more than tonight.

Emily toasted, "To friends, may they always bless our lives."

Lane tipped her glass in acknowledgment and in three large swallows nearly emptied it.

"Whoa! Looks like someone's on a mission tonight," Tara said, gazing intently at Lane.

"Is everything okay, Lane?" Carlina asked.

Lane looked at her glass, draining what little remained. "In about two more, it will be." She caught the waitress's attention.

Emily studied Lane. "Relationship trouble's my guess.

Tara added, "A man giving you problems, Lane?"

At the mention of a relationship, Lane felt some of her disquiet vanish.

"Definitely a relationship issue," Emily concluded. "Come on, dish. We all air our secrets here."

Lane hadn't ever thought of it that way, but it was true. That was why they gathered every month...to bare their souls. Well, except for her. There had never been anything in her life that she had wanted to be able to share. Until Ali.

"Ah, see—there is someone. Come on, Lane, tell," Emily teased.

She'd known these women for years and trusted them, but she wasn't ready for this. Carlina seemed to understand that. She reached over and grasped her hand on the table. "Don't feel any pressure to confess. Remember, Emily's been married for a century. Living vicariously through us is the most excitement she gets nowadays." Lane met Carlina's sympathetic gaze. "But...when you feel like talking, we're all here for you, darling."

Lane liked Carlina. When they'd first met, she'd had a bit of a crush on her, in fact. She put on her judge's face. "Like I said, there's nothing to tell." Carlina nodded, but something about the way she did it said she suspected otherwise.

Lane downed her second drink before their food arrived and made significant headway on her third one with dinner, which she barely touched. She knew she should quit, but when the other girls ordered coffee after dinner, she ordered another drink. As they stood to leave, Lane felt more than slightly light-headed. Carlina caught her by the arm as the other two headed for the door.

"I don't believe for a minute that everything is fine, but as your friend, I won't push you to talk if you don't want to." Lane felt herself melting into the dark eyes looking intently at her. "But if you need to talk—about anything at all, honey—don't hesitate to call." When Lane nodded, Carlina wrapped her in a comforting hug. "I mean it—anything."

The surprise embrace left Lane unable to respond.

Carlina released her, hooking her arm through Lane's. "Come on, let's get you headed home." As they stepped into the fresh night air and Randall appeared at the rear door of the Town Car, Carlina asked, "Your car?" Lane nodded. Carlina walked her to the car and squeezed Lane's hand. "Call me if you need anything."

Lane felt suddenly exhausted. Not physically from a long day and too much alcohol, but emotionally.

"Where to, ma'am?" Randall asked when he settled behind the wheel.

"Home," she muttered. En route, she lowered the privacy window. "Please drop me at the elevator in the garage." She extended her key card to him.

"Yes, ma'am."

Closing her eyes, she leaned her head back. Things began spinning, so she quickly opened them again and tried looking out the side window as the night passed by. That too created a dizzying effect, so she fixed her focus on the tinted one-way privacy window in front of her. When the car rolled down the garage ramp, she scooted to the door, ready to escape. The second Randall opened it, she swung her legs out. Standing a little too quickly, she fell back against the car's rear fender.

"Anything else, ma'am?" Randall was too polished to ask if she needed an escort upstairs. He handed over her key card.

She pushed off the car. "No, Randall. See you in the morning," she said, slurring slightly.

He rushed ahead to call the elevator, taking long enough to return to the car to make sure she got safely into it. It wouldn't be a wise career move for her—or for her driver, for that matter—if the judge were found passed out in her building's garage like a common drunk.

Lane stumbled slightly as she entered the elevator and slammed against its sidewall. She automatically punched the number eight button before remembering through the haze in her mind that she was presently residing on the fifth floor and punched that button too. It was lucky she did, actually. She couldn't have known it, but Randall had waited to get back in the car until he saw the number eight light up above the doors.

* * *

On the fifth floor Lane stepped out of the elevator on wobbly legs. Taking the short hall in the back she fumbled her keys from her purse and finally managed to unlock the apartment's back door. Light from the living room faintly illuminated the hall. She entered, bumping the small table inside the doorway. "Shit!" she mumbled as the collision nearly sent an accent vase crashing to the floor.

Ali was seated on the couch with her feet curled under her. At the sound she hopped up. When Lane swayed, she went to her and wrapped an arm around her waist. "Hi, baby. Rough day?"

"You could shay…say…that." *Damn*, Lane thought, knowing Ali had to have heard the slur in her speech. *Don't want her to see me like this. Don't need any more goddamn lectures.*

"Let me make you forget all about it." She guided Lane to the couch, got her seated and then straddled Lane's lap, reaching for the buttons on her blouse.

Lane watched blearily as Ali's fingers worked the buttons open and danced lightly over her skin. Her stomach muscles tightened in anticipation as she leaned in to kiss her below her ear. It never happened. Ali leaned back instead and intently studied Lane's eyes.

"What?" Lane asked through her fog.

"You had dinner with a woman."

"Three." Lane waved three fingers in Ali's face. "Waz wrong?"

"You only smell like one of them." She started to get up, but Lane caught her.

"They're jus friends. We meet once a month to catch up." Ali pulled against Lane's grasp. "One of 'em helped me to the car. I'm a little loaded if you din notice." Lane shrugged. "She hugged me." Her mouth was quirked in a tiny smile. "I almost told them about you tonight."

Ali kept her gaze leveled on Lane. "Why didn't you?"

"This whole relaze…relaze…this is new. I don wanna jinx it." She shrugged.

"They don't know, do they?"

Lane looked away and shook her head no.

Ali relaxed back into her lap. "So you and your friends get together once a month and get drunk?"

Lane looked again into Ali's eyes. She shook her head again.

"So why'd you drink so much tonight?"

She exhaled a frustrated sigh. "I had ta meet dear ol' Dad afore dinner."

Ali rested her hands on Lane's shoulders, rubbing her thumbs lightly over her collarbones. "Wow! I thought my dad was bad. Yours spoiled your mood that bad, huh?"

"Wha waz your dad like?"

Ali hesitated. Lane expected her to concoct some kind of story, but what she said sounded like the truth. "He was a minister."

"'Waz'?"

"Well, I suppose he still is. I haven't seen him in years." Ali lifted a shoulder. "He barely let me out of the house once I…"—her face was flushed with embarrassment—"you know, once I matured. He wouldn't let me go anywhere or do anything. I hated him. So I haven't seen him since I got out of high school."

Lane traced her fingers down Ali's neck. "An you did jus get out of high school, din you. How old you anyway?"

Lane's touch triggered a moan of pleasure. "Twenty-six, almost twenty-seven."

"Ah," Lane slipped her hands under Ali's top, brushing the underside of her breasts. "Wha day?"

Ali's breath was coming in short gasps as she settled deeper into Lane's lap. "Not...important. Just..." Lane stilled her hand. "A day." Ali gripped Lane's shoulders and rocked her hips.

Lane's eyes held hers. "So why secret?"

"Oh, God, baby. I need you." Lane tilted her head, but she made no move to acquiesce. "Please, baby," Ali begged.

"Date?"

"A little over a month from now, the tenth. Now, please," she pleaded.

When Lane captured Ali's mouth, she came easily, but that wasn't the case for Lane.

She caught Ali's wrist. "I can't," she said hoarsely.

"But baby, you feel so ready."

Lane removed her hand. "Too much booze...znot happenin'." The disappointment on Ali's face made Lane ache to think Ali might feel like she failed. "Ish not you." Lane stroked her fingers lightly along Ali's jawline. "You beauty. I sorry." Her head lolled back to rest on the back of the couch and she struggled to focus.

Ali slid over onto the couch, sitting sideways. She moved her fingers up and down Lane's arm. "What could your dad do to make you want to get drunk?" Ali had seen Lane drink, of course, but she'd never been excessive, always remaining in control. She couldn't imagine now what would drive her to give that up.

Strong emotions played across Lane's face and her whole body slumped. "Ah, baby. What'd he do to you?" Ali's concern for Lane wasn't born out of simply caring, but a shared knowledge of what fathers can do to a daughter.

Lane sighed. "Jus who he is."

"Is this is about your job?"

Lane nodded. "Partly."

"And the rest?" She couldn't help wanting to know the answers for the pain she was seeing in Lane's eyes. "He doesn't know the real you, does he?" She stroked Lane's arm. "He doesn't know this?"

Lane shook her head.

Catching Lane's hand, Ali stood. "Come on, I know what you need." Lane followed to the bedroom where Ali slowly removed her clothes, taking care to lay her things neatly aside before pulling back the covers for Lane to crawl into bed. Stripping off her own clothes, she slid in beside her, wrapped Lane in her arms and pulled her head to her chest. "Close your eyes and sleep, baby. It will all look better in the morning." She stroked lightly over Lane's back. Within seconds, Lane's eyes drifted closed. It took Ali thirty minutes longer to quiet her thoughts and fall asleep.

CHAPTER FIFTEEN

Lane woke alone and with a monster headache. Sitting up on the side of the bed with a groan, her hands braced at her sides, she struggled to keep her body upright. She wanted nothing more than to fall back on the bed and sleep until tomorrow. Ali appeared with a cup of coffee in hand, and Lane tried to smile, but everything above her neck hurt.

Ali walked over to the side of the bed and opened her hand. "These should help." She offered up two aspirins. "If you don't feel better in an hour, take two more." Ali placed the cup and aspirins on the nightstand and knelt in front of her. She stroked her fingers through Lane's disheveled locks. "I wish I could take the pain away for you, baby." She leaned in and kissed the corner of Lane's mouth. "Is there anything else I can do?"

Lane fought a wave of nausea. "Stand in the shower with me in case I pass out."

Ali stood and pulled Lane up with her. "I'll even wash your hair. But first, here," she picked up the aspirins and the coffee mug, "swallow these."

Lane swallowed the pills and padded naked into the bathroom. When Ali had the water hot and steamy, she dropped the robe she was wearing to the floor and grasped Lane's hand, pulling her into the shower. Next to lying in bed all day, Lane thought standing under the shower was a good second choice. She dipped her head under the spray. The water pelted her already aching head like tiny beads of hail. Seconds later, Ali was pressed against her back, lathering shampoo into her hair. Lane braced her hands against the shower wall while Ali's fingers massaged her scalp, Ali's pelvis pressed firmly against her ass to hold her steady. She felt the precise moment Ali's nipples hardened like pebbles against her skin. Hers followed suit seconds later. *Damn.* The rest of her might feel like absolute crap, but her libido was very much alive and well. Groaning, legs weak, she swayed to one side.

"What's wrong, baby?" Ali kissed Lane's back, wrapping an arm firmly around her waist. "Baby…"

Lane grasped Ali's hand on her abdomen, sliding it lower. "You see what you do to me?"

Ali murmured against her skin, "Let me take care of you." She rinsed Lane's soapy hair and turned her around. "Hold on to me, baby."

"It won't take much."

Ali kissed her neck, then lowered her mouth to a taut nipple. Lane's hips bucked as Ali's fingers found her swollen clit. Lane gasped. Ali's mouth moved lower. She knelt in front of Lane, but when she pressed Lane's thighs apart, Lane pulled away from her.

"No, don't." She pulled Ali back to her feet. "Please, just kiss me and touch me."

Lane didn't come hard, but it was a welcome release all the same. When she was steady enough to stand without bracing herself, she pulled Ali under the spray with her. "I'd say you've practiced shower sex." She thought she saw something flicker in Ali's eyes, but it was gone so fast, she barely registered it. She melted into Ali's lips.

* * *

Lane was seated behind her desk nursing the lingering headache when Jeremy knocked and poked his head in. "John Woods to see you, if you're available." She nodded a "yes," closing the folder in front of her.

John took a seat across from her, extracting several folded sheets of paper from his inside jacket pocket. "Good news is I tracked down where this mystery woman came from." He unfolded and offered the sheets of paper to Lane. "But there's more." He rubbed his hand over a day's worth of beard stubble. "As you can see she graduated from high school over in a small town in Indiana, then went off to the college listed there. In the middle of the second quarter of her first year, though, she dropped out."

Lane looked over the report, which included Ali's full name, her birthdate, which vaguely rang a bell, the schools she had attended and her parents' names. "A lot of people drop out of college, John. That's not unusual."

"You're right, but there was a missing person's report filed several weeks later, and between the time she disappeared from that college in Indiana and months ago when she bought that car she owns—there's nothing. It's as if she dropped off the face of the earth before magically reappearing."

"So where do you think she was for, what?" Lane's nail traced over the dates listed. She looked up at John. "Seven years?"

"I couldn't even guess."

Seven years was a large gap in a person's life. This was a question Lane needed to have answered. She wanted to trust Ali. She wanted to believe Ali was with her because she truly cared for her, the way she was beginning to care deeply for Ali. But she couldn't chance that there was something in Ali's past that could bury her. After all, wasn't that all she ever wanted? This distinguished career that would take her everywhere she wanted to go. That would fill her life, the way her father had always said it would? She tapped her finger on the pages. "How much?"

He shifted in his chair. "Seven hundred."

"If you can stop back after three this afternoon, I'll have it for you."

He stood. "Sure thing."

* * *

She walked down the block to her bank during the court's lunch break, mentally running through scenarios that might account for the gap in Ali's past. She could ask, of course, but that would reveal that she'd been checking on her. Would make her think she didn't trust her.

Did she trust her? She wanted to. She wanted Ali to be as squeaky-clean as she looked.

On the other hand, really, why did it matter? It wasn't like she could parade Ali around on her arm. She couldn't even acknowledge she knew her, because if you were in any kind of politics and there was any kind of skeleton in your closet, someone would find it.

She returned from court around two thirty. "Mr. Woods will be returning this afternoon. Please send him in when he gets here."

Jeremy opened his mouth, but Lane stopped him. "No questions. I've got a ton of work." She could feel his curious eyes on her as she disappeared behind the closing door.

John arrived a little before four o'clock.

"Do you have a few minutes?" She extracted the envelope from her case.

"Sure." He accepted the envelope, slipped it into his pocket and took a seat.

Lane leaned back in her chair, steepling her fingers. "I need more of your time, John, if you're available."

"Okay."

"There's fifteen hundred in that envelope. I need you to pursue this...investigation." He nodded. "I'd like you to look into the parents. See if there are any siblings too. And see if you can figure out what happened to the lost years in this woman's past."

"That might take a little time."

She nodded. "That's fine. If you can afford the time, I can afford you. Let me know when you need more."

"Will do." He pushed up from the chair. "I'll be in touch."

"Thanks, John."

He stopped at the door. "You wouldn't happen to have access to a photo of this woman, would you?"

"I'm sure I can get my hands on one. I'll get it to you as soon as possible."

"Great."

* * *

Lane arrived home to find a note that said Ali would be off at seven. "Dammit!" She was scheduled to attend some small local charity dinner. Jeremy's voice echoed in her mind. "You've got to have a presence at these small-time local affairs. This is the bread and butter for your future. These people will remember that Judge Lane Stanford wasn't too big or too busy to make time for them."

"Well," she muttered, "they're going to have to remember me for my big-hearted contribution instead." She found the invitation with the organization's name and number and made the call. Lane promised the gracious-sounding female who answered that her check in support of their cause would go in the following day's mail. She sat down the minute she hung up to make out the check, address the envelope and put a stamp on it.

Up in the penthouse, she poured herself a short drink, considering what to wear and where they might go for dinner. After selecting a comfortable pair of faded jeans and a navy oxford shirt, she sat on the bed. She was amazed at how a couple sips of the vodka had made her head feel better than it had felt all day. She smoothed her hands over the bed's silky satin comforter and wondered what it would be like to be able to have Ali in her own bed. The ringing of her cell phone, which was charging out in the kitchen, stirred her from the vivid daydream that inspired, but she didn't get to it in time.

The missed call was Ali's. "Shit," she muttered as the voice mail alert beeped. It was seven thirty, which meant Ali was probably already at the apartment. She grabbed her wallet and keys and rushed downstairs.

Ali was standing inside the kitchen door next to her note on the counter. "Hi! I just left a voice mail." Lane's brows went up in mock surprise as she dug the phone from her pocket. "Where've you been?" Lane stood there, her mind going a million miles an hour searching for a plausible answer. Ali curled her finger in a belt loop on Lane's jeans. "You're not in your work clothes."

"Uh..." Lane scrambled for a reply. "I was down in the garage looking for something in my car."

"Oh. I guess I was in such a hurry to get up here I didn't even notice." She smiled, tugging again on Lane's belt loop. "You look hot in these jeans." She pulled Lane in for a kiss. "I need a shower. Do we have dinner plans?"

Lane placed her hands on the counter on either side of Ali. "I thought we'd go out, but if you get in the shower I might not be able to resist joining you." She lowered her mouth close to Ali's. "After this morning."

Ali's eyes immediately darkened. "I might not be able to resist dragging you in there." She held Lane by her belt loop.

Lane took a step back. "But I'm starving. I felt too bad earlier to eat lunch, so I've got to eat something soon."

Ali gave her a quick peck on the lips and gave Lane another once-over. "I'll only be a few minutes."

"Perfect." Lane watched while she pulled her top over her head and headed into the hall. *Oh, God, I really do want to repeat this morning.* The thought that immediately followed, though—recognition of having just lied to Ali—started an ache in her heart.

Ali emerged ten short minutes later, also dressed in faded jeans and in a light blue blouse that hugged her full breasts. Lane could see her hands curving to fit those breasts. "All set."

She drove them to one of the lesser known restaurants across the river where she'd go when she didn't want to be seen by anyone who knew her or the person she was entertaining.

"So," Lane began, "you mentioned your father was a minister. I've always heard that can make for a tough childhood. He was pretty strict with you, you said?" The brightness in Ali's eyes vanished.

"I hated him. He was one of those fire-and-brimstone preachers. He thought it was a sin if I even looked at a boy."

"Did you look at boys?"

"Yeah." Ali shrugged. "Back before…"

"Before you discovered you liked girls instead?"

"Yeah," Ali repeated.

"So who was your first girlfriend?"

Ali looked away. "Nobody important, just someone I met—it doesn't matter."

"I'm sorry." Lane reached across the table and touched Ali's hand. "Judge Stanford?"

Lane jerked her hand back, looking up as a man stepped up to their table. "Mr. Conti," she said. "What a surprise." His smile more closely resembled a sneer as he stared at Ali. "This is my cousin," Lane blurted out.

"Vinnie," he extended his hand to Ali. "Very nice to meet you—"

"Sandy," Lane answered before Ali could. "This is my cousin, Sandy, on my mother's side." Lane wasn't sure why she lied about Ali, except that she couldn't have people questioning her sexuality and she wanted to protect Ali from the people out there, like Vinnie Conti, who her father wanted her to do business with.

"Well, it's certainly a pleasure to meet you, Sandy." He was holding onto Ali's hand far too long. The look in her eyes said as much, but he appeared to be oblivious. "You share the same beauty genes as Her Honor here." He released her hand and turned to Lane. "Forgive my interruption, Judge, but I just had to say hello." His reptilian gaze made her skin crawl. His purpose was plain. He wanted her to know she'd been seen. "I'll leave you ladies to your…family dinner." With that he slithered away.

Ali leaned over the table. "He seemed a little—"

"Creepy."

"Yeah." Ali wrapped her arms around herself. "Did you lock him up or something?"

"No."

"Can I ask how come you lied about my name?"

Lane leaned back in her chair. Her fingers tapped absently on the table. "Because he's a known womanizer, and I don't want him sniffing around you. I want..." Lane stared off, unsure how much she could afford to share.

"You want what, baby?" Ali's voice was low and only loud enough to reach across the table that separated them.

"I want you all to myself." She sat forward again. "I couldn't stand to think of anyone else ever touching you."

"You don't have to worry about that, I promise."

Lane wanted things with Ali she'd never wanted before, that she never knew she wanted.

"You know, I get the whole cousin thing. I get that a judge would need to keep *those* things about themselves private, unlike a lowly waitress."

"You are not lowly in any way whatsoever, and I wish you wouldn't think of yourself as such." Lane gazed off.

"What's wrong?"

"There's so much of my life that's so 'private' that I don't even know who the real me is anymore."

"Well, I know, and if you need reminding, I can do that." Ali eyed Lane with those perfect, heart-stopping, bedroom eyes. The curve of her lips so damn sexy.

"I..." Lane caught herself. "God, Ali, there is so much about me... you have no idea."

"So tell me."

It felt as if Ali was reaching inside her, turning her inside out. Lane wanted to share every part of herself.

"I hope that you feel you can trust me."

Lane heard her father saying, "Always remember, these people want something from you. They're not making offers out of the kindness of their hearts. They want to own you. You have to keep the upper hand, by any means necessary, so that you hold all the cards. So you have all the control." She stared off again.

"Baby..." Ali said softly.

"I do trust you." She knew as she said it it wasn't entirely true, but it was mostly true. No one—since her mother, she had to admit—no one had ever made her feel so safe. "I have something I need to confess to you since we're virtually living together."

"Okay…" She sounded worried.

Lane patted her hand. "Later and I promise it won't hurt. For now, let's enjoy the rest of our dinner."

When they got back to the garage and the elevator doors opened, Ali stepped in and automatically punched the button for the fifth floor. When it stopped there, however, Lane caught her arm before she could get out.

"Wait, I want to show you something." She hit the button for the top floor.

Ali assumed they were going to the roof to catch a romantic view of the city or to make a memorable moment of some kind. When the doors opened, though, Lane took Ali's hand, turned right into a narrow hall, walked ten feet and slid a key into a heavy steel door.

Lane pushed the door open. "After you."

"I don't think we should—" Ali stammered when her feet hit the polished marble floor. Her eyes went wide in surprise when she spied the photo on the small entry table. It was of Lane and an older man, both clad in black robes with a state seal on the wall directly behind them. Ah, her father the judge, the man she'd seen Lane dining with at The Inn. "We're in your father's home?" As Lane led the way down a long hall, Ali noted a landscape painting that looked an awful lot like the lake Lane had taken her to. And when they stepped into the large, open living room, she gasped, "Oh" and "Wow…" as she gazed through the floor-to-ceiling windows occupying all of one wall and part of another. The view of the downtown skyline, sparkling with lights, left her speechless.

"This is not my father's home."

Ali moved to the windows and gazed out in astonishment. "Then whose place—"

Lane stepped behind her, wrapped her arms around Ali's waist and pulled her firmly against her. "You are officially sworn to secrecy." Ali nodded. "*This* is actually my home, not the apartment downstairs."

"Seriously?"

"Seriously. And I'm sorry I didn't tell you immediately. I—"

"You had to be sure you could trust me. I get it."

"People always want something from me. I am overly cautious, always, but—"

"You don't—"

"No, please let me finish. I do know you're not after something."

Ali turned in Lane's embrace. "Well," she traced Lane's lips with a fingertip. "I am after one thing." She rocked her hips into Lane's thigh. "Mmm...take me to where you most enjoy having sex."

Lane smiled. "Sweetheart, I could enjoy you on a dirt floor in a barn." She leaned down and captured Ali's mouth in a hungry kiss while her hands moved up to cup Ali's breasts, her thumbs raking across Ali's already stiff nipples.

"Oh," Ali murmured into Lane's mouth. "If you don't stop that I'm going to come, standing here, fully clothed for all the world to see."

"Well, we can't have that." Moving her hands to Ali's hips, she steered her down the hall to the bedroom.

Ali took over then, took full control, and Lane submitted willingly. She possessed Lane totally, consumed her so completely that Lane didn't recognize the person inside her skin. No one had ever made her feel so satisfied and so—so replete. Nothing had ever, as long as Lane could remember, felt so right in every part of her. When she shuddered in release, Ali's arms surrounded her and held her tight.

"Lane, baby, you okay?"

Lane exhaled a long slow breath. "Yes...I am."

They took their time as they joined again, unrestrained in bestowing pleasure on each other, practiced and yet with everything new again. They lay in silence, arms and legs entwined, for a long time afterward. Lane's head rested between Ali's breasts. She listened to the steady rhythm of her beating heart—the heart, it seemed, that held her own—and thought, *I can't ever be without this.*

She raised her head and met Ali's focused eyes, more scared than she'd ever been in her life. "I've never..." Lane hesitated, swallowing her fear. "Never needed anything or anyone the way I need you."

Ali's gaze didn't waver, but tears glistened in her eyes.

"Oh, darling." Lane moved up to kiss them away. "I don't know exactly what this is or where it could possibly take us, but I do know I don't want to think about not being able to hold you every day and show you how special you are and so many other things I can't even put words to." She pulled Ali tightly into her arms. "I don't want to think about not being able to feel you this close...so close it feels like you're inside me."

Ali held onto Lane tightly, never wanting to relinquish the security of her arms. She thought she'd been in love once—because she'd been made to feel safe—but she'd been discarded later without a second thought. She realized now that she wasn't even sure what love should feel like. Lane was a strong, powerful woman who not only made her feel safe, but who had also only been gentle and caring with her. The realization exhilarated her and, frankly, scared the hell out of her.

She kissed Lane in the hollow of her neck. "I don't know how it happened. I wasn't looking…I didn't want to care for anyone like you. I mean…not like this." Lane stiffened against her and she cursed herself for speaking so clumsily. She scrambled for words, something, anything, to ease the tension claiming Lane's body. "It…I don't know…I'm sorry…"

Lane tightened her arms. "No, Ali, don't ever be sorry for feeling or for speaking your feelings aloud." She kissed the top of her head.

Listen to yourself, Lane mentally scolded. *What do they say? Practice what you preach?* She should heed her own words of wisdom and speak her feelings aloud. "I want you here with me…to stay with me. Here."

Ali raised her head. "Are you sure?"

Lane nodded. "But there are a few…things we need to discuss."

"Of course." Ali eased out of Lane's arms, rolled onto her side and propped her head in her hand. Lane turned onto her side too, leaning up on an elbow.

"This has to remain discreet, which I'm sure comes as no surprise." Ali nodded. "You must come and go from here through the back, same as always." Ali nodded again. "You can use the apartment address downstairs if you need to give an address for some reason. We'll make sure that building security knows you're living in the apartment."

"We?"

"Jeremy, actually. He'll tell them you're his steady gal."

"So I should act straight?"

"Simply act like you belong here, sweetheart."

"Okay."

"Remember: Always ride the elevator up and down from the fifth floor and make certain you're not seen using the rear stairwell to come and go from here. I've never seen anybody use those stairs, but there's always a first time."

"I won't get caught, I promise."

"I know, sweetheart. I trust you." And she did. Mostly. That didn't stop her from offering up a heartfelt prayer. *Please dear God, don't let this come back to bite me.*

CHAPTER SIXTEEN

Ali stirred when Lane kissed her the following morning. "I'm working noon to eight today."

"I will see you later." Briefly kissing her again, Lane hoped the feeling of Ali's soft lips would content her for the day.

She called Jeremy to her office when she heard him arrive at his desk, before he had a chance to begin his morning ritual.

"What?" he said, bustling in.

"I need you to do something for me after work today. I need you to swing by my building and notify whoever is on the security desk that you have a girlfriend moving into the apartment."

His eyebrows shot up so high Lane thought they might disappear into his hairline. "You're…" he stammered, "you're moving a woman into the apartment? Lane, I don't think that's—"

"I don't need you to think about this, Jeremy. I need you to take care of it for me." He glared at her, his mouth open as if he were about to protest. "Or should I hire a new assistant who will do as I ask without trying to manage my private life?"

"That wasn't your attitude when you told me to get rid of Caroline or when I was dropping everything to slip women in and out of 'my' apartment." She stared at him in silence. "Can I ask you something without pissing you off further?"

Lane exhaled a heavy breath. "What?"

"You've never moved any woman into the apartment. Not even one you really...enjoyed."

"Is there a question in there that I missed, Jeremy?"

"Well, aren't you afraid someone will somehow tie that apartment and whoever is living in it to you and ruin everything you've been working toward?"

He'd have a coronary if he knew what she was really doing. But to her the word "private" in reference to her life meant what it implied. Damn him and the rest of the world. She deserved some happiness. Didn't she?

"No, and as long as you don't let it out, no one will know."

Jeremy allowed a low whistle to escape as he stood shaking his head. "Whatever you say, boss. What's the name?"

"Ali Castle." She lowered her gaze to her papers, afraid Jeremy would see everything she felt for Ali in her eyes.

Jeremy stopped on his way to the door. "Don't forget you have a dinner meeting with Mr. Beckman this evening at seven."

"Fuck," Lane muttered. Tonight would be Ali's first night to come home to Lane's real home, and she wanted to be waiting there. "Can you call him—"

Jeremy took a quick step back toward the desk, shaking his finger. "You can't blow him off again, Lane. If you do and your father gets wind of it—and somehow he always does—he'll show up here himself. I for one don't want to be around for that." He very dramatically put his fist onto his hip. "I mean it, Lane. From everything I've heard this guy wields untold and unimaginable powers. He is a man you need in your corner."

Lane gritted her teeth. "Fine." She raised her hands. "Fine, I'll have dinner with the man. Don't forget what you need to do."

He waved his hand as he headed through the door. She watched as he settled behind his desk, drummed his fingers lightly on it, and scribbled something on a note that he slipped into in his pocket.

She called Ali during her afternoon recess, leaving a message that she would be late coming home.

* * *

Beckman had selected an obscure, out-of-the-way restaurant for dinner. That came as no surprise to Lane. She'd heard rumors about him long before her father introduced them. She knew he was smart enough to know that it wouldn't serve either of them if it were thought he had a judge in his pocket. He stood as she approached the table, offering a gracious handshake and charming smile.

"Mr. Beckman," Lane said. His smiled broadened as he released her hand and moved the chair out for her.

"Please, call me Tom." He eased the chair under her. "We'll be working too closely for such formalities. It's Lane, right?"

She half smiled. "Yes."

He took his own seat and leaned forward. "May I say how lovely you look this evening?" His smile was unquestionably flirtatious.

It never ceased to amaze her how appealing these men thought themselves to be to women. A shiver ran up her spine at the thought of a man, any man, touching her in the way she desired to be touched. "Thank you," she replied, forcing another smile.

The waiter appeared with drinks. "Vodka with two olives. I believe I got that correct." Lane simply nodded. He raised his own amber-filled glass. "To a long and fruitful relationship." She reluctantly clinked her glass to his.

During dinner he spoke mostly about Lane, reciting her many accomplishments and speculating on the potential for her future. By the time the table was cleared and they had been served their third drink, Lane had had enough of the little dance.

"Look, Tom, we both know what this is. You're going to offer a lot of money to help fund some kind of a campaign when I'm ready to move into a political position. The question is, what do you want in return?"

He tilted his head and smiled. "A woman who gets down to business. I like that." Lane stifled a sigh. "There's a trial on your docket set to start in a few months. The chief defendant is Harold Baker." He watched for an acknowledgment from Lane. When she offered none, he said, "Baker, as in Baker Contract Construction. One of the largest construction contractors in the tri-state area and contractor of choice for all my construction."

"The city has filed a suit against him." Lane was all-too-aware of the details.

"That's right."

She leaned forward, her tone deadly serious. "He was responsible for building a child care center that suffered a roof collapse after a snowfall this past winter." Beckman's eyes confirmed her statement. "I seem to recall dozens of children and workers were injured and several…"—she paused, recalling how horrific the news reports of the tragedy had been—"several infants died as a result."

Beckman became instantly defensive. "The supplier is at fault. They provided Harold with inferior product for the roof construction."

Lane's insides twisted in a tight knot, and her just-eaten dinner threatened to leave her stomach. She stood abruptly. "Excuse me a moment, Tom." She turned quickly, seeking out the ladies' room.

Inside it, she took deep breaths, willing her stomach to settle. She studied her reflection in the mirror over the sink and heard her father's voice, commanding her to get this done. "You are District Court Judge Lane Stanford but destined to be so much more. Nothing good comes easy. Sacrifice is the only means to achieve the greatest things possible." She let her father's words play in her mind over and over like a recorded loop, willing herself to believe them, then sucked in a final breath, threw her shoulders back and walked with authority back to the table. She had to do this to be somebody. Didn't she?

"Is everything okay, Lane?"

Tom Beckman was now looking at the Judge Lane Stanford that Weston Stanford III had been grooming for prominence for most of her life. "Yes, fine. Something I ate doesn't seem to be agreeing with me. Can we wrap this up? What exactly do you want from me, Tom?"

He downed the last of his drink. "I need you to make certain that Baker doesn't lose his business license or go to jail." He leaned in again. "By whatever means necessary. I don't care if it's a hung jury or an acquittal. We need you to make it happen."

She didn't allow her face to register the disgust she felt. This was, without question, the most heinous request that had been made of her to date, and the video of weeping daycare center workers carrying small bleeding bodies from the rubble of that building kept flashing in her mind. "That's a pretty steep request, Tom, but I'll do what I can to assist you."

He chuckled lightly. "You're a judge, Lane. You have all the power."

"Even a not guilty verdict can be overturned on appeal if the trial is not above reproach. And there's always the possibility of class action or civil suits."

"I have no doubt that you can do what needs to be done."

She pushed back in her chair. "I really must be going."

"I'll walk you to your car."

"That's not necessary. I have a driver this evening."

He tossed a wad of bills on the table. "I insist." He placed his hand in the small of her back as they stepped toward the entrance. The contact repulsed her, sending another shiver up her spine.

"Are you sure you're okay?"

She wrapped her arms tightly across her middle. "I think I may be coming down with something." She resisted the urge to throw up on his expensive polished shoes.

When Randall got out to open the car door for Lane, Tom held up a hand. "I've got this, buddy." Randall continued around the car to stand beside them. He would not be dismissed by anyone but her.

Tom took Lane's hand in both of his. "I'm very glad we were able to get together for dinner. I'm so looking forward to our next meeting." He leaned in and brushed a kiss on her cheek, so near her mouth she could feel his hot, alcohol-laden breath on her lips, and she thought for sure she might retch. Stepping clear of him, she pulled open her own door in one swift motion. "I have to go," was all she said before jumping into the car and pulling her door closed.

Randall scrambled around the car and into the driver's seat, where he simultaneously hit the door locks and powered down the privacy window. "I'm sorry, ma'am. I—"

"Never mind, Randall. Just get me home."

"Yes, ma'am."

The window slowly rose, leaving Lane to the dark quiet of the car's interior and the terribly unsettled feeling in the pit of her stomach. As the car approached her building, she lowered the privacy window and held her card through the opening.

"Please take me in through the garage." The last thing she wanted now was to have to make small talk with the doorman on duty. When the car stopped, she said. "Don't get out." She retrieved her card and opened the door. "Thank you."

"Good evening, ma'am."

"I'll see you in the morning," she called over her shoulder as she pushed the button for the elevator and its doors slid open.

* * *

Lane paused, key in hand, outside the back door to the penthouse. She'd left a key for Ali that morning, but as she stood there now, she hoped she might be down in the apartment instead. She felt disgusted with herself and dirty...too dirty to be around Ali. She took a deep breath, inserted the key and turned it. Seconds later Ali walked in from the living room, her smile lighting the otherwise semi-dark hall.

"Hi, baby." She was wearing cut-off running pants which perfectly outlined her shapely behind and a tank top over nothing more than her full breasts. Her hair was pulled back in a ponytail and her face was scrubbed clean of all makeup. Lane couldn't imagine anything more beautiful. She slid her arms around Lane's neck and pulled her head down to kiss her. Lane's arms slowly encircled her waist, the contact offering her a comfort.

Ali pulled back after a moment. "Rough day? You feel tense." She twined her fingers together behind Lane's neck and locked her eyes with Lane's. "Lane…baby."

Lane exhaled a deep breath. "Yes, it pretty much sucked." She steered Ali to her side and started down the hall. "How was your day?"

"Same ol' same ol'."

As they entered the living room, Ali caught her hand. "Let me make you a drink." She walked them to the counter separating the kitchen and living room, patting a stool before moving around to the other side of the bar. She grabbed a glass and poured in the vodka, adding two olives.

"Thank you," Lane said as she took a big swallow.

"If that doesn't relax you"—she dragged her nail lightly down Lane's arm to her hand—"I've got something else that might…"

Lane began to pull her hand away, halting when she saw the hurt in Ali's eyes. She felt like a heel. She drew Ali's hand to her lips and murmured against the soft skin. "I really need a shower. Would you excuse me for a few minutes?"

Ali smiled halfheartedly. "Sure. It's your place after all."

"I'll be right back."

Less than a minute after the warm water started pelting Lane's back, the shower door opened. Ali stood naked, hesitant and unmoving until Lane reached for her. Pulling her under the spray, Lane whispered in her ear, "You make me feel so grounded." She kissed the droplets of water along Ali's jaw.

Ali shivered as Lane's arms encircled her. "And you make me feel things I never imagined I could feel." Ali stroked her tongue over Lane's nipple.

Lane tilted Ali's head up, smothering her mouth in a passionate kiss. A moment later, Lane whispered against her temple, "So beautiful."

Ali looked up. "How do you do this to me?"

"Do what?" Lane felt relaxed for the first time all evening.

"Take me over." Ali kissed the valley between Lane's breasts. "Take control." She caught Lane's nipple briefly between her teeth. "And turn me inside out."

The word "control," innocently uttered, was the one that lodged in the forefront of Lane's mind. Controlling—that was who she was to the rest of the world. Not who she wanted to be with Ali. With her, she wanted to be only giving and sharing. She was flooded with shame. She was not the person Ali thought she was, the wonderful person she deserved. She held Ali at arm's length.

"We should get out before we shrivel up."

Ali grabbed a towel and began rubbing it over Lane's back as soon as the water was off. Lane responded by turning around, taking the towel and wrapping it around Ali and covering her own body with a heavy terry cloth robe. "I'll be in the bedroom," she said, after running a brush through her hair. She left the bathroom without a backward glance.

Ali stood before the mirror looking at her reflection and wondering what had happened—what she'd missed. It was like someone had flipped a switch. Lane suddenly had gone from a caring lover to someone so remote she didn't recognize her. Deciding to give her some time, she dried her hair before padding into the master suite. Lane was propped up on pillows in the bed, still in the robe. She had a stack of papers lying across her legs, but she was staring across the room at nothing. Ali stood in the doorway several moments watching her, trying to figure out where Lane's head was. Because it didn't feel like she was there.

Brooding, that's the way she seemed. Z used to get like that from time to time. Lane's dismissal was definitely much gentler than hers had been. She hoped it was also shorter. When Z got like this, it could last for weeks at a time. Ali didn't think she could handle Lane pushing her away that long.

She approached the bed, dropped the towel, pulled back the covers and slid in naked beside Lane, who slowly turned to look at her.

"I've got a lot of work I need to get done. I'm in court early tomorrow morning." She paused briefly. "I'm sorry."

"No." Ali touched her fingertips to Lane's lips. "You don't have to be sorry for having to work. I know how important your job is, baby." She caught a glimpse of something that looked a lot like pain in

Lane's dark eyes before she turned away. She reached out and gently turned Lane's head back toward hers. The wall that had been erected between them was tearing her apart. "Something's wrong and I feel like I caused it somehow." She felt her eyes well with tears.

Lane took Ali's hand, raised it to her lips and kissed it lightly. "No, darling, it's not you."

"Right, that's what they all say. 'It's not you, it's me.'"

"'They all'?"

"That's not what I really meant. I just feel..." A tear slipped down Ali's cheek.

Lane thought the pain in her heart would make it stop beating. "No, no. Oh God, no, Ali. Please, this really has nothing to do with you and everything to do with me. And it's not about us either. I'm so sorry if I've made you feel it is. It's...I've got a lot weighing on me right now, and I know, I shouldn't bring it home. It's overwhelming sometimes."

She sighed internally. Apparently she wasn't sorry enough to tell Ali the truth. She could explain the demands her career plans made on her and Ali would accept them, she was fairly certain. But she couldn't explain to her the things she'd have to do, the things she'd already done, to make those plans achievable. Hell, since meeting Ali she could scarcely explain or justify them to herself.

Ali slid her arm around Lane's shoulder, pulling herself against her. "I don't want to add to your burdens." She kissed lightly down Lane's neck, murmuring, "I'm here for you, baby, whatever you need."

In one swift movement, Lane swept the pile of papers over the side of the bed and relaxed in Ali's embrace. "What I need is to hold you."

"I'm right here, baby. I promise."

Lane held on until all she could see, all she could feel against her was Ali. Nothing had ever felt more real or right in her life. The arousal that had failed to surface before ignited between her thighs now. "You do such amazing things to me."

Ali kissed the top of her head. "It's nothing close to what you do to me." She pulled Lane on top of her, guiding Lane's hips between hers. Lane groaned, burying her face against Ali's neck as Ali's fingers moved over her swollen flesh and a wave that was achingly sweet washed over her.

CHAPTER SEVENTEEN

Lane woke, still lying half on top of Ali with Ali's arms holding her. She didn't want to move. She wanted to spend her life there. She glanced at the clock and slipped reluctantly from the bed. Thirty minutes later when she stepped out of the dressing room, Ali was still sleeping in the same position. She debated kissing her. She didn't want to wake her, but she couldn't fathom leaving for the day without one more sweet reminder of what she had to look forward to at the day's end.

Ali murmured softly and stirred. She reached for Lane's hand. "I don't have to go in until two today." She tugged Lane toward the bed.

"I wish I could. But..." Lane slipped her hand from Ali's. "I have to be in court early this morning." She leaned down and quickly kissed her forehead. "I'll see you tonight."

Ali stretched again, the movement exposing her breasts. Lane forced herself away from the bed. "I'll be late." Ali turned on her side, propping her head in her hand.

"Bye, baby."

Lane turned for the door. "Bye, sweetheart. Have a good day. I'll be here when you get home."

"Home." The word had a resonance to it today that was unfamiliar but welcome. After all these years, her big expensive penthouse was finally beginning to feel like a home.

* * *

"So how did the Beckman dinner go last night?"

Jeremy's question pulled the plug on Lane's exceptionally good mood and sent it circling the drain. She looked up from her papers to where he stood in the doorway. "It went."

"Come on, Lane, give me more than that. He's the one, isn't he? The kingmaker? Or should I say, 'queenmaker'?"

"I suspect that Thomas Beckman could get a former corrections inmate elected to the city council," she said sourly. "So, yes, if I decide to get deeper into politics he could be of help."

"*If?*" Jeremy scoffed. "Don't you mean when we—I mean, when you—seek political office? That's what you've been working toward, right?"

"How about you worry about your future and I'll take care of mine."

"Sorry, I—" She raised a hand, stopping him short.

He coughed and tapped his pen on the calendar in his hand. "You have an open evening. Do you want me to schedule anything for you?"

"No," she said flatly, returning to the brief she was reviewing. "Is there anything else?"

"Not really, except…is your guest having any trouble getting in and out of the building?"

"Don't you have work to do?" she growled. "Because if you don't, I'll find you some." He glared at her. "Go." She waved a hand in dismissal. She chose to ignore the grumbled remarks he made about returning to "his cage" as he exited.

Lane didn't return to her office immediately after adjourning court at four thirty. Instead she went to the jewelry store in the lobby of the building next to the one that housed hers.

"Something special I can help you find, Your Honor?" Katrina smiled and batted her long lashes at Lane.

Lane returned her smile. "I'm not sure exactly what I'm looking for."

Leaning over the glass display case between them, Katrina lowered her honey-smooth voice to a near whisper. "What's she like?"

Before Katrina had started working there, she and "Renee" had gone out on several dates. Weeks later, Lane had stopped into the store only to have Katrina wait on her—and have another customer greet her by her real name, blowing her cover. When Lane had explained the motives behind her pseudonym, however, Katrina had promised to keep her secret.

Lane smiled again. "She's beautiful and charming."

"Of course she is."

"Just like you."

"Flirt," Katrina replied. "Do you like her?"

"What kind of question is that?"

Katrina tilted her head. "It's a very simple one. Do you really like this woman? Is she going to be keeping you company for a while?"

"Oh, yes…" Lane clamped her mouth shut. She hadn't intended to answer so honestly.

"Well…" Katrina moved down the case, sliding a door open and pulling out a velvet square that held a simple gold chain on which hung a gold heart ringed with small diamonds. "I would recommend something like this." She held it out for Lane's inspection.

Lane held the necklace in the palm of her hand. The small, delicate heart made her think of Ali. "I'll take it." She pulled out her credit card.

"Credit?"

Lane gave her a puzzled look.

"You usually buy your little gifts with cash," Katrina reminded her with a gleam in her eyes.

For a moment, Lane was uncertain not only about giving Ali such an extravagant gift, but also about leaving a paper trail in the process. Eventually she nodded. "Yes, credit's fine."

"So, am I correct in assuming the good judge is about to become monogamous?"

Lane lowered her voice. "We saw each other a few times and I've shopped in your store." She tilted her head. "What makes you think you know me well enough to say something like that?"

"Because the woman I'm seeing before me today is a far cry from the other one I know." Katrina glanced around, making sure they were still alone. "The one I know intimately."

Lane felt her cheeks flush, like a schoolgirl's. She clasped her hands nervously behind her back while Katrina wrapped her purchase.

"Between you and me?" Katrina nodded. "I think I may have found that special someone."

Katrina handed her the package. "Well, there's a sea full of women out there that will be devastated to hear that." She winked. "But I'm happy for you, gorgeous. I hope it's everything you've ever wanted."

Lane dropped the small package into her case. "Let's hope."

* * *

Jeremy was gone when she got back to the office to Lane's relief. Then she saw the folded note he had taped to her door.

> Your father called, wanting to meet with you. He wormed out of me the fact that you have a free evening—sorry—and he insists you call him. I tried your cell numerous times without an answer. Guess court ran late. Anyway, please call him back.—Jeremy

She crumpled the note in her fist, wishing she could rid herself as easily of the duty she felt. Moving to the closet bar, she poured herself a short drink. After finishing it in several big swallows, she picked up the phone.

Jerald answered on the third ring. "Stanford residence."

"It's Lane. May I speak to my father, please?"

"Certainly, miss." She heard muffled sounds as he carried the phone down the hall. A moment later her father's voice came on the line.

"Lane, your assistant informed me you have a free evening. I want you to meet me for dinner."

Lane sucked in a breath, steeling herself for how he was likely to respond to her refusal. "I'm sorry, but I can't, Dad."

"Excuse me?" His voice rose.

"I'm sorry, but I really can't. I have this evening free so I can take care of some personal things."

"Personal things! What could you possibly have to do that's more important than your career?"

The anger in his voice sparked her own. "Do you really want to know? Because I will give you every detail, but I don't recall you caring about anything very personal relating to me after Mother died. You had Miss Clara take care of those things."

There was a long awkward silence before Weston finally spoke gruffly. "So you think taking care of all your little personal things is more important than strategizing on your future?"

She took a deep breath. "I think if I don't take care of my personal life, nothing else will matter."

"Well, young lady, this is where you and I disagree."

"I'm sorry, Dad, but I'm doing what I need to do. I'll talk to you again soon."

Lane hung up the phone without waiting for his reply and dropped into her chair. She'd planned to get some work done before heading home since Ali was working until the restaurant closed. But her father's call had derailed that. She loaded the files into her case and dialed the car service.

* * *

"Good evening, Henry. Having another nice, quiet night, I hope?"

"Good evening, Judge." The doorman rushed ahead of her to punch the elevator button. "Pretty quiet, though rumor has it Mr. Jeremy in five-oh-four finally has himself a steady gal."

Lane narrowed her eyes, fixing him with a steely gaze. "You don't talk about all residents this way, I hope." She stepped into the elevator, a frown fixed on her face.

"No, ma'am." His face turned beet red. "I'm terribly sorry, ma'am," he called to her as the doors closed.

She smiled as the elevator headed upward. At least the building staff appeared to believe the perky little blonde belonged to "Mr. Jeremy." Gossip among tenants and the staff was the very reason she kept her affairs so private.

Lane dropped her things inside the front door of the penthouse and poured herself a drink. She didn't feel like working and the thought of sitting alone in her lavish digs no longer held any allure either. She wanted Ali there so she wouldn't have to think about all the other things in her life that had nothing to do with the woman she was crazy about.

"Dammit!" She set the leaded glass down with a thud. Wandering toward the master bedroom, she saw an oversized canvas bag sitting inside the doorway of the guest room across the hall. Ali had stashed most of the contents from her car there earlier in the week. When she flipped on the light in the room, her eyes were drawn to a sketchpad sticking out of the top of the bag.

That's right. Ali said she wanted to be an artist. Her curiosity piqued, she reached for the pad. What she saw when she lifted the cover on the pad bowled her over. Stepping backward until her legs hit the side of the bed, she sat, mesmerized by the piercing dark eyes staring back at her. It was like seeing her reflection in a mirror. Ali had captured her face perfectly and with nothing more than a pencil. She was quite an artist.

She turned to the next page. There she found a prone nude female, face obscured, but so vivid it started her blood flowing. The page after that showed two women in a very intimate embrace. She quickly closed the pad, her heart beating rapidly. She felt like a voyeur. While she wanted to think the women were her and Ali, they probably weren't. She wasn't sure how she felt about that. Upset? Jealous? Actually, she was being ridiculous. It was art. Very appealing art. Something she would proudly display in her penthouse regardless of the artist. She put the pad back in the bag and returned to the kitchen to get her drink.

Her mind moving in fast forward, she went to her home office and brought her computer online. She quickly found what she was looking for, the Metropolitan School for Artists. Her excitement grew as she browsed their impressive website. After she'd learned what she needed, she leaned back with a smile and sipped her drink. When Ali came in right before eleven, she was seated comfortably on the couch in the living room, freshly showered and grinning inside in anticipation.

Ali leaned down, giving Lane a quick kiss. "Mmm...you smell good." She stood. "I don't. I need a shower."

Even doused in the smell of cumin and other spices from the restaurant, Ali made Lane's heart race. She wanted her to be comfortable, though. "Come join me here when you're done." She patted the couch. "I want to talk to you about something."

"Okay."

Ali hoped the sudden fear she had felt wasn't audible in her voice. As hot water sluiced over her in the shower she rubbed at the goose bumps Lane's request had raised on her skin. It had been quite some time since she'd experienced *that* sensation in the shower. Had Lane discovered her secrets? She'd driven home that evening on top of the world, anxious to be with Lane, but now she felt dizzy. Toweling her hair and pulling on a robe, she took deep breaths. Lane hadn't appeared to be upset or angry, after all. She'd actually looked more relaxed than she'd seemed all week. After one more calming breath, she walked to the living room.

Lane stood when Ali reappeared, wrapped her arms possessively around her waist and pressed her lips firmly to Ali's, teasing them with her tongue. Ali couldn't resist. She moaned, leaning into Lane's embrace. After a moment, Lane pulled back, gazed into Ali's eyes and brushed damp locks of hair behind her ear.

"Now that's a proper welcoming kiss."

Ali studied her, looking for a hint of what was going on, but she saw only the dark smoldering eyes that held her gaze.

"Let's sit. I have something I want to discuss with you." She lifted a glass of the sweet white wine that Ali liked from the coffee table and placed it in her hand.

Ali curled her feet under her on the couch and sipped her wine, trying to look relaxed.

"Remember when you told me you'd always wanted to be an artist?" Ali nodded. "You know there's an excellent art school right here in our city?"

"The Metropolitan, I know. It's like one of the most expensive schools in the country."

Lane handed Ali the page of information she'd printed out during her Internet search. "Would you attend it if you could?"

Ali laughed. "I couldn't afford to go there if I worked a hundred hours a week."

Lane laid her arm across the back of the couch, allowing her fingers to lightly massage Ali's neck under her hair. "If going there would help you achieve your dream of being an artist, would you do it?"

"That's a silly question. Of course I would. Who wouldn't? But Lane, it's way more than I could ever afford." She laid the sheet of paper on the coffee table.

"I want to make this happen for you."

Ali adamantly shook her head. "I can't, baby," she said. "I can't let you do that."

"I want to…"

"No," Ali repeated. "It's too much. I can't let you."

Lane took her wineglass, set it on the table and turned back to face her. "Please, let me do this for you. For all that you do for me."

Ali laughed. "Like what? Using your hot water and housekeeping services?"

Lane's eyes locked on hers, her expression was serious, but soft. "No, sweetheart. For making me feel all the things you make me feel. Wonderful things I've never felt before. I told you. I need you, and I want to do this for you."

"Oh, baby." She stroked her fingers over Lane's cheek. "You don't need to do this. Really."

Lane caught her hand, turned it and kissed her palm. "I do need to, and I so want to. I want you to become the artist you've always dreamed of being. I want to feel...I don't know..."—she shrugged—"like maybe I inspired you in some way."

"You do inspire me." Ali moved to straddle Lane's lap. "You're amazing. You make me feel things I never knew were possible. Beautiful things."

"Mmm..." Lane moaned as Ali pressed a deeper searing kiss to her lips.

Before it became too consuming, Ali pulled back, causing Lane to groan with disappointment. "I can't go to school. My job is—"

Lane hushed her with a finger to her lips. "We can figure this out, I promise."

"I have to keep my job."

"Why?"

"Because I need the money."

"No, you don't—"

"No, Lane, I won't be kept." She watched the hurt wash over Lane's face. "Oh, baby." She stroked Lane's cheek again. "You are the most caring and giving person I've ever known. You moved me in here after knowing me only a short time just so I wouldn't have to live in my car anymore. I appreciate more than you can imagine what you've done for me. I feel more like a whole person now...because of you. But..." She watched the dark eyes looking back at her. "I need to be self-sufficient. Can you understand that?"

Lane nodded. "I understand completely." And she did. Ali appeared on the surface to be vulnerable. The kind of woman people could take advantage of. Under the surface, though, she was so much stronger. Just how strong, Lane was only beginning to realize. She kissed the tip of her nose. "It's too important to pass up, so...let's talk about it more later. Okay?"

After some hesitation, Ali nodded. "Okay."

"You look tired. Let's go to bed."

"Yes." Ali's hot breath whispered across Lane's skin. "I want you."

Lane turned Ali's face to look at her. "Darling, the mere thought of you makes me ache, and when you touch me, I'm a goner. But it's late, you look completely exhausted and I have an early and very long day tomorrow." She moved her hand lazily up and down Ali's back. "How about if I hold you in my arms and we get some sleep?"

In bed, Ali kissed the corner of her mouth and laid her head just above her breast. "I am so happy to be with you."

Lane kissed the top of her head. "Sweet dreams."

* * *

Lane was busy at her desk well before eight the following morning. She was trying to catch up enough to have time to take care of a few personal things for herself. Before she had to head off to court, she completed an online preliminary enrollment application for Ali at the art school, which included a few photos she'd taken of Ali's sketches. She had also left a message at The Inn for Roscoe to call her.

When she returned after three o'clock, Jeremy hopped to his feet. "A Ms. Babbitt, dean of admissions from the Metro Art School, called regarding your application."

"Thanks." She took the slip he held out and headed for her office. *Crap! Where was my head this morning when I left the office number for a return call?*

"What are you up to, Lane? What's going on?"

She dropped a stack of files in the middle of her desk and settled into her chair. "What are you babbling about, Jeremy?"

He crossed his arms, which matched perfectly the expression on his face. "First this lady calls, from an art school of all places, and not fifteen minutes later Roscoe calls, saying he was returning your call. So again I ask, what's going on?"

"I'm thinking of taking up art." She shrugged. "To fall back on if this whole political thing goes south."

"Right." He nodded his head slowly. "You don't have an artistic bone in your body."

"You have to start somewhere."

"And you're calling Roscoe yourself because..."

"I'm thinking of having a dinner party. Roscoe is my favorite chef."

"And why am I only now hearing about it?"

"As I said, I'm thinking about it. And who are you today, Jeremy? My assistant or my mother?" She instantly regretted bringing her mother into their discussion. But she really did want him to back off.

"Fine, fine." He waved his hand dramatically. "Why don't you can me and get some intern in here to work for you?"

"Don't tempt me."

"Well, let me know if you have some bona fide work for me to do."
He flounced out of her office.

Lane glanced at the messages before picking up the phone. A perky
voice answered. "The Inn, this is Suzanne. How may I be of help?"

"This is Judge Stanford, Suzanne. Is Roscoe available?"

"I believe he is if you'll hold for a moment."

Several minutes later, Roscoe came on the line. "Lane, dear, how
may I be of service? Another private dinner at your home perhaps?"

She chuckled. "Roscoe, if I ate your food as often as I'd like, I'd
weigh three hundred pounds."

"You could never."

"I do have a favor to ask of you, though."

"How may I help?"

Lane had thought this conversation through all day. "I've taken
one of your employees under my wing. Ah…let's see. Ali Castle." She
paused. "Yes, that's her. She's a budding artist, and I have arranged
for her to be able to study at the prestigious Metropolitan School for
Artists. But"—she paused again—"for her to do that, she would need
to reduce her hours some and arrange her schedule so it works around
class hours. Is there some way the two of us could make that possible
for her?"

"For you, Lane, I would be happy to oblige. How much time would
you think?"

"It depends, I suppose, on her class schedule."

"I think we can work out what you need for her. I have students
from the college applying for work all the time, but they don't want a
lot of hours during a week. I could hire one of them to fill the hours if
need be. Let me know."

"Thank you, Roscoe."

"You're very welcome."

Before he could hang up, she said, "Oh, and I will be calling again
soon for one of your fabulous dinners, I promise."

"Always happy to serve the Stanford family. Have an enjoyable
day."

"You too, Roscoe. And thank you again."

Check, she thought. *One down.*

She dialed Ms. Babbitt next but was informed by her secretary
that she was in a meeting. Lane requested a return call, giving her
cell as the callback number this time. When she had completed Ali's
preliminary application, she'd included a note that she was making
inquiries on behalf of Ms. Castle. Wasn't that the kind of philanthropic

thing people with money and power did? Take "budding artists" under their wings?

Ms. Babbitt returned her call within the hour. "Judge Stanford, it is so wonderful to know you've taken interest in a promising individual and in our school. I've followed your career for a number of years now. You are quickly rising to become one the most powerful women in our city."

"Thank you. I'm honored that you think so."

"I've looked over the preliminary application you submitted for Ms. Castle, along with the photos of her sketches. She certainly possesses the level of talent the Metropolitan School of Artists is looking for in its students. I took the liberty of sharing the photos with several of the professors and the consensus is that she would be a welcomed addition to the student body."

"I'm pleased to hear that, Ms. Babbitt."

"I did notice there wasn't any information filled in regarding financials."

Lane leaned back in her chair. "I'll be covering any cost associated with Ms. Castle's curriculum. I'm more concerned with the availability of the classes she may require, given that the school year is already underway."

"I think we can accommodate her curriculum requirements. Might I suggest that you bring her in so we can get everything set up?"

"I don't think my schedule will allow that, Ms. Babbitt, but I'll have Ms. Castle contact you to make an appointment. Again, I will be covering her expenses, so that needn't be of any consequence. Let's just keep that between us and let her concentrate on her studies."

"Very well, Judge, and may I say it's been a pleasure speaking with you."

"Please, call me Lane. And thank you for your personal attention to this." Lane hung up the phone. *Two down and one to go.* She still had to get Ali to agree.

Jeremy knocked on her door precisely at five. "I'm heading out." She looked up briefly. "You're all set on your evening schedule, the drinks and that charity thing, right?"

"Yes," she replied.

"See you tomorrow." Lane said nothing.

"Have a good evening, Jeremy," Lane heard him mutter sarcastically beneath his breath as he left.

* * *

Ali was in the living room when she arrived home at ten thirty. "Oh, baby, you look beat." She slid Lane's suit jacket off her shoulders. "Sit down. Do you want a drink?"

Lane pinched her thumb and forefinger together, indicating a very small drink, as she eased her exhausted body onto the soft leather sofa. Ali placed the glass in her hand and sat next to her, her hand automatically going to Lane's neck and kneading the stiff muscles there.

"I've been thinking all day about what you proposed last night."

"And?" Lane tried to keep her muscles from tightening further.

"And I'd love to try the art school, but...*only* if you agree to let me pay you back for every penny you spend on it."

Lane gave her a tired smile. "I can live with those terms."

Ali smiled in return. "Come on." She stood, reaching for Lane's hand. "Let me put you to bed."

Lane placed her glass on the table, allowing Ali to pull her up. "That's the best offer I've had all day."

"And exactly how many offers do you get in a day, Judge?"

God...Lane thought about the part of her life she had been trying harder and harder to erase from existence—or at least memory—of late. "None that comes close to yours." She quickly captured Ali's lips.

"Mmm...," Ali murmured. "I'm glad."

CHAPTER EIGHTEEN

Ali began with two art classes a day. They were already a month into the quarter, but she assured her professors she'd make up what she'd missed. She was less concerned about the whole credit and grade business than in the chance to develop her talent. To do that in the past, she'd drawn female portraits, more than she could keep track of, always giving them to the women she drew. Not surprisingly, on her first day she spotted an interesting face in her noon class, a particularly beautiful one. Ali couldn't help stealing glances at her throughout class and got caught looking more than once. Embarrassed, she'd rushed from class, hoping to avoid the woman, even though the eyes that had met hers had been friendly. The following day, though, when she arrived, the gal was waiting outside the door.

"Hey." She had a low and sexy voice.

Looking up into her beautiful eyes, Ali got completely lost for a moment. Her face broke into a smile, jolting Ali back to awareness. "Uh…hi."

"My name is Jade." She extended her hand to Ali. "Welcome to our class."

Her hand lingered on Ali's. "Um…thanks." This woman was really throwing her off. She met strangers daily, attractive women too, some of whom flirted with her, and she'd never had trouble maintaining a cool, calm demeanor. This one had her rattled for some reason.

"So, new to town or just our school?" Jade stared at Ali's left hand, which was clutching the strap on her shoulder bag.

"I haven't been here long. In town that is. This is just my second day at school." She bobbed her head nervously. "But you already know that."

Jade smiled at her again and the whole picture—the eyes, the smile on very full lips, high cheekbones, strong jaw and a perfect dimple in the middle of her chin—left Ali blinking and swallowing hard.

Jade flipped her hair back off her shoulder. "Well, very pretty blonde whose name I don't know, do you think maybe—" Her words were cut off when their professor entered the room, bellowing as he passed them.

"Everyone to their seats, please. I have a number of things to cover before turning you loose today."

Ali stepped away quickly, moving toward a seat near the back of the room. If she didn't know any better, Jade was about to ask her—what, ask her out, ask for her phone number? Ali watched as she took her seat near the front left in the room, smiling a delighted smile at Ali as she did so. Nervously, Ali returned the smile.

Jade was one of the most beautiful women Ali had ever seen, with big, mesmerizing blue-gray eyes set in light coffee skin. Lane, with her smoldering dark eyes, was drop-dead gorgeous. Jade, on the other hand, looked like an artist, with braided dreads pulled together behind her head and hanging past her shoulders. She wore faded jeans, a loose-fitting, open-collar shirt with sleeves pushed halfway up her strong-looking arms and sandals. Ali pictured Lane again, remembering the first time she'd laid eyes on her, and her heart started fluttering. No question, Lane was the one who did it for her. Which didn't mean she could stop herself from looking at Jade.

Outside the building after class, Jade rushed up and touched Ali's elbow. "Hey there, um…"

Ali stopped. "Ali."

"Ali." Ali swore Jade's eyes twinkled when she said her name. "So, Ali, what I was going to ask before I was so rudely interrupted is if you'd like to grab a coffee or something after class sometime?" She rocked back and forth on her sandals.

If Ali weren't otherwise involved, she would have jumped at the invitation. But she was. "I have someone—at home, I mean. I don't think it would…"

"Hey, I'm only asking for coffee." Jade cut her off. "And maybe some conversation, you know."

"Just coffee?" Ali was reminded that Lane had invited her out "only for dinner."

"Yeah." Jade nodded. "Coffee or whatever you drink, public place, lots of people around." She leaned closer. "I even promise to try not to flirt. I can't guarantee that since you are some kind of beautiful, but I do promise, I'll try." She crossed her finger over her heart with a dazzling smile.

"Well, since you promised twice, and it's only coffee…okay."

"Cool. How about tomorrow after class?" Ali nodded. "Great. I'll see you in class tomorrow, Ali, followed by a harmless cup of something." She grinned ear to ear, turned and strode down the sidewalk.

* * *

Ali was in the living room doodling in one of her sketchpads when Lane arrived home. "Hey, baby." She jumped to her feet.

"Hi, gorgeous."

Ali slid into Lane's embrace. She smothered Lane's mouth in a kiss before leaning back in her arms. "I thought you had a dinner or meeting or one of those things that keep you busier than should be allowed by law. You're a judge. Can't you do something about that?" she asked playfully.

Lane sighed. "A dinner, then a meeting, but I pushed dinner back an hour so I could take a few minutes to come home and see you like this…" She winked. "Instead of simply naked in my bed."

Ali rubbed herself suggestively against Lane's thigh. "Well…I for one like seeing you naked in your bed. So, do you have time for naked now?"

"I wish. I don't have long. But I had to see you." Lane stroked a polished nail down Ali's cheek. "And to talk. It feels like we have too few opportunities to do that."

"Mmm…How about something else?"

When Ali leaned into her, Lane took a quick step back. "As wonderful as it would be, I can't now."

Ali was disappointed. At this point she would take a quickie. Their schedules had always been frustrating and they weren't likely to get any better, what with Lane working all day through the week and having some thing or other nearly every evening and on the weekends and her now working whenever Roscoe needed her in order to be able to go to school. As a result, they had little time to simply be together, except late at night when one or both of them were exhausted. She was sure Lane had fallen into a dead sleep the second after she climaxed the other night.

Lane led her over to the couch, glancing at the sketchpad Ali had tossed on the coffee table. "How are your classes going?" She settled into the leather with a mental "ah."

"Oh, baby, it's great. I love it."

"So...this school and classes are going to help you achieve your dream?"

"I sure hope so."

Lane leaned back, stretching out her long legs. "Well, are you going to tell me all about it?" Lane narrowed her eyes. "Or am I going to have to grill you?"

Ali sat beside her, curled her feet under her and began talking excitedly.

"Are all the students future famous artists like you?"

"I don't know. I've only really met one girl. She's in my second class." Lane noticed a slight smile curving Ali's lips. "I think she might be like us."

"Oh?"

"Well, artists can be...different. So it's hard to tell, but I think she might be gay."

"Really." Lane felt the tiniest bit unsettled. "Did she ask you on a date?"

"Oh, no, just coffee."

"I see."

"Baby." Ali's arm slid possessively around Lane's shoulder, pulling them close together. "I told her I have someone." She placed her lips on Lane's, kissing her tenderly. "You're more special than anyone I've ever had in my life. I don't even want to look at another woman."

Lane kissed her back, although briefly. "I need to get changed, Randall is waiting downstairs."

Ali gave her a pout. "I wish we could have one whole day off together. Just one."

Lane gazed at her. "Just one?"

Ali gave a sultry smile. "Okay, two." She moved closer.

Lane cupped her face in her hands. "We will, sometime...soon, hopefully. I promise." Ali tried to slide her arms around Lane's shoulders, but she leaned away. "You're too tempting and I've got to get going."

Ali trailed after her to the bedroom, plopping down on the bed. Lane caught glimpses of Ali watching as she stripped off everything but her bra and panties. "Ah, God," Lane heard her mutter.

She exited the dressing room, buttoning her blouse. "What is it?"

Ali got to her knees on the edge of the bed as Lane neared. "You make me so hot sometimes. It's unbearable."

Lane knew she needed to keep her distance or run the risk of being late. The deep shade of Ali's eyes told her that Ali was indeed aroused, and the thought quickened her own pulse. "How fast will you come if I touch you?" She took a small step closer, still staying out of Ali's reach. "If," she took another step, "you promise," then one more, "not to touch me…" Ali reached for her and Lane stepped back.

"Tease."

"If you promise not to touch me, I'll make you come." She watched as the color of Ali's eyes deepened to that familiar violet hue.

"Promise," Ali choked out.

Lane closed the distance between them. Catching the bottom of Ali's cropped shirt, she stripped it over her head, leaving her bare from the waist up. Her body rippled as Lane's fingers feathered a trail down her abdomen and shook when her hand dipped inside her waistband.

She whispered, "I'm going to fall."

Lane stopped. "You can hold onto my shoulders, but no other touching." Ali nodded.

"Please, baby, touch me."

Lane nipped at the tender skin on Ali's neck as her fingers slid into her wetness. Ali dug her fingers into Lane's shoulders and rocked against her hand.

"Inside," she gasped. "I need you in me, please."

Lane acquiesced and Ali climaxed quickly. She kissed her temple. "I've got to go now, sweetheart." Lane guided her gently down on the bed.

Completely sated, Ali gazed up at Lane. "Hurry home so I can take care of you."

Lane kissed her tenderly. "I will." She disappeared into the bathroom, emerging a minute later, tossing her jacket over her shoulders. It absolutely killed her to leave Ali in order to go have dinner with another self-aggrandizing businessman. "I'll be home as soon as I can."

She rushed through the lobby, finding Randall standing at the curb by her door. "Ma'am." He tipped his head.

"I'm sorry, I'm running late." She hoped Randall didn't notice the flush she felt coloring her cheeks.

"No problem, ma'am. We'll get you there in time."

Lane offered an apologetic smile. "I know you will. Thank you."

After dinner with yet another—yes, she'd guessed correctly—self-centered, egotistical male, she proceeded to a meeting at the Plaza Royal's lounge with half a dozen men from the state capital who were part of some kind of consortium. As the clock rolled around to nine forty-five, she stifled a yawn. She'd long since switched from vodka to plain club soda, unable to keep up with their drinking. She stood.

"Gentlemen, it has been a pleasure meeting with you this evening, but I must run. I have a very early court appearance in the morning, and I find counsel gets a little testy when I don't stay awake during proceedings." They stood, each offering a hand, thanking her and expressing the desire to meet with her again. She didn't say the same, though she didn't think they noticed.

* * *

Ali looked refreshed when Lane arrived home. Taking Lane's things, she led her directly to the master suite. "I want to relax you. It's all I've been thinking about since you left." She backed her to the bed, working at the buttons on her blouse. When it was open, she slid it and the jacket off in one motion. Unfastening her slacks, she slid them slowly down Lane's thighs, then knelt to remove them along with her shoes and stockings. Lane was left standing in only her bra and panties.

"You make my mouth water."

Lane felt her nipples straining against the thin material of her bra. Her skin flushed as Ali's eyes moved over her. Ali guided Lane down on the bed, shrugged off the robe she was wearing and lay down beside her. She drew her fingers lightly between Lane's breasts and down her abdomen. Lane groaned when she moved under her panties.

"God, baby, you're so wet." Ali straddled Lane's hips, which rose instantly, seeking Ali's heat. She slid the straps from Lane's shoulders, pulled the silken material from her breasts and leaned down to capture one, then the other nipple in her mouth. Lane groaned again, thrusting her hips to meet Ali's.

"I know what you need, baby." She slid down Lane's thighs, tugging off her panties as she moved. Once Lane was exposed, she feathered kisses up her leg to the tender skin at the top of her thigh. When her mouth moved toward Lane's throbbing center, though, Lane caught Ali's head in her hands.

"No," she said firmly. "Come up here. I want your mouth on mine when you make me come." She pulled Ali to her lips and quickly climaxed. Before her heart rate returned to a normal rhythm, she was fast asleep.

* * *

Lane waved Jeremy in the moment he arrived. "Close the door." She let him recite her day's schedule and then, as he stood to leave, said, "I need you to get me a weekend free."

"As in a Saturday and a Sunday?" His voice raised an octave.

"Yes, Jeremy. Saturday and Sunday are considered the weekend."

He flipped through the pages of her calendar. "I don't know how I can, Lane. Weekends are when a lot of your meetings and charities and fund-raisers take place."

She let out an exhausted breath. "Make a way. Find the first weekend that's empty at the moment and block it out. I don't care what charities, fund-raisers or otherwise come up between now and then. That weekend is to be off limits. Is that clear? Do you think you can handle that?"

"Yes, Lane, but—"

She cut him off. "No buts, Jeremy. Make it happen."

"Got it." He placed big Xs over two days that were three weeks away, then cast a questioning gaze upon her.

"What?" she asked impatiently as she jotted down the date of the weekend he'd given her, which seemed an eternity away.

He took a breath. "That's what I want to know. What's going on Lane?" A look of deep concern settled on his face. "Are you sick?"

Why did people automatically assume if you changed your attitude or routines you must be sick or dying? "Yes, Jeremy…" She paused a long few seconds, watching the worry lines deepen on his face before deciding she tortured him enough. "I'm sick of working sixteen hours a day and never having a moment to myself unless I'm sleeping."

"Well, I don't understand what's so important all of a sudden that you need time to yourself when you never seemed to want any before." It was obvious he was fishing. "I thought at first it could be that woman you installed in the apartment, but this has been going on for weeks and your little flings never last that long. You've put off meetings and repeatedly rearranged your schedule at the last minute. And I know you blew off that charity event recently, sending a check in lieu of attending." When Lane didn't respond, he said, "A donation of that size warrants a personal thank-you, and the woman handling the fund-raising called to thank the Honorable Judge Stanford." He planted a hand on his hip.

Lane stood abruptly. "In case you've forgotten what your job is, Jeremy, let me remind you. It does *not* involve questioning everything I do or don't do. Am I understood?"

"Of course," he snapped. "Anything else?"

"No." She wouldn't fill Ali in until she knew everything was set in stone. In the meantime, she began to consider what they could do with two consecutive days together.

* * *

"Hey, Ali." Jade was waiting for Ali inside the door for their class. She had to admit, she liked the way her name sounded when Jade said it.

"Hey."

"So, uh, we still on for coffee or something after class today?" Jade asked nervously.

"Sure."

A grin spread over Jade's face. "Cool." She bounced her head. "Let's meet up out front after class then."

Jade's eyes seemed to be on her every time Ali glanced her way during the two hours that followed, and her face seemed to be wearing a perpetual grin. The effect, Ali decided, was sexy as hell.

"I know a neat little coffee shop/bookstore a few blocks from here if you don't mind walking," Jade said, stepping up to Ali out front.

"Walking is okay."

"Unless you have a car and would rather drive. It's kind of a hassle finding parking, though. Heck, I don't even have a car. I walk everywhere." Jade flipped her braids over her shoulder, rambling nervously.

As they walked, they talked about their class, the professor and some of the other students. Ali's gaydar pinged the moment they entered the coffee shop. She watched two girls at another table talking, and the way they looked into each other's eyes suggested much more than simple friendship. She envied their openness, knowing there was nowhere she could go with Lane and be herself.

I have Lane to come home to every night, though. And that's something.

"Here." Jade held a coffee cup in front of Ali, curtailing her thoughts.

"Thanks." Jade smiled that damn sexy smile in response and Ali couldn't help smiling back.

"Come on." Jade caught her hand and led her past bookshelves to a small sitting area. "It's quieter back here," she said, before releasing Ali's hand. "So we can talk."

Having Jade's hand clasping hers had unsettled Ali. What did it mean when a complete stranger could affect you like that with a touch and a smile?

Jade picked up her cup. "Here's to new friends." She tapped her cup to Ali's and leaned back in the chair, stretching long muscular legs to the side of the table. "So you just moved here from somewhere else. Where would that be?"

Ali shook her head. "I've actually been here about six months now."

"Oh." Before Jade could continue her inquisition two young girls, looking to be barely out of high school, came in. Giggling, they moved to the farthest corner and stood holding hands, face to face.

When they kissed, Ali looked away. She felt her face flush. "Is this a lesbian bookstore or something?" she asked, whispering.

"Yeah, it's owned by a couple of women that have been together for like twenty-five years. That a problem?"

It felt like Jade's eyes were burning into her. Ali looked down into her cup to break the effect. "No, uh…I just…didn't know."

Jade reached across the table and touched Ali's hand briefly. "Sorry, I thought you were…you know. Like me. It was stupid for me to make that assumption. I'm sorry. So I guess you have a boyfriend?"

Ali looked at her hand on the table, still feeling the warmth from where Jade had touched it. "No…I…." Ali couldn't meet Jade's eyes. "You don't have to be sorry. You're not wrong."

"So the someone at home is a woman."

"Yes," Ali said softly.

"Well, just so you know, I go for women too. So we have that in common. You seemed, I don't know, like someone I could talk to."

Someone to talk to…that was okay, wasn't it? Even though Jade was so hot looking? Ali steered the conversation back around to art, but got an anxious feeling every time Jade smiled at her.

Jade insisted on walking Ali back to her car. "So what does your girlfriend do? Is she a student here too or over at the city college?"

Jade assumed she and Lane were close in age, Ali realized. She wondered if Jade thought Ali was about the same age she was. She guessed Jade to be in her very early twenties. "No, she's in the legal profession."

"Cool. If I ever get into trouble I can call her," she said jokingly, taking the last few steps to Ali's car backward.

"She doesn't defend people. She's kind of responsible for putting them away." That was sufficiently vague, she thought, while still being true. She would not be responsible for outing Lane, but she didn't want to make a habit of lying either. She tossed her bags over to the passenger seat and slid behind the wheel.

Jade leaned on the top of the door. "It was nice today. Talking and sharing a cup of coffee and all." She shrugged. "So maybe we can do it again?"

"Sure. See you tomorrow."

"Yeah." Jade smiled that signature smile. "Stay safe." She closed Ali's door, offering a flick of her hand in goodbye.

Ali headed to The Inn. She had brought her serving clothes with her, knowing she wouldn't have time to stop at home before going to work. *Home*, she thought. How nice it was to have a place that she could not only call home, but where she felt as though she *were* home. Where she felt safe and didn't have to constantly look over her shoulder. A place where she belonged. She wanted to do something to show Lane how much she appreciated that, how much she appreciated *her*. She made a mental note to check with Lane about her schedule. Maybe they could do something on Sunday, her next day off.

CHAPTER NINETEEN

Jade was waiting in the parking lot for Ali the following day when she arrived for her first class. "How'd you know I'd be here?" she asked as she gathered her bags.

"You told me which class you had. All I had to do was check the schedule."

"You're not stalking me, are you?" Ali started to walk away from her.

Jade caught her arm. "No, I like you. I like hanging with you, but if you don't want me around say so."

Ali saw something in her eyes that made her regret joking about the stalking. "I'm sorry, Jade, it must be PMS. I didn't mean anything by it. I like hanging with you too."

"Good. So I shouldn't have to do much arm twisting to get you to go to the coffee shop with me again after class."

"I can't today. I have to be at work." Noticing that she was running late, Ali quickened her pace. Jade stayed right with her.

"Why don't you have the legal babe support you while you go to school? People do that all the time."

"Not me."

"If I had someone to foot the bills, you can bet I wouldn't be working all the little nitpicky jobs I have to so I can afford classes."

"I've got to go," Ali said, cutting short their conversation and beginning to run. She called over her shoulder, "Next week, we'll do coffee again next week." Before she turned the corner, she saw Jade stop in the middle of the crosswalk, nearly causing a collision, her face still wearing that sexy smile.

Ali sat in class doodling, not paying much attention to her professor or what was taking shape in her sketchpad. She kept seeing Jade staring after her as she rushed to class. When Ali finally looked at what her hand had unconsciously created, she found that face staring at her again, its unbelievable blue-gray eyes filled with reverence.

When Ali arrived home after her shift, Lane was propped up in bed with papers strewn across her lap, drowsing but to all appearances sound asleep. As she began quietly gathering up the mess, Lane jerked in alarm. "Stop! Don't!" she croaked. Ali jumped back, clearly startled by the abruptness of Lane's rousing and the chilly tone of her voice. Lane hastily began pulling the papers together herself. When she finally looked up at Ali, she saw the hurt in her eyes. "I'm sorry."

Ali stepped away from the bed. "It's okay. I know what you deal with is not for everyone's eyes." She headed for the door. "I didn't mean to startle you," she said stiffly. "I'm going to jump in the shower."

If anyone saw this stuff, Lane thought, securing the documents in her briefcase, *my life would be over. My career, anyway.*

She was waiting again in the bed when Ali returned drying her hair, but this time she was wide awake.

"I'm really sorry," she said again. "I didn't realize I'd dozed off with all those confidential documents out." She patted the bed beside her. "Come to bed and tell me about your day." Ali gave her a forgiving smile as she dropped the towel tucked under her arms and slid into the bed beside her. "Now that's hardly fair," Lane said. "How am I supposed to think about what you're saying with your naked body pressing against me?" Lane was wearing a pair of silky pajamas.

Ali settled into Lane's arm, resting her head against her shoulder, her hand lying between Lane's breasts. "Class was very interesting today." She began undoing the buttons of Lane's pajama top. "As for work, it was grueling. You know what serving dozens of people can be like." She slid her hand up to graze her fingertips over a nipple, which hardened instantly under her touch. "So how was your day, baby?" she asked before leaning over and capturing the nipple in her mouth.

Lane moaned, her legs clenching and hips rising at the sensation that tingled all the way to her toes. "I…uh…" Ali's mouth moved to give the other nipple equal attention. "How, uh…" Lane cleared her throat, caught Ali's chin and, raising her head, tried again. "How am I supposed to talk when you do that?"

"Do what?" Ali asked innocently. Her fingers skated down Lane's abdomen to the top of her pajama bottoms, dipped below the silk and combed through the triangle of hair. "Touch you like I want you?" She stripped off Lane's silk pajama bottoms and settled over her hips.

"God, you feel so good…right there." Lane groaned.

"You don't want me to stop?" Ali slowed her movement.

"No, please…don't stop."

The intensity of Lane's orgasm was as fierce as a storm's surge, crashing its waves onto a beach. "God!" Lane said breathlessly as Ali lowered herself against Lane's sweat-soaked body. "I've never…"

"Me either," Ali murmured against her skin.

"Never what?" Lane's limbs felt like rubber.

"Come that way—from touching like that."

"Oh! Maybe you're a top." Lane tried to turn them over, but Ali resisted. "Sweetheart, what's wrong?"

"Mmm…nothing." Ali settled her head against Lane's chest.

She pressed her lips to the top of Ali's head. "I really want you."

Ali sighed contentedly. "You just had me."

"But—"

Ali placed her lips against Lane's damp skin. "Relax, baby. I'm perfectly content."

Lane pulled her arms tighter around her. *You're perfect, all right. I could spend the rest of my life here in your arms. Damn the rest of the world.*

After a while Ali moved beside her and settled her head into the crook of Lane's arm, their bodies fitting together like two puzzle pieces. Ali traced lazy circles over Lane's chest, intermixing the fragrance of Lane's earthy perfume with the scent of their lovemaking.

"You know I'm off this Sunday."

"I remember you mentioning that." Lane ran her hand slowly up and down Ali's back.

"How much do you have going on? I thought we could do something. I don't know what…something."

"I have a late afternoon meeting at my father's house and an early dinner." Lane knew if she tried to worm her way out of their Sunday get-together after refusing to meet him earlier in the week the sky would probably come crashing down on her. "I'm sorry. I seem to have so little time for us."

Ali turned her head to look up at her. "It's okay. I understand what you do is important."

Lane was beginning to wonder why it suddenly seemed that what she did, everything she did, was important to everyone but her. "I'll be home Saturday evening by dinner time."

Ali sighed. "I have to close Saturday night."

"How about…" Lane considered the time frame, "if I pick you up at the restaurant and take you out somewhere?"

"I'll smell like—"

"You can change in the car."

"Are you sure you want to take me out somewhere public?"

"I'm dying to. And we can stay out late, because we can sleep in Sunday morning."

"That sounds great." Ali stretched up and gave her a slow, lingering, goodnight kiss.

* * *

The city was still sleeping, but Lane was hurrying around the following morning when Ali entered the kitchen. "Gotta run," Lane said regretfully, pausing only long enough to brush her lips over Ali's before she rushed out for the day.

"Have a good day," Ali called after her. She grabbed a cup of coffee and curled up on the living room couch to watch another day dawn. She wondered if Lane's life would always be so hectic and demanding. Probably, she decided, given that Lane was already a judge and was aiming for even bigger things. Her heart grew heavy at the thought that Lane might move on one day and leave her behind.

These new worries were still plaguing her when Jade caught her arm on her way to class.

"Hey, Al."

"Hi," Ali said distractedly. They walked along in step.

"Why the long face? You look like you lost your best friend, but that can't be. I'm still here." Jade grinned.

"Still a little hormonal, I guess."

"Sure, I get that. Want to grab coffee after class today? Might make you feel better."

Ali leaned against the wall outside the classroom door feeling incredibly tired—emotionally as much as physically. She looked into

Jade's amazing blue eyes. "I'm not good company today. My mood pretty much sucks."

Jade shrugged. "It's okay." She shoved a hand in her pocket. "We can sit and people watch or something."

Ali felt exposed under Jade's intense gaze. It was nice having a woman look at her with desire, but she was unnerved by the twinge of longing she felt in response. After all, she was with Lane.

"Come on, Ali." Jade leaned closer. "I'm not going to bite."

Ali's skin prickled as her out-of-control mind imagined Jade's mouth on her skin. *No*, Ali told herself, *I want Lane that way. In every way. Not this woman.*

"Sorry. Can't," she said. "Have to go to work." Brushing past her quickly, Ali headed into the classroom. She kept her eyes focused on her things as she settled into her seat, fearful if she looked at her again Jade would see the uncertainty she was feeling but couldn't explain.

"Maybe one day next week when you're feeling more like yourself?" Jade's hand brushed across her shoulder as she passed.

More like myself? And exactly who is that? Ali wanted to know. She didn't recognize herself lately.

* * *

Lane should have stayed at the office working, but the desire to do so simply wasn't there. She felt confused. Confused in a way she hadn't felt since an oncologist at the Cleveland Clinic turned her childhood upside down. It was unsettling. She arranged for the service to pick her up at home instead of the office and hailed a cab ten minutes later.

When she walked into the penthouse, she felt it. Ali's presence was palpable even when she wasn't there. Lane could smell the fresh floral scent of her hair and her skin…oh that skin. Lane's fingers twitched involuntarily. No one had ever been here, in her sanctuary, until Ali. Inviting her to share it with her, though, had seemed as normal as anything in her life. Not that she had much normal in her life.

She dropped heavily onto the couch, watching the shadows on the buildings across the street stretch toward nightfall. *How did I get here? How did I fall, so hard, so fast, for a woman I knew so little about? Still know so little about.* A woman who could turn everything she'd worked for since her mother died into a raging inferno.

She shook her head. The fact was, nothing mattered in her life now as much as sharing it with Ali did. When she thought of the petite blonde, her heart swelled so much she thought if she pressed on her chest it might explode inside her.

"Oh, God," she groaned. Was she falling in love? "Fuck."

She stood abruptly, pacing to and fro in front of the windows, contemplating the goals her father had set for her. Was she prepared to give up her dream of achieving them? She might have to, because she certainly wasn't prepared to give up Ali.

She'd have to find a way to make having both of them work. If anyone could do it, she decided, she could. She was Judge Lane Stanford. She wielded power equal to any man, and she was resourceful to a dangerous degree.

As she returned to the couch, she noticed one of Ali's sketchpads leaning against the end of it. Feeling slightly guilty, but unable to forget what she'd seen in there before, she picked it up, sat down and flipped open the cover. To her untrained eye, it looked like doodling, but in the corner of every page, in Ali's precise handwriting, was a date, her name and a notation about something like texture or contrast.

Her breath caught in her throat when she flipped to the next page and found herself looking at a pair of light-colored eyes set in an arrestingly beautiful face. The drawing was only pencil, but Lane could tell by the features and the hair that the woman was African-American, at least partly. She wondered who she was. A model for the drawing class? Only models were that beautiful.

She closed the pad and returned it to its spot, sighing deep and long. She wanted Ali home, not that she was going to be there long herself.

An hour later, changed out of her work clothes into something slinkier, she headed off to an event in support of the women's self-defense league. Maybe afterward she'd have Randall drop her at The Inn so she could sit at the bar and drink until Ali was done working.

As she made her way across the ballroom to where Tara and Carlina were standing, she was stopped every few feet by some well-meaning individual who wanted a few minutes of her time. They were lucky her own self-defense skills were rusty. This wasn't where she wanted to be. She wondered if it was obvious.

When she finally reached her friends, Carlina extended a martini glass toward her. "Here, darling. You look like you need this."

Lane took a breath and pasted on a smile. "It's lovely to see you too, Carlina."

Carlina narrowed her eyes before looping her arm in Lane's. "Come on and let's get you a real drink." When they were at the bar out of Tara's earshot, she asked, "What's going on, Lane? The last time I saw you, you were drinking to drown something. Tonight you look like you're itching to get out of Dodge."

"Honestly, I'm not sure I even know," Lane said, placing her drink order with a cute little redheaded bartender. When she had it firmly in hand, Carlina led her to a tall table sheltered from the noise of the ballroom. "I told you before, you don't have to talk to me, I don't expect you to. But honey, I've never seen you like this. You need to find someone you can confide in." She slid her hand across the table and patted Lane's.

She looked up. "I've met someone. I…I think it's pretty serious, but…" God, she thought, she wasn't sure if she could say this out loud.

"But," Carlina interjected, "it's not the kind of relationship you can allow to become public and still pursue your career aspirations." Lane stared at her in stunned silence. "Oh, darling, don't look so shocked. I've had my eye on you since we met."

"I didn't…I mean…" She shook her head. "I would never have guessed."

"Well, I only had a suspicion, given the attraction I felt for you when we first met. But you know, that's the way it is with femme lesbians like us." She winked. "It's hard to tell." She lifted the martini glass toward her mouth. "Since I have outed myself, you might as well unburden yourself."

"I've met this woman." Lane gave a sardonic laugh. "It doesn't really matter who she is. Hell, it doesn't even matter that she's fucking beautiful because a relationship like that, well, I can't…It would kill everything we've planned."

"'We'?"

Lane took a hearty drink of vodka. "Me and former State of Ohio Supreme Court Justice Weston Stanford III."

"So—you reassess accordingly, reevaluate your options, plan a different course."

Lane laughed again. "As if it were that easy."

"Honey, nothing in life is easy, but sometimes you have to make sacrifices for the greater good."

Lane sighed. "Somehow I don't think my father would accept the sacrifices I'd have to make so I can live my life as I would choose. Actually, I'm pretty sure that if he learned I'm a lesbian, he'd have another stroke."

"You really like this woman?" Carlina kept her voice low.

"I do."

"I can't tell you what to do. I can only be your friend and lend an ear when you need one. And I will."

"Thanks. That means a lot."

Making her admission to Carlina didn't change Lane's circumstances, but she felt a tiny bit lighter when she got home, like part of the burden had been lifted from her shoulders. She still didn't have any answers, but at least she had someone to talk to if she needed to.

She was waiting in bed, propped up on the pillows and trying without success to read a book, when Ali came home. She looked worn out.

"Hi, baby." She placed a brief kiss on Lane's lips. "Back soon. Gonna take a quick shower."

Lane released a contented sigh when Ali went into the bathroom. This was what she wanted. The only kind of life she'd ever really wanted…a happy home.

When Ali returned, snuggling in beside her and stroking her fingers lazily down her abdomen and thigh, Lane kissed the top of her head. "Why don't we save the lovemaking for tomorrow night when I'm sure we'll both be more energetic." Ali gave her a tired smile, kissing Lane as if she had enough strength to devour her, but she was sleeping in a matter of minutes.

CHAPTER TWENTY

Lane wasn't interested in what the speaker at the city's Women in Leadership Group's luncheon was saying. She was daydreaming about what to wear on her date later with Ali. When lunch and the speeches finally ended, she shook an appropriate number of hands, uttered an adequate amount of small talk and rushed out. She still had a late afternoon meeting to endure before she could think seriously about her evening plans. By the time she muddled through drinks—sticking to club soda—in the downtown hotel lounge with yet another bunch of developers, she was more than ready to rid her mind of any and all thoughts of business.

Finally home, she picked out a pair of faded jeans, a forest-green button-down shirt and comfortable pair of loafers. After appraising her image in the full-length mirror, she removed the clothes, returned them to the bed and pulled on jogging pants and a T-shirt. Food, her growling stomach reminded her. She needed to have dinner if she intended to have a drink while they were out. She called for delivery from a favorite Asian restaurant, and forty minutes later was sitting at the counter sampling a new dish the girl on the phone had recommended. She showered afterward, applied a scant amount of makeup and eventually dressed. With one last glimpse in the mirror, she grabbed her wallet and keys and headed for the elevator down to the garage.

She pulled her little sports car out into the night and was sitting across the street when Ali emerged from the restaurant. She was wearing a dangerously short skirt that came barely below the curve of her hips, a tight stretch top that left no question how full her breasts were and ankle boots with three-inch heels. Lane's heart rate doubled as adrenaline pumped through her body. When she went around the building to the parking lot, Lane started the car, easing it into the lot behind Ali's car while she stowed her bag. After Ali climbed in, Lane rolled the convertible around to a dark place in the lot and leaned across the narrow console to kiss her.

"You look simply delectable."

Ali slipped her finger in the front of Lane's shirt, holding her close. "And you look so damned sexy."

"We should probably table this conversation or I'm pretty sure we're not going to make it out of this parking lot."

"I can't help myself. You are so hot."

Lane leaned away from her. "Buckle up, darling, and let's go have some fun." Fifteen minutes later they had crossed the river and were driving south, while they caught up on each other's doings.

"So, they bring in good-looking models for you to draw, right? I mean I always imagined that's what art classes were."

"No, none yet," said Ali. "And if they do have any, I hope they don't pose nude. That would be way too embarrassing for me."

Who did the beautiful face in Ali's sketchpad belong to, Lane wondered, if not a model? And if she were embarrassed by the idea of a nude model, how did she happen to sketch the two drawings of naked women Lane had seen?

"Wow!" Ali commented. "This must be some kind of place for you to drive us so far."

"It's not much farther, about twenty minutes." Ten minutes later she turned off the four-lane route onto a two-lane road.

When Lane turned from that onto a narrow gravel road, Ali asked, "Gosh, baby, are we going to a barn dance?"

"Something like that." Seconds later, out of the darkness, lit only by the car's headlights, an enormous barn appeared.

"You're serious."

"Kind of." Lane threw the shifter into park.

The second she turned off the engine they heard heavy bass music emanating from the barn. It grew louder, loud enough to feel it, when they opened the car's doors.

"C'mon." Lane took Ali's hand as they walked toward the structure. It was wondrous to hold her hand. Lane longed for the freedom to do that whenever she wanted, wherever she wanted.

"Is there some sort of party going on here?" Ali asked as they neared the heavy-looking door set into the front of the barn.

"Something like that," Lane repeated. "And listen, it can be kind of a meat market in here sometimes, get kind of wild, but don't worry—I'm with you…" Stepping up to the door, she released Ali's hand and fumbled with her keys. "I'm with you. I only want you tonight." She inserted a key into the door lock, then looked into Ali's eyes under the faint overhead light and brushed her fingertips over her cheek. "For tonight and longer—for forever—if that's the way life turns out." She turned the key in the lock. "Let's go have some fun."

Inside they were greeted by the thundering sound of techno dance music and the bouncer, a large, very butch woman with short hair, a black T-shirt with rolled-up sleeves, black jeans and black motorcycle boots. She gave Lane a cheeky grin.

"Hey, pretty lady," she yelled over the music. "Haven't seen you here for a very long time." She gave Ali a thorough once-over. "Someone has been keeping you busy, eh?" She nodded her approval.

"Just life," Lane responded.

"Some life," the bouncer said, giving Ali another look and winking at her. "Enjoy your night and remember to drink responsibly."

Lane squeezed Ali's hand. "Come on, let's get a drink and find a table."

Ali looked around, her eyes wide in amazement. And why not? thought Lane. The dance floor in the middle of the space, with its strobing and roving lights, could have been transported from one of the New York City clubs from the disco era. It was surrounded by tables on all sides, and the bar at the end stretched nearly the length of one wall. At the opposite end was an elevated area with intimate seating areas and small tables. Definitely not your average barn.

Lane steered Ali to an opening at the bar and stood behind her. "What would you like?" she asked, her lips brushing Ali's ear.

"You." Ali pushed her hips, which were already moving to the rhythm of the music, back into Lane.

A brunette bartender who looked like she spent as much time working out as Lane spent in court, slapped napkins down in front of them. "Whadaya having?"

"A white wine." Lane considered her choices. "Make that two white wines."

The gal disappeared, returning minutes later with their drinks. Lane slid a twenty across the bar. "Keep it. Thanks."

The brunette nodded. "Enjoy." And like the bouncer, she too winked at Ali.

Taking Ali's free hand in hers, Lane threaded them through the mass of bodies. It didn't escape her notice that many of the young, and even older, women, appeared to be undressing Ali with their eyes. Lane twined her fingers tighter in Ali's and pulled her closer.

"Let's sit up there." Lane tilted her head in the direction of the raised lounge area.

Once seated, Ali took a sip of her wine and leaned close to talk. "This place is amazing. How did you ever find it?"

"I know the owner. We went to school together a long, long time ago. It's private, members and their guests only. Most of us require anonymity."

"So I don't have to keep my hands off of you?" When Lane shook her head, Ali stroked her fingers over her cheek. "Good." She gave Lane a quick kiss. The second it ended the music went from loud and jumping to soft and slow. "Let's dance." She placed her glass down, hopped to her feet, and practically dragged Lane to the dance floor, where she threw her arms immediately around her neck.

"I've been dreaming about holding you like this. I wish there were more opportunities to do it." Lane rested her cheek against Ali's temple, their bodies swaying to the music's rhythm. By the time the song ended, Lane's body was on fire. She caught Ali's hand, intending to lead her off the floor as a fast dance number queued up.

"Stay and dance with me."

Lane dipped her head. "This isn't exactly my kind of dancing."

"Please, baby, just one dance." Ali placed her hands on Lane's hips, rocking against her. "You don't have to do anything but stand there. I'll dance for you."

Ali began a rhythmic grind against Lane's thigh, causing the flame Lane was feeling to burn hotter still. The throb became so intense by the time the number ended that Lane was sure she could come if Ali simply looked at her "that way."

It turned out Ali was feeling the same way. Back at the table Ali wiggled into Lane's lap. "That was so hot," she whispered into Lane's ear. "I think if you kissed me I would come, right here, fully clothed." Her lips curled into a devilish grin. "Come on, baby. Kiss me."

Against her better judgment, Lane cupped the back of Ali's head and brought their lips together in a blistering kiss. A moment later she felt Ali shudder in her lap. The sheer thought of what had happened nearly took Lane over the edge with her.

Ali leaned her forehead against Lane's. "God, baby, I can't believe you can do that to me."

Lane's hand moved down to Ali's luscious backside. She struggled for breath, her heart thundering in her chest to the beat of the music. "I don't think I've ever done that with anyone, not in public anyway. You're the first. The only."

"Mmm...I like the thought of that." Ali pecked her on the lips.

"Renee, darling," a voice above them shouted. "I can't believe I'm actually seeing you. It's been such a long time."

Ali watched Lane's lustful expression eclipse in an instant to one of—well, a look she'd never seen before. She whipped her head around looking for the source of the distraction. Towering over them was a slender blonde in very tight, low-cut jeans that showed a peek of bare belly, complete with a navel piercing not quite hidden under a short-cropped top. She had pale green eyes surrounded by the longest lashes Ali had ever seen, high cheekbones and very full lips. She wondered who the hell Renee was. The woman's gaze was fixed intently on Lane.

"Uh, yes...yes, it has been a long time," Lane finally said.

"Well, I can see what you've been keeping yourself busy with." The woman stroked a long, French tip painted nail over Ali's cheek.

Ali recoiled. She didn't appreciate being touched by a total stranger.

"This is Sandy," Lane told the woman. "We've been together for a while."

The woman took Ali's hand. "It's so nice to meet the woman that reined in Renee. You're a lucky woman, Sandy." Her eyes shifted to Lane's. "She's very beautiful, Renee. Luck is on your side as well."

She stroked her thumb over the back of Ali's hand, another gesture Ali found unsettling.

"So...Renee, do you still like to play?" Neither Lane nor Ali missed the slight thrust of her hips that accompanied her question.

Lane's face turned a deep crimson. "I'm not playing. This relationship is very important to me."

The woman's eyes locked on Ali's. "Such a shame. You look like you'd be fun to play with."

Being leered at like she was a piece of prime rib was making Ali more than a little uncomfortable.

"If you'll excuse us," Lane said, "we were engaged in an important conversation. It was nice to see you. Perhaps we'll see you around."

The woman's seductive expression faded quickly. "Perhaps. It was a pleasure to run into you, Renee, and to meet you, Sandy—" She looked as if she might touch Ali's face again, until Ali glared at her. "So beautiful." She ran her tongue over her glossy full lips. "You ladies enjoy yourselves." With that she slinked off. Ali kept an eye on her until the throng of women enveloped her. She looked at Lane.

"I'm sorry," Lane blurted.

"Who was that woman?"

Lane dropped her gaze. "Honestly, I don't remember her name." Her face colored again. "It was a long time ago, though, I can assure you."

Ali read the discomfort in Lane's expression. She placed a finger under her chin, tilting her head up to see into her stormy dark eyes. "It's okay, baby, we all have a past."

When Lane's eyes met Ali's eyes, Ali hoped she saw in them how much she cared about her—and how little she cared about past transgressions. Apparently, she did. "God," she asked, "how did I get so lucky?"

Ali was about to say something when the music slowed once more. She stroked her fingers through Lane's hair. "Dance with me again."

Lane caught her hand and kissed the back of her fingers tenderly. "Your wish is my command." She pulled Ali tight against her and they started to sway.

Ali wanted this moment, this feeling, to last forever. Wanted them to stay wrapped in each other's arms forever, nothing except the two of them and the soft music.

"Fate," Ali said against Lane's ear.

"Hmm…" Lane murmured.

"It wasn't luck, baby. We were meant to be here."

Truer words had never been spoken, Lane thought. She tightened her arms around Ali and breathed a breath of deepest contentment.

When the number ended and another loud, upbeat song began, Ali grasped her hand and said over the loud drone of bass, "I have to pee. Any idea where the bathrooms are?"

Lane led her past the end of the bar to a short hall. The ladies' room was small and cramped, with three already occupied stalls, one woman waiting ahead of them and a single sink.

When a stall finally opened up, Ali disappeared into it, saying, "I'll wait out in the hall for you." A minute later another stall opened up and Lane went in.

Lane washed her hands in the tiny sink afterward and checked her reflection in the old cracked and peeling mirror. She couldn't remember enjoying herself this much since she and Ali had spent that day at the lake. She realized she was having "fun." The concept was foreign to her or had been since early childhood. This was what life was supposed to be like. Two people, doing things and spending time together, enjoying each other without pressures or expectations.

"Hey," a voice called over her shoulder, "you taking a bath there or what?"

The reflection in the mirror showed who was speaking, a punk-looking, twenty-something with a tongue piercing and a nose ring. She grabbed a paper towel and stepped aside. "Sorry." Lane watched her in the mirror as she dried her hands.

"Well, if you're that sorry you can make it up to me." She turned toward Lane, running her tongue over her bottom lip so Lane could see the stud in center of her tongue. "I'm sure I could rock your world tonight."

A schoolgirl blush warmed Lane's cheeks. At another time in her life, she would have obliged. She wasn't Lane's type, but she was cute with her short baby butch hair, leather vest and tight jeans. Lane tossed her towel in the trash. "I'm with someone, but thanks for the offer."

"Your loss, pretty lady." The gal shrugged.

Lane exited the bathroom—and stopped dead in her tracks. The forgettable blonde from earlier had Ali practically pinned to the wall a few feet away. Lane's hands clenched into tight fists.

Ali caught sight of Lane, her eyes pleading for help. Lane stepped so close behind the woman she could smell the scent she was wearing. She pressed forward until her breasts touched the woman's back and placed her mouth a breath away from her ear.

"I do hope you've not touched her in any inappropriate way. I'm feeling a little hormonal tonight."

The woman stepped from between Lane and Ali and reached up to touch Lane's cheek. "Don't." Lane caught her hand in a death grip. "Whatever we may have shared was a very long time ago. My partner and I are exceedingly happy, so be a lady and leave us the hell alone."

"Relax, Renee." She raised her hands. "I got it." She turned and left.

"Are you all right?" Lane put her arm around Ali. "What did she do? Did she hurt you?"

"No," Ali said, answering only her last question. She rested her head against Lane's chest. "I realize we haven't been here very long, but would you mind leaving now?"

She rubbed her hand lightly up Ali's back. "Let's go." She kept Ali close at her side as she led them toward the exit.

* * *

Ali was quiet on the ride out to the main road. Too quiet, Lane thought. When she'd still not uttered a word twenty minutes into their drive, Lane said, "I'm so sorry about that woman back there." She glanced over briefly to see Ali's shrug.

"Like I said before, we all have pasts." Her tone was flat.

"I hate that you had to be subjected to something unpleasant from mine."

"Not a problem."

Yes, it was. Clearly something was wrong. Lane reached across and settled her hand on Ali's thigh. "I told you that I'd been with a number of women. A fact I'm not proud of. By most standards, I would probably be called a user. I'm…not sure why I became that person."

Was that true? Or was it about power and control, things she'd been taught to admire and desire?

"It's who I was, and it was always about sex. And always understood to be only about that. I'm not that person anymore, Ali. Because of you." She slipped her hand higher on Ali's leg. There was no reaction. No twitches, no tensing muscles, no nothing. Lane glanced over again. Ali was staring blankly at the windshield. She slowed the car, searching for a place to pull off. When she found one, she eased the car onto the shoulder and shifted into park. She unbuckled her seat belt and turned to study her lover.

"What's wrong?" Ali asked finally.

"That's what I want to know. I thought we had some fun back there, dancing, being able to be together, being able to be ourselves."

"Are you sure you were yourself?" Ali asked bitterly.

"Of course." Lane reached out to stroke Ali's cheek, but she drew away. "I am only ever myself with you. Is this about that woman I can't remember?" Lane saw Ali's jaw clench. "She did something to you out in the hallway, didn't she? Please, Ali, tell me what happened."

Ali turned icy blue eyes on her. "You really don't remember her or what you used to do to her, do you?"

Lane dropped her head in self-loathing. "No, regrettably, I don't."

"Well, please, allow me to refresh your memory." Ali's gaze pierced her like a razor-sharp knife. "You fucked her. You fucked her really good, with a big fat strap-on dick that filled her so fully. A man could never hope to compete with how magnificently you fucked her." She couldn't stop her tears. "Is that your plan for me? Get poor homeless little Ali all comfortable and feeling secure with you so you can rape me like a man?"

"Oh, sweetheart." Lane reached for her hand, but Ali jerked it away. "No. Please believe me, Ali, I could never—"

"She doesn't even know your real name, which makes me think I don't either. What do I really know about you anyway? About us? She thought you were going to fuck her silly for the rest of her life. You say I'm going to be yours forever. Why should I believe you? How can I trust you?"

"Please, let me explain," Lane pleaded. A sheriff's car passed them going the opposite direction. "But first, let's find a better place to talk. That was a sheriff's cruiser."

Ali whipped her head around, catching only the taillights of the passing car. She continued to watch behind them as Lane eased them back onto the road, tears continuing to roll down her cheeks.

Lane pulled into a car pool parking lot near the intersection with the highway. At the edge of the lot she shifted the car into park and turned to face Ali.

"First, let me assure you that my name *is* Lane Stanford. Actually it's Elane Renee Stanford. I *am* a criminal court judge. We've already discussed my reasons for remaining anonymous and out of the spotlight. And yes, I've been with a lot of women. More than I could ever hope to recall. I know how 'playboyish' this sounds, but I never did anything with a woman that she didn't invite. You have to believe me, Ali. I may have been less than forthcoming with them about who I am, but I swear to you, I have never physically hurt a woman. I've only ever pleasured them in ways that they wanted. And I would never consider doing any such thing with you if you didn't ask me to. I care for you far too much."

"You didn't care for any of those women in your past?" Although Ali's tone had softened, there was still an edge in her voice.

"No. Not a one of them." She lifted her eyes to meet Ali's. "But when I met you the first time, that night at the restaurant, it was different. You were different from everyone before. *I* felt different than I'd ever felt before." Lane waved a hand between them. "I would have told you eventually. Once I had no doubt that our relationship was unbreakable, I would have told you everything about my past affairs, as despicable as they are. I wouldn't want anything but the truth between us."

Ali reached over and grasped Lane's hand. "I'm sorry," she whispered.

"Shh..." Lane drew her hand to her lips. "Please don't ever be sorry for sharing your feelings with me, sweetheart. I want us to always talk—about anything."

Ali's heart ached painfully and tears welled in her eyes. Not because she was hurt or angry now, but because she was afraid—afraid she may have damaged what they'd begun to build. Fear was quickly replaced by guilt. As she'd said to Lane, everyone had a past. She said a silent prayer that her past would remain there—in the past.

"Let's go home, baby." She pulled Lane's hand against her heart. "I want to show you what you mean to me."

CHAPTER TWENTY-ONE

The ride home was filled with anticipation. They barely maintained restraint as they took the elevator to the penthouse. Once inside the door, though, all self-control vanished.

Lane pulled Ali into a hungry kiss, allowing her to spread her legs as far as the short skirt would allow and grip Lane's thigh between them. While Ali's hips rocked, Lane threaded her fingers into the silky strands at the base of Ali's neck and held their mouths together in a hot tangle of tongues.

Ali slid her hand between them, moaning. "I need to touch you, right now."

"Oh, God, Ali, if you do that again I'm going to come." Lane tipped her forehead against Ali's.

Ali pulled her hand back. "No, baby, not here." She stepped back a pace and tugged her toward the bedroom.

Twenty minutes later, Lane's head was resting gently on Ali's thigh while her hand stroked her other thigh. Ali's muscles twitched under the touch. "So beautiful," Lane murmured.

"Come up here." Ali reached out for Lane.

Lane moved up, stretching on her side and situating a leg between Ali's. Ali pulled her into a kiss, groaning at the taste of her own sweet pleasure on Lane's lips. She pulled back. "God, I feel like I could come all over again."

"Well, maybe you should."

"Uh um." She urged Lane onto her back and sat astride her hips. Lane responded by lifting them and pressing into Ali. Ali watched as desire turned Lane's eyes dark as a starless night sky. She leaned forward, teasing her tongue over Lane's lips.

"Ah...I'm close." Ali moved down her body, but not quickly enough to get her tongue on Lane's clit before Lane grabbed her shoulders. "No," she grunted hoarsely. Ali tried to resist, but Lane pulled at her arms until she moved back up her body.

Ali could feel Lane's body clamoring for release under her, so she pressed her lips to Lane's as she stroked her to orgasm. When Lane relaxed, Ali moved to her side and stroked her fingers over her abdomen, doing her best to keep her disappointment under wraps.

"You make me feel like spending every minute here, like this, with you."

When Ali didn't reply, Lane tipped her chin. "What's wrong, sweetheart?"

"Nothing..." Ali looked away.

Lane rolled onto her side and rose up on an elbow. "Ali," she touched her fingers to Ali's chin again. "Please look at me. You're saying 'nothing,' but there's something in your eyes."

"I..." Ali hesitated, "it's nothing. Forget it."

"Tell me, please."

Ali couldn't possibly look Lane in the eyes and admit to what she was feeling. She rolled to her other side, pushing her back into Lane and pulling her arm tightly around her. "I don't know why you won't let me go down on you."

Lane tightened her arm around her. "Oh, sweetheart, you don't have to do that for me."

Ali let out an audible breath. "I don't want to do that just for you...I want to do it for me too." She felt Lane tense along the entire length of her spine.

"I simply don't want you there...like that."

Ali heard the finality in her voice. It made her heart ache to think she'd never be able to make Lane feel the indescribable sensation she experienced when Lane brought her to orgasm that way. It felt as though she were actually melting into Lane when Lane did it. She'd had enough orgasms to know how one felt, but—never before had she experienced the euphoria in an orgasm that Lane enticed from her with her mouth.

Lane kissed Ali's shoulder. "Tired?"

"Resting a minute. You said we could play all night." She drew Lane's hand to her lips, kissing across her knuckles.

"That I did, but we can take a little break."

"A little one," Ali agreed, snuggling more firmly back against Lane. Lane pulled the corner of the sheet up to cover them before enfolding Ali in her arm again.

* * *

The next thing Lane was conscious of was the sliver of light streaming through a small gap in the drapes. It heated her face, and Ali's body, cocooned against her in the precise spot she'd last remembered them lying in, heated her body. She wasn't aware she'd even closed her eyes as she held Ali after their lovemaking. The arm stretched under Ali's neck was stiff, her fingers tingled and her shoulder screamed to move. She shifted slightly, trying to slip her arm out.

Ali emitted a tiny murmur. "Where you going?" she asked in a groggy voice, pulling the arm Lane had draped over her tightly between her breasts.

"My hand's asleep." She wiggled her fingers.

Ali rose up and turned to face her. "It's morning?"

Lane worked the last of the pins and needles from her fingers. "It appears it is."

"I don't remember falling asleep."

"Me either." Lane smiled. Even with her eyes still heavy with sleep, she didn't think Ali could look more irresistible. "Well, in any case, good morning, beautiful."

Ali kissed her tenderly. "Morning."

Lane gathered her closer. "I'm sorry our time out got cut short last night. We are okay, right?"

"We're okay."

"Are you sure?"

Ali guided her over on her back, positioning herself on top of Lane. Her hips began the familiar movement on Lane's thigh. "You lay right here and I'll show you how okay." She coated Lane's thigh with her wetness as she rocked gently. "Are you sure I didn't wear you out last night?" She kissed up the column of Lane's neck.

Lane chuckled lightly. "Not a chance."

Ali shifted enough to slip her hand between them and pressed her lips to Lane's neck. Lane came fast—too fast. When Ali looked up, her eyes were heavy lidded.

"Good morning again." Ali kissed the corner of Lane's mouth.

Lane's lips curved. "Mmm, allow me to return your wonderful wake-me-up."

"In a bit. How about you make us some coffee now."

"Your wish is my command." Lane stretched before extricating herself from the bed. She grabbed the robes from the bathroom door, tossed one on the bed beside Ali and pulled on the other. "Coffee in five," she called over her shoulder as she headed from the room.

Minutes later Ali stepped behind Lane at the kitchen counter. She wrapped her arms around her waist and pressed her cheek between Lane's shoulders. "I've got to say I really like waking up like that."

Lane turned in the embrace, cupping Ali's face. "I can't seem to be anywhere near you and not want you."

Ali pressed against the length of Lane's body. "You're pretty hard to resist yourself, you know." She stood on her toes to kiss Lane while the coffeemaker gurgled away. When it stopped, she pushed back. "Coffee's ready."

Lane kept her from moving very far. "The coffee's not the only thing."

"Baby, I think you need a cold shower. Don't you have places to be?" She slipped from Lane's arms. "And I have to get my car picked up," She retrieved coffee mugs and poured them each a cup. Lane scowled at her. "But...we don't have to rush yet." She caught Lane's hand and tugged. "Let's take a shower."

After the shower, Ali insisted Lane remain in the dressing room while she took her clothes to the bedroom to dress, saying she didn't trust either one of them to keep their hands off the other and reminding Lane that she had something important to do with her father. They met in the kitchen again over toast and juice.

"I'll drop you by the restaurant to get your car on my way to my father's."

Ali looked lost in thought. "Ali, sweetheart?" Lane watched her intently. "Are you certain everything is okay?"

"Uh...sure, I was trying to figure out what I was going to do today."

The ride was quiet. When Lane reached across for her hand, though, Ali twined her fingers into hers. The contact was comforting, Lane thought, so she didn't question Ali's silence.

When they got to the restaurant the lot was full. Obviously Roscoe's Sunday brunch was a huge success. Lane fantasized about how wonderful it would be if she and Ali could have a leisurely Sunday morning, followed by brunch somewhere like this. They'd have to drive hours away, however, to be able to truly enjoy it, which diminished the romance.

Lane pulled to the exit from the lot and waited for Ali to pull behind her. When she didn't, Lane backed up and circled the lot. Ali was getting out of the car, cell phone in hand. "Something wrong?" Lane called out while lowering the window.

Ali's shoulders slumped. "It won't start. I'm going to call the kitchen guy and see if he can look at it for me."

"You don't need to. I'll call for a tow. I know a good garage." She glanced at her watch. "Let me run you back home."

"You'll be late." Ali walked to the open window. "It's okay." She lowered her voice. "I'll ride the bus back home, baby."

Lane pulled out her phone and a card from her wallet. "You're not riding the bus," she said firmly as she waited for the call to be connected. After giving the information to the towing service, she called the garage and left a message, dropped the phone and card back in her purse and pulled out some bills. "No bus," she repeated. "Call yourself a cab after they pick up the car." Ali frowned. "Please? I'd feel better knowing you're not on a bus."

"Okay." Ali took the money. "Thanks. I'll talk to you tonight."

"I've got to go. Enjoy your day off." Lane waved.

She had to break a few speeding laws to keep from being late to meet with her father, and the run up the front steps left her breathless. Try as she might, she was finding it harder and harder to be as enthused as her father was about their Sunday strategy get-togethers. She wanted to be with Ali on her day off. She wanted to help her deal with the car and snuggle with her on the couch.

Domesticity, that's what she wanted, Lane realized as her father lectured her on what he wanted her to do next. She wanted a home life. A family. That didn't fit into her father's vision for her, unfortunately, and that was the only one that should matter, according to him. Anything else was simply…unacceptable.

She wondered if that was how he had viewed her mother. Whether he would give her the same dark looks she was getting now when she would refuse to be his trophy wife in order to spend her time with Lane. She stood abruptly and raised her hand to her mouth. "I don't feel very well." She rushed down the hall to the bathroom and locked herself inside.

"Damn," she muttered before dropping onto the small vanity chair. If she hadn't left her phone in the car she could call Ali. For a minute, she could hear her voice, could reaffirm that there was more to her life than her father's stratagems and schemes. It was depressing to think their relationship would have to remain in her little dark closet for… well…for forever. She took a few more minutes to compose herself and then opened the door. When she emerged, Miss Clara was waiting.

She immediately put her hand to Lane's forehead and her neck. "You don't feel feverish. That's good. What's wrong, child?"

Lane dropped her head. "I don't want to be here."

Clara cocked her head. "You ain't sick?" Lane shook her head. "Get into my kitchen. I'll be right there." Clara headed toward her father's study. When she returned to the kitchen minutes later, Lane was sitting at the table, her face in her hands. She sat down across from her. "Tell me what's goin' on." Her voice didn't demand, but comforted. This woman truly cared about her.

"I don't know," Lane said through her fingers, answering with her favorite childhood line.

"Tsk." Clara got up and went to the stove. Placing the teakettle on the burner, she retrieved cups from the cupboard. "That didn't work when you were a young 'un and it certainly doesn't now." She turned back to Lane, her meaty hips leaning against the counter. "Does this have anything to do with the person you mentioned before?"

Lane sighed and lifted her head. "I suppose."

Clara nodded slowly, but said nothing.

Lane angled her head toward the front of the house. "He has all these plans for me." She interlocked her fingers in front of her on the table, her thumbs fidgeting nervously. "Plans that don't—and won't—include the kind of personal life I'm interested in."

"You mean like being married with kids?"

"Yes, you know…I think I'd be okay with the whole having kids thing. Being a mother. It's the marrying a man part. That's never going to happen." She shook her head. "I want to share all that with a woman, not the man he expects me to marry someday."

Clara frowned. "Tell him."

Lane snorted. "Oh sure, break his heart and lose the only family I have."

Clara turned back to the stove, fixed the teacups and carried them to the table. She placed her hand on Lane's shoulder as she set the cup in front of her. "You got me, sugar, and you always will." She dropped a kiss on the top of Lane's head.

Lane patted her hand. "Thank you."

"So, this must be pretty serious." She sipped her tea, watching Lane over the cup. "I haven't seen you...so affected by anything in a very long time."

Lane stared into her own cup for a long moment before responding. "Yes. I suppose it is."

Clara gave a slight nod. "You in love with her?"

Lane met her eyes. "I'm not sure I'd know if I were."

"How does she make you feel?"

Lane didn't hesitate. "Like there is no place I'd rather be."

"Yep, I think you've been bitten by the love bug, sugar." Clara smiled across at her.

"You think so?"

"No question about it. What's important now is not to let it slip away." She reached over and placed her hand on Lane's. "You know your momma was head over heels for your daddy when they first met."

Looking back, Lane could only recall how her mother had argued with him every time they prepared to make their getaway to the lake each summer. It was hard to believe there had ever been any love between them. "What happened?"

"Your daddy let stuff become the focus of his life, instead of the woman that was devoted to him. That's why she started taking you away whenever she could. You became the love of her life." Lane watched as a single tear trickled down Miss Clara's cheek. "God rest her soul." She swiped the moisture from her face. "Don't be your daddy, sugar. He's become a malevolent old man. Don't let him stop you from making the kind of family you deserve."

Lane wished she could find the courage to take Miss Clara's advice, could resist the demands that her father and society were placing on her. She could only nod. When the silence stretched too long, she rose from her seat. "I should be going."

"You're always going." Clara cleared the cups away. "You need to come back when you have time for a proper visit—soon."

"I will, I promise." As she snuck out the back door, she reflected on the fact that she didn't even have the courage to leave the way she'd come in for fear of running into her father. District Court Judge

Lane Stanford, age thirty-six and a State Supreme Court justice in the making, was slinking out the service entrance like a child guilty of some unspeakable act. Well, she supposed, as she made her way around the mansion to her car, that was appropriate. If she followed her heart instead of his instructions, that's what she would definitely be seen as in his eyes.

* * *

Her afternoon meeting with cocktails and conversation dragged on endlessly. She finally managed to excuse herself around six. On the drive home, her rumbling stomach reminded her she'd missed lunch at her father's. The thing she wanted, though—more than she wanted food, more than air to breathe—was Ali Castle.

Lane stood in the doorway watching Ali as she lay stretched out on the couch listening to Lane's iPod with earbuds. She had a book open against her legs and her feet were tapping out a beat to the music. Wearing cut-off sweatpants, the ones Lane thought perfectly accentuated her behind, and a cut-off T-shirt, she was nothing short of beautiful.

Lane cleared her throat as she approached to gain Ali's attention. She plucked the earbuds out, dropped the book and jumped to her feet. "Hi, baby!" She moved into Lane's arms. "I missed you today." She pulled Lane closer. "Missed you a lot," she murmured. Her lips brushed over Lane's, the kiss uniting them in a way that was more consequential than simply the touch of two bodies.

Lane pulled back slowly. "I've thought of nothing but you all day." She leaned her forehead against Ali's. Her fingers slipped beneath her T-shirt and brushed over the lace covering Ali's breasts. She felt her nipples harden at the touch.

Ali dragged her to the couch where they hurriedly stripped away enough of the physical barriers between them to explore their swelling passion.

Spent, her mind free of every thought but the exquisite sense of having been completely fulfilled, Lane dropped her head back against the couch. Gazing at Ali, she said softly, "I love you."

She couldn't decide later whether or not she'd made a conscious decision to say that aloud, persuaded by Miss Clara's advice, but it really didn't matter. In the end, she couldn't stop the words from tumbling out. She turned to Ali, trying to gauge her reaction. She didn't necessarily expect her to return the declaration, but she didn't expect what she did see in Ali's eyes. Fear—that was the only way Lane could describe it.

CHAPTER TWENTY-TWO

Ali's mind reeled as she slid naked between the sheets beside Lane. Those three words kept repeating in her mind. Words she'd never heard a woman say to her, and, truthfully, ones she wasn't sure she ever would hear from someone.

She didn't want to think about it anymore. She was wet and she wanted Lane. She positioned herself on top of her, leaning up on outstretched arms. If she moved just so—*yes, right there*—she could touch her clit to Lane's clit. She guessed when Lane grabbed her hips, holding tightly as she thrust up to meet her, that it was pleasurable for her too. Ali's lids drifted closed as she rode Lane until she collapsed onto her chest, spent, sweat coating both their skins.

"I can't get enough of you, baby," she said, trailing her lips along the underside of Lane's jaw, down her neck and very slowly to her breast. Lane groaned in pleasure, signaling the possibility of another climax. When she tried once more to move further down, though, Lane again stopped her.

"No" was all she said.

"You don't like to come that way?" She felt the shrug of Lane's shoulder.

"I've never tried, and we don't need to discuss it any further."

She was on the verge of tears when she rested her head against Lane's chest, listening to the strong steady beat of her heart. She couldn't understand how Lane could say she loved her and refuse to let Ali show her how much she desired her.

* * *

Ali was curled against Lane's pillow when she sat on the bed to kiss her goodbye Monday morning. "Randall will pick you up here to take you to class. He'll also take you into work when you need to go. Just give him the time. I have a late business dinner so I left you cab fare to come home tonight."

"You don't—"

"Please don't argue about this. I have to go." Lane kissed her forehead. "I'll see you later tonight."

Ali dragged her body from bed, tired, but unable to turn her mind off enough to fall back asleep. She was still frustrated about Lane's refusal to let her go down on her. She hoped a long, hot shower would wash away the unsettling feelings, but it didn't help. She ended up sitting at the counter doodling, killing time while she waited for the arrival of her ride to class. Ten minutes before it was due to arrive, she hurried down the back stairs and snuck around the gate arm post in the garage. She was leaning against the corner of the building when the Town Car pulled up.

Lane didn't have court till afternoon and was attempting to clear a few things from her desk. It was a fruitless effort. She kept thinking about last night's admission to Ali.

Jeremy knocked. "That John Woods guy is here again."

It took Lane a moment to recall why her investigator would be here. "Send him in, please." She grabbed the documents spread on her desk, shoving them into their folder.

"Judge," he said by way of greeting as he entered.

"Can I get you anything?" Jeremy stood holding the door.

Lane looked up at John where he stood, clasping a manila envelope in his hand. "No, thank you, I'm fine." She redirected her gaze to Jeremy in the doorway. "Nothing for me either, thank you, Jeremy." She motioned John to one of the seats opposite her.

He sat silently until the heavy door clicked closed, then offered the envelope to Lane. "It wasn't easy, but I found Ms. Castle's missing seven years. She actually spent them right here in our state."

Lane slowly pulled the envelope open, removing its contents. The small photo of Ali that she had provided to John was paper clipped to a form clearly identified as a Department of Corrections document. The color drained from Lane's face as her eyes skimmed it.

Dated more than seven years ago it indicated that one Cassie Allen had been convicted on a charge of second-degree murder in the death of Darrell M. Davis and sentenced to Middleburg Women's Correction Facility. Allen was described as being nineteen, five-feet-four inches tall and one hundred-ten pounds, with blonde hair and blue eyes. It sounded like Ali. She unclipped the pages and looked over the next one in the stack. "There's no Social Security number for this girl."

He shrugged. "She had no identification on her at the time of the arrest. I tracked down the prosecutor, and he said she was a 'nobody.' They couldn't find a thing to corroborate or dispute her claim to the name, no fingerprints in any system anywhere—nothing—so they went with the name she'd given them."

Lane knew from past cases that it was possible for someone to fake an identity if neither their fingerprints or DNA were registered in any databases and there was no one to dispute their claim. Ali was from Indiana, so assuming another identity in Ohio wouldn't be impossible. Which would explain why John hadn't found any criminal record here for Ali Castle.

She knew John was thorough, but she asked anyway. "You went to the facility?"

He nodded. "I showed the photo around and got several confirmations. The girl in that photo is the one they knew as Cassie Allen."

A wave of nausea washed over her. Lane fought the urge to vomit. This couldn't be happening. She loved Ali, had confessed that to her only last night. Only to discover now that she'd murdered someone and spent seven years in one of the maximum security prisons in the state.

She called upon every bit of self-control she possessed. "Well," she said, "my friend is going to be terribly disappointed to learn this information."

"Sorry it wasn't better news." John sounded genuinely sympathetic.

"I'm sure they'll deal with it." She slipped the papers back into the envelope and laid them aside. "Until I hear what they intend to do, let's forget the information you uncovered even exists, okay?" He nodded.

"One more thing…Could you get a copy of the trial transcript and any other evidentiary information available on the case? On the q.t.?"

"That shouldn't be a problem."

"Very well, how much more do we owe you? I'm certain this required a lot of man hours."

"Twelve," he said, a little nervously.

From her wallet she handed him the three hundred in cash that she had. "Stop back later for the rest." He tipped his head. "If I'm not here, I'll leave it with Jeremy. He's here until five." She eyed the envelope, wondering what other bombshells it might hold, then glanced back at him. "Thanks, John. My friend will appreciate all your hard work on this."

"Sure thing, Lane." He stood. "If you need anything else…"

Seconds after he left, Jeremy knocked again. "Everything okay?"

"Everything is fine."

"It's…I don't know." He hesitated in the doorway. "You don't look like everything is fine."

"I have a lot of work, so please shut the door. With you on the other side of it. I'll call you if I need anything. Isn't that what this intercom button is for on the phone?"

He backed away and closed the door.

She slid the envelope in front of her, nausea threatening again as she removed its contents with shaking hands. The photo wasn't the best. Lane had snapped it hurriedly with her cell phone and printed it from the desktop printer in her home office. Maybe that was the problem: the photo was so poor the people John showed it to thought it was this Cassie.

She began to read through the information John had gathered. In addition to the corrections intake form was the document that reported that Cassie Allen had been released from Middleburg eight months ago. The arrest report was there as well. Ms. Allen was found passed out in the victim's room in a fraternity house on the college campus in Alton. The victim's blood was found on her clothing and her fingerprints were on the kitchen knife embedded in his abdomen. The initial autopsy report indicated he had fallen after being stabbed inches from his navel and had cracked his skull on the corner of a heavy wooden chest at the foot of the bed. The actual cause of death was ruled to be blunt force trauma to the head.

DNA on the bed linens indicated that there had been sexual activity. There was also a note made by the intake nurse at the hospital where the girl had been taken for examination. She indicated there appeared to be faint ligature marks on the girl's arms but that no rape kit had been requested or performed. In their report the arresting officers wrote that the girl had kept repeating that she didn't know what had happened or how she'd gotten there. The lead detective on the case had decided that that warranted a trip to the hospital for a psych evaluation.

Lane was still absorbing the information in John's file when her phone rang. "Yes," she answered, her eyes still focused on the arrest report.

"The attorneys for the Curtis case are here and would like a few minutes of your time," Jeremy said.

"Give me two minutes and send them in." She hung up, quickly restacked the documents, shoved them in the envelope and dropped it into her bag. She felt as though she'd been shifted into someone else's body on a completely different world.

The attorneys entered and immediately began bickering about exculpatory evidence. Unable to get her brain to process what she was hearing, Lane finally raised a hand. "Stop! You both are to have your motions on my desk by two p.m. this afternoon. Notify any witnesses that you have scheduled that we'll resume tomorrow at ten a.m. I'll rule on your motions at that time."

The defense attorney started to speak, but Lane again raised a hand. "Save it, counselor. I don't want to hear from you until I've ruled on this matter."

He huffed a sigh and gave his rival a sidelong look. As they exited, she heard him mumble "Bitch" under his breath.

* * *

Thanks to the squabbling attorneys, Lane's afternoon had been cleared. She gathered her things and left, knowing she couldn't possibly get any other work done until she read all the pages John had brought her.

"Court's canceled this afternoon, reconvening at ten tomorrow," she said, stopping briefly at Jeremy's desk. "I'll be back later." She hailed a cab out front. When the cabbie asked where to, she realized she had yet to get the remainder of John's money.

"National Bank." He waited at the curb while she ran inside and made a withdrawal, then dropped her at her home. Retreating to her office, she took an empty DVD case from a desk drawer, fanned the hundred dollar bills inside the top and snapped it closed. She shoved it into the unmarked manila envelope John had given her and secured his paperwork in a zippered compartment in her bag. Licking and sealing the envelope closed she quickly scrawled John Woods' name across it. Hailing another cab, she headed back to the office. She ran back up and deposited the envelope on Jeremy's desk. "Mr. Woods will be returning this afternoon for this. I forgot to leave it on my way out before." She caught one more cab and headed home again.

The penthouse had always been her sanctuary, her refuge, which is why she'd instinctually come here. It wasn't private now, though, was it? She'd opened it up, opened herself up, to a woman she realized now she'd never really known.

She poured a short glass a third full of vodka and swallowed the contents in two large gulps, feeling it burn all the way down. Opening her bag, she extracted the information John had gathered and stared at the photo she'd secretly taken of Ali as they sat on the sofa one night. Focused on the sketchpad that was propped in her lap, she had had no idea that Lane had snapped it.

Lane had barely enough time to get to the sink as the vodka erupted in her empty stomach and came violently back up. She ran cold water, splashed her face with it, then swiped at it with a dish towel. Her makeup was ruined, but what did that matter?

"Fucking idiot!" she yelled as she threw the wadded towel across the room. She leaned against the sink, staring again at the pile of papers from John. One second she wanted to know every detail of Ali's past. The next, she wished she knew nothing of it. She was frustrated and mad as hell.

No, not angry, she realized. Hurt. And feeling utterly helpless.

She grabbed her cell phone, scrolled through her contacts and punched the button. Her call was answered on the second ring.

"This is an unexpected, but pleasant surprise," the low, sexy voice chuckled. "Need a girls' night out?"

"I…" Lane hesitated, suddenly unsure why she'd called Carlina. "Actually, I'm not sure why I'm calling."

"Oh, honey, what's wrong?"

"I'm not certain I know that either."

"Do you have lunch plans?" Carlina asked.

"No." Lane rubbed her thumb over an imaginary spot on the counter.

"Would you consider meeting me for a late lunch?"

Lane pondered whether curling up in her bed and hiding from the world the way she had as a child might not be a better idea than going out somewhere.

"Lane...honey," Carlina said, "why don't we get some lunch?"

"Sure...all right."

Carlina recited the name of a place and asked, "Is one o'clock too late?"

"No."

"I'll see you there."

"Okay."

* * *

Ali waited out in the hall for Jade after class.

"Would you...uh, maybe, I don't know...want to get some coffee?" She nodded her head in the direction of the main door.

"Sure, sounds great." Jade grinned wide. "I wasn't sure you'd even be here today. I didn't see your car in the lot."

"It's in the shop. It kind of died."

"Oh," Jade responded. She was walking with an extra bounce today, though she didn't say much more until they got their coffee and sat at their usual table.

Ali didn't say anything. She'd lost her nerve. Jade might be the only person she really knew besides Lane, but opening herself up to her now seemed like a bad idea.

"I did this amazing sketch over the weekend. I'll have to bring it in to show you sometime."

Ali stared, unfocused, at the cup she cradled in her hands.

"I also got a pet panther."

Ali nodded. "Okay."

"Ali, hey." Jade reached across the table and touched Ali's hand. "What's going on with you today?" She wrapped her fingers around her wrist. "Whatever it is, you can tell me."

Ali swallowed her apprehension and shrugged. "It's nothing. Actually...I'm sure it is. In fact, it seems kind of stupid now."

"It might make you feel better if you talk about it." Jade leaned back in her chair. "Talk to me. It's not your girlfriend, is it?"

"It's not a big deal. Not really."

"I would think anything about a relationship is a big deal."

Ali took a deep breath and lifted her eyes to Jade's again. "When we're...you know in bed—you know..." Ali felt a blush rising in her face. "It's good between us, don't get me wrong. Very good. It's..."

She swallowed. God, why was it so hard to talk about this? Because as a preacher's kid you didn't talk about these things. You didn't even think about them for threat of burning in hell. And Z, well, she had always laughed at how uncomfortable Ali had been about talking about sex when she was so damn good at doing it. She leaned over the table and said very quietly, "She won't let me go down...down *there*, you know."

Jade nodded slightly. "And that's a problem why?"

"I...don't know." Ali fumbled for words. "When we're together it's awesome. It's never felt this way before. It's like she touches a part of me that's never been touched before. And I—I want to make her feel that too, like I do." She shrugged. "I know. That sounds totally lame."

"I don't think anything in a relationship should be taken for granted or left to chance. Talk to her about it."

"She'll think I'm nuts."

"Maybe. Then again, she might not."

Ali shrugged. "Or maybe I should leave it alone. It's not like she can't get off without that."

"I hear some women feel they relinquish too much power if they let someone go down on them. Is she into domination? Maybe she's a control freak. Or maybe..."

"Maybe nothing," Ali said, her face on fire at Jade's lack of inhibition. "I think I'm thinking too much. Let's talk about something else."

* * *

Lane was already waiting when Carlina arrived.

She slid into the seat across the small table, stirring Lane from her daydream. "Oh honey," she reached across, placing a hand over Lane's. "I've never seen you looking so defeated. What on earth is going on?"

"Have you ever been with someone you care so much for, only to realize they're not who you think they are?" Lane raised her weary eyes to Carlina's.

Carlina gave a small chuckle. "I'm sorry. Unfortunately I have, more times than I'd like to admit." They grew silent when the waitress appeared.

When she left them, Lane said, "What I'm about to share with you could come back to bite both of us someday."

"Please." Carlina waved a hand. "I know nothing."

Lane exhaled a slow breath. "Do you remember the beautiful blonde waitress at The Inn the last time we had dinner there? You flirted with her."

She gave a bemused smile. "I remember. She was gorgeous and, I seem to recall, a bit flirty herself. Oh…my." Carlina's eyes went wide. "Oh, darling, it's her you're having this thing with?"

Lane nodded. "Long story short—" she stopped as the waitress delivered their drinks. "I'd never noticed her before, not that she wasn't there. I just never noticed. But that night, when she was taking care of us…" Lane gazed down into her glass, remembering that night. "I don't know." She turned the glass in her hand. "Something happened I can't explain. I couldn't get her off my mind, so I asked her out. It took several weeks of pursuing before she finally said yes." Carlina smiled across at her. "What?"

Carlina curled her fingers around her wrist. "You're crazy in love with her." Lane stared at her in disbelief. "Oh, darling, I can see it in your eyes and hear it in your voice. You are, believe me."

Lane wasn't sure how to respond. It would be stupid not to admit it. Hadn't she told Ali she loved her. Would denying it make it less true? "I do care for her. But she's the last thing I should have in my life right now."

"Don't cheat love, Lane. Does she feel the same?"

She nodded slowly. "I think so, she hasn't said as much, but…"

"But something's happened. Talk to me. Perhaps I can help somehow."

"I don't think anyone can help with this."

"You might be surprised."

Lane leaned in over the table. "Like I said, it could easily come back to bite not only me, but you as well."

"I'm a big girl." Carlina shrugged.

Lane took a deep breath. "I have to be especially careful about whose company I'm seen keeping." Carlina tipped her head. "I saw where she lived after our first dinner date, and it's not a good neighborhood. It was in the warehouse district." She hesitated. "I have to be very careful," she reiterated, "and I *really* wanted to see her again." She smiled fleetingly. "So taking precautions, which are second nature to me, I had a friend from my days on the other side of the bench check her out."

Carlina's expression remained unchanged.

"Turns out she was lying to me about where she was living." Carlina's face finally reflected her surprise. "I know, I know. How stupid can I be? But we'd already been out again. It was hopeless. I couldn't get her out of my head."

"Or yourself out of her pants." Carlina squinted across at her.

"No! We hadn't slept together yet. We didn't do that until our third date."

Carlina leaned close, a tiny smile playing on her lips. "Don't all of us lesbians sleep with each other on the first date and move in together on the second? We may have to revoke your membership card. Really? No sex until the third date?"

Lane nodded. "None. Except for a kiss or two. But we did move in together, in a manner of speaking."

"That sounds interestingly sketchy."

Lane waved a hand. "That's a whole other matter. I kind of have two places."

"Kind of?"

"We're getting off track here and the fewer details you know the better." Carlina sat silently. "When I received the information from my guy everything looked perfectly normal for the life of a twenty-six-year old, except there were about seven years of her life unaccounted for."

"So you asked her about it and she said what?"

Lane shook her head. "I sent my guy on a more intensive search. He came back this morning and accounted for the missing years."

Lane halted the conversation while the waitress placed their lunch salads before them. "Another drink for either of you ladies?"

"Just water, thank you," Carlina answered. When the waitress was gone, she asked, "So?"

"She spent seven years as a guest in our state prison for women." She swallowed hard.

"Oh, God, Lane." The color washed from Carlina's rich complexion. "I'm so sorry...so...oh, honey, you must be devastated. What can I do—is there anything I can do to help?"

Lane swallowed again, fighting to hold the tears at bay. "I..." She nearly choked. Clearing her throat, she tried again. "I don't know what to do." She looked at her trembling hands on the table, watching as Carlina's fingers curled around hers.

"And you're head over heels for her." Carlina's words were soft, but probing.

"Yes," Lane all but whispered. When she raised her eyes to meet Carlina's, she felt a tear roll down her cheek. She didn't care. Her heart ached in her chest. She'd never felt so empty inside, not this empty, even when her mother had died. She swiped at her tear-streaked cheek.

"You should talk to her, Lane, or this will slowly eat you up inside. Maybe she's innocent. It happens, as you well know."

Lane sat silent. Twenty-eight years ago, having barely survived the pain of her mother's death, she'd promised herself that she wouldn't ever give her heart to another soul as long as she lived. And yet, here she was again.

Carlina's voice brought her back. "You have to talk to her, honey."

Suddenly, like a switch had been flipped, her chin lifted, almost defiantly, and her eyes focused on Carlina. "Yes." Her words lacked any emotion. "I'll get answers." She pulled her shoulders back. "After all, that's what I do."

She touched her napkin to her lips and dropped it on the table. "I appreciate your time." She lowered her voice. "And discretion. Thank you." She rose and moved around the table to place a light kiss on Carlina's cheek. "Enjoy the rest of your lunch. I'll take care of the check." She walked off with a confidence in her stride that she didn't feel.

CHAPTER TWENTY-THREE

Lane went home with the intention of changing clothes and taking a nice long drive. Once there, though, she remembered the motions she had to rule on in the morning. "Dammit!" She hurriedly reapplied her makeup and drove to the office. Jeremy looked up as she approached.

"I'm not here to stay. I need the motions from the Curtis trial attorneys."

"They're on your desk. What is going on, Lane?" His question startled her. "You look terrible."

She picked up the folders and spun around abruptly. "What is going on? How about none of your goddamn business, Jeremy?" She brushed past him, then paused in the doorway. "I'll be back in the morning for court. If there's anything on my calendar for this evening, you'd better get busy and get it canceled, because I *won't* be showing up for it." She left.

Her car didn't take her away from the city as she had wanted, but to one of the highest points in the city instead. The park there held the city's conservatory, a history museum and any number of quiet out-of-the-way spots where a person could easily lose herself. After locating such a place, she grabbed her bag and walked the short distance from the parking area to a nearly secluded picnic table that was situated in a stand of towering old oak trees. Clad in an expensive suit, she wasn't dressed for an outing, but she brushed a hand across the bench and sat anyway.

She pulled out the half-inch stack of papers John had brought and unclipped them, glancing again at the photo on top before flipping it over and laying it aside along with the corrections intake form and the release form. The arrest report which followed was the most disturbing of the documents she'd scanned at her office. Evidence pointed to sexual activity between the man and woman, and the woman had evidence on her that indicated that she had perpetrated the stabbing. She was otherwise unharmed. The only reason for taking her to the hospital was because she kept claiming to not know or remember what happened, where she was or what day it was.

Lane's skin prickled again when she read the nurse's note that indicated the woman's wrists had visible ligature marks. And yet no physical examination had been performed, including one to determine whether the sexual activity had been consensual or forced. Nor were there any blood tests to check for drug or alcohol use.

She flipped to the following page, which contained only information on the court proceedings. "Slam dunk," she muttered aloud. An assistant DA had seen the opportunity to close a case quickly with a conviction and hadn't bothered to look closely at anything that didn't fit his scenario.

It didn't make any sense. Ali had grown up in a small town in Indiana, had gone off to a college in the same state and yet somehow had ended up in a college town hundreds of miles away, with evidence of a possible homicide on her person and no memory of what had happened. Or so it appeared. It made Lane furious. She roughly shuffled the papers, shoved them into her bag and headed for home.

When she plugged her phone in the charger in the kitchen, she saw a note on the counter that she must have missed earlier. She forced herself to the opposite end of the counter where she made herself a drink. Then, glass in hand, she picked it up.

"Hi, baby! I wanted you to know how much I liked going out with you over the weekend. Last night was something else. I miss you." Lane took a drink and fought back tears. "I can't wait to be in your arms tonight. Yours alone, Ali."

In one more gulp, she finished the drink and closed her eyes against the persistent, consuming pain in her chest. "Ali, who are you?" she whispered.

After making another drink, she carried it, along with the trial motions, back to her home office and forced herself to sit at the desk. She could blow off charities, fund-raisers and any other kind of obligation someone had seen fit to commit her to, but she couldn't ignore her responsibility to the people she was elected to serve four years ago. She immersed herself in the documents. This is what she did—who she was. She wasn't some mush-minded, hormone-driven woman, as her father would have so crudely put it. She was Judge Lane Stanford, and she conducted every aspect of her life with unwavering resolve.

Several hours later she finished. She should probably eat something. When she met Carlina for lunch, she'd left her food virtually untouched. The thought of food wasn't enticing, but her rumbling stomach reminded her she needed something in it if she intended to have another drink. She opened her newly well-stocked refrigerator and pulled out a cup of yogurt, a package of cheese and a luscious-looking red apple, then set about cutting cheese and the apple on a cutting board she had never used before. Piling a plate high with the food, she carried it to the living room. She made another drink, grabbed her bag and returned to the living room to watch the city slowly turn in for the night.

She ate several spoonfuls of yogurt before removing the now familiar stack of papers. Flipping over the pages she'd reviewed earlier, she focused on the first of the many handwritten pages John had compiled for her, complete with dates and times. Once a cop, always a cop, she mused, as she read his interviews with several prison officials and more than a dozen inmates who knew Cassie Allen.

The warden had declared Ms. Allen to be a "perfect inmate." A corrections officer had confirmed the warden's statement, adding that they, the COs, had given the young woman the nickname of "Quiet Cassie," but the inmates called her "Al." She never caused a moment's trouble and seemed to get along with every other inmate without any problems. She wasn't ever a disruption to the order of things, conformed without question and was always respectful to the officers and other personnel charged with running the facility.

She read through his interviews with numerous other prison officials and inmates. Each one said Cassie was a sweet girl—considerate and polite. No one mentioned that Cassie had ever made the claim that she was innocent, as nearly all convicted felons did.

The last interview John had documented was with a "lifer" by the name of Zelda Reese. She too agreed that Cassie Allen was a sweet girl, never made trouble and seemed to know her place in the order of things. John had also noted that the hard-edged, rough-looking woman with muscles that exceeded his own, had winked at him and said, "Yep, she could be a real pistol, that Al." John wrote that he took the comment to mean that while incarcerated, this Zelda and Cassie had spent time together in a "conjugal" way.

John's notes about Zelda sent a shiver up Lane's spine. Her gut feeling was that Ali might in fact be innocent, as Carlina had pointed out. Zelda, however, appeared to be a hardened felon, a bad egg. It was all too easy—and stomach-turning—to imagine her preying on someone like Ali. Oh God, Lane thought. Had she been Ali's "someone?"

* * *

The sound of the door lock snapping closed and the clink of keys on the table sent Lane's eyes searching for the wall clock. It was going on ten. She shoved John's report into her bag a moment before Ali entered the room.

"Hey, baby." She gave Lane that killer smile and dropped on the couch beside her.

"Rough day?"

Ali exhaled a long, audible breath. "The longest." She reached for Lane's hand, sliding her fingers between hers and curling them under.

Lane looked at their conjoined hands. Warmth enveloped her, as it always did when Ali touched her. Closing her eyes, she forced herself to raise their hands and lightly kissed the back of Ali's. "Why don't you shower, I'll clean up my mess here, and we'll meet in bed."

"That's the best thing I've heard all day," Ali said as she popped up and headed down the hall.

Lane wanted to run. Run as far away as she could get from her present mess of a life. She had no idea how she could lie in bed with Ali. As she carried the remains of her dinner to the kitchen, the words of one Zelda Reese, incarcerated by the state for life, replayed in her mind, the ones declaring Cassie—Ali—a "pistol." The few bites of food she had consumed for dinner tumbled violently in her stomach.

She dressed in silk pajamas and slid beneath the sheets. Ali returned a short time afterward, one towel tucked closed between her breasts, the other draped over her shoulders. She skimmed her fingers through her wet hair, watching Lane's eyes as she dropped first the towel from her shoulders, then the one wrapped around her naked body. She hesitated a long moment before climbing beneath the sheet, pillowing her head against Lane's shoulder and resting her arm across Lane's waist.

"Feel better?"

"Mmm," Ali responded, skimming her hand under the silk of Lane's pajama top. "Bet we could both feel better." Lane trapped her hand before it could move much farther.

"I'm completely beat tonight, Ali. Can we go to sleep?"

"You okay?"

"I'm fine, sweetheart. Just really worn out." She kept her tone light, carefree.

"Hold me?"

"Of course." Lane wrapped her arm around Ali, hoping to convey somehow the sense that everything was right in the world—with both of their worlds. It seemed to work. Ali drifted quickly to sleep.

She didn't. Her mind kept replaying the words she'd read and reread earlier. Especially the comments made by that crude Zelda woman. Had she held Ali in her arms the way Lane was now doing? Or had she just taken what she wanted? Did Ali call her "baby"? Did she come for Zelda the way she came for Lane?

The images the questions conjured in her head wouldn't stop, causing her stomach to once again roil violently. Quickly extracting herself from Ali's hold, she ran to the bathroom. There, over the porcelain bowl, she vomited the limited contents of her stomach. She continued to heave even after her stomach was empty, gutted by the pictures running riot in her mind.

The knock was gentle at first. Lane flushed and heard it again, more assertive this time.

"Baby, you okay?" Ali's voice was soft, sleepy and caring.

"Yes," Lane croaked, her throat raw.

"I..." Ali hesitated a moment. "I don't think you are. I'm coming in."

Lane, too weak to stand, fell against the wall and grabbed a towel from the bar above her head. She held it to her nose and mouth, hoping the floral scent of laundry soap would stop the nausea in her stomach.

"Baby." Ali knelt beside her, stroking Lane's sweat-covered forehead, brushing the hair from her face. "You're sweating, you're sick." She stood, grabbed a washcloth, soaked it in cold water and knelt again. "Let me take care of you." She ran the cloth tenderly over her face. Lane closed her eyes. Ali's voice was a soothing caress. She gently ran the cloth behind Lane's neck, under her hair.

Lane was reminded suddenly of childhood and her mother. Of how tenderly she had always taken care of Lane.

And of how suddenly she had left her. The person here now who spoke so softly, professing to care, she would leave Lane too. She was no ministering angel. She was a woman who had sex with convicted criminals. A woman who was a convicted criminal herself. Her stomach roiled again.

She grabbed for the wet cloth. "I'm fine." She injected a strength into her voice that she didn't feel. "Must have been something I ate." She got off the floor, praying that her legs would hold her. "Go back to bed. I'll be there in a minute."

Ali turned hurt eyes to Lane's in the mirror. Lane held her gaze only a second before leaning over the sink and turning on the water. Once Ali was gone, she splashed cold water on her face, brushed her teeth and stood several long minutes staring at her reflection. She had always been a force to be reckoned with, someone who exuded strength and unwavering self-confidence. And here she was, brought low by a woman she cared for with all of her heart—but didn't really know. She barely recognized herself.

Ali lifted the sheet when she returned to the bedroom. She forced herself to relax and clear her mind as she slid beneath it. Ali reached for her, guiding Lane's head to her breasts. "I'm worried about you." Ali stroked Lane's hair. "You never seem to even get the sniffles."

"I'll be fine."

"Are you…are you mad at me about last night?"

Last night? Last night, they'd made love and she had fallen into slumber, completely sated and happy with life. She'd awakened feeling the same way. No, last night all had been right with the world. It was today that everything had come crashing down around her.

"Why would I be mad at you about last night?"

"I…I thought maybe…I don't know…you're mad because I keep trying to love you the same way you love me—you know…down there."

Before today Lane would have chuckled and made passionate love to Ali to prove she was happy with the way things were between them. She was guarded now. She couldn't afford to have anything more unravel in her life.

"No, sweetheart, I'm not mad at you for that." She lifted her head to look in Ali's eyes. Even in the dim light, she could see the familiar sparkle in them and the innocent solicitude they also had. Ali stroked her fingertip across Lane's cheek, bringing it to her lips where she let it linger. Lane couldn't breathe.

Ali's voice was a whisper. "I love you...I want to take care of you." She replaced the finger resting on Lane's lips with her own lips. The kiss—tender, soothing—underscored the words Ali had just spoken.

Lane felt the truth in Ali's words in every part of her soul and, desperately wanted to believe that Ali's love would make everything right again in her world. She tried to relax in her embrace.

"Go to sleep, baby, so you'll feel better in the morning." She guided Lane's head down again to be pillowed on her breasts, continuing the light caress up and down her back until Lane fell asleep.

* * *

Lane only slept a few hours before waking, still in Ali's arms. She tried to return to sleep, but pieces of the day kept tumbling through her mind. After an hour she slipped from the bed. Ali murmured but didn't wake. She walked to the living room and stared into the black night. It was two a.m., and unlike her, the city beyond the penthouse windows was sleeping peacefully.

She exhaled long and slow, then wandered into the kitchen. She couldn't drink. She had to be in court in eight hours, and, well, she admitted to herself, she'd been turning to alcohol too often of late, trying to escape...something. Grabbing a bottle of water and her bag from beside the front door she went to her office.

One more time she pulled out the papers that John Woods had gathered and scanned them once again. The arrest information kept nagging at her. The assistant DA's case was based almost entirely on circumstantial evidence. The police investigation had been full of holes. The suspect had been held for over eight hours in a tiny cramped room, interrogated off and on during that time.

The result, Lane suspected, was a coerced confession, followed by a plea deal for a charge reduced from murder one. With the right cop handling things, it was easy to see how a scared and very confused nineteen-year-old might be convinced she'd done what they kept telling her she had.

Lane couldn't picture Ali as a murderer. The name change was perplexing, of course, and more than a little concerning. Even that, though, could have a plausible explanation.

"Baby..."

Lane's head snapped up. Ali, sleepy-eyed and clad only in the blouse Lane had taken off earlier and forgotten to hang up, was yawning in the doorway. Lane quickly gathered the papers of the report and placed them upside down on the desk.

"I know what you do is very important, Lane, but…I saw the vodka bottle on the counter when I stopped home between class and work. I'm worried that working this much is going to make you sick. Or worse." She rested her hands on Lane's shoulders and kissed the top of her head. "What's going on, baby? Tell me how to help. I need you to stick around, you know."

Lane shut her mind down and allowed herself to feel. Her heart to search. Ali's touch to reach inside her.

She's no murderer. She's not. She's the woman I love.

"I'm sorry I woke you," she said hoarsely, overwhelmed with emotion. She took one of Ali's hands and placed a soft kiss in her palm. "Go back to bed, sweetheart. I'll be right there. Promise."

As Ali drowsily made her way back to bed, Lane secured the documents in her home safe. She didn't need to look at them anymore. Everybody had a past. If Ali was guilty of anything, it was of being too naïve to know she was being taken advantage of, being railroaded.

Lane shed her pajamas before climbing in bed this time. Ali rolled against her and wrapped an arm around her waist. "You feel so good right here. Get some sleep, 'kay…?" Lane settled back into the pillows, her eyes already heavy. Her heart finally felt at peace.

Movement beside her startled Ali out of a deep sleep. Lane's body was jerking violently, and her deep, low voice was repeatedly crying out the word "no."

"Baby." Ali gently shook Lane's shoulder before flipping on the bedside light. "Baby," she repeated softly. Lane slowly opened her eyes. "Lane…what's wrong?"

"I…" Lane scrubbed her hands over her face. "Bad dream." She shook her head.

Placing her hand on Lane's chest, Ali felt her heart thundering beneath it like the stampede of racing horses. "God, you're trembling. What on earth were you dreaming about?"

Lane pulled her close, pressed her face into Ali's neck and took several deep breaths. "You…" She stopped and tried again. "Someone had you. They were holding you and hurting you…" Lane's body shook violently. "You were calling for me to help you. And I…I couldn't get to you…couldn't protect you, keep you safe." She was nearly crying. "I'm so sorry…"

"Shh." Ali held Lane to her, rocking her gently. "I'm fine." She squeezed Lane tighter. "Feel me. I'm right here, and as long as I'm with you, I'll always be safe."

Ali felt the warm wetness of Lane's tears on her skin. Lane, this big powerful woman, was as vulnerable as she herself felt at times. "It's okay, baby. We're here together, and no one is going to hurt us." Ali wanted to believe her words of assurance more than she had ever wanted to believe anything in her life. Lane finally drifted off.

CHAPTER TWENTY-FOUR

Lane woke the next morning feeling as though someone had poured sand under her eyelids. She'd slept little after her nightmare, which had not been exactly as she described it to Ali. Someone had had Ali, all right. A very large, burly butch who had one arm wrapped tightly around Ali's waist and with her free hand was exploring Ali's body, finally landing between her legs. Ali had cried out for help, called for Lane to save her. But Lane couldn't move, and the beast of a woman had pulled her farther and farther away.

Standing under the shower spray now, she allowed its hot beads to beat away at her exhaustion, hoping it would also pound the dream out of her thoughts. She pressed her hands to the tile and rested her forehead between them. *Let it go*, her mind repeated over and over. "Let it go," she muttered aloud.

"Baby, you okay?" Startled by Ali's voice, Lane pushed off the shower wall and turned too quickly, almost losing her balance. Ali stepped into the shower and caught her around the waist. "Lane, baby, I think you're really sick. You need to go back to bed."

Lane braced one hand against the wall and the other on Ali's shoulder. "I'm okay. Really." She removed her hand from Ali's shoulder and ran it through her wet hair.

Ali reached around Lane to turn the water off. She was soaked to the bone and the clingy wet fabric of Lane's discarded pajama top accentuated every curve—and two noticeably hard nipples.

"I'll be okay after I've had coffee and something to eat." Lane kissed Ali's forehead. "I have to go. I have court this morning."

"I'm seriously worried about you."

Lane cupped Ali's face. "I'm okay. I promise." She reached behind Ali, plucked a towel off the bar and wrapped it around Ali. "Go back to bed, sweetheart. It's incredibly early and you couldn't have gotten too much sleep either."

"I'm fine." Ali grabbed another towel and pressed it into Lane's hands. "Finish getting ready. I'll meet you in the kitchen." She got out and peeled off the wet pajama top, preparing to slip into one of the robes hanging on the door.

Lane's eyes fastened on Ali's naked body. For everything she'd gone through in less than a day's time, emotionally and physically, she couldn't suppress the swell of arousal that the sight caused. She dressed and, feeling only mildly steadier, made her way to the kitchen. Ali—sans makeup, hair pulled back loosely at her neck and wearing only an oversized robe, its sleeves pushed up to her elbows—was one of the most beautiful things Lane had ever seen.

She stared at her, transfixed, knowing that whether or not everything else would work out, she would never want another woman this way—with every piece of her being. She slipped behind Ali and pressed her mouth to the side of her neck.

"Oh!" Caught unaware, Ali pushed back into Lane's body. "You shouldn't do that. You might not get the kind of breakfast you need."

"What makes you think this isn't what I need?" Lane nuzzled her neck.

"You need food." She turned in Lane's arms and looked closely at her. "The makeup helps, but you still look like you're not well."

"You look tired yourself. Why don't you go back to bed?"

"I'm up. I might as well get something done." She pecked Lane on the lips before slipping away. "Eat your breakfast. I'm going to make the bed."

Lane added another splash of coffee to the cup sitting there to warm it up and started in on the toasted muffin Ali had made for her. It was sitting fairly well on her iffy stomach—until she glanced at the newspaper that Ali had brought in from the hall. "Criminal Trial of Harold Baker to Begin in Six Weeks" read the headline. It was followed by a statement from the district attorney's office's lead prosecutor Anita Carson: "Baker Contract Construction's complicity in the deaths of two infants when the childcare center's roof collapsed under the heavy snowfall isn't what is in question in this case. What is in question is when big business will stop putting profit above building codes and the safety of human life."

Lane decided to read no further. There was no point in thinking about the Baker situation until she had to. She finished the muffin, set her cup in the sink and went to find Ali. She found her curled up and snoozing on the half-made bed. Smiling, she walked quietly to the bedside and kissed her on the temple.

"Oh, shoot." Ali jerked awake. "I just sat down for a minute. I nodded off?"

"It's okay, sweetheart." Lane pulled the corner of the comforter over her. "Go back to sleep. I'll see you tonight."

Today was going to be a better day than yesterday, Lane decided as Randall drove her to the office. She'd make it so. And she did, upbraiding Jeremy when he nagged her again about her activities and less than sharp appearance and showed unjustifiable interest in the package that she had left with him for John Woods to pick up. There was an extra spring in her step as she walked through the courts building and renewed verve in her voice as she made her ruling on the submitted motions and testimonies began again. The morning flew by.

During a break she powered on her phone to find a missed call and voice mail from Ali that explained that the garage called and her car was ready. She intended to have Randall drive her there after class to pick it up before she went to work. She was going to work out a payment plan to pay for the repairs. "I miss you, baby. I hope you feel better when I see you tonight." Lane gave a contented sigh.

* * *

Ali wanted to thank Jade for her advice the day before, but she wasn't in class. When she arrived at the garage, she found the charges for her car's repair had already been taken care of. Killing time at the penthouse before she had to be at work, she decided to clear out some of the stuff that had been hurriedly stashed in the guest room when she moved in. She carried a bag with sketchpads, other drawing supplies and a small box with a few brushes and paints down to the apartment, making a mental note to ask Lane where she preferred Ali to keep them.

Lane let the afternoon session run late, hoping Jeremy would be gone when she got back. Unfortunately he wasn't. He was standing beside his desk, arms crossed over his chest. "I would have come and found you, you know."

Lane sighed. Lady Luck wasn't smiling on her this afternoon.

"Your father has called three times to remind you that you are meeting him for dinner this evening. He did not sound happy. I'm no psychic, but I'd guess it has something to do with your canceling with Mr. Beckman at the last minute last night."

Lane thought the use of "Mr." in front of Beckman's name was an abuse of the title. Thomas Beckman was anything *but* a man to be respected. She snatched the messages from his hand. "Don't worry. I will be seeing my father for dinner."

"And Beckman?"

"I haven't decided. Has his office been bugging you?"

"No."

"Then don't worry about it, Jeremy. Go home."

She tossed the first three messages, the ones from her father, into the trash. Four others couldn't be returned until the morning, and the last one was from Emily, reminding her of a charity affair the next day that she'd agreed to go to months ago. She dropped into her chair with a deep sigh. Dinner with her father tonight, charity something tomorrow night, it was always something. When would it ever end?

Her phone rang as Randall pulled them into the evening rush hour traffic. She was pleasantly surprised to see it was Ali calling. "Good evening," Lane answered.

"Oh, God, baby. That voice of yours makes me want to reach through the phone and touch you."

"Darling, please, please refrain from saying things like that. I'm on my way to meet my father for dinner."

"I was on my break and took a chance I'd catch you. Seems the car fairy paid to get my car fixed." Lane chuckled. "Thank you, but you shouldn't have done that."

"I wanted to."

"Well, anyway, thanks again."

"You're very welcome."

"Do me another favor?"

"Certainly."

"Could you tell your father not to ruin your mood tonight, please?"

Lane wanted to laugh at the utter absurdity of Ali's request. *As if...*

"I'll try not to let him get under my skin. I'll save that for you, sweetheart."

"Mmm." Ali's voice purred through the phone and into Lane like warm honey. "I'm going to be walking around all evening now thinking about that."

Lane thought that was only fair since now she'd be walking around throbbing as well. "I'll see you later."

"I'm closing tonight."

"Okay."

"Bye, baby."

There was no way Lane was going to allow her father to ruin her night. She was happy...yes, that's what she was feeling. She leaned down and kissed his cheek. "Hi, Daddy."

"I'm not sure what you're so happy about. Sit," he waved a hand, "we have important things to talk about."

The waiter appeared to take her drink order. Weston sat there stoic, swirling the amber liquid around the ice in his glass. He started on her the second the waiter left her drink.

"You canceled on Thomas Beckman again last night. Your career is going to go straight to hell in a handbasket if you don't start taking care of things." He held up his hand to stop her from talking as he had when she was a child. "I don't care what kind of excuse you have to offer, Lane. I haven't been working to connect you with the individuals who will help further your career for my health, you know. And you think what—having a date or God knows what—is more important than what we're trying to accomplish? More important than meeting with someone as powerful as Tom Beckman?" His hand shook as he pointed a finger at her. "You're screwing up."

Lane's anger, which had been simmering since he started in on her, began to boil. She could feel the heat of it in her cheeks. She swallowed a gulp of vodka for courage and leaned over the table so she wouldn't have to raise her voice. "For your information, Dad, Thomas Beckman is a creep. And though I'm being forced to deal with him, it's going to be on my terms." His mouth dropped open. "As a matter of fact, from here on out I'm taking charge of my career myself. I'm not

going to be bullied or railroaded into anything, anymore, by anyone."
She pushed back from the table. "Thanks for the drink, Dad. I've lost
my appetite for dinner." She was gone before Weston Stanford III
could utter another word.

Lane was preparing to call a cab when she spotted Randall in the
Town Car half a block down the street. She heard the baseball game
on the radio through the open driver's window as she let herself in the
back.

"I'm sorry, ma'am. I didn't expect you so soon."

Lane tossed her purse across the seat. "Seems everyone's
experiencing the unexpected this evening. Especially my father. I'm
definitely going to be written out of the will after tonight. I'd bet my
Social Security on it."

"Uh, yes, ma'am. Where to next?"

"Take me home, please."

"Certainly, ma'am."

Lane sat forward and spoke over the noise of the drive. "Do you
have children, Randall?"

"Yes, ma'am."

"How old?"

"Thirty-eight and forty-seven, ma'am."

"And do you still treat them like children?"

"No, ma'am, even though the oldest still acts like he's twelve years
old. The missus and I didn't think we were going to have any more
after him. She spoiled him terribly. The younger one is much more
mature."

She leaned back. "I bet you're a great father too."

"Ma'am?"

"Nothing...talking to myself."

Lane tried to decide whether she cared if her father spoke to her
again. He had been doing this to her since her mother died, cajoling
and coercing her to do things she was supposed to believe were for
her own good, for her future. She doubted all of that now. By the time
Randall pulled up in front of her building, she had convinced herself
that she wasn't going to do it anymore.

"Sit tight," she told him. "I'll let myself out. Have a good evening."

"Have a good evening yourself, ma'am."

The second she entered the penthouse her cell rang. She checked
the caller ID and sighed. "Hello, Car."

"Goodness, you don't have to sound so thrilled," Carlina said
sarcastically. "I wanted to check in and see how you're doing."

Lane dropped her purse and bag inside the door and dragged her tired self to the living room couch. "If you'd asked me, oh, maybe an hour ago, I would have told you life is good."

"And now?"

"Well, I may have tanked my future, among other things."

"How so?"

"I pretty much told my father off."

"Wow! Well, in your defense, Your Honor, I'm sure you had a very good reason." She laughed lightly.

"I believe I did. God, Car, he treats me like I'm eight years old, not thirty-six, and incapable of making my own choices."

"I assume you're talking about your personal life choices?"

"Are you kidding? He thinks I shouldn't have a life outside of this career he has all mapped out for me."

"So he doesn't know about your 'lifestyle'?"

"Oh, hell no! He'd probably have another stroke."

"Well, speaking of your lifestyle, that's why I called. Have you spoken to your mystery woman and worked things out?"

"No." Lane headed to the kitchen to fix a drink.

"What aren't you telling me?" Carlina asked.

"I probably won't."

"Won't what?"

"Talk to her."

"So you're going to throw away the potential love of your life?"

"Oh no. No. I'm going to throw away what I know about her past—forget it."

"You think, all things considered, that ignoring it is a wise move?"

"Car, she loves me and I love her. You can't fake what's between us. I don't want to jeopardize that."

"By letting her know you had her checked out."

"That too." Lane sipped her drink, heading back to the couch.

"What else?"

"I'm afraid she'll decide she shouldn't be with me because of it, that her past is going to harm me. I can't..." Lane pressed her hand to her chest. The thought of losing Ali made her heart hurt. "I can't lose her. I'll sacrifice everything else I have if that's what it takes to keep her."

"Oh my, you truly are head over heels for her, aren't you?"

"A total goner. I'd give everything up this minute if she asked. Hell, I'd become her slave if she wanted me to."

"You mean sex slave?" Carlina laughed.

"Sex slave, house slave, any kind of slave she wanted." Lane laughed too. "Yes, I love her that much."

"Well, darling, you are one of the smartest women I know so I'll trust that you know exactly what you're doing."

"Actually, Car, I'm stumbling along in the dark…following my heart. I have never felt this way before in my life."

"In that case, dear friend, I wish you and your heart well."

"Thanks."

"This isn't going to keep you from our monthly singles clique meeting, is it? After all, Em's married and she still sticks around."

"No, I'll still join you gals for the monthly dish." They laughed together.

"All right. I shall see you at the next one, if not before."

"Have a good evening, Car. Thanks for checking in on me."

"You're my special friend, darling. I'm only sorry the beautiful blonde caught your eye before I could."

They ended the call, which Lane was grateful for, considering Carlina's last comment. Could it be that Carlina had actually wanted something more with her?

Back in the kitchen she fixed another drink and something to snack on since she'd abandoned dinner with her father. *God, he'll probably never speak to me again.*

As she worked on her second drink of the evening, she asked herself if she really cared that much.

As she went for her third drink, she hoped that Ali got home before she ended up drinking too much.

At eleven ten, when Ali finally arrived home, Lane's fourth drink was long gone, "Hi, baby." She dropped her purse inside the door.

"Hi!" Lane responded with a smile. She was laid back on the couch, legs stretched out across the cushions, wearing comfortable old faded jeans and a front button shirt.

Ali eyed Lane's empty glass on the coffee table as she sat on the edge of the couch, her thigh pressing into Lane's. "Did you start the party without me?"

"Nope, no party, just waiting on you to come through that door."

"I've got to shower."

"I could help." Lane smiled again.

Ali pressed a hand on Lane's shoulder when she stood. "No, you stay right here. I'll be back before you know it."

Ali disappeared and Lane went to the kitchen to pour herself one more drink, which she absolutely knew she didn't need, and a glass of wine for Ali.

"So now the party's starting?" Ali's voice startled her. She was wearing one of Lane's oxford shirts now and teeny bikini panties.

"Most definitely."

Ali brought her lips to Lane's. The kiss started tenderly but became urgent so quickly that it created a spark in Lane's belly that spread like wildfire. When Ali's hand drifted toward her crotch, however, she caught it. She wanted to go slow. She needed to go slow. Needed to take her time. To feel everything, so she could justify the decisions she'd made regarding what the future would be for them both.

"Whoa," she said, gazing at Ali. "There isn't a fire."

"You wanna bet?" Ali grabbed Lane's hand and pressed it between her legs. "You feel that?" Ali's wetness had already soaked through the thin fabric. "I took a very cool shower and the second I thought about you sitting out here, well…this is what you do to me."

Lane stroked the backs of her fingers over Ali's cheek before putting the glass of wine in Ali's hand. She picked up her own drink. "To memorable nights." Lane clinked their glasses together.

"May we have many more." Placing the glass to her lips, Ali took two small sips before setting both hers and Lane's glasses aside. "I want to come, baby. If you touch me, I will."

There wasn't another thing that Lane wanted more than she did Ali at that moment, and she was certain she would want her like that forever. She pulled her over to the couch and, lying back on the couch cushions, pulled Ali on top of her. She tenderly held her face in her hands. "You are extraordinarily beautiful, Ali Castle."

With a turn of her head, Ali pressed her lips into Lane's palm. "You make me feel beautiful and so many other things I never knew were possible."

Lane smiled. "I hope I can always make you feel that way."

Ali moaned softly as she pressed into Lane. "I want to make you feel things now." Her lips parted.

"You already have." Tears sprang forth in Ali's eyes. "Ah, sweetheart."

"I love you so much." Ali swiped away the tears that escaped.

"I can't imagine my life now without you," Lane said. And she couldn't. She wrapped Ali in an embrace. She'd never known that being in love could be so damn wonderful. "I hope you plan on hanging around for a while."

Ali lifted her head to look Lane in the eyes. "I'm not going anywhere. I think this is where I've always belonged."

They dozed off on the couch, Lane waking hours later when she couldn't move under Ali's weight. She pressed her cheek to the top of Ali's head, shaking her gently. "Ali, sweetie, let's go to bed." They crawled into bed. "Sweet dreams," Lane murmured. Ali answered with a gentle snore.

CHAPTER TWENTY-FIVE

Lane felt like a new woman. Well, not a new one. Simply the one she was sure she was supposed to be. Ali was still sleeping when she reentered the bedroom. Sitting on the bed she lightly brushed back the hair obscuring Ali's face.

"I have to go, sweetheart." She placed a kiss on her temple. "I'll see you tonight."

"Come back to bed." She reached out for her arm.

"I would if I could." She stood. "Have a good day. I'll see you later."

"I love you," Ali murmured.

Lane was warmed from the inside out. She was so crazy in love with the woman in her bed.

Her day was progressing marvelously until right before the noon break when the opposing attorneys began to bicker back and forth again. She called order, once, twice and when they started in for the third time, she called, "Counselors—in my chambers—now!" The second the door was closed they started in again, their voices rising with each word, trying to be heard over the other.

She slapped her palms onto the desktop. "I've heard enough from both of you. You sound like children." She was fed up. "You're both going to submit motions—yes, again—and I want them in my office by five p.m. today. I'll rule on them in the morning." She stood. "And if you pull this crap again, I'm going to slap both of you with contempt charges. This trial should have finished yesterday afternoon, but you two," she pointed back and forth between them, "are trying to turn it into the trial of the century. Are we understood?" They both nodded before returning to the courtroom where she adjourned until the following morning.

Despite the aggravation from the attorneys, she found herself humming. She had a break and knew exactly how she wanted to spend it. From inside a cab, she called the service to cancel her after-work ride. Once home she rushed down to the garage. There'd be just enough time if she bent a couple of speed limits. She found Ali's car in the parking lot and parked across the street from the art school's entrance. Ali would have to walk right past her. They could grab a quick bite somewhere before Ali had to go into work.

The first person to catch her eye as the students began to file out was the beautiful woman from Ali's sketch, the one she'd thought might be a model. Stepping off the walk, she casually leaned against a lamp post a few feet from the door clutching a sketchpad to her chest. A moment later, Ali came through the door. Before Lane could catch her attention, her eyes turned to the beautiful girl, and she smiled and went over to her. They talked, back and forth, Ali leaning very close at one point as though she were sharing some secret. The girl laughed, then Ali laughed.

The exchange suggested a little too much familiarity to Lane. That was nothing, however, compared to her reaction when the girl with the coffee-colored skin caught Ali's hand in hers and leaned dangerously close, bringing her lips a mere breath from Ali's ear. She spoke and Ali laughed. Lane's blood thundered in her head and her stomach heaved as it had two days ago.

She'd seen enough. She started the car and drove off without another look back. She couldn't bear witness to this. Her heart was breaking all over again. The words the prison woman had used to describe Ali echoed in her head. She pointed her car away from town with no clear idea where she was heading.

* * *

"So glad you could join us today, Ms. Martinez." The professor glanced at his watch.

"Sorry," Jade apologized and glanced Ali's way.

Ali mouthed, "Let's talk." She had been beginning to think Jade wasn't coming to class again.

Jade simply nodded a "yes."

Jade was already outside when Ali exited the building. "Hi."

"Hi back."

"I was kind of worried when you didn't make class yesterday."

"I had something I couldn't not do, you know." Jade lifted a shoulder. "Sorry to worry you."

"It's no big deal. It wasn't like a mothering kind of worry." They both laughed.

"So what's up?"

"I asked my girlfriend whether she was mad at me for..." Ali felt the blush in her cheeks. She leaned in. "You know, trying to go down there in bed."

Jade laughed. "Sorry. You're so damned cute when you're embarrassed." Ali laughed too, mostly to hide her embarrassment. "So everything's good between you two?"

Ali nodded. "Thanks for the advice."

"Hey." Jade caught Ali's hand and leaned in closer. "Tell her she'd better take real good care of you 'cause I'm waiting on a chance to woo you away."

Ali laughed again to hide a new embarrassment. "I'll tell her."

* * *

The landscape passed in a blur as Lane sped down the two-lane road and whipped into the parking lot to the side of the building. Stuffing her phone in a pocket, she wandered around the old house. She couldn't imagine why she would need it. Ali wouldn't be calling her. She would be otherwise engaged with her model.

Lane couldn't get the sight out of her head. What she witnessed between Ali and this other girl was too intimate, too similar to things she had thought and believed Ali only shared with her.

She made her way down to the water, stopping when she cleared the trees that surrounded the small lake. This was the first real thing she'd shared with Ali. Their dinner had simply introduced them to one another. When they'd gotten together that second time, though, and she'd brought her to this place, Lane had opened a deeply hidden part of herself to what was then—and apparently still was—a virtual stranger. She still didn't understand what compelled her to share so much with Ali on that day. Ali hadn't felt the need to do the same.

Shouldn't she have noticed that Ali was guarding information about her past like some kind of state secret? Did having serious feelings for someone turn your brain into mush?

She headed down to the dock but couldn't make herself walk out to where they had sat, the sun shimmering on Ali's beautiful face. The memory caused an ache so deep in her chest she thought she could die. *Better here than in a courtroom*, she supposed.

If she died now, she wondered, would she join her mother in heaven? Or would the person she'd been thus far keep them forever separated?

She kicked off her shoes and stepped off the boardwalk into the soft sand along the edge of the lake. The weather was a little cool for many vacationers, so she had the area to herself. When her phone chirped in her pocket, she looked at the screen, but she didn't want to talk to anyone, including Emily. A breeze whipped up as she walked along the small beach. The waves it created on the water sparkled like so many tiny diamonds in the bright afternoon sun, but she felt empty inside, desolate and more alone than she'd ever been in her long, lonely life. She wrapped her arms tightly around herself to ward off the chill inside her, longing for a warm embrace.

A young couple raced down the boardwalk and across the dock in the opposite direction toward the boathouse and the rentals. She watched in envy as they ran hand in hand, carefree and probably in love. When she reached the boardwalk again she brushed what she could off her dirty stockings, slipped into her shoes and headed back to the gardens. After she took a seat on one of the benches, her phone chirped again. The screen confirmed another call from Emily, which was followed a moment later by a voice mail alert. She ignored it. She couldn't talk to anyone, didn't want to talk to anyone. Except possibly the woman she loved.

She stared at the luscious floral gardens but saw nothing but Ali's face. Ali's face that first night at dinner when she had looked across the candlelit table at Lane. Ali's face when she'd exchanged whatever it was today with that beautiful young woman.

She looked at her watch. It was nearing three thirty and she needed to head back into the city. Twenty minutes down the road her phone rang once again. It was Jeremy. She definitely did not want to talk to him. The ringing ended abruptly and it gave an alert for a text message. Jeremy's message said, "Please call." She tossed the phone onto the passenger's seat. It rang again in five minutes, followed by the same text message to call him. She waited a few more minutes before grabbing it off the seat and hitting the return call button.

"Judge Stanford's office."

"What is so damned urgent?"

"Where have you been all afternoon? I heard you recessed court before lunch."

"I'm pretty certain my mother's dead. So I'll ask again. What is so urgent?"

"You have two more motions for the trial here. Are you coming by to pick them up?"

"No, have the messenger service deliver them to my place."

"Okay…" There was a lengthy pause. "You've been acting kind of erratic lately. I'm…I'm worried about you."

"You mean you're worried I'm screwing up my future—and therefore your future."

"I don't want to see you ruin everything you've worked so hard to accomplish."

Accomplishments. Is that what I've been doing with my life? Making accomplishments. It didn't feel much like it. "I'll make a deal with you, Jeremy."

"What's that?"

"You worry about yourself and I'll worry about me." He huffed out a breath. "I do not need someone, anyone, watching over me. Got it?" She didn't wait for his response. She disconnected the call.

When the phone began ringing a mere five minutes later, she wanted to toss it out the window. It was Emily, so she ignored it and another voice mail alert sounded. Home before rush hour, she went to her walk-in closet and selected her evening attire. Stripping off her clothes and donning a robe, she went to the kitchen for a much-needed drink. She didn't gulp it, but sipped it, standing at the counter until it was finished. Ali's sketchpad, set on the end of the couch, caught her eye. Her glass and bottle in hand, she picked it up and went to her office. Seated on the leather sofa there, she poured more vodka before opening the pad to the perfect likeness of the beauty she'd seen Ali talking to. The liquor settled like a hot coal in the pit of her stomach.

When she had first learned of Ali's incarceration and the apparent relationship she'd had inside with a hardened, lifetime criminal, she'd been physically sick. This—having her gut telling her that Ali was sleeping with another woman—made her feel like someone had ripped her heart out. She wanted to pull the sheet from the pad and tear it into tiny little shreds. Instead, she drained the glass and returned the pad to the living room.

Her cell phone rang in the kitchen, where she was charging it. She blew out a frustrated breath and answered. "Hello, Em."

"I've been calling you for hours."

"When I'm in court I'm unable to answer."

"It's six o'clock, so you couldn't possibly be in court. Be that as it may, I don't have time for you to explain *why* you haven't called me back. You are coming this evening, aren't you?"

"Yes, I'll be there." She headed down the hall to the bedroom.

"Thank the gods. My husband backed out earlier. I've called the other girls, but·no one is calling me back. You know how I hate going to these things alone."

Lane dropped onto the side of the bed with a sigh. "Yes, I know, Em. I'll see you there."

"Love you, Lane, you're a dear." She clicked off before Lane could say goodbye.

She sat staring at the outfit hanging on the door, a tight-fitting navy skirt with matching jacket which required nothing underneath but underwear and stockings. She kept that in mind as she selected the bra and panties and, while dressing, mused about finding some hot young chick who could make *her* come and forget all her troubles. She checked her image in the floor-length mirror one more time, smoothing a hand over her slim hip and eying the curve of her backside under the skirt's silken fabric. Perhaps she should take a ride across the river after the charity affair and see if she could get lucky at one of the lesbian bars. "Affair," she said aloud with a harsh laugh. "Anything you can do, I can do better." She snatched up her clutch on her way out the door.

* * *

Randall dropped her in front of the luxury downtown hotel at precisely seven o'clock. "What time shall I pick you up, ma'am?"

"Nine."

"Very well. Enjoy your party." She gave him a nod.

Emily spotted her the second she entered the ballroom and rushed to greet her. "Lane, dear." She hugged Lane lightly. "I should say that you look like every man's dream girl tonight." She leaned in. "But on closer inspection, I suspect something's amiss under that well-maintained façade of yours."

"Too much to do and not enough time for half of it. You know how it is."

Emily threaded her arm through Lane's. "Isn't that the truth? Come on, I thought I saw the girls when I came in." They edged up behind Tara and Carlina, who were in deep conversation at the bar. "Good evening, girls."

As they exchanged greetings, Carlina held Lane in a hug longer than customary and whispered in her ear. "Okay, you're clearly not the same happy in love Lane from last night. What's happened now?"

"Later." Lane didn't want to think about it, let alone put words to it, for fear that her emotions might take over.

"I'm going to hold you to that, darling." She released Lane. "Let's get you ladies a drink."

They moved to a tall table away from the flow of mingling bodies. Lane felt fortunate no one had singled her out. She wasn't in a mood for any glad-handing or shoptalk. She wanted to numb herself. She was well on her way to that when they were directed to the adjacent hall for dinner. Carlina slipped her arm through Lane's as the crowd began moving. When neither Emily nor Tara was close enough to hear, she said, "I think you might want to slow down a bit on the alcohol, Lane, darling."

Lane tried to withdraw, but Carlina held her arm tighter. "I can see you're hurting, and I'd probably want to do the very same thing in your situation." She gave a warm smile. "I am here for you. We can talk or drink all you want after dinner, privately, without prying eyes."

Lane met her eyes as they took their seats. "Sure, Car." It didn't stop her from requesting additional drinks throughout the course of the dinner, however.

During the speeches, first Tara and then Emily excused herself. Carlina scooched her chair close next to Lane's and draped an arm across the back of it. "Whenever you're ready, darling…"

The press of Carlina's breast into Lane's arm made her want to nuzzle against Carlina's side and drop her head on her shoulder. She swiped her napkin across her lips. "Les go." She swayed slightly when she stood. "Sorry."

Carlina slipped a hand under Lane's arm. "Let's get you home. Did you drive?"

Lane shook her head. "I haf a car." They cautiously made their way to the sidewalk.

"Do you see your driver?"

Lane grinned. "Jus wait." A moment later the Town Car pulled up and Randall hopped out, hurrying around the car to open the door. Carlina assisted Lane into the backseat and followed.

When Randall was again behind the wheel, he powered down the privacy window. "Where to, ma'am?"

"Home, Randy."

He glanced in the rearview mirror. "Very well." He powered the window back up.

Lane's head dropped back on the seat. "I thing I drunk too much."

Carlina patted the thigh that rested beside hers. "That's probably an accurate observation, darling."

Lane murmured something softly before her head lolled sideways and rested against Carlina's shoulder. A few moments later her head jerked up. "Sheze cheatin'…"

"I'm so sorry, Lane." Carlina took her hand.

Lane squeezed her eyes shut to hold back unshed tears. "Yeah—me too." She dropped her head back against the seat again.

Randall pulled into the drive for the underground garage, lowered the partition again and quietly said, "If you'll get the swipe card from her purse for me, we'll go into the garage and avoid the lobby."

When they pulled up in front of the elevator doors, Carlina shook her gently. "Lane, darling, wake up, we're home." Lane moaned and opened her eyes to the harsh glare of the interior light when Randall opened the door. "Come on," Carlina patted her thigh, "let's get you inside." Lane followed Carlina out, but nearly fell back inside the car when she tried to stand. Carlina quickly caught her under the arms, pulling her up and practically into an embrace.

"Shall I help you in, ma'am?"

Carlina turned, slipping an arm around Lane's waist. "I'm sure we can manage. Thank you. I would appreciate it if you'd wait and drive me back to my car, though."

Randall tipped his head.

CHAPTER TWENTY-SIX

Lane grasped the handrail and leaned against the wall inside the elevator the second Carlina released her.

"Which floor?"

"Top." Lane braced for the movement to come.

"And your keys?" Lane fumbled with the flap on her clutch. When she finally flipped it open, it dropped to the floor, spilling its contents. Carlina held up a hand. "Don't move. I've got it." She stooped and retrieved Lane's belongings. The elevator stopped, the door sprang open and Carlina slipped her arm once again around Lane's waist.

"Back door…" Lane swung her arm to their right, almost throwing them both off balance before she bumped herself into the wall.

Carlina dropped Lane's keys and clutch on the entry table. "Where's your room, darling?" Lane indicated with a sweep of her arm and they moved cautiously down the hall. Inside Carlina flipped the wall switch to turn on the lamps on each side of the massive bed. "Very nice," she commented. "Where's the bath?"

Lane pulled from Carlina's steadying hold, swaying as she crossed the room and disappeared through a door. She emerged a few moments later having unbuttoned the jacket of her suit and started to work the zipper down the back of her skirt. She kicked her heels off, dropped the skirt, and miraculously stepped out of it without tripping. She flopped down on the bed in her bra, panties and thigh-high stockings. Carlina removed Lane's stockings, urging her, unsuccessfully, to move under the covers.

"You're probably not going to feel very well in the morning." Carlina stood for several moments at the bedside before sitting. "Your little blonde beauty is a damned fool," she muttered quietly. "Lane... darling..."

"Mmm." Lane barely managed to open one eye a tiny slit.

"You call me if you need anything at all. Understand?" Lane's head nodded ever so slightly. She pushed the hair off Lane's forehead and leaned down to lightly brush her lips there. "We'll talk soon." She let herself out.

* * *

Ali stepped through the back door with an unsettled feeling in the pit of her stomach. She entered the bedroom to find Lane sprawled on the bed covers in her underwear. That was an unusual sight, but even more peculiar was how her clothes were strewn about on the floor and her shoes appeared to have been haphazardly kicked off. She moved quietly and picked up the expensive jacket, noticing a lingering fragrance there that wasn't familiar. She laid it with the skirt across the back of the chair at the window. She set the shoes inside the closet and went to shower.

Later, wrapped in a towel, she stood at the vanity in the walk-in closet, looking at Lane's collection of fragrances. Curiosity wouldn't let her ignore the uneasy feeling in her gut. She picked up each of the four perfume bottles on the vanity, giving each one a sniff. Her hands trembled as she put the last bottle back in its place, switched off the light and returned to the bedroom. She crossed to the chair at the window, picked up the jacket there and pressed it to her face to again inhale the unfamiliar scent. Her stomach did a slow roll. Settling on the side of the bed, she shook Lane's arm gently.

"Baby." Lane didn't respond. Ali shook a little harder. "Lane, baby, wake up. Let's get under the covers."

"What?" Lane mumbled.

Ali caught her hand and tried to pull her up. "Let's get this off." She started to undo the front clasp of Lane's bra, but Lane slapped her hand away.

"I get it." Ali could smell the alcohol on her breath. Lane fumbled with the clasp, finally releasing it and tossing the bra to the floor. She pushed the covers down and flopped back into the pillows.

Ali didn't doubt she was drunk. She picked up the discarded bra, rounded the bed and dropped it on the chair with Lane's suit. The suit that smelled of another woman. Her heart squeezed in her chest as she recalled that the last time Lane arrived home drunk she had smelled like another woman too. She climbed into bed and scooted over to lie against Lane's side as she did every night, but Lane turned her back to her. Ali didn't try to cozy up again. Instead she turned away so Lane wouldn't hear the sobs that were sure to follow the torrent of tears soaking her pillow.

* * *

Lane woke with a monster headache. It was early enough she thought she might be able to nurse herself to some kind of functioning state. Leaning heavily on the counter as the coffee brewed, she tried to recall how she made it to bed last night. She thought she'd arrived home before Ali, but she wasn't certain.

Ali. Her name made Lane's head pound all the harder. She was the reason Lane had chosen to drink herself into oblivion. She carried a cup of coffee in a shaky hand to the bedroom, preparing to dress for the day.

A sliver of early-dawn light filtered through the blinds, illuminating her discarded clothes. She picked them up and carried them to the closet, catching a whiff of a familiar scent on the way. She closed her eyes, briefly recalling Carlina's presence in her bedroom. "Oh, God," she whispered. "What the hell have I done?" She wanted to rush out before Ali got up. She couldn't confront her now—not the way she was feeling and not without knowing if she herself had things to atone for—but she wasn't able to. Every part of her was moving in a slow motion.

She dressed and quietly closed the bedroom door where Ali was still sleeping soundly, if not peacefully, her brow knitted in worry and her lips twitching. At the kitchen counter she scribbled a note for her. Then she called Carlina.

"Lane, darling, I'm glad to know you're alive this morning. I would require at least a day to recover from the liquor you put away."

"Well, if it makes you feel any better, I feel like I spent the night with a sadist."

"I couldn't possibly feel better knowing you are suffering."

"Suffering is an understatement." She paused a moment. "I don't really remember coming home last night."

"It's no wonder, darling. I've never seen you quite so intoxicated."

"Well, thank you for getting me here."

"That whole 'friends' thing you know."

Lane sipped her coffee. "Speaking of friends. I woke pretty much naked. We didn't...do anything...did we?"

Carlina chuckled. "I was certainly willing and able, but you, my darling, weren't in any condition. Not to mention how distraught you were. I would never take that kind of advantage of you."

Lane exhaled in relief. She liked Carlina. She was a beautiful woman, sexy and desirable, but not her type. "I'm sorry for being such a burden last night. Thanks again for getting me home."

"You're welcome, darling. Aside from being physically ill this morning, are you doing any better?"

"Absolutely," Lane said with determination. "Listen, I've got to get going. I'll talk to you later."

"Call anytime."

With great effort Lane bent to pick up the messengered briefs from the floor beneath the mail slot next to the front door. She was waiting on the sidewalk out front when Randall arrived, still looking to avoid Ali.

"Good morning, ma'am." He opened and held the door.

"Good morning," she responded, even though it was anything but good.

She opened her bag and pulled out the briefs. The thought of facing the bickering lawyers in court made her head pound hard enough to register on the Richter scale, but she managed to skim their arguments on the ride in. Court seemed endless and she still had a cocktail meeting to attend, followed by dinner. She wanted to blow it off, but a voice in the back of her mind which sounded a lot like her father's warned that she needed her career now more than ever.

* * *

Ali woke to an empty bed and an emptier feeling inside. She thought for sure she'd hear Lane get up. But she had laid there for so long last night crying that she'd slept through it. She poured a cup of cold coffee, microwaved it and spied the note on the corner of the counter. Her heart stopped a beat, then two, before she picked it up.

"Ali, sorry we missed. I have a busy evening.—Lane."

The tears came again automatically. She couldn't stop them. Something had happened in the last twenty-four hours, something awful, and Ali didn't have a clue what it might be. The microwave dinged, drawing her attention back. She showered, dressed and left for class with little time to spare and even less enthusiasm or inspiration. She rushed in at the last minute, hoping to avoid Jade, and again hurried out afterward. Almost to the street, she heard her name being called over the racket of hordes of voices and noisy cars passing.

"Ali!" Jade caught hold of her hand at the curb. "Hold up a sec." Jade sucked in deep breaths. "Hey you." She reached for Ali's arm and turned her around. "Hey, Al, you okay?"

"Sure." Ali shrugged.

Jade cocked her head. "Really?"

Ali's eyes teared up. "I will be."

"Come on, let's get coffee and talk."

She relished, for a moment, the feel of the warm hand holding hers before pulling it away. She wrapped her arm across the one clutching her things to her chest. "Can't. I have to get to work." She forced a smile. "I'll see you tomorrow."

She hurriedly crossed the street amidst honking car horns and locked herself in her car, allowing the tears to flow she'd held back in front of her friend. She should have had coffee with Jade. She could have talked about the insecurities she was feeling as a result of Lane's behavior. She could have. Jade was her friend. But she felt too raw and vulnerable.

She had the same empty feeling when she got home. She had hoped against hope that Lane had stopped home and possibly left a reply in response to the note she'd written. That was still on the counter where she left it. The tears threatened as she read her words again. "Baby, I'm off this evening and will be waiting anxiously for you to get home. Love—Ali."

She crumpled the paper in her fist and tossed it toward the wastebasket, then dragged her arm across her tear-stained cheeks. She wandered down the hall, glancing into the bedroom, then down the hall to the room that served as Lane's home office. She stepped in the doorway there and flipped the switch. On the small coffee table in front of the couch stood an opened vodka bottle and, beside it, an empty glass. She sat down on the couch and stared at the bottle, trying to imagine why her lover had sat there and gotten drunk.

* * *

Lane tensed upon entering the penthouse. She could feel Ali's presence and hear the faint sound of voices. Pulling a stack of files from her case, she clutched them to her chest and headed down the hall. Ali was in the guest bedroom seated in the overstuffed chair in front of the small television. She noticed Lane a few seconds later, clicked off the TV and jumped to her feet.

"Hey, baby. I missed you today." When she reached Lane in the doorway, she stretched to kiss her. Lane made no attempt to rid her arms of the files and enable any kind of embrace. Ali leaned back. "You look really tired. You want me to run you a bath or something?"

Lane steadied herself against an onslaught of emotions. The logical part of her brain said to back away and wash her hands of this mess of a woman she'd let into her life. But her heart saw, or rather felt, something different. It saw honesty in Ali's bright eyes and caring. It saw trust. *Give me the strength.*

"I've got a lot of work I need to do tonight." She leaned away from Ali and temptation.

"Okay." Ali stepped back. "I'm going to hang out in here. Let me know when you're ready for bed."

Lane gave only a slight nod. In her office she dropped the files on the desk, glad for the vodka bottle and glass that remained on the coffee table. She would stay sequestered here in hopes that Ali might fall asleep in the guest room. She poured two fingers of alcohol in the glass and took a swallow. She grabbed one of the files from the desk, kicked off her heels and settled back on the couch. Should Ali look in, she wanted to appear to be occupied with work. When, in fact, she was simply trying to ignore the elephant in the room. She knew she should go confront Ali. This…situation…needed to be resolved so they could each go on with their respective lives.

Lane heard Ali's sob from the next room. It was a sharp knife that penetrated flesh and muscle, reaching her heart. She felt like her life was slowly draining from her. "God dammit," she mumbled as she tossed the file from her lap across the room and dropped her head back on the sofa. Where was the Lane Stanford of old? She would have come home, stormed through the penthouse collecting the few belongings Ali had and tossed them into the hallway, to be carted by their owner to the beater down in the garage and driven…someplace. Instead of sitting here impotent. What the hell was wrong with her?

Ali heard a faintly muttered curse and what she could only assume was the strewing of papers in Lane's office. She swiped her cheeks roughly on her arms and stood. A quick glance in the mirror over the small dresser confirmed she looked almost as bad as she felt. She took several deep breaths to settle the queasy feeling in her stomach, and stepped into the hall anyway. She hoped she wasn't about to destroy everything they had built, but she couldn't sit by any longer without knowing what was wrong between them and continually thinking the worst.

Ali stood silently inside the doorway. Lane's head was tipped back, eyes closed, and her hand was wrapped around the tumbler of vodka. Ali wrapped her arms tightly around herself, hoping to hold everything together inside her. Very softly she said, "Lane…baby," and Lane's head snapped up. Ali's hands trembled at her sides. "Something's wrong. I can't…" Her voice quivered. "I don't know what to do." A lone tear escaped and slid down her cheek. "I'm scared."

Lane raised the drink to her lips, watching Ali over the top of the glass. The elephant was demanding to be recognized. She couldn't avoid it any longer. She set the glass down, fearing otherwise she might throw it. Her eyes remained trained like lasers on Ali's.

"Who is she?"

Ali's lip trembled. "Who?"

Lane's fingers curled into tight fists. "The woman you're fucking when I'm not around." Her voice boomed in the small room.

"There isn't anyone, Lane. I swear to you."

"Really?" Lane jumped to her feet and moved toward Ali at lightning speed. Ali stumbled out of the way, arms raised as if to shield her torso, as Lane brushed past her to the back entry and grabbed the bag Ali had dropped beside the door there. Roughly pulling out the sketchpad, Lane found what she was looking for, returned to the office and shoved it at Ali.

"Who the fuck is she?" When Ali didn't respond, Lane shook it at her. "I asked you a question."

Ali dropped her eyes to the sketchpad. "That's…" Her voice shook. "That's my friend, Jade, from…from class." Tears raced down her cheeks. "There's nothing—"

"When do you fuck?" Lane felt the heat in her face. "Where do you do it?" She didn't give Ali a chance to answer. With angry steps she backed her against the wall. "Have you brought her here?" Lane shook the sketchpad in Ali's face.

Ali gasped. "Baby, no." Her breath caught. "There's no one...I would never..." she sobbed. "Never, baby. There's only you." She swatted at the sketchpad. "Only you...I love you." She sucked in gasps of air. "Please believe me," she pleaded.

The muscles in Lane's jaws were clenched so hard they hurt. She wanted to destroy something with her bare hands, to demolish it. She stood statue still, one hand clasping the pad and the other balled into a tight fist at her side. She took a long deep breath as she stared into Ali's frightened eyes. She wanted to smash something to pieces, yes. But not the woman before her. She could feel her pulse beating at her temples while her mind battled her heart. The words of the prison inmate echoed again in her head. No, she told herself, that wasn't Ali—not her Ali. She sucked in another breath, trying to quell the storm raging within.

Suddenly there was another voice in her head. "The best things in our lives truly are worth working for." That's what her mother would say when Lane was frustrated and ready to give up. Her sweet, gentle voice was no match for the first, malicious one, however. She tried, but she couldn't shake off the overwhelming emotion it provoked.

"Please, baby..." Ali reached a shaking hand up to cup Lane's tight jaw, gently stroking her thumb over her cheek. "I would never cheat on you. Ever."

Lane didn't move a muscle. Rather than attempt to live up to the lessons her long-gone mother had tried to teach her, she turned to the ruthless tactics she had learned at her father's knee.

"How about Cassie then?" she asked. "Would *Cassie Allen* cheat on me?"

She watched Ali's face shatter into a million pieces. Lane's heart shattered with it. Only days ago she had told Carlina she was willing to bury the secret of Ali's past forever because she loved her so much, and here she was now, throwing it in her face, on the flimsiest of evidence, because she felt hurt and betrayed and...yes, she admitted to herself... jealous and afraid of being abandoned again.

Ali dropped onto the couch, drew her legs to her chest and wrapped her arms tightly around them. Lane watched as she began to rock back and forth.

"I'm so sorry, baby," she whispered. "So sorry." She continued to rock, eyes closed. "Told the truth…" She sucked in a breath. "Not the whole truth." The rocking was almost maniacal now. "Swear…hasn't been anyone but you." She sobbed. "No…one…just you." She stopped rocking and whispered again, "I'm sorry, baby."

As a prosecutor Lane had been known to turn strong men into sniveling babies. She had thrived on the rush that power gave her. But what was happening here—it was tearing her up.

"You don't deny the Cassie Allen alias?"

Ali shook her head slowly. "It was me." She brought her swollen eyes up to meet Lane's. "I don't know who she was, though. And what they said she did," her voice quivered, "I don't remember. I knew it was bad. I…I felt it." She wrapped her arms tightly around her waist. "Felt it in here." She rocked again. "I couldn't let my father find out… anyone…so I lied. It's the only lie, I swear."

It went against everything she'd been taught about rules of evidence in law school and in the courtroom, but when Lane looked into Ali's eyes she saw it. Innocence. The innate innocence she had seen the first time she looked in those eyes weeks ago and the trust in her that was somehow still shining in them, despite what she'd just done. There was more she wanted to know, so much more, but…

"I…" She couldn't get her voice past the knot in her throat. She tried clearing it and began again. "I believe you," she said quietly. "About Jade. And about…the rest."

Ali's eyes welled again with fresh tears. "I'm so sorry. I was trying to make a fresh start, get past all…that. Should have stopped things as soon as I found out you were a judge, but you were so beautiful and…I knew you'd be hurt if you found out, if anyone found out…"

She fell silent. After a moment, she swiped at the wetness on her face and uncurled her legs, preparing to stand. "I'll get my things and go."

"Don't."

"I'll ruin your life. Everything you're working toward. I can't do that."

Lane inhaled sharply. This was it, the tipping point in her life. She could cut her losses right now. Ali would go away quietly, she would stay away from The Inn for a while, she'd never have to deal with her again. But she couldn't begin to comprehend how big a hole that doing so would leave in her heart. She didn't want to.

"I can't let you…" Lane managed to choke out. She went to the couch and wrapped her arm around Ali's quivering shoulders. "Shh…"

Lane pulled Ali's head against her. "I'm sorry," she whispered. "I didn't want to hurt you this way. I was jealous and I was scared. I don't want to lose you. I only want to love you."

Ali sobbed uncontrollably, shaking them both. Lane only held her tighter. This was necessary, Lane reasoned. They needed to get this dark secret out in the open, get it out of the way, so they could go happily on with their lives.

Is that possible? she wondered. She was not convinced that Ali had been guilty of the crime she'd served time for. She knew for sure, however, what *she* had done. If revealed, the skeletons in her own closet could take her down in a flaming inferno, along with anybody within arm's reach. Was it fair to continue keeping Ali in the dark about *her* secrets?

They sat for what seemed like forever. Finally Lane pressed her lips briefly to Ali's forehead.

"Everyone has a past, you once told me. I'm not that different from you. There are things I've been involved in, Ali, that could potentially hurt me—and you, because you're with me."

"Nothing can hurt me if I'm with you," Ali said with quiet conviction.

"You don't know what…"

Ali stopped her with fingertips to her lips. "I know your stuff is confidential and really important and I won't mess any of that up, I promise. I want you to have everything you've been working for. I'm okay staying in the closet too as long as I get to love you."

Without another word Lane rose and led her across the hall. There they slowly, reverently undressed each other and made love until they fell into an exhausted heap. As Lane drifted to sleep, she made a silent vow to spend the rest of her life pleasing Ali in every way possible.

CHAPTER TWENTY-SEVEN

Lane smiled. The unbearable weight of days past was gone, replaced by the knowledge that she had the love of a woman, someone who was beautiful outside and in, who had been willing to walk away to protect her. Their morning together had been sweet but much too short. Hoping she wouldn't disturb Ali's peaceful slumber but unwilling to leave without connecting with her again, she had leaned carefully over the slumbering blonde and placed a kiss on her temple.

A smile tugged at Ali's lips. "Mmm…" She slowly opened her eyes. "Good morning, beautiful."

"I was dreaming about you," she said with a seductive wiggle.

"Were you now? Well, I'm going to be dreaming of you all day. Now, though, I've got to get moving. I have a jam-packed schedule today. And tonight too, no doubt. Jeremy would never let me have a Friday night for myself. Are you working?" Ali nodded. "I'll see you when you get home." Lane kissed her tenderly.

"I love you," Ali said, tears shimmering in her eyes.

Lane kissed her again. "I love you too." Would she ever get tired of hearing those words or saying them?

Lane's musings were interrupted by a loud knock on her door, which was followed by Jeremy's entrance. He advanced to her desk uninvited, a scowl on his face.

"By all means, Jeremy, barge right on in."

"So…you don't want to know that the gossip mill is really churning this morning and you're the one that's being ground up?"

She laid down her pen and sat back. "What on earth are you talking about?"

"The rumor yesterday was that you were inebriated at the Community Outreach Charity. That wasn't too hard to handle. It's not like nobody else has ever gotten blitzed at one of those boring events. The rumor today, however, is that you were seen leaving *in that condition* arm-in-arm with a very attractive woman with whom you are having a torrid affair." His eyes bored into hers. She stared back unflinchingly.

"I might have had one too many." She gave a wave of her hand. "The 'very attractive woman' was a dear friend who saw to it that I got home safely. I should think for a judge that would be seen as very responsible behavior."

"No." He shook his head so hard Lane was sure he'd rattle something loose. "What it is seen as is a chance to capitalize on the fact that there's no regular male presence in your life and label you as a lesbian."

She shrugged. "How can you sit there"—he sputtered—"so blasé?"

"I don't know what you're so worked up about. It's just gossip."

"This could ruin your career." His neck was turning red.

"It's my career, Jeremy. If there were anything to substantiate it, my face would be splashed all over the TV or at least in the papers." She picked up the newspaper she'd read on the ride in and tossed it across the desk at him. "See for yourself." He stared blankly at it. "Again," she reiterated, "*my* career and *my* call. How about you concentrate now on doing what I pay you for." Her hands clenched briefly.

He said nothing as he stomped to the door and closed it louder than necessary. She smiled. It was wonderfully liberating to finally be taking charge of her own life. Her day in court also held the promise of being a short one—only one more witness and then closing arguments. With any luck she'd be done early and maybe…

She snatched up her cell phone, hitting a familiar number on speed dial.

* * *

The defense attorney wasn't the only one who noticed when the answers from his key witness suddenly started favoring the prosecution.

It made Lane sit up and take notice too. What she saw was a middle-aged Hispanic woman who looked very nervous and who spent more time looking at the assistant district attorney than at the man who was questioning her.

Lane reminded her of the penalties for perjury, but when she denied having been coached by anyone about her testimony there wasn't much more Lane could do. Thankfully, in the process of that exchange, the defense lawyer had caught a clue and shifted to a line of inquiry that revealed that Mrs. Hernandez was not a U.S. citizen and was working without a work permit.

The fresh-faced, just-passed-the-bar prosecutor had objected, but Lane had overruled her. When the witness finally admitted she'd been promised a visa in exchange for changing her story, Lane acquiesced to the defense lawyer's request and dismissed the case for misconduct by the prosecution.

Lane's cheeks burned with anger. She had had no doubt that the accused was guilty as charged. The prosecution's unfathomable move, made for the purpose of securing a win that was already only a breath away, had resulted in his release to perpetrate crimes on more innocent victims. It was also going to cost the prosecutor dearly, as Lane reminded her before ending the trial: "There are reasons we have laws, Ms. Sloan, and lawyers and courts to uphold those laws. Prosecutors may have full immunity from civil liability regardless of how egregious their actions are, but I promise you, you will pay for what you have done. Your reputation may never recover, in fact. I hope it was worth it. We are dismissed."

She was no better than Ms. Sloan, Lane realized, pacing back and forth in the cramped quarters of her chambers like a caged animal. She ripped her robe off, wadded it up, tossed it in the chair and went into the bathroom. When she leaned over the sink to wash her hands, she took a good long look at herself in the mirror. She didn't like what she saw. She needed to make changes in her life, and she needed to do it now.

She called her office as she walked toward the elevator.

"Judge Stanford's office."

"The case finished early. I'm going to be out for a while. I'll be back in this afternoon. No need to send out the bloodhounds." She snapped the phone closed before Jeremy could say another word. Fifteen minutes later a cab dropped her off in front of her building. Fortunately the elevator was waiting when she punched the button so she didn't have to endure any banal conversation with the doorman.

She didn't need the distraction. Not that kind, anyway. She was hoping Ali would stop home between class and work.

Once inside the penthouse she went to the kitchen. She stared a long minute at the cupboard before going to the refrigerator and pulling out a bottle of water. For the first time in a very long time, she didn't feel the need for a drink. She leaned a hip against the counter, smiling. She was about to alter her life in ways that would raise eyebrows and burn some bridges. It was likely to be a rough trip, but she was looking forward to it.

She was leaning in the same spot when she heard the back door open and close. A moment later, Ali turned the corner into the kitchen.

"Oh," she exclaimed, putting her hand to her chest. "I didn't expect to see you there. You scared me."

Lane moved toward her. "I stopped in to surprise you. I guess I accomplished that." She put an arm around Ali's waist. "I'm sorry."

Ali turned into her, slipping her arms around Lane's neck. "Well, you have my heart pounding double-time. You want to try for more?" Her eyes sparkled, and Lane forgot about her plans to talk with Ali about the changes that lay ahead.

Lane backed Ali against the counter and dipped her head to kiss the tender skin below her ear. Her fingers tugged the top from Ali's skintight jeans and touched the warm flesh of Ali's stomach, eliciting a moan, then moved up to capture her breasts. "You feel amazing." She kissed the column of her neck. "Always amazing." Her thumbs rubbed the thin lace of Ali's bra, calling her nipples to attention.

"Oh, God, baby." Ali rocked her hips into Lane's.

Lane stripped Ali's top over her head, then dropped her hands to Ali's jeans. She unbuttoned, unzipped and forced them down to her knees, and gently lifted her by the waist onto the counter. She worked her shoes off along with her jeans and panties, pushed her legs apart and moved between them, pulling her hips forward until she could feel the heat radiating off Ali's center.

Ali's eyes slammed shut and her head fell back as Lane's fingers stroked her to completion. Her body was boneless afterward and her breaths came in ragged gasps. "I love what you do to me." She turned her head and pressed her lips to Lane's neck. "I love *you*." Tears brimmed in her eyes.

Lane brushed away the tears. "Ali, darling, please don't cry."

Ali pulled Lane into a tight embrace. "I can't help it. I've never felt so happy in my life." They continued touching and kissing until Ali finally reluctantly said, "Baby, I have to go to work."

Lane leaned back, stroking her fingers over Ali's cheek. "I know. I need to go back to my office too."

Ali touched her fingertips lightly to Lane's lips. "I don't ever want anything but this."

"What," Lane asked, "lovemaking on the kitchen counter?" She reached for Ali's top, which she'd tossed behind her on the counter.

Ali swatted at her playfully. "No, silly. This…feeling. This connection." She waved her hand between them. "This thing between us."

"You mean this feeling of love?"

Ali shoved her arms through her top and settled it down to her waist. "Yes. This is all I'll ever need. Please don't ever forget that."

"I won't."

"Promise?"

Lane snatched Ali's panties and jeans up from the floor, holding them for her to put her feet in. "I promise."

Ali hopped down, wiggling into them. She slid her hand down the center of Lane's chest. "God, I wish we had more time."

"There's always bedtime." Lane gave her a wink.

* * *

Lane made it back into the office before four, about the time Ali would arrive at the restaurant. Jeremy looked like he was ready to bust at the seams. "We have to talk." He stood beside his desk.

"Yes, we do." She opened her office door. "Bring my calendar in." He snatched it off his desk and followed. "Please sit." She rounded the desk. "What's on for tonight?"

"You're scheduled for a dinner with a league of business professionals from around the state."

"Am I slated to speak or present anything?" He shook his head no. "Cancel it, please."

"Lane, I don't think—"

She raised her hand. "Jeremy, do you like your job?"

"Uh," he stuttered, "yes, but…"

"Then I suggest you do it." He started to interrupt, but she cut him off again. "We need to look at my schedule. I have a feeling I have many more commitments to break." He stared at her, mouth agape. She settled her arms on the desk, locked her fingers together and leaned toward him.

"I'm making major changes in my life, Jeremy. A lot of those will impact things that everyone else, aside from me, thinks I should be doing with my life." Jeremy sat silent. "I don't like who I've become. I don't like being groomed by others for something I'm no longer sure I want to do."

"You're giving up on a future in politics or the State Supreme Court?"

"I'm already in politics, Jeremy. I didn't get elected to this position only because I was a top prosecutor and had the same last name as a State Supreme Court justice. I 'campaigned' for it. I'm going to give myself a chance now to have a life that might provide more than a bank account."

"Is this about the blonde living in *my* apartment?"

Lane tried to keep her expression impassive, but she could feel her jaws clenching. "It is."

He smacked his hand down on the calendar. "I knew it. That's why you've been acting irrational and reckless as a sixteen-year-old boy with a perpetual hard-on. Lane, this is ludicrous. You're jeopardizing your future, which may I remind you will last infinitely longer than all your trysts put together."

Lane's anger boiled over. "Enough!" She stood abruptly, forcing her chair to slam into the window frame behind her as she slapped her hands down on the desk. "I am sick and tired of everyone else deciding what's right for me, my future and my life. If you value your job and you want to keep it, now is a really good time to start doing it. You want to be in politics—throw your hat into the ring or find another coattail to ride on. I'm hanging mine up."

She felt a tiny stab of guilt for blasting him for simply doing what she invited him to do in the past. And, of course, he was right. She'd never lasted more than a month with a woman. She wondered if she even had what it took to hold onto Ali. Ali was everything she'd never been. And there was their ten-year age difference. Would Ali quickly tire of her? Would she love her still if she knew Lane's secrets, the deals she had made and the lies she had told?

"Fine," he replied tersely. "What else do you want to jettison?"

In the next fifteen minutes they reviewed her schedule for the next month and scratched all but a few charity and fundraising affairs that Emily had made her commit to. Lane started thinking about which cause she might want to give her time to simply because she cared about it and not because someone thought it would be a good career move for her. She decided to talk about that later with Ali, ask her what she was interested in.

When Jeremy left she called The Inn.

"This is Judge Stanford. Is Roscoe available?"

A cheery voice replied, "Please hold on and I'll find him."

She drummed her fingers to the music.

"Lane, so good to hear from you." Roscoe's voice boomed in her ear. "What can I do for you? An elegant dinner party, something intimate for two?" He laughed robustly.

"Actually, Roscoe, I am calling to ask a favor, but I promise I will order one of your special deliveries very soon."

"Very well. What can I do for you today?"

"I know this is very short notice, Roscoe, but I was wondering if there was any way Ali Castle could be relieved of her shift on Sunday. There is an exhibition in town that I think she might enjoy, given her studies, but it only runs through Sunday."

Lane could tell by the background noise he was moving through the restaurant. "Let me see what I can do for you." There was a minute of silence before he asked, "May I call you back in a bit?"

"Of course, Roscoe. I appreciate anything you can do. If you can't, not to worry, the world won't end. Thank you."

"I will call."

She hoped as she gathered her things and headed home that Ali wouldn't be upset with her for presuming she'd like an extra day off. She was entering the penthouse when her cell phone rang. "Yes, this is Lane."

"I have arranged for your artist extraordinaire to have Sunday off."

"Thank you so much, Roscoe. I'm sure Ms. Castle will benefit greatly from this experience. I owe you, sir."

"You will order something special for a special occasion very soon, yes?"

"You have my word. Thank you again."

Lane turned off the water when she heard the back door open and close. She stepped out into the hall where Ali's tired eyes looked up at her. "Your bath awaits, my darling." She lowered her lips to the tender skin at the base of Ali's neck.

"God, baby." Ali gave Lane a little nudge. "I smell like the shrimp dinner special. I need—"

"You smell good enough to eat alive." Ali groaned and Lane grabbed her hand, tugging her into the bedroom and beyond it to the bathroom. When she was naked, Lane guided her to the tub. "I'll be right back."

Lane returned from the kitchen with a bottle of sparkling wine and two champagne flutes. She filled both, handed one to Ali and placed the other on the edge of the tub before slipping off her robe and sliding into the steamy bath with her. She reached for her glass, pressing her breasts into Ali's back and eliciting a sweet groan.

"What's the special occasion?"

"You." Lane touched her glass to Ali's. "I want to celebrate how special you are and how very important you are in my life."

Setting the glasses aside after a few swallows, Lane slipped her arms around Ali's waist and settled them back into the bubbles. Ali rested her head against Lane's shoulder. "You know," she began while Lane's fingers started a soft caress of her slick skin, "never in my life could I have imagined that I would be here...with someone as wonderful and loving like you."

Lane pressed her lips to her temple. "Nor I." She shifted Ali in her arms, tilting her head up and capturing her lips in a kiss so full of passion and desire it threatened to erupt in a scorching hot blaze.

"I love how you make me feel," Ali said, pressing into Lane's teasing strokes. Lane kissed her eyes, nose and lips again and picked up the bath sponge. "Let me wash away the day." She drew the sponge quickly and methodically over every inch of Ali before stepping from the tub and holding out one of the thick terry robes for her. Donning her own, she led the way into the bedroom. Once there, she slipped the robe off Ali's shoulders and pressed her lips briefly to Ali's breast. "I want to make love to every part of you." Ali let the robe pool at her feet, and Lane guided her down onto the bed.

CHAPTER TWENTY-EIGHT

Lane woke early, the whisper of Ali's breath warming her chest. It was a sensation, she decided, that she wanted to experience every morning for the rest of their lives. She pressed her lips to the blonde head beside her and stroked the arm draped around her waist. "Do you know how much I love you?"

Ali stretched. "Maybe, but why don't you tell me again so I'm sure I have it right." She smiled a thousand-watt smile.

That smile, those eyes, her beautiful face, turned Lane's insides to liquid. "I want to spend my life falling in love with you again every day."

"Mmm, I was hoping you'd say that." She lowered her mouth to Lane's. When they separated, she sighed. "I wish I could stay here all weekend."

Lane stroked her hands up and down Ali's back. "I can. I took it off."

"No fair!" Ali pouted. "I have to work."

"I do have something to take care of on Sunday, but I have a little surprise for you too. I hope you're not going to be upset with me."

"Why would I be upset?"

Lane braced herself. "I talked to your boss."

Ali's eyes narrowed. "About…"

"About you having tomorrow off. Please don't be mad for not asking you first."

"How long are you going to be tied up?"

"It depends on how it goes." She exhaled a long breath. "I've made some life-changing decisions in the last twenty-four hours. Maybe we can discuss them over breakfast?"

"Okay." Ali gave Lane a quick peck. "I'd love to have breakfast with you." She popped out of bed and tossed one of the robes to Lane before pulling on the other. "I'll start the coffee. You want to shower before or after?"

"Before or after what?" Lane replied suggestively.

"Baby," Ali whispered, moving to where Lane stood. "You're insatiable." She slipped her hand inside Lane's robe.

"Sweetheart, when you're around, I can't help myself." Lane caught Ali's wrist and grinned. "If you start the coffee, I'll start the shower."

"Deal." Ali gave the sash on Lane's robe a tug and headed off to the kitchen.

"It's a good thing we both have jobs or we'd wear our bodies out before we even hit middle age," Lane joked later as they were dressing.

Ali wrapped her arms around Lane's waist and pressed her cheek to her chest. "It's the perfect exercise. We're gonna live forever."

Lane kissed the top of her head. "Let's go have a breakfast meeting."

"So, tell me what you've been up to." Ali blew steam away as it rose from her cup.

Lane sipped her coffee slowly, trying to decide where to start. "I haven't done anything drastic yet. I've only cleared extra things from my calendar. I want more time for myself," she said matter-of-factly.

Ali's eyes went wide. "Is everything all right?"

"Everything is perfect." She reached over and tucked a few strands of hair behind Ali's ear. "I do have to meet with my father tomorrow, if he'll see me, and figure out a way to tell him that his dreams are not my dreams." Lane caught the faraway look in her lover's eyes. "What is it, sweetheart?"

Ali shook her head. "I have no idea if my father had any plans for me, other than controlling my life."

"Does that bother you?"

"I…uh…no," Ali stuttered. "Is this going to turn into a battle of the Stanfords?"

"I don't think so. He may be as tall as I am, but he's pretty frail anymore. I think I can take him if I have to." She winked. "Anyway," Lane took another sip of coffee, "I thought I'd take you along, since you have the day off."

Ali's face went pale. "Do you think that's a good idea?"

Lane gave Ali's now-trembling hand a pat. "No worries. I don't intend to throw you to the lions. I want you to meet the woman who raised me after my mother died." Lane turned on her stool and turned Ali to face her. "And she very much wants to meet you."

Ali's eyes narrowed. "Why does she want to meet me?"

"She knows how happy you make me. I told her about you."

"You sure it won't cause problems?"

She took Ali's hands in hers. "Darling, I have never been more sure of anything in my life." She kissed her softly.

Lane had dinner delivered and waiting in the oven when Ali returned from work at eight thirty. Ali showered hurriedly and met Lane at the dining table, which was complete with candles and her favorite wine.

"So this is what married life's kind of like."

"I imagine so." Lane paused a heartbeat. "Would you?"

Ali set her glass down. "Would I what?"

"Marry me." Lane reached over and curled her fingers around Ali's hand. "Would you marry me, Ali Castle?"

"Lane, baby." Tears appeared in Ali's eyes. "I would do anything, go anywhere or be anything you wanted in order to be with you forever and always."

Lane lifted their joined hands to her lips. To think she'd denied herself this for so many years. She stared off at the night beyond the windows.

"Baby?"

"Hmm…"

"I'm suddenly not very hungry for food." Ali stood, pulling Lane up from her chair. Lane carried her off to the bedroom, their dinner forgotten.

* * *

Sunday morning dawned with Ali still cradled in Lane's arms. How, she wondered again, how she had gone all these years without this? The simple answer, of course, was that it was because she hadn't met Ali.

Her bliss dissolved quickly at the thought of what she planned to do today. It could very well be the catalyst for many more life-altering changes. She twitched, a chill of crushing fear racing through her. Ali muttered softly in her sleep, and the barely audible sound grounded her once more. She didn't want to live her life without her. She wouldn't.

She tried to reclaim sleep but decided to give up after half an hour. Standing before the windows out in the living room, she imagined another life. She was a million miles away on a beach with Ali. They were soaking up the sun and enjoying tropical cocktails, and she was lost in the magnificence of the woman at her side.

"What's wrong?" Ali wrapped her arms around Lane from behind and pressed her cheek against Lane's back.

"Nerves, I guess. I'm a little afraid to have this 'come to Jesus' meeting with my father."

"Then don't."

Lane turned in the circle of her arms. "Don't?"

"Don't do this because of me. I can stay away if you need me to. I can wait until you're ready, whatever you need."

Lane felt the tears threaten, thanking the darkness for hiding them. She cleared her throat. "You are what I need." She cradled Ali's face. "You're all I'll ever need. I would live in that car of yours if that were the only way I could be with you. But I can't live without you."

"Come back to bed." Putting herself in the hands of the woman who held her heart, Lane followed Ali to the bedroom and finally found rest in her embrace.

After breakfast, they sat out in the living room. Lane was working to catch up a on few things for work, while Ali sat, legs propped on the couch, with a sketchpad in her lap. Lane couldn't concentrate. The impending meeting was still weighing heavily on her mind. She tossed the file aside.

"What are you drawing?"

Ali turned the pad around for Lane's inspection. "Something I saw the other day."

Lane admired the smooth lines of the face developing on the page. "Who is she?"

Ali smiled. "I drive past this park on the way to work from class. I stopped the other day to kill some time, and this adorable little girl was there with her mother. Her face stuck in my mind." She shrugged. "It kind of reminded me of my childhood. Before my dad started keeping me captive in his house because all the boys were hell-bent on taking my virginity." She laughed. "Little did he know he had nothing to worry about with the boys." She looked at Lane and shrugged again. "I'm sorry. My childhood is anything but interesting."

"I want to know everything about you."

Ali dropped the pad to the floor, got on her knees and crawled the length of the couch to Lane's lap. "What would you like to know?" She batted her lashes.

Lane eased her away. "Sweetheart, you turn my insides liquid when you're this close. I can't think about facing my father in this state."

"I'm sorry." She leaned away. "You think it will always be like this? You know, us craving sex like it might evaporate if we stop?"

"I can't imagine why it wouldn't be. It's certainly not going to happen today. For the sake of my sanity, though, we can't act on it now. My brain will become mush."

* * *

After spending more than thirty minutes deciding what to wear, Ali came out of the dressing room. "Well?"

Lane tilted her head and assessed Ali's outfit—a short-sleeved blue stretch top the color of her eyes, a backside-hugging skirt that fell slightly above her knees, and peep toe heels. "You look beautiful. If I thought I could walk you down the street on my arm without being accosted, I would." She gave a wink. "Come on, let's go meet the family."

Before Ali could protest or delay their departure by another second, Lane coaxed her out the door.

While she drove, Lane mentally rehearsed the lines that she'd been preparing the last day and a half. After fifteen minutes Ali broke the silence. "So who's this woman you said raised you?"

"Miss Clara filled my mother's shoes after she died. Well, as much as my father would allow her to. She's the housekeeper, the cook, whatever she needs to be. My father would never admit it, but since his stroke, he doesn't run the house. She does."

Ali turned in her seat. "Except he still runs you."

Lane let out a long breath. "Yes. And that certainly does not speak well about me."

"But—"

"That ends today, though. I am going to become my own woman." She flashed a quick smile at Ali. "Or *your* own woman, as the case might be. You can do with me what you want, as long as you let me out to go to work so I can pay the bills."

Ali slapped her leg playfully. "Don't talk like that before you drag me into your family's house." Lane turned off the street and headed down the long drive. Ali's eyes grew big as saucers. "You grew up... here?"

"Unfortunately, yes."

"It's like...like...a palace in a fairytale."

Lane chuckled as she pulled along the wide set of steps. "That's interesting. I always thought of it more as a prison after my mother passed away. There was no fun, no laughter..." She paused. "No real love."

Ali caught Lane's hand before she could get out of the car. "I'm so nervous I feel like I'm going to throw up."

She drew Ali's hand to her lips. "Relax, sweetheart. You have nothing to worry about."

"God, I hope so," she whispered as she pushed her car door open.

Lane saw the shadowy figure through the etched glass panels in the doors, one of which opened the moment they stepped onto the wide front porch. "Ma'am," Jerald said, tipping his head. "I don't believe Mr. Stanford is expecting you."

"He's not, Jerald, but would you let him know I'm here?" She stepped past him and headed down the hall with Ali hot on her heels. "I'll be in the kitchen."

"Yes, ma'am," he said to her back.

Ali hurried up beside Lane. "They call you ma'am?" she whispered.

"Yes," Lane sighed audibly. "Jerald does." She pushed through the kitchen door, startling Clara where she was seated at the table.

"Well, well, child." She jumped to her feet. "What brings you by here unexpected?" Lane took a step sideways, revealing Ali. Clara stopped where she was and sized Ali up and down.

Ali straightened under the woman's scrutinizing gaze and held her breath, waiting for the woman's verdict.

The penetrating eyes finally turned to Lane's. "Well, sugar, who do we have here?"

"Miss Clara, I'd like to introduce you to Ali Castle." Lane glanced at Ali. "Ali, this is Miss Clara."

"Well, aren't you the prettiest little thing." She reached for Ali's hand, taking it in both of hers. "It's very nice to meet the one responsible for puttin' that smile on Miss Lane's face." Clara's mocha-colored eyes twinkled.

"It's very nice to meet the person responsible for turning Lane into the amazing woman she's become," answered Ali.

Clara squeezed her hand, acknowledging the tribute. "She's pretty amazin' if I do say so myself."

Lane felt her cheeks flush at the compliments they were passing back and forth, then smiled. They were going to get along wonderfully.

Jerald pushed through the door. "Mr. Stanford will see you now in the study, ma'am."

"Wish me luck." Lane followed Jerald out.

When Lane was gone, Clara took Ali's arm and steered her to the kitchen table. "Come now, honey, and tell me about yourself."

Ali would normally have been nervous being left with a complete stranger and in a mansion of a house no less. But Clara's warm eyes and inviting smile made her feel…well…like Lane did.

"What would you like to drink, sweetie?"

Ali looked toward the door that Lane had disappeared through. "What does Lane usually drink here?"

"She drinks that old hard liquor. You don't strike me as that kind of drinker."

Ali wrinkled her nose. "I'm not."

"I got just the thing." Clara busied herself at the stove.

"So you helped raise Lane after her mother passed away."

Clara turned from the stove, crossing her arms over her ample bosom. "I did what I could. Her father is…" She thought for a moment. "Well, I don't like to speak ill of anyone, but he's a stubborn, difficult man. Her momma found more peace where she is now, God rest her soul."

She turned back around and finished the cups of tea, topping each off with a shot of brandy. She placed a cup in front of Ali. "See if you don't like this now. I used to fix this up for Miss Lane when she'd get herself a cold. There's sugar there," she pointed to the bowl in the center of the table, "if you need to sweeten it up. Or I've got honey if you want. You're not one of them that puts milk in your tea are you?" When Ali shook her head, Clara took a sip.

"So…" she began when the raised voices from the other end of the house shattered the quiet of the kitchen. Her brows shot up, disappearing under the curly gray locks on her forehead. Ali turned her gaze toward the door. "Don't pay any mind to that. Miss Lane will hold her own with him just fine." She leaned in over the table. "I've been waiting a lot of years for her to finally do this. So…where is it you're from, sugar?"

"Indiana." Ali took a sip from her cup and nearly choked.

"What part of Indiana? I've got some family that lives down along the river."

Ali relayed only as much information as was necessary to satisfy the woman's curiosity.

"And how is it you're here?"

That was a loaded question. "I go to the art school downtown."

The loud discussion echoing through the long hallway ended suddenly with the reverberating slam of a door. Clara and Ali stared across the table at each other in the ensuing silence. Lane came through the door a moment later, her face and neck a bright crimson.

Clara pushed up from her chair. "Sit, honey," she instructed. Lane dropped with a thud into the chair beside Ali. Clara grabbed a short glass from the cabinet, slipped into the pantry and returned with a bottle of bourbon. "You okay, honey?" she asked as she poured. Lane nodded a slow yes. Clara pushed the glass in front of her.

"He's impossible! Downright pigheaded, unyielding and unforgiving." Lane took a drink and slammed the glass to the table.

"Apple don't fall far from the tree sometimes."

Lane looked shell-shocked. "I can't possibly be as bad as that man."

"Well, not anymore, honey, but you used to be. I think your momma's genes have finally taken hold, though."

Lane looked to Ali, waiting for her assessment. She slipped her hand onto Lane's thigh under the table. "You okay? Really?"

The compassion and caring in the blue eyes looking into hers so earnestly squeezed at her heart so fiercely Lane thought it might explode in her chest. "Yes," Lane managed to whisper. Without thinking, she leaned over and pecked her on the lips. "Thank you."

"You two don't be getting any ideas about doing anything on my kitchen table," Clara said, chuckling as she moved back over to the counter for the brandy bottle. Ali's face blushed a bright pink while Lane simply shrugged and winked at her. Clara stood with the bottle poised over Ali's cup. "Another little sip, sugar?"

"Why not."

Clara poured another shot into her own cup, raised it and said, "Here's to lives full of happiness."

Lane swallowed down the last of her drink. "Are you ready to go?" Ali nodded.

"You two don't need to be running off."

Lane stood. "We do, but I promise we'll come back." She stepped beside Clara to place a kiss on her cheek.

Clara grasped Lane's hand. "You better come back soon...both of you." She looked over at Ali and gave Lane's hand a shake. "She's a keeper, honey. Don't be running her off."

"Never." Lane gazed at Ali. She took note of the study door as they passed it. Still closed. Well, if that's the way he wanted to play it...

Once in the car and headed home, Ali asked again, "Are you okay, baby?"

Lane reached across and took her hand. "Couldn't be better."

Ali turned her hand, entwined her fingers with Lane's and raised their joined hands to her lips, kissing her knuckles. "I think I might have to find that out for myself."

Stopped at a light, Lane turned to look at her. "I won't disappoint."

"Promise?"

She couldn't get back home or get Ali naked in their bed fast enough.

CHAPTER TWENTY-NINE

They had just finished Lane's abbreviated schedule on Monday morning when Jeremy called back into her. "John Woods would like a few minutes of your time."

"Send him in."

Jeremy opened and held the door for Mr. Woods as he entered with a large file box under his arm.

"John…" She nodded, clearing her throat to get Jeremy to leave them.

He dropped the box onto one of the armchairs in front of her desk. "This is everything I could get my hands on from the Allen case."

Lane stared at the box, its contents now inconsequential. She had meant everything she had said to Ali about giving it all up, the job, the car and the penthouse, to be with her.

"Lane?"

"Uh, thanks, John. How much?"

"Three hundred." Lane tipped her head to the side. "I met a very nice admin assistant in the prosecutor's office." He smiled sheepishly and his cheeks colored.

"Oh."

He tapped his fingers on the box top. "You know, I looked through some of this, and I've got to say this investigation was botched from the get-go."

"I suspected that from the preliminary information you found for me."

He rubbed his hand over the back of his neck. "If I had something invested in this girl's situation, I'd be looking to get it overturned. The initial investigation and evidence gathering are questionable at best."

"I agree. I'll make sure that gets passed along." She dug out her wallet. "Thanks again for the assistance, John." She handed over the bills.

"Sure thing." He gave a nod by way of a goodbye and let himself out.

Lane secured the box and instructed Jeremy to send it over to the penthouse. "Will you bite my head off if I ask you what this is about?"

"It's really none of your business. Let's say that it's a case that is ripe for appeal."

"One of yours?"

She laughed. "Of course not!" She prided herself on following the letter of the law in court. At least she had so far. Her personal reputation might be about to take a hit, but she'd bet every last cent she had that she would never be overturned on a case.

Before she could leave for court, Jeremy knocked and entered. "I know you're on your way out, but Beckman's on the phone and he's insisting on speaking with you."

"I don't have time, Jeremy." She grabbed up her case. "I've got to go now or be late for court."

"What should I tell him?"

"Maybe the truth. That I'm extraordinarily busy."

"But he's going to want to know when he can—"

"Jeremy, please, handle it. I have to go. I'll deal with it later."

"Well," she heard him mutter to her retreating back, "at least her old man has quit calling and harassing me."

When she returned from court at four thirty, he was anxiously waiting. "He called again." He trailed her into the office.

"Who?"

"Beckman, and I mean him, not an assistant."

She dropped her things beside the desk, knowing in her soul that she no longer had a choice. There wasn't any way now that she could do the kind of things a man like Thomas Beckman wanted her to. Her conscience wouldn't allow it.

"He makes me nervous," Jeremy said. He was actually trembling. "I mean, I'm really creeped out. He's a scary-sounding man."

Lane motioned him to one of the armchairs. "What did he say? Did he threaten you?"

"No, no real threats. Not in so many words. He made some cryptic comment about the world blowing up when no one's watching. He kept going on and on about how you've been avoiding him and he called you—" He stopped talking.

"Called me what?"

He twisted his fingers. "He called you a coward."

She'd been called many things over the years, but coward wasn't one of them. "I hate to put this on you, but I need you to call him tomorrow. Set up a time that works with my daytime schedule and his." He scribbled. "Also, this needs to take place in the fifth-floor apartment." He looked up, clearly surprised. "I don't want to meet with the man anywhere public, in case—"

"In case?"

"Never mind. Please get it set up as soon as possible."

"Do you want me there for this meeting?"

She laughed. "Not unless you want to flirt with the possibility of perjuring yourself or going to prison."

His mouth fell open. "What the—?"

"Jeremy, the less you know the better. I can handle Beckman. I only need you to set up the meeting for me and make sure the doorman knows you'll be expecting a guest whenever that is. Please." He nodded silently. "Don't look so damned grim, Jeremy. There is nothing for you to worry about." *At least, I'm going to try to make sure it's* only *my ass on the line. Thanks for caring though...*

* * *

Ali sauntered naked into the bedroom after her evening shower and slipped into bed beside Lane. "You look tired."

Lane set her book aside and kissed the top of her head. "I'm never too tired for you, darling."

"All the same, I think I could go to sleep without any encouragement tonight."

Lane chuckled. "'Encouragement,' that's what we're calling it now?"

Ali kissed her neck. "No, what I call it is the best thing that's ever happened in my life."

"You flatter me. It's no wonder I like you so much." She tipped Ali's head up and captured her mouth for a brief, but passion-filled kiss. "Goodnight, darling."

"Night, baby." She snuggled tightly against Lane and within a minute was sleeping soundly.

Lane might have looked tired, but when she closed her eyes she saw Thomas Beckman behind her eyelids. She dreaded confronting him, knowing the move could cost her everything she had.

Well, almost everything. She'd still have Ali, and that's all that really mattered. Ali was her raison d'être now, her reason for existing. Nothing she could lose would cost her more than losing the woman she loved. She tried focusing on the warm body in her arms, but sleep was a long time coming.

* * *

When she returned from court the following afternoon, Jeremy handed her a note that had Friday's date written on it along with the letters T.B. and a time of three o'clock.

"I have Friday afternoon free?"

He watched as she wadded the note and tossed it in his trashcan. "One of the attorneys had a conflict with another case, so yes, that afternoon is clear. Well..." He glanced at the crumpled note in the trash. "Mostly clear."

She was almost asleep that night when Ali spoke. "Baby?"

"Hmm?"

"Are we turning into an old married couple?"

"Why would you think that?"

Ali shifted her leg between Lane's. "Because, this is two nights in a row that we've gone to bed—to sleep."

"Do you think that we should make love every night?"

"I...I don't know. I've never had this with anyone before."

"Do you mean a relationship?" Ali nodded. "I think a relationship is what two people make it. If you want to make love every night, we can."

Ali propped herself up on her elbow and looked into Lane's eyes. "You're so damn sexy, I always want you. But..."

"But what?"

"I don't know." Ali shrugged. "I don't want to screw this up like I've screwed up everything else in my life."

Lane cupped her hand to her cheek. "Sweetheart, there is nothing you can do to screw this up." She pulled Ali to her and claimed her mouth as if it were the lifeline that would sustain her. She tried to pour her heart into the connection, so Ali would feel all that Lane felt for her and her insecurities would be quelled.

"If you want to make love you need only touch me." She pecked Ali's lips. "Anytime, my darling."

"Just a touch. You mean like this?" Her eyes twinkled as her fingers skated across one of Lane's breasts. "Or..." She drew her fingers down Lane's abdomen to the juncture of her thighs. "Here?" Lane's eyes closed as she pushed into Ali's hand, finally able to shut everything out of her mind, except having the woman she loved in her arms.

* * *

Wednesday was a repeat of the day before. Life, it seemed, was settling into a routine for them. They went on their way each day knowing that they'd be together again sometime in the evening. Lane was happier than she'd ever thought she could be, kissing Ali goodbye and going off to work every morning. And Ali, well, she was thrilled with life for the first time since she was a very young girl. She felt loved. Passionately loved. This connection with Lane was something she could have only dreamed of. It was as if she had a place where she belonged, finally, after so many years. She felt grounded. And Lane believed her—believed *in* her. Lane was making it possible for her to explore and reach for her dream. She never believed in fairy tales, but without a doubt, Lane was her knight in shining armor.

Ali was waiting for her in the kitchen as she prepared to leave the next morning. She slid her arms around Lane's waist. "I always want you the most first thing in the morning."

Lane pressed her cheek to the top of her head. "Why do you suppose that is?"

Ali's hands wandered up and down Lane's back under her suit jacket. "Because I've spent all night having your body pressed against mine. I am forever aroused."

That was precisely what Ali's hot little body did to Lane. And the reason that more often than not she ended up taking a colder shower in the morning in an effort to cool the fire that seemed constantly to be simmering. "I can assure you, sweetheart, that's exactly what you do to me."

Ali's hands moved down over Lane's backside. "We should do something about it tonight. I'm off early. Seven thirty, I think."

Lane caught Ali's hands and moved them in front of her. She didn't want the throb of need now when she couldn't do anything to assuage it. "I think that's a perfect plan for *tonight*, but you can't touch me like that now or I'll be walking into walls all day."

"Sorry, baby." Ali giggled. "Not!"

"I'll make sure we have something special for dinner when you get home."

"Mmm, sounds good." Ali gave a sultry smile that made Lane's fingers twitch. "No kiss goodbye?"

Lane pecked her on the lips and quickly moved out of range. "Have a good day."

"You too, baby."

Not long before Ali got home, the dinner for two Lane had arranged with Mario had been delivered and was warming in the oven. "Take your shower, darling. Dinner will be waiting." Lane stood in the kitchen doorway casually dressed in soft brushed cotton trousers, an emerald-green shirt with sleeves rolled up several turns and her favorite loafers.

Ali looked awestruck when she returned and Lane was standing at the dining table with the lights dimmed and candles glowing softly on the perfectly set table. She'd tried to make it reminiscent of the first dinner they'd shared. She slid the chair out for her.

"This is so romantic, baby."

As they ate, they talked about everything and nothing. It was comfortable—natural.

Ali leaned back from the table. "Can I ask you something?"

"Of course." Captivated, Lane leaned in.

Ali fidgeted with the napkin in her lap. "I don't want you to get mad at me, but I was, uh, wondering, when you used to entertain women, did lots of them want you to..." She looked down at her lap. "You know...do them, uh, like, uh...like a guy, I guess?"

Lane paused a long moment before replying. "Can I ask why you would want to know this?"

Ali's cheeks colored and she shrugged. "I guess I've never thought about two women having sex that way."

"I believe it's a preference, not because of a woman's sexuality, but because she finds it pleasurable being intimate in that way."

"So, uh…" Ali couldn't meet Lane's eyes. "You've, uh, been with more than one gay woman who likes to do it that way?"

"I have, and as I said, I believe it's a preference. Some women can only achieve an orgasm that way."

"Does it have anything to do with why you won't let me…you know, go down there?" Ali's cheeks were bright crimson.

"Not at all." Lane was remarkably unfazed by Ali's curiosity. "I don't mean to embarrass you, sweetheart. But again, is there a reason you're asking me this?" If her suspicions were correct about what had led to Ali being in prison, Lane couldn't imagine she would have any desire to be intimate in that manner.

"When your fingers are inside me…" Ali looked at her hand fiddling with the napkin. "It's the most wonderful thing I've ever experienced."

Lane's breaths became so shallow she almost stopped breathing.

Ali shrugged. "I don't know. I thought you might like doing that with me." She finally raised her eyes to meet Lane's.

"I would only ever want that if it's what you wanted."

"Would you enjoy it, though?"

Lane's blood ran liquid hot through her veins and pooled between her legs. She managed not to let that influence the answer she gave, however. "I would only enjoy that if you enjoyed it."

Ali's gaze was intense. "I think…"

Uncertain, Lane thought.

"I think I'd like to. If you want to."

Lane felt beads of perspiration on the back of her neck. Her mouth was so dry she wasn't sure if she could even speak. She cleared her throat. "Only if you're absolutely sure about this." Ali nodded. "I… uh." Lane was suddenly more nervous than she'd ever been with a woman. "It's downstairs."

"I'll clean up."

"No," Lane said quickly. "Leave it."

Lane looked over at Ali, noting how the candlelight sparkled in her eyes and bathed her face in its soft glow. She had only ever strapped on the phallus to fuck a woman whose primary interest was in having Lane please her, down and dirty. Every time she made love to Ali, she had allowed herself to be a part of the intimacy. She was having a hard time reconciling the way it had been with the way it was now. She needed to figure out where she was with all of this.

"Why don't you fill our glasses and get comfortable in the bedroom? I'll be right back." She trotted down the three flights to the apartment and grabbed the small bag from the bathroom vanity there, taking her time returning to the penthouse. Unlike the cavalier way in which she'd behaved with other women, this—with Ali—would have to be so very tender.

When she entered the bedroom, the lights were off. Ali had placed the candles from the dining table on the bedside tables. It was heavenly and made even more so by the vision of Ali stretched across the bed in a robe. Ali's eyes fixated on the bag in Lane's hand.

"I need a few minutes," Lane said in a raspy whisper before disappearing into the bathroom. Her hands trembled as she undressed and secured the harness. Again, she hadn't been this nervous at the thought of being with a woman since her first time in high school. *And I've gained decades of experience since then.* Of course she'd never been in love before. Pulling on a robe, she willed her nerves to settle and, careful not to expose herself, she climbed into the bed on her side next to Ali.

Ali's gaze met Lane's. "I want you so much." Her hand slid behind Lane's neck and pulled her into a kiss. As it deepened, she eased her leg toward Lane's, brushing against the bulge at the top of Lane's thighs.

Lane moaned deeply. She'd forgotten how arousing this was. They were both gasping for air when Ali pulled her mouth away.

"God, you make me so hot." Ali guided Lane's hand between her legs and pushed into it. "You're going to make me come." Lane's hand stilled. "Can I touch you?"

Lane nodded, and Ali pressed her palm against the phallus. "Ah, God," she gasped, her hips jerking.

"Does it feel good if I touch you like this?" She curled her fingers around the phallus and increased the pressure on it.

Lane nodded slowly.

Ali continued to caress the phallus. "I want you, baby," she murmured. "I want to feel you inside me."

Lane felt like she might combust. Easing Ali onto her back and parting her robe to expose her soft skin, she kissed down the column of her neck to her breasts. When she moved her hand between Ali's thighs, Ali opened herself to her. She moved back up Ali's body and braced herself on one arm while she placed the tip of the soft rubber against Ali's center.

"Make love to me."

Lane hesitated, caught in a struggle between need and fear.

"Baby, please," Ali begged.

"I don't want to hurt you."

"No, you could never. Please…I need you."

Lane gently, slowly, entered her, all the while watching Ali's eyes— so trusting. She wanted nothing more than to pleasure her.

"Yes," Ali groaned.

Lane felt her own heart beating everywhere. And when Ali began to tremble beneath Lane it rocked like an earthquake through every part of her. She let go. She let herself tumble over the edge and free fall with Ali. She knew, in that moment, that nothing would ever be more natural or move her in the way this had. She watched Ali's eyes, hooded with pleasure. "You are so incredibly beautiful," she whispered.

"Mmm," Ali kissed the corner of Lane's mouth. "I could do this every day of my life."

"As you wish, my love." Lane knew she'd be putty in Ali's hands hereafter.

CHAPTER THIRTY

Ali hummed as she went about getting ready for her class on Friday. She was a little sore, but she decided that would remind her throughout the day how absolutely incredible their lovemaking had been last night. She was still humming absentmindedly when she was stopped by her professor as she started to enter her second class.

"Ms. Castle, may I have a word with you after class today?"

"Uh…sure…okay." Her euphoria began to dissolve.

A second later she felt the press of a body at her back and a whispered, "Ali's in trouble."

She spun around and snapped, "Why would you say that?"

Jade took a quick step back, raising her hand defensively. "Whoa, easy there. I was only joking."

"I'm sorry."

Jade angled her head toward the front of the room. "Any idea what's up?"

"No clue." They approached Ali's usual seat.

"I'm sure it's nothing," Jade said, heading to her own seat.

Ali fretted for the next two hours that she was about to get booted from the class. Worse than her own disappointment, she knew, would be Lane's. Lane believed in her more than she believed in herself. By the time class ended and he asked her to follow him to his office at the other end of the building, she was anxious to get it over with.

"Please have a seat," he instructed as he rounded the desk and sat down himself. She did so, albeit nervously. "I've had some interest in some of your work." He smiled.

"Seriously?"

He chuckled. "Yes. I share my students' work around whenever possible, so…" He slid a business card across the desk to her. "This particular gallery owner was very interested in your pieces. She's interested in having you work with her at her gallery here in town. I believe she has another in some other major city as well."

"I…uh…" Ali was dumbfounded.

"She asked to see more of your work. I told her I would inquire. She was particularly interested in your nudes. She said they are so realistic that they have a heartbeat."

Ali's mind was spinning. "Uh, sure, I can bring in some others on Monday."

"That would work perfectly, my dear. I'll see Ms. Tyler again next week." He leaned back, locking his fingers together at his waist. "This is an incredible opportunity for you, Ms. Castle. I would like to see you pursue it, in fact, even if it meant dropping my class to do so." Ali looked on, surprised. "Yes, I believe you're that talented."

"Thank you." She stood, nodding her head. "Thank you *so* much."

He tipped his head. "Bring me more of your work on Monday and let's jump start your future."

"I will. Thank you so much, professor."

He stood briefly. "It's too soon for gratitude, and even then it would go to Ms. Tyler."

She was practically walking on air as she made her way out of the building.

"Hey, Ali," Jade called from outside the building. Ali stepped off the walk to join her. "Well, I'm guessing by that look they didn't kick you out."

She grabbed Jade's hand excitedly. "There's a gallery owner here in the city that wants to see some of my work. I might be able to get a job there. It's so cool! Just think! I could quit waiting tables for a living."

Jade squeezed her hand lightly and withdrew hers. "I'm really happy for you, Ali. I hope it works out. You'll still be my friend when you're a big famous artist, won't you?"

Ali slapped her arm playfully. "Of course, silly. I'll never forget where I've come from." It was mostly true. "Listen, I've got to go. I need to stop home and see what all I can come up with for Monday." She started away. "See you. Have a good weekend." She didn't really need to rush—she had plenty of time before work—but she couldn't suppress the excitement bubbling inside.

* * *

As the clock ticked closer to three, Lane paced between the bar and piano in the apartment, her stomach in knots. She'd poured herself a drink, out of habit more than anything, but had only taken a sip. She didn't want her senses dulled for her meeting with Thomas Beckman. She hadn't been this nervous facing her father.

She jumped when the doorbell chimed. Taking calming breaths as she neared the door, she pulled it open and forced a smile she hoped appeared genuine. "Mr. Beckman, come in, please." The leer he gave her in return sent an unwelcome chill racing up her spine. She motioned him toward the bar as she closed the door. "Would you care for a drink?"

He slipped off his suit jacket and hung it on the back of a barstool as he sidled up to the bar. "Only if you're joining me." Lane picked up her glass from the piano on her way to the bar. He slid onto one of the other barstools. "I see you got a head start on me."

She didn't want to look at the man and wished he'd quit talking. "What would you like?"

He crossed his hands over his chest. "I'm hurt that you don't remember. Scotch neat."

Oh, God, please let this be over. She fixed his drink and again avoided looking at him.

When he had his glass in hand, he toasted, "To partnerships with benefits."

Lane thought she might gag. The man was married, for crying out loud! *The absolute gall of some people.* She took a small sip of her drink. No time like the present. Rip off the bandage and be done with it. She set her glass on the bar. "This whole notion of a partnership is why I wanted to speak with you today."

"Oh?"

She took the leap. "Unfortunately I'm not going to be able to assist you with your 'Mr. Baker' problem." She watched red rise from his tightly buttoned shirt collar to his hairline. He looked like a pressure cooker about to blow. She forged ahead before he could speak. "I'm changing the direction of my future, and these types of arrangements don't fit in my plans."

He shoved off the barstool. "You can't do this!" She stood perfectly still, her insides shaking, attempting to exhibit the calm countenance she always wore in the courtroom. "You can't do this," he yelled again.

She exhaled slowly. "I already have, Mr. Beckman. I've had myself recused from the case since we are known to be social acquaintances."

He slammed his fist down hard on the bar. "We had an agreement."

Lane gripped the edge of the bar to still her trembling hands. "Agreements are set aside all the time, Mr. Beckman. That's one reason our courts are so bogged down."

"This is unbelievable," he spat. "I'll be speaking to your father about this."

Lane stifled a smile. "My father won't be changing my mind. We've already discussed it."

"Dammit, Lane." He pounded his fist on the bar again. "You can't do this! You have skeletons in your closet that will bury you— permanently."

"Take your best shot." She crossed her arms over her chest. "I'm in charge of my life and my career now, and my plans no longer include doing business with men like you, Mr. Beckman." She tossed out a threat of her own. "If you make trouble for me, I will be ready. Remember, please, that even if I am forced down and disbarred, I can still be a witness."

"This...this..." he stuttered, "is far from over. I promise you that." He jerked his suit jacket off the barstool beside him, sending it sailing to the floor with a deafening crash.

"I'm not going anywhere," she said calmly.

A moment later the door slammed loudly. She reached a shaky hand for her glass, finding it took both to hold it steady enough to take a drink. After a couple of sips, her insides calmed considerably. She walked around the bar, righted the stool that had been tipped over and grabbed his glass. On her way to the kitchen she called downstairs for the doorman to hail her a cab. She checked herself in the bathroom mirror before gathering her things and heading back to work. Feeling another weight falling from her shoulders, she even smiled at Henry as she crossed the lobby. This new life was going to suit her nicely indeed.

* * *

Ali rushed into the penthouse, dumped her things inside the door and went in search of the piece she wanted to show her professor, a nude she'd done shortly after she and Lane first met. She hadn't yet seen Lane nude at that point, but she had had a feeling what she might look like under her business attire. As it turned out, she'd not been too far off in her imaginings.

She searched frantically through the master bedroom, guest room, the living room, under the obvious furniture, couches and beds—but nothing. She even peeked into Lane's office. Finally it dawned on her. She had stored some of her things down in the apartment. She took the back steps quickly but paused, key in hand, when she reached the back door and heard raised voices coming from inside. Very quietly she slipped the key in the lock, turned it and the knob slowly and opened the door a crack.

Something slammed loudly and a male voice reverberated down the hall. "You can't do this! You have skeletons in your closet that will bury you—permanently."

"Take your best shot." She heard Lane's voice respond firmly.

Someone was threatening Lane, her lover, the woman she'd come to love more than anything she'd ever known in her life. It didn't take a Harvard lawyer to know that the angry man had to be threatening Lane with revealing the fact that she was a lesbian. A lesbian with a lover who'd been convicted of murder. Ali's hands trembled uncontrollably as she tried to close the door without making a sound. Her legs shook so fiercely she knew she never be able to climb the stairs. She staggered to the elevator.

"I can't ruin her life," she said softly to herself. "I won't."

She went to the closet in the bedroom and rummaged for her bag. Into it, she shoved every piece of clothing she'd come with, leaving behind only the nice things Lane had paid for. She grabbed several garbage bags, filled them with her sketchpads from school and all the art supplies she could find and placed them at the back door.

In the kitchen she wrote a note and placed her keys and garage card beside it. Her tears flowing freely, staining the front of her top, she took a slow walk around the penthouse before picking up the bags at the back door. The fear she'd felt twenty minutes earlier was gone. In its place was resolution—and a grief so deep that she thought she'd be sick.

Lane's Miata had been in the garage when she had come home. *Home*, she thought, sadness filling her completely. *Not anymore*. She didn't know if Lane was using her car today or the car service, but to avoid running into her in the elevator Ali decided to walk down. The stairwell was empty and cavernous. The way she felt inside. Her footsteps echoed as she descended flight after flight of stairs. After peering out the door into the garage to make sure Lane was nowhere in sight, she hauled her things to her car and drove off. It was twenty minutes until four. She could still make it to The Inn if she rushed, but she couldn't go there. She could barely breathe, much less work. Something unimaginable tore at her insides. As she drove aimlessly through town the only thing she could manage was one sob after another.

* * *

Knowing Ali had to work until closing and not wanting to spend the evening home alone after her confrontation with Beckman, when she got back to her office Lane called Carlina.

"Lane, darling, how are you?"

"Couldn't be better."

"I don't doubt that for a moment." Carlina chuckled.

"I know it's short notice, but are you free after work for a drink or a bite to eat?"

"Hmm," she purred. "Are you on the menu?"

Lane laughed. "Sorry, no."

"Well, a girl has to ask." Lane could hear papers shuffling. "I have a call I can't make until after five thirty, but I can meet you when I'm done."

"Perfect." Lane thought she could force herself to do some work of her own now that she knew she wouldn't be spending the evening alone. "Where shall we meet?"

"Let's see…how about the lounge at the Regency? The bartender pours divine drinks, and we can have appetizers for dinner if we get hungry. They're not what I'm salivating for, but they'll have to do since I can't indulge in you."

Lane shook her head. "You're incorrigible."

"What can I say?"

"That you'll see me around six thirty-ish at the Regency."

"Count on it, darling."

Lane was laughing with Carlina's favorite bartender, drink in hand, when Carlina arrived. "Hello, darling," Carlina's breath whispered in Lane's ear.

"Your friend here was filling me in on some of your best pickup lines." Lane winked at Ricky.

"Ah, but I save the best for you." She squeezed Lane's arm and climbed onto the stool beside her. When Ricky moved out of earshot, she said, "You look as though you're glowing, darling. Married life must agree with you."

"I suppose it must." Lane sipped her drink.

Ricky returned with Carlina's drink. "Thank you, darling." She gave Ricky a heart-stopping smile.

"So, it's Friday night and you're having a drink with me instead of your gorgeous blonde. What's that all about?"

"She's working. She won't be home until eleven or so."

"And so you're settling for me." She gave a pout.

"Not settling, Carlina. I consider you my friend, and we should all spend more time with our friends. I like you, aside from the fact you are a relentless flirt."

Carlina simply batted her eyes. If Lane hadn't known the woman better, known that she was a high-powered wheeler-dealer at the brokerage firm, she might believe her innocent come-on. They talked about work and about mutual friends, ordering something to munch on before ordering more to drink. When they finally stepped out of the hotel into the cool night air, Lane was feeling quite pleasant…just the right amount of high. She was anxious to get home.

"We should do this more often, Lane. I have so much fun with you."

"Agreed. It should be easier to do. I've freed up my schedule considerably."

"Call me anytime." She leaned in and kissed Lane's lips lightly. "Goodnight, darling."

"Goodnight."

* * *

As the elevator rose she began planning their night. She wanted to dim the lights, put on some soft music and sway with Ali in her arms. She was humming a romantic tune and floating on a cloud when she unlocked the door, dropped her things beside the table and headed to the bedroom.

After a quick shower she made her way to the kitchen for a glass of water. She wouldn't drink any more alcohol unless Ali wanted some. Flipping on the light, she grabbed a glass and filled it at the refrigerator. Only then did she notice the note, keys and card lying on the counter. Instantly grasping what they could mean, she felt like she was falling into a dark abyss.

She picked up the paper, but her hand was shaking so violently she couldn't read what was written on it. She laid it down and read through vision blurred by tears.

Lane, I'm so sorry to take the coward's way out and do this this way. But I believe it's for the best. I can't ruin your life like I have my own. Please always know that no one has ever or will ever again capture my heart like you have. I'll love you forever.—Ali.

"No." She pounded her fists on the granite countertop. "No... no...no..."

Wrapping her arms around herself to try to stop shaking, she stumbled out into the dark living room and leaned her forehead against the cool glass of the floor-to-ceiling windows. She cried so hard she thought she would be sick. When she managed to stop the tears, she found her cell phone, sat in the corner of the couch and called Ali's phone. Her call went straight to voice mail.

"Ali..." She did her best to sound put-together. "Sweetheart, please call me as soon as you get my message. I don't know what's happened, but whatever it is, we can fix it. I...love you."

She exhaled a long breath and dialed the phone again.

"Missed me that much, darling? Has it even been an hour?"

"Oh, Car." Lane couldn't get out anything more before her voice broke and a sob escaped.

"Lane, my God, what's wrong?"

Lane's lips trembled as she tried to speak. "She's...she's gone."

"What?"

"She left me," Lane answered through her tears.

"Oh, darling, I'm so sorry. Do you want me to—"

"Please come over...I need..."

"I'm on my way now." Lane heard the jingle of keys and the slamming of a door. "Are you okay until I get there?"

"I...yes?"

"You have to promise me you won't do anything but sit there and wait for me, Lane."

"I won't. I mean…I will. I'll wait." She closed the phone and clutched it to her chest, willing it to ring. Praying for Ali to call her. Hearing the rumble of the elevator, she stumbled to the door and looked out, hoping to see her face. The hallway was empty. Leaving the door unlocked, she returned to the couch and sat in the darkness crying softly. Twenty minutes later Carlina knocked and let herself in.

She settled down beside her friend. "Oh, darling." She pushed the hair back from Lane's face and drew her into a comforting embrace. "Shh…" she soothed. She smoothed her hand up and down Lane's back. "I know it seems impossible now, but you're a very strong woman, Lane. You will get past this."

Lane shook her head, slowly withdrawing from Carlina's arms. She swiped the wetness from her cheeks. "She stole my heart, Car. I'll never care this way again as long as I live. I don't want to…" she whispered.

"You said earlier she was working late." Lane nodded. "Did you try calling her there?"

"No," Lane whispered.

Carlina noticed the phone clutched in her hand. "Call her, darling. What could it hurt?"

Lane's hand shook visibly as she found the number for the restaurant in her contacts and raised the phone to her ear.

"The Inn, this is Suzanne. How can I help you?"

"This is Judge Stanford," Lane said, trying to keep the pain and fear out of her voice. "I was wondering if I might speak with Ms. Castle."

"Uh…" Suzanne hesitated. "I think she must be out sick this evening. She didn't come in."

"Okay." Lane cleared her throat. "Thank you." She snapped the phone closed, allowing it to fall from her hand to the floor. Carlina looked at her expectantly. "She's gone." Lane sucked in a breath, trying to stave off another round of tears. "She didn't show up for work." She bent over, gasping for breath. "I can't do this, Car."

Carlina grasped her by the shoulders. "Look at me, Lane." She coaxed Lane's eyes up to meet hers. "You can't do anything more tonight. We'll figure things out tomorrow." She stood, slid her hand into Lane's and gave a gentle tug. "Come on, let me put you to bed and we'll start fresh in the morning."

"I'll never sleep." Lane's legs shook.

Carlina slipped an arm around her waist, steering her toward the hall. "Yes, you will. I'll make sure of it." In the bedroom, she pulled back the covers. "Get in. I'll be right back." When she returned a minute later with a pillbox and a bottle of water from the refrigerator, Lane was precisely where Carlina had left her, on her side of the bed, staring blankly at the place Ali should be. Carlina sat beside her and shook a tiny tablet from the box. "Here, take this." She turned Lane's hand and placed the pill in her palm.

"What is it?"

"It's for anxiety," Carlina explained. "Hazards of the job. It will relax you and help you sleep some." She uncapped the water and handed it to her. Once Lane had successfully swallowed the pill, Carlina placed the bottle on the night table. "Come on, darling. Get in under the covers."

When Lane was settled into the pillows, Carlina pulled the sheet and covers to her waist and sat at her side, gently running her fingers through Lane's hair. "Now close your eyes and sleep. We'll figure something out tomorrow." She touched the back of her fingers lightly to Lane's cheek. When she pulled her hand away, Lane caught it.

"Please don't go," Lane whispered desperately. "Don't leave me alone, Car."

"I would never abandon you, Lane." She lowered their joined hands and held them between her breasts.

"Could you hold me again while I try to sleep?" Lane pleaded. She knew somehow that what she was asking was injudicious and possibly unfair to Car, but never before had she felt so raw, so vulnerable.

Carlina managed a nod, though, and said, "Be right back." She eased from the bed and slipped off her jacket, shoes, skirt and stockings. She unbuttoned and removed her blouse as she slid beneath covers on the other side of the bed. Lane moved into Carlina's arms and rested her head on her shoulder.

Carlina sighed deeply, settling her cheek against Lane's hair. "It's going to be okay, somehow, some way, my darling." She gently stroked up and down Lane's arm, soothing her into sleep before dozing off herself.

CHAPTER THIRTY-ONE

The sun was beginning to dip in the western sky when the drive that Ali had thought was directionless brought her to a very familiar, very special place. Propelled by some force she didn't recognize and couldn't explain, she walked around the mansion and, going on memory, made her way through the garden and the wooded area to the lake. It was picturesque, but Ali, the artist, couldn't see the beauty. She could only feel the loneliness that was consuming her.

As she stepped off the boardwalk and onto the path into the woods, vivid memories came flooding back, too intense to outrun no matter how fast she ran. Lungs burning, eyes blurry from her tears, she dropped to the cold, hard ground, braced herself against a tree and sobbed. She had thought that being locked away for seven years was the worst thing she'd ever experience. She understood now how wrong she had been.

She closed her eyes, remembering the day she'd spent here with Lane. They'd shared their first kiss here, tentative as it was. She touched her fingers to her lips, recalling the softness of Lane's. She realized now that her initial reluctance to accept Lane's invitation had been fear of giving herself over to the kind of woman she'd only ever fantasized about. She had known when she went into the woods that day with Lane that she was a goner where she was concerned.

When darkness began closing around her she made her way back to the boardwalk. The sky was awash with deep reds, an artist's dream vista, but she didn't take even a moment to enjoy it. She sat in her car trying to come up with some kind of a plan for what to do next but came up empty. When she started the car this time and began driving, she truly had no idea where she was going.

* * *

Nestled in Ali's arms, Lane shifted her head so her lips were but a breath away from the soft flesh of her breast. She stretched her arm across the warm inviting skin at her waist and pulled her closer, moaning softly as her hand slid lower toward her hip and to the top of her thigh.

"Lane, darling, I think you're dreaming." Carlina gave Lane's shoulder a gentle shake, bringing her closer to full consciousness, reminding her whose arms were holding her. She rolled away.

"I'm sorry, I thought..." Her voice was rough as gravel.

Carlina shifted onto her side, resting her hand on Lane's shoulder. "Darling, it's all right." Lane's muscles tensed. Carlina must have felt it. "I mean, it's not all right, I'm sure of that, but please don't give it another thought. How are you feeling?"

Lane heaved a sigh. "Like I was hit by a bus last night and dragged across the city."

"Not surprising, considering." Carlina sat up and moved to the side of the bed. "I'll make coffee while you jump in the shower." She pulled on her discarded blouse, which barely came to the top of her lace panties, and padded out of the room.

Twenty minutes later Lane made her way to the kitchen, reemerging with two mugs and a carafe of coffee. She took them to the living room where Carlina was curled up on the couch reading her email. She put down her cell phone and accepted the cup of coffee Lane offered her. Lane couldn't help noticing what a striking woman she was, disheveled hair, yesterday's blouse and all. She was also a damn fine friend.

"I saw the note on the counter. Do you want to tell me what happened?"

Lane took a drink from her mug, putting it aside when she felt the acidic burn in her stomach. "I gather from her note she thinks she's going to somehow ruin my life."

"Why does she think that?"

"She has her past."

"Don't we all…"

"I told you she'd been in prison. I didn't tell you she'd been sent there for second-degree murder."

"Oh…" Carlina gasped. "I had assumed it was something…oh hell, I'm not sure what I thought."

"Yeah," Lane finally said in the ensuing silence. She gazed out the window. "I finally reach a decision to take back control of my own life so she can be a part of it, and…" She swallowed, trying to control her emotions. "She's gone," she finally managed to say, somehow keeping the tears at bay. "Her past is her past. It couldn't hurt me enough to matter now."

She exhaled slowly. "Not to mention the fact she's not guilty of what she was convicted of. Of that I am certain. Her case should have been thrown out by the presiding judge. Instead, they threw her away." She rose and walked over to the windows, her eyes searching the city beyond the glass. "I can't live without her now, Car." She shook her head. "I don't want to."

Carlina moved to stand next to Lane. She rested her hand on Lane's shoulder. "We'll find her, darling. And when we do, you can charm her right back into your life."

Lane wanted to take her friend's words to heart, but her heart felt like a black hole. "I don't know, Car."

Carlina slid her hand down Lane's back and around her waist. "I do. I also know that I'm famished. Let's go get a bite to eat and figure out how to search for your lover."

Carlina drove them to a quaint little cafe along the river. When they'd settled into the cozy booth, with cups of steaming coffee before them and their orders placed, she asked, "Where do you think she would go?"

Lane stared at the cup cradled in her hands. "I honestly don't have a clue."

Carlina took a sip of the strong black coffee. "Where did she live before she moved in with you anyway? Would she go back there?"

Lane shook her head, ashamed to admit the truth, because when you put all the truths together it sounded an awful lot like she'd taken in a stray. "In her car."

"As in homeless?" Carlina blurted out. "Not that that has any bearing on anything," she quickly added. "You must know people who could track down her car using the license plate."

In all the time Ali had been living with her, she'd never paid any attention to the license number. "I don't know what it is," Lane admitted. "But I know a guy who does. He can look into it for me."

"Good. After brunch we can go to the restaurant. You can ask again about her…or I can ask for you."

Before they went to The Inn, they went to Carlina's condo so she could shower and change clothes. Lane paced like a caged animal as she waited. They made it to the restaurant around eleven thirty in the middle of the Saturday luncheon crowd.

Lane made her way to the hostess stand where she was greeted by the redhead's cheerful smile. "Judge Stanford, so happy to have you joining us for lunch today."

"I'm sorry. I'm not here to dine. I was wondering if Roscoe's here, and if so if I could possibly speak with him."

The hostess waved a hand. "Absolutely. Let me find him." She disappeared toward the dining area. Lane and Carlina moved aside to wait. When she returned, she said, "Roscoe said he'd be a few minutes, but if you wouldn't mind waiting please enjoy a mimosa on the house. He'll be with you as soon as possible." She motioned to the empty end of the bar.

Carlina sipped the sweet drink while Lane simply stared at hers. What she really wanted couldn't be found in a drink glass.

Roscoe appeared finally, wearing a look of consternation. "Your artist seems to have flown the proverbial coop," he said without his usual good humor.

"I've very sorry, Roscoe."

He waved a hand. "How could you possibly be responsible for any of this?" He didn't wait for her answer. "She was one of the best servers I've ever had and several of our regular customers are asking for her. She's left me in a real bind. I imagine she's hung you out to dry in some way or another as well?"

"I'm hoping she'll turn up," Lane said, swallowing the anguish trying to force its way out of her throat. "Perhaps for a paycheck. Could you let me know?"

"Yes, yes, of course. I will tell her to call you immediately."

"No," Lane stated, a bit too abruptly judging from Roscoe's startled expression. She took a calming breath. "I mean if she should show up or even call with a forwarding address, I would appreciate it if *you* would let me know. There's someone interested in speaking to her."

"Certainly, Lane, I will contact you if I see or hear from her."

As Lane slid off the barstool, anxious to leave, an image of Ali at the other end of the bar flashed in her mind and nearly stopped her heart. Suddenly dizzy and weak, she grabbed for the back of the barstool.

"We should run, Lane, or we'll be late." Carlina caught her arm and helped her through the crowd to her car.

"Anywhere else you think she might possibly go?"

Lane had no idea why, but she directed her friend to drive the few blocks to the abandoned building Ali had tried to pass off as her residence. When the car stopped at the curb, Lane was out of the door almost before Carlina could put it in park.

Lane leaned against the side of the car, staring up at the dilapidated structure. "Lane?" Carlina joined her, standing close enough that their shoulders touched. "What is this?"

"Where she told me she lived when I first started seeing her."

"Because she didn't want you to know she lived in her car."

"Was everything a lie, Car? Like telling me she lived here? Did I simply imagine that she cared as much as she said?"

Carlina's eyes were warm with compassion. "What does your heart tell you? Do you really believe it was all a lie?" Lane slowly moved her head side to side, tears welling in her eyes. "There's your answer," Carlina said quietly.

"Why?" Lane managed before the tears slipped from her eyes. "Why would she tear me apart like this if she truly loved me?"

Carlina pushed closer until they were touching along the length of their bodies. "Love is a mystery I've yet to solve. I don't have any answers for you, darling. I'm sorry."

Lane stood there only a moment longer. "Let's get out of here."

"Where to now?"

"Take me home."

* * *

Carlina followed her up to the penthouse. "You don't have to hang around. I'm sure you have things to do." Carlina settled down on the couch. "Nothing of any importance." Her eyes shone with concern.

"I'm all right. Really. You don't have to stay and hold my hand."

"Well, of course I don't. But I can't help being a little worried about you, Lane. Last night you were completely devastated. Now you're acting like you couldn't care less."

"I *was* devastated. I probably still am in some deep place. But I also realize I can't live pining after a woman I'll likely never see again." She avoided Carlina's eyes. She didn't want her worrying about her or, worse, hovering. No, the best thing she could do would be to lock away the pain and get back to "normal." That would allow her to continue to hunt for Ali without having to deal with everyone's solicitousness. She'd never accept that Ali had been conning her. The words in the note she left had not been contrived. She had meant them.

Carlina interrupted her thoughts. "Look at me and tell me I have nothing to worry about."

"I'll be fine, Carlina." She squeezed her hand gently. "I promise."

Carlina gazed at Lane a moment longer. "All right." She stood. "But if I call and you don't answer, I'll be here breaking down your door."

Lane gave a small smile. "That might be worth ignoring your call."

Carlina narrowed her eyes. "Don't mess with me, darling. I'm being serious."

"I know you are." Lane led her to the door. "I appreciate your friendship more than you can know."

Carlina tugged her hand, pulling her close enough to place a kiss on her cheek. "I'll be checking on you, but if you need someone, don't hesitate to call me."

Lane closed the door and leaned against it, crossing her arms over herself. After a minute she pulled her phone from her pocket and dialed Ali again. It rang and rang and finally went to voice mail. "Ali, please call me, sweetheart. We need to talk."

Ending that call, she scrolled through her contacts and made another. It too went to voice mail. "Hi, John, it's Lane. I need your assistance for some additional work regarding Ms. Castle. Please call me at your earliest convenience."

She blew out a breath in frustration. She hadn't a clue if John even checked his messages on the weekends. If he didn't, she was certain this would be the longest one of her life.

So she sat a while, paced a bit and scanned the penthouse looking for some kind of a clue to Ali's whereabouts. She even considered getting in her car and driving around looking for Ali's beater, but without any idea of where to begin, it would be like trying to find a needle in a haystack. She managed to tough it out until seven o'clock before she poured her first drink. By ten she was sufficiently inebriated to fall asleep.

At ten the next morning she was awakened by an incessant noise, a far-off ring that took several minutes to identify. When she did, she stumbled from the bed to the living room and grabbed up her cell from the coffee table. The screen showed the missed call was from Carlina. She quickly phoned her back, hoping Carlina wasn't already in her car.

Carlina answered instantly. "I was on my way."

Lane tried for a chuckle. "I guessed as much. Sorry, I was soaking in the tub and forgot to take my phone in."

"Need any company?"

"Thank you for the selfless gesture, but I'm good, Car."

"What are you doing today, darling? Do you want to go out for a bite, catch a movie, go shopping?"

"I actually have a lot of work to catch up on that I should have done yesterday. Thanks for the invite though."

"Thank-yous aren't required. Are you really all right, Lane?"

"Of course. You know me, Car, tough-as-nails Judge Stanford. Nothing gets to me."

"I'll take you at your word," Carlina said. "This time." She ended the call with a promise to touch base again soon.

The day turned into a miserable one for Lane. She tried to do some of the work she'd chucked into her case Friday as she left the office but found it impossible to concentrate. When she couldn't pace any more, a thought occurred to her. They had lived a short time down in the apartment. There might be some kind of clue there. She rushed down the stairs to check.

A search of the bedroom turned up nothing. As she started down the hall, though, she caught sight of the bag stashed in the guest room and the sketchpad peeking out of its top. She flipped it open on the desk. The pad was the one she'd seen before. She turned the pages until she found the sketch of the nude female figures embracing each other intimately. The emotionally intense depiction brought tears to her eyes again—and gave her another idea of where she might search for Ali.

She tucked the pad back into the bag and carried it upstairs. If she couldn't find Ali—correction: *until* she found her—she'd have to be content looking at the sketch, which she desperately wanted to believe was of the two of them.

CHAPTER THIRTY-TWO

Lane made certain Monday morning that she was in a work frame of mind before Jeremy arrived. He'd been increasingly difficult since she had him clear her schedule and start declining invitations. When he entered with her calendar, his demeanor was stiff and too professional not to be forced. He wasn't pleased with her decision. She wouldn't be surprised, in fact, if he had done as she had suggested and started putting feelers out for a new up-and-comer to latch on to.

He poked his head back into the office minutes after he'd left. "That John Woods fellow is on the phone for you again."

"Thank you." She refrained from picking up the line until he closed the door. "John, thank you for getting back to me."

"No problem, Lane. What can I do for you regarding this Ms. Castle?"

She exhaled. "It seems Ms. Castle has vanished once again. No one is able to locate her, so I'm hoping to employ your expert sleuthing skills, John."

"No problem, Lane. Any ideas on where I might start?"

She was reluctant to reveal anything that might link her to Ali personally, even though John had always been very discreet and didn't appear to be a judgmental man. "I checked at the restaurant. I know the owner personally. He said she didn't show up for work Friday and has not been seen or heard from since."

"That's not much to go on."

"I know. I'm sorry." She rotated the pen in her hand absently between her fingers. "I understand if you have no interest or the time to chase after this."

"I've still got the info on the car. I'll have my buddy down at the precinct see if he can turn up anything. Is there anything else you can think of that might provide a lead?"

Seeing the sketches yesterday had reminded her of the one Ali had done of the beautiful coffee-skinned woman she had class with. Jade, Ali had called her. She hated to lie to John—he had always come through for her—but she didn't want him asking questions at the art school. "Nothing at the moment, John. If I think of anything, I'll give you a call."

"Okay, Lane, we'll talk soon."

Off the phone she did some calculations. Even if she could time today's lunch break from court to coincide with a trip to the art school, she wouldn't have enough time to get there and back and find Jade and talk to her. She blew out a breath. The only option, it seemed, was to try to lose herself in work. The less she thought about Ali and the emptiness she felt, the less likely she would be to completely lose her mind.

* * *

After she called for an extended lunch recess on Tuesday, Lane rushed from the courthouse, hailed a cab to take her the dozen or so blocks to the school and told the driver to wait at the curb across the street. When she saw the students filing out, she jumped out and crossed to the sidewalk. The beautiful girl emerged a moment later. Lane approached her with an air of confidence she wasn't feeling.

"Excuse me, are you Jade?"

The student scrutinized Lane in her work clothes, a Saks Fifth Avenue suit. "Any reason you're asking?"

Lane gave what she hoped was a smile that could be trusted. "We have a mutual friend." The artist narrowed her exquisite, blue-gray eyes at Lane. Lane wondered how many men and women had fallen into them.

"Yeah?"

"Ali Castle."

Jade's skeptical expression dissolved into a smile. She shoved a hand in the pocket of her worn, torn jeans. "You're her woman." Her eyes slowly traveled the length of Lane's long body before returning to her eyes.

"Yes, I am." Lane swallowed against the tight knot in her throat. "Have you spoken with her recently?"

Jade shook her head. "No, she hasn't been to class since last Friday." Her eyes studied Lane's, questioning.

"What?" Lane almost didn't recognize her own voice, it was so filled with despair, hurt and need. Jade regarded her with uncertainty. "Please, I have to find her."

Jade tipped her head toward the building. "Our prof stopped me after class asking about her too. Friday was when he told her about the gallery owner who was interested in her work."

Oh, God, Lane thought, she is that good. She wouldn't have to spend her life waiting tables. She could have her dream. She wouldn't need me any more and probably wouldn't want to associate with me anyway, given what I've done. Lane's eyes began to tear.

"I'm sorry, I don't have a clue why she quit coming to class or where she might be." She blew out a breath. "Heck, you're the only one she ever talked to me about." She shook her head. "I'm kind of worried about her."

Lane withdrew two cards from her purse. "We should stay in touch." She offered both cards to Jade, flipping one over to its blank side. "How about a number where I can reach you if I find her."

Jade pulled a pencil from the bag slung over her shoulder, wrote down her number and handed it back. "Ali is some kind of an awesome artist. She probably just took a drive somewhere in search of some inspiration or something. We artists can be kind of"—she shrugged again—"I don't know, weird that way, you know."

Lane gave her a tight smile. "Hopefully that's all there is to it." She turned quickly before Jade had a chance to read the doubt in her eyes. She called out over her shoulder as she stepped away, "Please call if you hear anything."

"Likewise." Lane waved the card in her fingers over her shoulder in reply.

* * *

The cab took her back to the courthouse, but she had to force herself back inside. She would have much rather headed to the nearest bar for a drink—or several. She managed somehow to push thoughts of Ali to the back of her mind long enough to tend to work. The evening was like the one before, filled with tears and memories of their time together. The way Ali could so easily inspire her laughter. How nervous she'd been to meet Miss Clara and how enamored Miss Clara had been with her. Her unselfish willingness to walk away when her past was revealed. "Oh, God." Lane sniffed. Their first kiss in the woods. No, she had not imagined something more than simply sex between them. But why...what had driven her away?

Wednesday mirrored Tuesday and Thursday turned into the day before. During lunch recess Lane called John's number. She got his voice mail. "John, it's Lane. I was checking to see if you've found any clues as to Ms. Castle's whereabouts. If there's no news, there's no need to return my call. Thanks." By day's end, she was restless and irritable. Jeremy knocked minutes after she'd returned to her office.

Despite the fact that she gave no answer, he cracked the door open and poked his head in. "Lane?" She was standing behind her desk chair looking out the window.

"What?" she snapped.

"I, uh..." He stepped inside and closed the door. "Is everything all right? Are you all right?"

She spun around and gripped the back of her leather chair so tightly her knuckles went white. "Don't I look all right?" Her tone was terse and she didn't care. "What do you want, Jeremy?"

He slipped his hands in his trouser pockets. "I'm concerned about you. You haven't been yourself all week."

"Jeremy, I'm busy and I don't need another damned distraction. Is there something work-related you need to talk about?"

"No, but—"

"No buts. Leave now so I don't have to fire you to get rid of you."

Raising his hands in a gesture of surrender, he retreated. "I'll see you in the morning."

She dropped into the desk chair. Taking her frustration out on him should have helped, but it didn't. She was staring blankly at the wall when the ring of her cell phone startled her. She viewed the screen, saying only "hey" by way of greeting.

"Hey, yourself. How are you, Lane?"

"Well, I just threatened to fire my assistant, if that's any indication."

"Oh! Come on, darling. Meet me out for a few drinks. Some company will do you good. I promise, I'll let you vent as much as you like."

Lane gave it a moment's thought. "All right. Where?"

"Same place as last time…say a quarter of seven? I've got to finish something here."

"See you there."

* * *

To Lane's relief, Carlina didn't inquire about the status of Lane's search for her missing lover. She was simply her usual flirty, amusing, diverting self. The drinks went down easy, and the conversation—about anything and everything except Ali—flowed even easier.

Three hours later as they waited for a cab on the sidewalk in front of the hotel, Carlina held tightly to her arm to keep her from toppling over. "I'm going to ride with you, darling, to make sure you get tucked in safely." Lane rested her hand on the one gripping her arm in a wordless thank-you.

The ride home was silent. Lane's head was swimming—with vodka and with strange thoughts about how good it felt—well, better than good—how arousing it felt to have Carlina's thigh brush against hers each time the cabbie took a quick corner.

After Carlina sent the cab on its way, she helped Lane upstairs and steered her toward the bedroom. When they got there, Lane turned and slipped her fingers into the long dark hair at the back of Carlina's neck. "I been dyin' to do this for the last two hours." Unsteadily she leaned toward Carlina, eyes closing and lips parting slightly in anticipation.

Carlina pulled back. "Lane," she said abruptly, bringing Lane's eyes open. "What are you doing?"

Lane's smile was probably lopsided, though she hoped it was sexy. "You always flirt, Car. I'm jus takin' you up on it."

Carlina disengaged herself and stepped back, leaving Lane swaying in a drunken haze. "No…" she said softly. "You're not."

Lane stumbled back several steps, dropping onto the bed. "Why?"

Carlina took only a step closer. "Because, Lane"—her voice was gentle—"the woman you're in love with has left you, and you've had entirely too much to drink. Only a predator would take advantage of you in such a vulnerable state. And that I am not. I am your friend.

And," she hesitated, "if I were ever to sleep with you, it would be when we were both very sober and you weren't pining after someone else."

Feeling rejected and embarrassed, Lane looked down at her feet. "I'm sorry," she whispered.

"Think nothing of it, darling. It's vodka under the bridge." Carlina gave her a rueful smile. "Get some sleep. I'll let myself out."

Lane flopped back on the bed. Had she made a complete fool of herself? She kept her feet firmly on the floor to keep the bed from moving and promptly passed out.

* * *

She woke very early Friday morning, dry as the desert and still fully clothed. Sometime during the night she had at least crawled up into the bed. She groaned at the faint pounding in her head when she tried standing. "God," she grumbled on her way to the bathroom. "Will I ever learn my lesson?" She filled a glass at the sink and swallowed two aspirins, following them with orange juice to combat the hangover, rather than the alcohol she ached for. She needed only to survive the day and she'd have the weekend to recuperate.

The morning was a rough one, but Jeremy let her be and court was relatively uncomplicated for a change. Back in her office after the afternoon session, she heard a knock on the door. Jeremy poked his head in. "John Woods on the phone for you. And don't forget you have a fund-raiser tomorrow evening. Your doctor friend called while you were in court this morning to remind you."

She nodded and waited for him to leave. "Hello, John," she said around the big lump in her throat. Her intuition told her he was calling with bad news.

"Afternoon, Lane. Listen I know you said I didn't have to call if I didn't have any news, but I wanted to let you know where things stand. This gal has vanished like Houdini. I haven't been able to come up with anything on the car, which tells me she may have ditched it. I've been sitting on the restaurant on the off-chance she'll come in for her final paycheck, but nothing. Do you want me to keep looking?"

Lane felt as if the world was sitting on her chest, unbelievably heavy and painful. "If you don't mind…but only as you have time to, John. No need to make it a primary focus. Let me know how much and when you need to be paid."

"No problem. I'm good on funds at the moment. I'll be in touch if I turn anything up."

"Thank you, John."

She replaced the receiver and gathered up her things. On her way out she told Jeremy she was leaving for the day and he could go whenever he wanted to. Once home, she kicked off her shoes and headed straight to the cupboard where the liquor was. She had failed at getting what she truly wanted in her life and in the process had all but thrown away the only thing she'd ever been good at. She needed now what she had achieved last night—mind-numbing relief.

* * *

Friday morning's hangover paled in comparison to the one she woke with Saturday. She barely made it to the bathroom in time. She splashed her face with water afterward and took a hard look at the person in the mirror. Her face was drawn, her eyes bloodshot and accentuated by dark half-moon shadows below them. "I have to quit drinking away the pain," she murmured. She vowed to her gaunt reflection that she was going to quit punishing her body for what her heart saw as her greatest failure. She wondered if she'd be able to keep her promise.

She forced down some dry toast, then some juice and yogurt. By eleven she felt human enough to shower and dress. She holed up in her office after that, concentrating on the work she'd brought home, but by midafternoon was restless again. She couldn't help thinking of Ali, the only woman she'd ever loved, and of Carlina, the woman she had tried to substitute for her, and the look on her face as she pushed Lane away. When she went to the living room to clear her head by gazing out at the city her eyes were caught instead by the drawing of the nude in the sketchbook lying open on the coffee table. She dropped on the couch, her mind taking her back to the last night she and Ali had made love. The memory burned fiercely, painfully in her chest.

Maintain control, she warned herself, as she prepared to administer the only anesthetic she knew. She poured two fingers of clear liquid in a short glass and added the olives. She'd have only one, the way she did on any given Saturday as she prepared for an event. When she had trouble deciding what to wear, though, she went back for another. When she discovered she had thirty minutes to kill before her ride arrived, she poured a third one. She felt in complete control as she made her way downstairs to the waiting car.

Emily was waiting inside the doors to the banquet hall. "Thank heavens you're here. I was beginning to think all you gals were going to stand me up."

Lane allowed Emily to lead her across the large room to the bar. "Who else is coming?"

"Tara and Carlina."

Lane mentally cringed at the mention of Carlina's name. She had hoped to avoid her for, oh, the next year or so. They were standing with their drinks in the bar area when Tara arrived, followed in another ten minutes by Carlina. They exchanged their usual friendly hellos and hugs.

Lane braced for a stiff hug from Carlina, but she was perfectly relaxed. "How are you, Lane?" she asked as if she'd not seen her two days ago.

"Fine, and—"

"Really?" Emily asked pointedly. "I don't mean to sound critical, but you look ill." She reached up a hand and touched the back of her fingers to Lane's cheek. "No fever." She cocked her head.

Lane averted her eyes. "I've been tired lately. Too much work." In her peripheral view she saw Carlina turn from their tight circle.

Emily grasped Lane's arm gently. "Promise me you'll get in to see a doctor and get checked out. I'm really concerned about you, honey. You don't look well."

"Fine, fine, Em. I'll work that into my already crazed schedule."

Damn. She was certain she'd applied enough makeup to cover the signs of her recent dissipation. Perhaps she should consider adding better lighting to the bathroom or one of those enormous magnifying mirrors.

Dinner was uneventful, with Lane pacing her drinking to avoid attracting the attention of her friends. When she had endured all that she could, she stood. "Well, ladies, as enjoyable as this evening has been, I must run along for another engagement."

Carlina stood too. "I need the ladies' room. I'll walk to the lobby with you." Lane sighed. She wasn't sure she was ready for a conversation with Carlina, but it looked like she was going to have one anyway.

"Are you sure you're okay, Lane?" Carlina's eyes were warm and welcoming when Lane gazed into them.

She nodded. "Little by little, I'll get past this."

"Given time, darling, I don't doubt that you will."

Carlina's comfort reached deep inside Lane. "Listen, I'm sorry about the other night. I—"

Carlina stopped her with a squeeze of her hand. "Think nothing of it. Too much alcohol can make any of us do things we normally wouldn't. I've already forgotten it."

Lane smiled weakly. "Thanks, Car."

"Keep taking care of yourself, darling, and call if you need to talk or want some company."

Lane stepped out into the night and once Randall was seated behind the wheel, he asked, "Where to, ma'am? Home?" He'd been attuned to her solitary mood of late.

"No, Randall." She gave him directions for her next destination.

CHAPTER THIRTY-THREE

Randall double-parked in front of the nondescript bar across the river, which wasn't located in the best of neighborhoods. Lane powered down the privacy window and leaned forward. "I need you to hang on to this until you pick me up Monday morning."

"Yes, ma'am." He took Lane's clutch from her.

"Feel free to drive by my place and charge the time and mileage to my account." Exiting the car, she added, "I'll see you Monday." She folded half a dozen twenties and tucked them into the pocket of her slacks after paying the cover charge inside the door. Stepping aside, she gave her eyes a few minutes to adjust to the dim lighting before making her way to the other end of the bar, where she waited her turn to order a drink.

A young brunette seated on the barstool beside her gave a low whistle. "Hey, good-lookin'," she said over the music reverberating around them. She looked Lane up and down. "I think you might be in the wrong bar."

Lane accepted her drink from the bartender before turning to give her appraiser the same once-over. She wore a white collared shirt tucked into skintight leather pants and black boots. Her eyes appeared gray in the dim light or may have been a very pale blue, and she had a strong, handsome face. She was a looker. Lane lowered her eyes to take in how the black leather hugged her crotch. When she looked up, the woman was grinning.

"Or...maybe you're *not* in the wrong kind of bar."

Lane backed away from the bar and slowly sipped her drink, keeping her gaze on the woman. She finally lowered the glass and leaned close. "Do you have a name, hotshot?"

The brunette took a long pull on her beer and leaned closer. Her lips only a breath away from Lane's ear, she said, "Nicole, but anyone who knows me, calls me Nic." When she leaned back, again meeting Lane's eyes, her expression was cocky. "Maybe you'd like to know me."

"Is that all they call you, or do you have a pet name, like Stud?"

Nic's lips curled in a smirk. "Maybe later I can *show* you what women know me for."

Lane reached past Nic, setting her empty glass on the bar. "Perhaps you can." Her lips brushed Nic's ear. "But for now, maybe we could try dancing."

She figured Nic for an in-control top. Turning her would be fun. She was going to leave her face down on her bed, her body limp with exhaustion from too many orgasms. Lane probably wouldn't come, thanks to all the alcohol she'd consumed, but that wasn't what she was looking for, was it? She was looking for power. For dominance. That was the tried-and-true way to keep her heart safe.

Dancing was followed by more drinking and an invitation to go back to Nic's place. It was just like the old days, thought Lane. She couldn't be more in control of this woman tonight if she had a whip.

She couldn't control her mind as well, unfortunately. And when they left the bar to go to Nic's car, an older model black Firebird, her mind thought it saw Ali standing in a doorway across the street, watching them. It wasn't her, of course, just the reflected lights of a passing car. But it had all the impact of a punch to the gut. The results were predictable, given how much she'd imbibed.

She wasn't clear on exactly what happened after that, except that Nic, who turned out to be a pretty decent sort despite all the posturing, had not only stood by her as she threw up on the curb but had also waved down a cab for her and helped her into it. Before that, though, she'd written her phone number on Lane's wrist.

"I'm ready when you are, Renee. But that's clearly not going to be tonight." She smiled compassionately at her. "Give me a call when the time's right. We'll find a quiet place to talk." She leaned forward and brushed her lips along the edge of Lane's jaw. "Or, better yet, a place to make a lot of noise of our own."

* * *

The near-miss with Nic didn't exactly serve as a wake-up call, but it and the haunting image she'd had of Ali that night did encourage Lane to try to curtail the drinking that she blamed for both of them. She wasn't very successful. Although her daily routines came and went as usual, alone at home in the evenings she was restless—to the point that she was actually thinking of recommitting to some of the deals she let go when she decided she wanted to commit herself to Ali.

Before she could examine that idea further, her phone rang. It was Carlina.

"Good evening, gorgeous."

"Well, hello, darling. I was calling to check on your state of mind, but you sound perfectly pleased with life. Are you entertaining this evening?"

"No. I'm home alone on a Friday night."

"I'm at the office but *so* ready to be somewhere else."

Lane's desk clock read seven-twelve. "Perhaps we should go out?"

"Whatever did you have in mind?" Carlina's words were flirtatious as usual, but she sounded tired.

"Dinner and drinks somewhere?"

"Sounds divine. Where?"

"You decide," Lane said, walking to her bedroom to slip into something a little less comfortable.

Forty minutes later they were seated at the bar waiting for a table at a favorite restaurant downtown. They caught each other up on their work and their lives, with the conspicuous exception once more of neither of them saying anything about Lane's AWOL girlfriend. Lane also omitted mentioning anything about her indiscretion the week before, though when Carlina commented that she seemed to be drinking less, she did admit that she was taking care to see that it didn't become problematic.

"I adore your company, darling. We should make a standing date to get together every Friday," Carlina said as they stood on the walk out front after dinner.

"I'd enjoy that. Should be easier to arrange than in the past. I *do* tend to have a lot more free time these days." She snuck a look at Carlina, hoping she didn't sound too self-pitying.

Carlina chose not to respond to the comment, instead giving Lane a peck on the cheek. "Thanks again for rescuing me, darling. Let's talk on Monday and arrange our next Friday evening."

"I'm looking forward to it already." Lane gave her hand a quick squeeze before they headed off in opposite directions for their cars.

* * *

Ali was watching the building at six thirty when the familiar Town Car passed in front of the building and turned at the corner to circle around for the garage. An hour later she spotted the little blue sports car coming around the corner. She wasn't completely sure what had brought her here tonight. The chance for a glimpse of Lane? Because it was her birthday and this was the only gift she was likely to get?

In any case, she found herself, without conscious thought, following at a discreet distance and watching without detection as Lane entered a posh restaurant downtown. Her clothes said "social occasion" and not "business meeting." She drove around for a bit before finding a parking spot that gave her a view of the door to the restaurant but would keep her safely out of sight when Lane emerged.

"What am I doing?" she asked aloud. She should leave. She'd seen Lane now, seen she seemed to be doing okay. Why stay? Because… She wanted more—needed more. She wanted to take care of her. To "baby" her and protect the tender, vulnerable core of her that nobody else saw.

Wasn't that the real reason she hadn't left the city? In case Lane needed her to do more than disappear so she could pursue her dreams? Yes, she'd had to let go of her own dreams—art school, the gallery job—but Lane deserved all that and more. As long as she stayed in Columbia she'd have to keep working at dives where they wouldn't check out the fictitious information she gave them and they'd pay her in cash or she'd work in exchange for room and board like she was doing now. She was used to having nothing in her life. It's all she'd ever had really, and she would get used to it again. She hoped. Eventually— once she was sure Lane was no longer at risk—she'd move on.

She picked up the buckeye from her console, rolling the smooth nut between her fingers. Lane had given it to her the first day they had kissed, had said they were good luck. This one had been, if only for a little while. She had known when that kiss had melted her insides that Lane was the "one" in spite of the fact that Lane was a judge and she was an ex-con. In spite of the difference in their ages, in their social standings. She squeezed the buckeye. It was pretty much all she had left of the love of her life. That and her voice on her phone.

She returned the buckeye to the cup holder and pulled her phone from the glove box. She kept it off usually, unsure if Lane could track it down since she'd been able to dig up her prison past. Then again…it was her birthday. She turned the phone on and replayed Lane's messages, savoring that smooth low voice again even though it sounded increasingly frantic and more than a little scared. It was painful to know that her leaving had hurt Lane so deeply, but it felt kind of good, too, to know that Lane had viewed it as a catastrophe and not a stroke of good luck.

She turned the phone off, put it away and picked up the sketchpad on the passenger seat. She was bone-tired, though not too tired to keep checking the door every time someone exited the restaurant. To keep from drifting off, she drew intermittently on the pad. Drew that oh so familiar face. Those eyes that turned dark as the darkest night when she was aroused.

When Lane finally came out two hours later, when she was finally able to get a really good look at her, her heart skipped a beat. She was so incredibly beautiful. As was the woman at her side. Ali recognized her. She was one of the women who had been there on the night she first noticed Lane at Roscoe's restaurant.

Ali watched the woman kiss Lane's cheek, jealousy and envy clawing at her insides. An innocent enough gesture, perhaps. Until Lane grasped her hand. Ali could sense the intimacy between them from the other side of the street half a block away. She pressed her fist to her mouth to stop a sob.

It hurt, but she understood. Lane needed to be with a woman with the right social stature. With a past that would pass scrutiny. That was the reason she'd left. This was the way it had to be.

She sat paralyzed as Lane walked to her car. "Oh, God, baby," she whispered in the darkness. "I miss you so much." She stopped breathing when Lane stopped abruptly a few feet from the Miata and looked down the street in her direction. Her face was perfectly lit by the light of the nearby streetlamp. Ali wanted more than anything to race up the street and throw herself into her arms.

Quickly, she reminded herself again why she couldn't have the only person she'd ever truly loved. Lane was a powerful woman, was on her way to greater things. Ali was nothing but an anchor that would prevent her from doing that, that might even sink the ship. She watched the convertible's taillights disappear up the street, then dropped her forehead against the steering wheel and yielded to the tears she'd staved off earlier, sobs that shook her to her core.

* * *

It was nice having the standing date with Carlina each Friday, Lane thought as she strolled up the street. It was good having someone she could share part of her real self with. It didn't hurt either to have someone that beautiful flirting with her, albeit in a teasing way. She was still a little uncomfortable about the drunken overture she'd made several weeks ago, but Carlina seemed to have forgotten about it, thank goodness.

As she neared her car she thought she heard someone call out to her. She turned, thinking perhaps Carlina had forgotten something and called her name, but she was already out of sight. Strangely, though, out of nowhere, Ali's face popped into her mind.

It will never be gone, she sighed as she drove home. *I'll always see that face, always long for her touch.*

When she entered the penthouse, she went straight to the couch, pulled out the sketchpad she had stashed under it and stared at the drawing of the two women. Finally forcing herself to put it—and her thoughts—away for the evening, she went to the kitchen and poured herself a drink. Before she could finish it, she was overwhelmed by the memory of the way Ali had looked the afternoon they'd made love there. Memory upon memory was followed by drink after drink. Eventually she numbed her mind enough and staggered to her lonely bed.

* * *

She spent the bulk of Saturday nursing a hangover, but by evening she felt like a big cat trapped in a small cage. Out—she needed to be out and about. But calling Carlina didn't seem like the thing to do. After dressing in jeans and a V-neck sweater, she called a cab to take her across the river. She didn't look for Nic in the bar, though

Lane suspected she was probably around somewhere. Spying a petite blonde standing off to one side by herself, Lane got a drink and drifted toward her instead.

She smiled as Lane neared and said, "Hi" as if they already knew one another.

"Hello." Lane stopped short of encroaching on her space. "Tell me that you're not here alone and I'll walk away."

"I am. Would you like to keep me company?"

The corner of Lane's mouth lifted. "I believe I would."

"I'm Andrea." She shifted her drink glass to her left hand, extending her right.

Lane took her delicate hand and kept her gaze on the blue-green eyes looking up at her. "Renee. It's very nice to meet you, Andrea. Do you live around here?"

"Just off-campus. I share a house with some people."

Off-campus? Damn, she was a student. Lane took a closer look. Younger than Ali, by all appearances, and even more innocent, judging from the way she was nervously biting her lip. She shook her head as a slow number began playing on the jukebox. She stuffed the comparison away and prayed it would stay put. "Would you like to dance, Andrea?"

"Uh, sure."

On the dance floor, Andrea reached around Lane's neck and rested her cheek against Lane's chest. When Lane slipped her arms around her slim waist, she felt Andrea shake slightly. "Are you all right?" She was a lot of things when she was with a woman, starting with controlling and dominating, but a predator she was not.

"I...uh...yes." Andrea gazed up at Lane.

"Are you sure?"

Andrea swallowed. "Yes, I am. I've just..." She paused, "I've never been...Oh, God." She shook her head. "You're so damn gorgeous."

Lane chuckled easily. "Thank you. You're quite beautiful yourself." Andrea's cheeks blushed bright pink. Lane placed her lips close to Andrea's ear. "Relax, and let's enjoy the dance."

When the song ended and an up-tempo number began to thump from the sound system, Lane led Andrea to the bar and ordered them fresh drinks. After a few sips, Andrea relaxed and sidled closer to Lane.

"I'm sure I've never seen you here before. I mean, I'm not a regular, but I come in occasionally."

"I don't often go to bars."

"You're a lesbian, though, right?" Andrea's cheeks turned rosy again.

"I am." Lane's mouth curved into a smile as she leaned down and again placed her lips against Andrea's ear. "And a good one too. Would you like me to show you how good?" Lane was standing close enough to feel Andrea's shiver. This was going to work out fine, she thought. The girl might be relatively inexperienced, but she looked to be a quick learner—and Lane had lots to teach her.

When her response finally came, Andrea's voice was breathless and about half an octave higher than it had been. "Okay."

Lane led her to a semidark corridor off the main bar area, the hall where the restrooms were located. The music's pounding bass was half as loud here, making it a good spot for two willing women to get better acquainted.

On familiar territory again and determined not to let any phantasms get in the way of getting off this time, Lane reached up to stroke along Andrea's jaw. "Is this okay? I don't want to make you uncomfortable."

Andrea nodded, and Lane dipped her head, preparing to retrace with her lips the path her fingers had just taken. Even as she was anticipating enjoying the velvety softness of Andrea's skin, though, her mind was taking note of the additional stretch the action was requiring. *Must be about five-two*, she calculated, *an inch or two shorter than...*

Before she had time to quash the thought and continue her explorations, the restroom door opened. The light from within it lit up Andrea's platinum hair—and enough of her face to make it clear that it was not the one Lane had been mentally picturing. She stepped back hurriedly, knocking into the woman who was exiting.

"Hey! Watch it!" Lane swerved to face the young woman, automatically shielding Andrea from...well, you never knew what kind of person you might run into in a joint like this, though there was something familiar looking about this one.

"Oh, hey, Renee! I was hoping to bump into you again. Except, you know, without an actual collision. At least not here," she said with a leer. "You got home, all right, I guess?"

It was Nic, and she was looking just as fine as she had a week ago. And as polished as her black Firebird, in another pair of flattering, form-fitting leather pants and with her short hair spiked. Lane's face heated as she remembered the condition she'd been in when Nic had poured her into a cab last Friday and sent her home.

"I don't think I said before, but thanks for that," she said with a rueful grin. "It wasn't my best moment."

"Neither was the next day, I bet," Nic said, laughing. "Don't worry about it. We've all been there. If you're looking to make it up to me, though…oh!"

Andrea had poked her head out from behind Lane, looking to see what was going on. Nic's eyes widened. "Never mind. I see you're already taken tonight. Didn't mean to interrupt."

"Nothing to interrupt," Lane answered, before realizing how that might sound to the young blonde. She looked down, ready to apologize, and found Andrea's eyes glued to Nic and a hungry, decidedly *not* nervous look on her face. *Ah…*

"Have you two met?" The answer to that would be no, she decided, watching their faces. "This dashing young thing, my dear, is Nic, rescuer of inebriated lesbians. And this fair lady, Nic, is Ali…I mean… *Andrea*. This is Andrea."

As she watched them gravitate toward one another, she couldn't help but compare it to the way she'd felt the night she'd first seen Ali. As if there was nobody else in the room. As far as these two were concerned, she was invisible.

The observation, oddly enough, didn't unsettle her the way it would have once. She was not meant to be here, it seemed. She shook her head. Of course she wasn't. She was supposed to be enjoying this weekend with the love of her life. She should have been celebrating Ali's birthday with her yesterday instead of drinking herself to sleep. Spotting an exit at the end of the corridor, she made her way quietly to it and eased out into the alley behind the bar. There'd been no point in saying goodbye, judging from the amorous glances they had exchanged as they began speaking to one another. Nic deserved something for the way she'd helped Lane out last week, and Ali—not-Ali!—deserved someone better than a one-night stand with an aging drunk nursing a broken heart.

Real Ali deserved better too, she thought, berating herself as she made her way to the street to hail a cab. What did it say about their relationship, about the love she'd sworn to Ali would last forever, when mere weeks later she was ready to screw almost anything with two X chromosomes.

Instead of controlling others, maybe she ought to try controlling herself. *Yeah*, she thought with a snort. *Look how well that worked when I decided to control my drinking. Still…*

When she actually stopped and searched her heart, she knew she'd never again want to lie with a woman who wasn't Ali. Wasn't that why'd she'd gotten so blasted drunk with Nic a week ago? Because that was the only way she could fathom having sex with a stranger now? She couldn't give up on finding Ali—not this soon. And until such a time that she was certain beyond a doubt she'd never have Ali back again, she needed to get a handle on her drinking or lose what little she had left of a life.

And so it went. On Friday evenings she and Carlina would get together for drinks and dinner. She spent Saturdays prowling the city looking for things to distract her from her devastating loss. She rarely if ever succeeded. An ill-considered trip to an exhibit at a local museum had her reflecting on how much Ali would have loved seeing it—and spending the rest of her visit scanning the crowds to see if she might be there. Long drives in the country invariably ended up places that they'd gone together. She considered visiting Miss Clara, but didn't want to risk running into her father—or the breakdown that might follow having to tell Miss Clara what had happened.

John wasn't having a lot of luck either. Although he did manage to track down and make contact with Ali's father. The preacher and his wife had relocated to another church in another small Indiana town.

"Yeah, that guy is a real piece of work," John had reported, his voice filled with disgust. "He said they had to move because their 'disgrace of a daughter had seen fit to run off with the devil.' Can you believe it? He didn't pursue the missing persons report he filed either. He just assumed...hell, I don't know, Lane...assumed the worst, I guess. Whatever he wanted to think. Like I said, a piece of work."

Following her conversation with John, Lane's curiosity had driven her to the computer to search for the pastors in Ali's hometown. She managed to find an archived photo of Pastor Castle and his family. The grainy color image showed a man that looked more like a predator than a preacher. The cold stare and sneer he wore gave the appearance of something demonic versus something godly. Beside him stood a very dour-looking wife and mother, and in front of the pair, a smiling towhead that couldn't have been more than six or seven years old. She'd recognize those sparkling eyes anywhere. "Oh, Ali," she whispered. "Where are you, sweetheart?" She printed the photo, staring at it a long time afterward.

John checked in periodically—less and less frequently as one month passed, then two—but the messages he left were essentially the same. He still hadn't found a single crumb of information to follow.

CHAPTER THIRTY-FOUR

Lane's phone vibrated on the table as she and Carlina were sharing their usual Friday evening drinks and dishing about their week. It rarely rang any more and when it did it was usually a robocall or some other annoyance. Lane ignored it, not once, but three times. The fourth time it began, Carlina picked it up and asked, "You're not going to answer it?"

"There's no one I want to talk to more than you," Lane said, giving her a wink.

She held the phone so Lane could see it. "Good choice. You talk to enough Johns in court as it is, right?" Lane stared for a moment at the name on the screen and then snatched the phone out of Carlina's hand, accepted the call and headed to the alcove where the restrooms were.

"John!"

"Lane, I'm glad I got hold of you. I didn't think I was ever going to turn up anything on the elusive Allison Castle, but I finally got a lead."

The roar this produced in Lane's head made it hard to hear. "I'm sorry, John. It's kind of noisy here. Could you repeat that? I didn't hear you."

"I said—I finally got a lead on Ali Castle."

Lane swallowed and attempted to speak around the lump that had formed in her throat. "That's good news."

"You know, I'd have sworn she left town, maybe even the state, since she seemed to disappear without a trace. But I got a call today from one of my buddies at the PD with a lead on her car."

She could hear him now, but she was having a difficult time wrapping her brain around what he was saying. "So...you've found the car? Only that?" She dreaded his reply. After all, it could be he'd found it abandoned, wrecked or, worse, with something indicating Ali had come to harm. She swallowed again. Her heart hammered double time, leaving her lightheaded.

John's voice interrupted her hazy state. "...probably needed it if she was job hunting or anything else for that matter."

Lane couldn't stand any longer not knowing where the other half of her heart was. She hoped for nonchalance in her tone when she was feeling anything but that. "So where exactly is she, John?"

"My guy says the car's parked in an alley behind this sad excuse for an Italian restaurant on the east side of the city. Not the best of neighborhoods, and I guess the restaurant is pretty much a dive. Anyway, he says he spotted the car this morning, went back right before his shift ended, and it was still there. He figures maybe she works there or is possibly living upstairs. They rent rooms by the week over the restaurant. I'll run by tomorrow and check it out."

"No," Lane said sharply. She was beyond caring if her old friend suspected anything. "It's probably best if you give me the address. She might get spooked if she suspects anyone has tracked her down."

"You sure, Lane? 'Cause it's no trouble for me to run out there and take a look."

"No, I think the location will suffice, but thank you for the offer. If for any reason I do need you to check out the situation, I'll certainly let you know. In the meantime...I'm not where I can take down information at the moment. Can you text the address to my phone?"

"Yeah, sure, Lane. Let me know if you need anything else."

"Thank you for your persistence on this, John. Call me next week and we'll arrange for you to get paid."

"No urgency. I do know where to find you." He laughed, garnering a chuckle from her as well.

"I'll talk to you next week." She ended the call, her heart still racing, and felt some of the heaviness that had oppressed her for the last two months lift. If it wouldn't have caused a scene, she would have danced back to the table.

"So," Carlina asked when she returned. "Is John really a—you know—a john?"

Lane gave a wry smile. "You know better than to think that, Car."

"A Jane perhaps?"

Lane shook her head and put the phone back on the table, setting it down almost reverently. "John is a friend," she explained. "And an investigator. He worked for us when I was with the prosecutor's office. He does contract work." She sucked in a deep breath as the phone vibrated again.

"Let me guess. John?"

Lane opened the text and viewed the address before turning the phone so Carlina could see it. "This…" Her hand trembled. "This is the location of a certain someone who went inexplicably missing a few months ago."

Carlina's mouth fell open, and she silently mouthed an "oh" of understanding.

"It's the first lead we've had since she left."

"What do you plan to do with it?"

Lane's heart began to race again. "First, find out if it's her." She read the address again, committing it to memory. After all this time, there was a glimmer of hope, something to hang on to.

"So where is this?"

Lane took a small bite of her artichoke risotto. She forced herself to chew and swallow, even though food was the last thing on her mind. "The east side of the city."

"Tough neighborhood."

Lane agreed with a nod. "I have to ask a—"

"You don't have to ask. Of course, I'll go with you. That's what friends do for each other. I wouldn't let you go to someplace that dangerous by yourself."

Lane laid her fork down. She couldn't make herself eat any more. "Too dangerous for an evening ride." She stated it as a given.

Carlina reached over to touch Lane's hand, which trembled ever so slightly. "Oh, darling, if you want to go now let's get up and go. It will be so *Thelma and Louise*."

"Are you sure?"

Carlina smiled and signaled for the waiter. "Of course, nothing would please me more than to help you reunite with the love of your life." Outside the restaurant, she said, "Let me drive. In case you decide," her shoulder lifted slightly, "on a sleepover...or something."

"That's not likely." Lane was mentally calculating her approach to the situation as they pulled from the curb.

"So are you going to storm this place and take your woman captive?" She flashed a playful smile at Lane before turning her eyes back to the road.

"I'm...I'm not sure what I'm going to do."

Carlina left her to her thoughts, the ride silent save for the female voice of the GPS unit offering directions. As they entered this less than savory part of the city, Lane hit the button to lock the already locked doors. Carlina pulled to the curb across the street from the dimly lit restaurant, left the engine running, turned in her seat and looked expectantly at Lane.

"I...uh..." Lane stammered.

"What, darling? Tell me."

She stared at her fidgeting hands in her lap. "I'm not sure I should go walking in while she's working, if she's even there. If she sees me, I'm not sure she won't slip into the kitchen and disappear again, maybe forever this time..." Lane sighed deeply. "And I have to at least talk to her, Car—face-to-face."

Carlina patted her hand. "Not to worry. I'll pop in to ask for directions or something and see if she's in there. I certainly remember what she looks like. A blue-eyed blonde, about five-four-ish, oh, and carrying your heart around." Before Lane could protest, she said, "Be right back." She exited the car, relocking the door, and headed for the restaurant.

Lane watched Carlina cross the street while the now-familiar anxiety sat like a heavy weight on her chest. She could barely make her out through the grimy front window, talking to someone at a small counter inside the door. Carlina half turned and waved her hand around. When the man she was speaking to walked off, Carlina turned to face the front window but did not look in Lane's direction. A moment later the man returned and handed Carlina a piece of paper. Lane hit the unlock button as she approached. When Carlina settled back behind the wheel, she handed the piece of paper to Lane. It smelled faintly of garlic.

"What's this?"

"Directions to the performing arts center." Lane looked at her quizzically. "Well, I couldn't walk in there, stare at everyone and walk out. I asked for directions."

Lane continued to look at her. "Well?" she finally asked impatiently.

"She's definitely in there working. She was busy with some customers, though, and didn't see me. What's next?"

Lane's stomach did a slow roll. She wanted to burst in there, sweep Ali into her arms and carry her away. Wasn't that how every love story ended? That only happened in the movies, her common sense told her.

"Tonight doesn't feel right. I need to think about it. Figure out the best way to approach her."

Carlina dragged her seatbelt across her body and shifted the car into gear. "Okay." When they reached Lane's car, Carlina asked, "Are you up for a drink inside or maybe a nightcap at your place?"

"I'm going to pass." Lane touched her arm briefly before getting out. She leaned back in through the open door. "I want—I need to think on all of this."

"Of course. Call if you need anything."

"Thanks for being such a good friend, Car."

"Think nothing of it. I'll say a little prayer for you tonight." Carlina gave her a wink. Lane took a deep breath when she stepped back.

Her hands shook as she unlocked her front door. Nerves—she'd never been a nervous person in her life, until a few hours ago. And now, she had butterflies as big as bluebirds fluttering about in her stomach. She went straight to the kitchen and poured a drink before returning to sit in the darkness of the living room and watch the city's night lights. She let her mind conjure up the image of Ali working the first night she had noticed her. She considered the latest developments while she sipped the vodka.

* * *

She tossed and turned all night. At six thirty she gave in and got up. She showered and dressed, poured coffee into an oversized mug with a lid and headed downstairs. Gritting her teeth, she endured annoying conversation with the doorman while she waited for a cab. She tried to formulate some kind of plan while her cab ride took her north of the city to the airport. She had only gotten as far as deciding a rental car would be the only way she could avoid being spotted while being parked on the street where Ali worked. She purposely requested the oldest economy car they had available as she took her first shot at stalking.

After a quick cruise down the alley behind the building and confirming that Ali's car was, in fact, there, she parked within easy view of the unopen restaurant, but far enough down the street that if Ali appeared she might go unnoticed. It wasn't quite eight thirty. She donned her baseball cap and sunglasses and tried to get comfortable on the car's stiff vinyl seat. She barely sipped the coffee she'd brought along. She couldn't imagine using a public restroom anywhere in this neighborhood and there certainly weren't any woods nearby.

Hours later and going stir-crazy, she began to think that she might not get the chance she desperately wanted with Ali. But seconds later, she appeared in the narrow alley beside the restaurant. Ali looked up and down the street, before heading off in the opposite direction. She's still keeping an eye out, Lane thought, but why? She watched as Ali neared the corner and disappeared around it to her left.

"*Go*," Lane's mind ordered. She hopped out, locked the door and jogged to the corner. She peered around it before following. Ali was a little over halfway up the long block. Lane continued at a quick pace, remaining silent until she was fifteen feet behind her.

"Ali." She said her name loud enough to be heard over the din of traffic. Ali's steps faltered for a second before she started to walk faster. Lane jogged to catch up. "Ali," she called again. "Please stop. Give me a minute, please." Finally closing the distance, she lightly touched Ali's arm. "Please, Ali."

Ali stopped, but she wouldn't turn to look at her. Lane breathed deep, trying to still her pounding heart. "Thank you," she managed as she caught her breath. Lane stepped in front of Ali. Her head was down, but there was no mistaking the wet spots on the front of her top. "Oh, sweetheart." Lane slipped her finger under Ali's chin and tipped her head up to meet those brilliant blue eyes. Her heart clenched at the sight of Ali's dull, lifeless eyes and the dark smudges beneath them. Her face was expressionless, but the tracks of her tears glistened in the sun.

When Ali had heard her name, uttered in that unmistakable low voice, the tears had started automatically. She'd thought she was done with them, at least in the light of day. How had Lane found her? Why had she even been looking?

Instinct told her to run, but she knew she couldn't outrun Lane, not with her long legs. Much like she wouldn't ever be able to outrun her past, even though she once thought she'd done so. Here was another past back to haunt her.

When Lane made her look up, Ali's breath caught. Lane's eyes, normally filled with life and passion, were now portals to an endless dark abyss. Her face was drawn and her expression one of pain. *God, I did this to her.*

"I'm sorry" was all Ali could say before she looked away.

Not seeming to care that they were in public, Lane stepped close and wrapped Ali in a tight embrace. She froze when Lane's arms came around her. Her heart wanted nothing more than to melt into the sensation. Her brain registered where they were, however, and more importantly, why they were there.

She pushed against Lane's chest and stepped back from her. Gathering her runaway emotions, she looked away. "You shouldn't be here," Ali said, shaking her head. When Lane took a step toward her again, she took another step back.

"Ali," Lane's voice pleaded, "we need to talk."

She couldn't meet Lane's eyes. "No," she said with as much conviction as she could muster given the emotional battle going on inside her. "I thought my note was clear." The lump was back in her throat, but she forced her words past it. "We can't be together."

"But why?" The anguish in Lane's voice was palpable.

"I told you."

Lane reached out to her. "Ali—"

"No," she stepped back again. "I can't do this."

Lane caught Ali's arm before she could turn away. "Look me in the eyes and tell me this is truly what you want—to throw away what we have—and I will walk away."

"I can't do this," Ali said again, trying to pull from Lane's grasp.

"Ali, please," Lane persisted. "Please, talk to me. At the very least we owe each other the respect of a conversation. We need closure."

Ali's shoulders slumped, a sign to Lane she might give in to at least talking. "I have to work in a little while." She tugged again at Lane's hold on her.

Lane's heart hammered. "I'll come back when you're off work. We'll go somewhere for a drink or a cup of coffee." Ali didn't move. Lane prayed that her heart was fighting her resolve to end what they had had. "Please," Lane whispered. "I know you still care, at least a little. I only want to talk."

Ali nodded a barely discernable yes. "I should be done by eleven."

Lane's butterflies fluttered again. "Okay, I'll be back then." As she released Ali, Lane trailed her fingers up her arm. "Promise you won't run away again before that?" Lane said softly. "Please? I couldn't take that again."

Giving another slight nod, Ali started back the direction she'd come from. Lane walked slowly and crossed at the corner so Ali wouldn't feel like Lane was following her. Lingering on the corner, she watched as the love of her life turned into the alley before continuing on to the rental car.

Lane's phone was ringing in the little console between the seats as she slid behind the wheel. It had stopped by the time she got it out. The missed call was from Carlina.

"Darling, how are we today? Any news on your beautiful girlfriend?"

Lane sighed. "I just saw her."

"Oh, Lane, what's wrong?"

"God, Car, when I saw her nothing in the world mattered but her. Then she…she acted like I was the last thing she wanted." Lane dropped her forehead against the steering wheel.

"I'm sorry, darling. What will you do now?"

Lane took a deep breath. "She agreed to talk. I'm going to come back and meet her when she's finished working tonight."

"And then, my friend, you'll sweep her off her feet with all that charm of yours. I predict she'll be back in your arms by tomorrow."

"I hope you're right."

She didn't recall much of the drive back to the rental car lot. Thoughts of Ali consumed her. There'd been an inkling of hope when she'd taken Ali in her arms, but it had faded to despair when Ali pushed her away. Though, when she forced Ali to look into her eyes, for a moment the veil had lifted and she'd seen…something. "No," Lane muttered as she waited for a cab to take her back home. "It's not over—not by a long shot."

Carlina called again around six. "How are you, darling?"

"Fine, Carlina." Lane's thoughts were a million miles away.

"I'm checking on you, in case you're wondering. Are you eating? Would you like to grab some dinner? Should you be driving to that place by yourself tonight?"

"Thanks, but no. Please don't worry. I'll be careful, I promise. Actually, as a distraction I'm trying to get some work done." That was a lie, of course, but Lane justified it as a way to ease her friend's mind.

"Will you let me know how things are tomorrow?"

"Sure, and thanks, Car."

"Anytime, darling. Call if you need me."

She hung up, went to the kitchen and poured a drink. She also called the deli down the block and ordered some soup and a sandwich. Her stomach felt like a hollow pit. Forty minutes later she was forcing herself to eat.

Around nine, tired of pacing aimlessly through the penthouse, she poured a single shot and sat on the couch staring at the sketchpad Ali had left behind. She should probably give it to her. It would be the considerate thing to do, but deep down a tiny part of her was afraid that it might end up being the only tangible piece of Ali she'd ever have. The thought made her heart…just hurt.

She gave herself plenty of time to make the drive and tried her damnedest to think positive thoughts. She had to convince Ali to come home, because the alternative, well…she'd been living it and living without Ali just might kill her.

* * *

Ali was a nervous wreck. So nervous, in fact, that her hands were shaking, which prompted the waitress working with her to ask if she was ill. Irene was close to her own mother's age, but friendly and nurturing by nature, and they had gotten along splendidly from the moment they'd met. Ali was thankful for the distraction Irene provided. The heartache had begun to ease the tiniest bit, but every day was a struggle. Today, though…today was an all-out battle to stay sane and to stay put.

I am so stupid, she admonished herself. *I never should have agreed to see her again.* Her heart hadn't been able, though, to deny the pleading she saw in Lane's eyes.

She looked again to the window that fronted the street, though she knew she wasn't going to be able to see anything beyond its fly-specked glass. She should have insisted they meet in a safer part of town. Considering the number of streetlights that were out up and down the block, Lane could be putting herself in harm's way by coming there late at night.

I could call her, she thought fleetingly, *and tell her we should meet another time.*

No. She needed to see Lane one last time, so she could say goodbye, face-to-face, and get the closure they needed to go on living their separate lives. "Hell," she cursed under her breath. Who was she kidding? She wouldn't be living anything after this—only existing.

A flash of headlights hit the front window as a car turned the corner, but she couldn't tell where it had gone or if it had stopped somewhere out front. She glanced at the clock on the wall behind the small take-out counter. Ten thirty. She never wanted a shift to end more than this one, even though what she had to do tonight *would* rip her heart out all over again.

CHAPTER THIRTY-FIVE

Lane arrived at the restaurant thirty minutes early. Her convertible stuck out like a sore thumb in this neighborhood of rusted-out, wrecked old junkers and pickup trucks. Like Ali stuck out from all others, at least to her. This was definitely not a good place for her to be, she thought, directing a combative glare at a scruffy passerby who appeared to be calculating what her tires and audio system might be worth and whether she was going to be stupid enough to leave them unguarded long enough for him to remove them.

If nothing else, she thought, maybe she could help Ali get her job back at Roscoe's. Sleeping in her car in that part of town had to be safer.

She went over the argument she'd been mentally preparing all day. This was the toughest case she'd ever have to try and she had to sell it like her own life depended on it. Because, in truth, it did. If she couldn't have Ali in her life, it wouldn't be worth having. She'd never again find the kind of happiness that she had brought into her life.

"God, sweetheart," she murmured. "Just let me take care of you. The rest, as they say, will fall into place."

Finally, a few minutes after eleven, Ali stepped out onto the sidewalk. She spotted Lane's car and walked slowly over to it, dropped into the passenger seat when Lane reached across and opened the door for her.

"Are you crazy, driving this car into this neighborhood? I can't believe no one's tried to jack it yet." Ali kept her voice tight, virtually emotionless.

Lane chuckled nervously. "The courthouse parking sticker probably scared them off."

"Right." Ali stared through the windshield. Even in the car's dim interior she could feel Lane's dark eyes searching her face. If she had any hope of making this breakup final, she had to avoid those eyes.

Lane started the engine. "Would you like to have a drink or coffee?" She drove down the barely lighted street, stealing a glance at Ali when they passed under one of the few lit streetlights.

Ali didn't think a drink was the best choice, but she was already so keyed up that coffee might push her over the edge of the precipice she was standing on. A few sips of wine might actually help calm her jumbled nerves. "I guess a drink would be okay."

Lane drove slowly, wanting to prolong their time together if this was the last they were going to have. She had promised herself that she would fight tooth and nail to convince Ali to return, but she had also resolved to let Ali go, once and for all, if she wasn't in love with Lane and didn't want a relationship with her. Their knack for easy conversation now seemingly lost, the trip was filled with long silent moments which Lane filled with heartfelt prayer. The silence was broken finally when she turned onto the street that led to her building six blocks away.

"Where exactly are we going for this drink?"

"I thought we'd go to the penthouse." She placed her hand over Ali's where it rested on her thigh. "It'll be quiet. We can talk."

Ali jerked her hand from under Lane's. She hadn't imagined that Lane would take her home. *Home*. The word caused an unwelcome longing. She closed her eyes, took a long slow breath and rehearsed what she was going to say. She needed to look Lane in the eyes and tell her that she didn't want her. That she'd been wrong to think she could settle down. It was just that simple. Surely Lane would understand that.

In any case, she thought, it's not going to be that hard for Lane to go back to her old life. Judging from how happy she'd looked when Ali had seen her with that "friend" of hers, she was already halfway there.

She took another deep breath as the car rolled down the garage ramp and Lane swiped her card. Memories washed over her, so painful that they threatened to steal the breath from her lungs.

As they entered the penthouse, Lane brushed past her and headed down the hallway. A jolt shot through Ali's body. She rubbed her arm, where the sensation lingered. *Oh God*, Ali thought, *if I don't do this I'll ruin Lane's life the same way I have ruined my own.*

Lane led her to the kitchen, where she pulled glasses from the cupboard. "Is wine all right, or would you prefer something else?" Ali, in the doorway, was staring at the counter where the garage card and keys she'd placed there two months earlier still lay next to her note.

"Uh...wine's okay." Ali turned her back to the counter and stared at the floor.

Lane took her time preparing their drinks. She wanted every possible second with the woman who held her heart, wanted to deliver the most important argument she'd ever make. She handed the wine to Ali. "Why don't we sit in the living room?" she said, waving Ali toward it.

Ali took a gulp of wine and led the way, a look of determination on her face.

Lane had the lights set to the soft, inviting glow that they'd enjoyed in the past, hoping it would help relax Ali. But en route to the couch, Ali stopped abruptly—as though someone had struck her—and with a sharp, audible intake of breath. She hurriedly set her wineglass on the end of the coffee table and crossed to the windows.

Glancing around to see what might have upset her, Lane noticed she'd left the sketchpad open on the table. She watched Ali in silence until she saw her shoulders begin to shake. When she moved behind her and she lifted her hand toward her shoulder, Ali stepped away.

"Please don't," she said through her tears.

Lane curled her fingers in a tight fist as she lowered her hand. "Ali, sweetheart, please talk to me. Make me understand how this happened. Please!"

Ali's body jerked involuntarily as the memory came flooding back. The sight of the missing sketchpad had brought it back with such clarity. The loud slam, the male voice that yelled, "You can't do this! You have skeletons in your closet that will bury you permanently."

She was Lane's skeleton, the thing that would bury the woman she loved. She needed to save her, even if it killed her.

She covered her mouth and leaned against the cool window glass, her body shaking. Lane moved again to stand behind her and Ali could feel the heat of her. Desire tore at her insides. The desire to be held. The desire for Lane's strong arms to make her feel safe again.

When Lane slid her arms around Ali's waist, she stiffened in response, but Lane held on. "Ali...please, sweetheart. Talk to me. Tell me why you're so upset."

Ali sucked in a breath. "Where did that come from?"

"What—? It's yours."

"No." Her voice quivered. "*Where* did you get it?"

"It was down in the apartment where you left it."

Ali's eyes glistened with new tears, reminded of the pain of the decision she'd made that day. It ripped her heart out to walk away from what she and Lane had begun to build. But the memory served as a reminder of how she could ruin Lane's life.

"I can't do this." She twisted out of Lane's arms and raced toward the door.

Lane caught Ali before she could open the door and leave. Her hand was gentle around Ali's arm. "Ali, please stop!" Ali's body went rigid.

"Please..." Lane softened her tone. "Please tell me what's going on." Lane's own tears threatened. "Whatever I've done to drive you away, please tell me. I'll fix it," she whispered. "I promise."

Lane felt Ali tremble, saw a pain in her eyes that was so deep that it pierced her very soul. She couldn't speak. She pulled Ali into her arms and held on fiercely.

"Oh, sweetheart," Lane murmured. "Whatever it was, I promise I'll make it right. I only want you to be happy." Her words drew deep sobs, until Ali was literally shaking in her arms. "Shh..." She pressed her cheek to the softness of Ali's hair. "Please, just let me take care of you." Ali went slack and Lane scooped her up in her arms and carried her to the bedroom.

Lane walked to the bed and sat down, keeping Ali in the cradle of her arms. Ali's tears seemed endless, but Lane held her tightly, rocking them in a slow motion.

Ali got her tears controlled and sniffed. "I'm sorry," she whispered. "I didn't mean to lose it like that." She swiped at her tear-stained cheeks.

"You have nothing to apologize for." Lane cupped her cheek, stroking her thumb across the damp skin.

Ali turned her face away. "I shouldn't have agreed to this...I shouldn't have come here." She tried to stand, but Lane kept hold of her.

"I'm not letting you go until you talk to me. Please, Ali. If you don't, I will stalk you forever."

Ali let out a breath. "I can't be with you, Lane. I thought maybe I could settle down with one person, but I can't. I'm sure you understand." Her chin quivered. She only met Lane's intensely dark eyes for a fraction of a second. The words had a practiced, wooden sound to them that was familiar to Lane from listening to herself as she rehearsed what she wanted to say to Ali.

"I don't believe you," Lane replied flatly. "Ali, look at me." When she wouldn't, Lane lifted her chin. "Please, look at me." Ali finally raised her red-rimmed eyes to meet Lane's. "What happened in there, in the living room, when you saw that sketch?" Lane didn't wait for her reply. "It reminded you of how good we are together, didn't it?" Ali shook her head. "Then why did you lose it?"

"I can't be with you." Ali's misty eyes drifted away. "I can't be responsible for ruining your life."

Lane reached up and turned Ali's face so she could look at her. "God, Ali, why would you think you could ruin my life? This—" She waved between them. "This is ruining my life. I can barely breathe from the pain of being without you. I need you. I thought you knew that."

Ali shook her head again. "No...I heard that man threaten to expose you. If I'm not here, though, there's nothing to ruin the future you planned before we met."

"What are you talking about? What man?"

Ali's eyes dropped to the button on Lane's blouse. "I came home between class and work that day to find that sketchpad. Because the professor knows this gallery owner who wanted to display some of my drawings—"

Lane drew in a pained breath. Things made more sense now. This wasn't about something she'd done. It was about Ali having the opportunity to go on to fame and fortune as an artist and not wanting to be tied to a lesbian relationship with a stodgy old judge. Well, it would hurt like hell, but if that's what Ali needed, she'd...

"...couldn't find it here anywhere, so I went down to the apartment, and I—" Ali paused, her voice tight with anxiety and remembered fear. "I heard you arguing with him, and I heard him say you had skeletons that could bury you."

Beckman...that crazy, stupid bastard.

"I'll take responsibility for totally messing up my life, but I won't do it to yours."

Ali pushed up, preparing to leave. Lane caught her arm and stood with her. "No, Ali, please, listen to me. You're wrong about what you heard."

Ali pulled against Lane's grasp, frantic.

"Ali," Lane whispered, unable to stop her own tears. "It was business, an arrangement with that man that I refused to carry out. Something...that could have ruined my career." She looked at her feet. "Something I would have lived in shame with the rest of my life. Not about you..." She raised her eyes to Ali's. "Never you. You are everything—everything I want. I want to be with you. I want to build a life with you. To let everyone know you're the thing that makes my life worth living. The rest, none of the rest, compares with having you in my life."

Ali saw the truth in Lane's eyes—felt it in her words. "Oh, God... baby...I'm so sorry."

That simple little endearment opened the floodgates of Lane's own tears. She pulled Ali to her.

Ali's arms slid around Lane's waist and held her as sob after sob racked her body. "I'm sorry."

"Shh..." Lane stroked her hands up and down her back. "It's okay. It will always be okay now as long as we're together."

Lane's voice, so sure, so full of promise, lifted the heaviness from Ali's heart. "I love you so much," Ali whispered.

Lane shook her head, realizing at that moment the depth of Ali's love. She had sacrificed what meant more to her than anything in order to protect Lane. She didn't think she would ever equal that, but by god, she was going to try. She tightened her hold on Ali and whispered back, "I love you too. More than I can ever put into words."

They held on to each other, anchored in that spot, for a very long time. The contact was soothing, a welcome touch, a safe harbor…a promise for eternity.

Lane took Ali's shoulders finally and held her at arm's length, savoring the sight of her. She stroked her fingers over Ali's cheek and was rewarded with a tiny smile.

Ali leaned into Lane's soft caress. "I must look a wreck."

"No." Lane brought her other hand up to cup Ali's face. "You're beautiful." She kissed her forehead. "Always beautiful." She kissed her cheek. "You take my breath away." She brushed her lips over Ali's.

Ali slid her fingers into the hair at the back of Lane's neck and brought their lips together in a soft, lingering kiss.

"Stay with me tonight." Ali nodded.

"And every night."

"Forever, if that's what you want."

Lane grinned like a schoolgirl. "I want." She pulled Ali firmly against her for a kiss that spoke of love, of want, of unrelenting desire.

Ali groaned against her mouth. "You're making my knees weak, baby."

Lane's heart danced in her chest. She murmured, "And you leave me defenseless."

Ali brushed her fingers over Lane's jaw. "Defenseless? Never. You are strong, powerful…"

Lane grinned. "I'd argue that point with you, but…" She slid her hands up Ali's sides to her breasts.

"Baby," Ali whispered breathlessly. Lane watched her eyes darken to that familiar shade of violet.

"But I have much more important things to do." Lane dipped her head to capture Ali's mouth in another kiss.

Ali pressed her hands to Lane's chest to hold her off. "I smell like garlic and grease and sweat."

"Ah, but I love Italian." Lane leaned into Ali and restrained her hands.

"No," she said firmly. "I have to have a shower before I can show you how much I've missed you."

"You've got ten minutes and I'm coming in." Lane couldn't get what she could only assume was a stupid grin off her face.

"I promise to be quick." She pulled out of Lane's grasp. "Why don't you get more comfortable." She inclined her head toward the bed as she left. "Like there."

Lane stripped off her clothes, tossing them aside with abandon. When she slid between the cool sheets she felt how heated her skin was.

Ali came out of the bathroom five minutes later, wet hair framing her face and wearing only a bath towel wrapped under her arms and tucked into her cleavage. She stood at the side of the bed. Lane's gaze was a soft caress on her skin. The sensation was so real, it sent a shiver up Ali's spine.

"I need you," Lane said, her voice low and raspy.

Ali dropped the towel and slid in the bed beside Lane, who filled her lungs with the fresh scent of soap and shampoo. Her arms pulled Ali closer. "God, you feel so good." She shivered. "I was so afraid I'd lost you forever."

Ali brushed her fingers across Lane's chest. "I'm here, and I'm never leaving."

Lane closed her eyes. "Promise?"

Ali pressed her lips to Lane's collarbone. "Oh, God, baby, I promise you." She kissed across her chest as she shifted on top of her. "You"—she kissed her chin—"are going to have to"—she kissed the underside of her jaw—"throw me out"—she kissed her neck below her ear—"with the trash to get rid of me."

"Never." Lane turned her head and captured Ali's mouth briefly. "Never."

Ali looked into Lane's eyes. "I want to please you so bad right now."

Lane's eyes were heavy lidded. "I need you." Their mouths came together in a passion-filled exploration.

Ali pulled back after several moments. "God, I love you so much."

Lane held her tightly. "I love you more than life. Never doubt that."

Ali wanted Lane, all of her, more than she wanted to breathe. Her lips painted feather-light kisses down Lane's abdomen, hesitating only briefly before lowering her mouth to Lane's slick center. Ali couldn't stop the groan that rose from deep inside when her lover let her claim her.

Having decided before meeting Ali tonight that she was prepared to give her anything her heart desired, if it was within her power to do so, Lane now wanted to give her everything. She'd seen the hurt in Ali's eyes every time she tried to go down on her and she had refused. Lane had spent time over the last few months going through the reasons why she never allowed anyone to do that. The obvious answer was her need for control in every part of her life. Especially the closeted part where she kept the women she had been using to feed that need for control. Relinquishing control left a person vulnerable.

Lane fisted the sheet in her hands. She'd never done this—never wanted to surrender herself to a woman—ever. Never wanted to be so exposed, this vulnerable to another woman's touch. But she wanted it now with every cell of her being. She wanted to share every part of herself with Ali. And it was every bit as powerful as anything she could have imagined, even more so because it was Ali who was making her feel so vulnerable and so loved. She begged for more.

Ali gave Lane what she begged for and was rewarded with deep throaty moans and a paroxysm so intense that it almost bucked her off the bed when she climaxed. As Lane recovered, Ali kissed her lightly everywhere, finally resting her cheek on Lane's thigh and watching the rapid rise and fall of her chest as her breathing slowed. She wrapped her arm possessively around Lane's thigh. "I love you," she murmured. Ali never wanted to move from this spot. Lane had opened herself to her with complete abandon. She had allowed herself to be vulnerable to Ali and allowed her to be Lane's first. Lane trusted her with every part of herself. *This is what happy ever after feels like.*

Lane's head felt deprived of oxygen. Her body hummed with total euphoria. A single tear slipped from each eye as Ali's breath whispered soft and warm across her skin. She stroked Ali's hair. "Come here."

Ali crawled up and planted a lustful kiss on Lane's lips.

"I love you." Lane tightened her arms around Ali. Ali smiled wide while her head shook slowly. "What?"

Ali shifted to Lane's side and rested her head in her hand. With her other hand she traced random patterns over Lane's chest and down her abdomen. "You're perfect," she said, almost shyly. "The perfect woman. The perfect lover." Lane's cheeks heated. "How is it that no woman has snagged you before?"

"Because…" Lane stroked her finger over Ali's cheek to her full lips, outlining their delicate shape. Ali quickly kissed the tip of her finger. "I've been going through life, day to day…" her fingers slipped into Ali's hair, "waiting for *you*, sweetheart."

Ali's breath caught. Lane's deep penetrating gaze spoke of so much promise. "I'm yours forever," she said softly.

"And for always," Lane added before their lips came together again, solidifying the promise—their destiny.

* * *

They drifted in and out of a love-induced haze for hours. Lane woke when Ali moved from the bed. "Ali?"

Ali stood naked at the bedside and stroked her fingers down Lane's arm. "I'm going to the bathroom. Do you want something?"

Lane smiled up at her. "Only you...back in my arms."

Once the bathroom door closed, Lane reached into the bedside table and took out the gift she'd bought months ago. She palmed it and slipped her hand under the sheet. When Ali returned to her side in the bed, Lane held the little velvet box out to her.

"What's this?"

"A little something I picked out for you. A while back, actually."

Ali gasped when she opened the box. "Baby, I can't take this, it's... it's too..." She gazed in wonder at the delicate heart ringed with diamonds.

"Oh, but you must." Lane sat up and took the necklace from box. "You've already captivated the living, beating one." She slipped the chain around Ali's neck without further protest. "It will be a reminder that you have my heart and how very much you will always mean to me."

Tears shimmered in Ali's eyes, then spilled over. "I can only give you this." Ali leaned in and placed her lips to Lane's.

The kiss melted Lane all the way to her toes. She pulled back after a lingering moment. "It's enough...more than enough. And it will always be."

Bella Books, Inc.

Women. Books. Even Better Together.

P.O. Box 10543
Tallahassee, FL 32302

Phone: 800-729-4992
www.bellabooks.com